I0601989

The Sonora Springs Tales

A Collection of Ellis Worth Short Stories

Edited by
Dean O. Smith

Annandale Press

Published by Annandale Press
Spokane, WA 99224

ISBN-13: 978-1-7364534-0-7

Printed in the United States of America

For inquiries, contact Annandale Press at
annandalepress@gmail.com

This book is dedicated to Everett E. Smith (1911-1972).

Contents

Acknowledgments

I should like to thank Curtis F. Smith for his role in the preservation of these stories and Karlene A. Hoo for her invaluable encouragement and support during the preparation of this anthology.

Some of the stories were published previously in small literary magazines. I thank the present-day editors of *Snowy Egret,* the only one of them still in business, for permission to publish these stories: Ellis Worth, "The Bull of the Mountain," *Snowy Egret* 27, no. 22-24 (1963); "Cold Day," *Snowy Egret* 29, no. 1 (1965); and "A Night on Knob Mountain," *Snowy Egret* 34, no. 2 (1971).

In memoriam, so to speak, I thank the editors of the now-defunct magazines for publishing: "The Witch of Gridley," *Simbolica* 26; "Landing Party," *Simbolica* 31; "The Black Prince," *The Editors* 2, no. 1 (1966); "School in the Sky," *Gong* 1, no. 6 (1966); "The Ordeal of Mr. Merriwell," *Verb* 3, no. 3 (1966); "The Sinner," *Canadian Lights* September(1967); "The Heckler," *Iota* 2, no. 1 (1968); "Etiquette and the Cattleman," *Latitudes* 11, no. 1 (1968); "A Simple Case," *Cloven Hoof* 1, no. 3 (1969); "Bert and Clotilde," *Erratica* 1, no. 2 (1971); "Da Orla," *Quixote* 4, no. 9 (1972); "Short and Sweet," *Erratica* 1, no. 4 (1973). Their contributions to the literary arts are not forgotten.

Also in memoriam, I should like to acknowledge DeForrest H. Judd (1916-1992) who painted the ceramic cover art, "Winter Mts." He was Elllis Worth's brother-in-law.

Foreword

B orn in 1911, Ellis Worth grew up on a farm in Minne- sota. After receiving his law degree from the Univer- sity of Minnesota, he practiced law in Minneapolis and then Washington, D.C. During World War II, he served in the Judge Advocate General's Corp under General George Patton. Following his discharge, Worth resumed a career in the legal profession, as a lawyer in private practice and as an editor for a publisher of law books. He died at the age of 61 in Colorado Springs. At the time of his death, Worth had published over thirty-five short fiction stories plus a dozen or so professional legal articles.

After Worth's death, his writings—magazines con- taining published stories and unpublished manu- scripts—were placed in storage, where they remained "out of sight, out of mind" for nearly 45 years. I acquired the trove, along with his diary, in 2015 and curated the musty treasures.

Worth wrote this selection of stories between 1955 and 1972. Accordingly, they refer to people, events, and objects in the vernacular of that era: President Dwight D. Eisenhower, Soviet Union Premier Nikita Khrushchev, costly operator-assisted long-distance telephone calls,

Hudson automobiles, and so forth. In that regard, they provide a sometimes nostalgic glimpse of the history of those times.

During this period, Worth lived in Colorado, first Denver and then Colorado Springs. Many of the stories refer one way or another to Sonora Springs, a mythical city that presumably was his hometown in Colorado: hence the title of this anthology. They express a sense of place, his fondness of the Rocky-Mountain geography and culture.

Characteristically, most Ellis Worth stories are quite short. Indeed, they belong to the "short-short-story" genre. In his diary, Worth commented on their brevity. "Thinking about my stories, I realized two distinguishing characteristics. From the beginning, I have known they were extraordinarily brief, compact, condensed. Am I writing sketches instead of stories? It may be so. However, I often feel that many authors of longer stories have put so little into their soup that the soup though copious is tasteless and weak. I try to give a concentrated, nourishing, meaty story." Also, most stories are rife with symbolism, inviting readers to stretch their imagination answering questions such as: What was the meaning of that? What comes next? Thus, the Worth stories often linger consciously or subconsciously beyond their brevity as readers process their meaning, often with a smile.

All of this is not to say that the stories are abstruse or heavy reading. To the contrary, many of them are satirical, light-hearted fables sometimes featuring squirrels or crows while others are amusing narratives about boss and employee, man and woman, love and sex—maybe. Altogether, these stories lend themselves to reading during a brief pause in the day or before bed-time at night.

Other books by or about Ellis Worth include another collection of short stories, *Once Upon a Farm: Tales of Discovery* (Annandale Press) and a memoir based on his diary, *Ascent from the Maelstrom: The Dynamics of Recovery from Mental Illness* (Annandale Press).

Dean O. Smith
January, 2021

The Sonora Springs Tales

An Affair of Art

There may be one born every minute, as Barnum said, but the new ones can't hold a candle to those who have been around long enough to learn the ropes and gain experience. Van Hummel Holst, for example, is thoroughly convinced of that ever since his little affair of the heart last summer. Just between us, and with only the names changed here and there to save embarrassment, here's what happened.

I've known Van ever since we went to Downing Elementary School together. In those days I had a positive propensity for getting into scrapes. It wasn't that I was more mischievous than the average: I just tripped and plunged headfirst into deep water, automatically. Not Van Hummel Holst. He kept his nose clean, his shoes shined, and his hair brushed. If there was an empty tin can on the sidewalk as he came along, he didn't kick it so it hit the old lady ahead of him in the back of the knees the way the rest of us did. He left the can right where it was and carefully navigated around it. He didn't pick it up and carry it to the public waste-disposal container at the corner in the smirking fashion of Percy Marble, but he skirted around the thing as I've said.

Van's always been like that: kept trouble at a distance. He was that way at Hilliard High, too. He was a good-looking fellow and wore his hair straight and long in the greasy pompadour style that was all the rage at that time. He was tall enough to play a bang-up brand of basketball, and all the sweet, sweatered, sixteens liked him. The popularity didn't go to his head, though, so that he tried to have fun with all the girls the way the footballers did. He had a sense of proportion: enough was enough, and plenty would go a long ways.

If Van hadn't told me himself about his little misadventure at the musical festival last summer, I wouldn't have believed it; I mean not altogether. As I say, I've known Van for years and never heard of him going even to one of those jazz jam sessions, let alone a high-brow concert. A more level-headed lawyer there never was, but a long-hair? It wasn't in him. That's what I would have said. Why, Van has helped nearly every organization in town raise money: Goodwill, the United Fund, the Cancer Society, everybody. He's that civic-minded. Just the same, the local symphony orchestra never tried to line him up on its side when it campaigned for funds. No wonder; he wouldn't have known a trombone from a tuba.

Of course, quite a number of fellows I goofed around with in school and college turned out differently than anyone would have guessed. There's Dick Moser, for example. He went to West Point, and in a few years he'll retire as a Major General. But, at Montgomery Junior College, Dick used to drift by the old Gopher Hole Harbor practically every night to see if Hammond—we used to call him Ham Hoskins—would get moody enough to start pounding the piano. And Dick worshiped electric guitar players that Van never knew existed.

It's hard to tell what will change a man. Maybe it's not just one single thing, event, but a succession of things. Van had been happily married to Betty for twenty years, at least, when they surprised everybody by getting a divorce. Their only child, Elsa, was just married, and bingo, the Holst's got divorced. One move leads to another. Then, Van left the law firm he was with to become executive secretary of a trade association. The chairman of the association was president of one of the law firm's biggest clients, and I happen to know Van didn't lose financially by the step. Still and all, the Holst name was the name around which all the others in that get-up revolved, and the legal situation in the Sonora Springs Bank Building never would be the same without Van.

Betty Holst went back where she came from originally, the college town of Bolton, a scant hundred miles away. That was three years ago, right after the divorce. Van continues to live in Sonora Springs, but he has to travel a bit in his new job. I guess he likes that; he says he does. It gives him a shift in scenery, he says. I said once "Yeah, the time a guy reaches forty, he likes to see some new sights and faces now and then."

"Forty," he said. "Thanks for the compliment, but who are you trying to kid? Boy, you're as old as I am, if you're a day."

I clapped him on the back and went on. You can't really rib Van, but it's fun to try.

As I get it now, there was a guy in Van's old set-up, Schweinhaupt, Holst, Hopkins, and Peters, that Van didn't take to at all. Peters wasn't in Van's way at the office. He was a good man who knew his business and knew his place. But, he rubbed Van the wrong way. It wasn't anything special, and Peters was Schweinhaupt's protégé and fair-haired favorite, so Van kept silent. Van said he hadn't even met Peters' wife at the time he pulled out of the partnership to go with the trade association. I don't know; that's what he said.

I do know this: that Evangeline Peters — Vangie, they call her — is a knock-out. But trust her, I wouldn't. Come a new fashion in hairdos, and, Mister, she's the very first to try it out. With all her rakish, rusty-brown hair, she makes it look good, too, better than any of the others who come along afterwards and try it. The same with the sack dress or what-have-you. On her, the sack was effective. No matter how new or how careful her get-up, there is a casual disorder about Vangie, a sultry insouciance, a kind of pouting, challenging, green-eyed insolence that is fetching, that makes a man want to straighten her out, if you know what I mean.

I suppose it doesn't matter whether Van Hummel Holst got to know Vangie Peters when Holst and Peters were partners, or later. He didn't become well-acquainted with her till afterward — if he ever got well-acquainted. In June last year they both were guests at a small dinner-party at the Schweinhaupt home. Wickford Peters was in Chicago on the business of a cement company client at the time. In a natural gesture of friendliness, with no devious plots whatever in mind, Van asked Vangie if he could drive her home. She accepted. It was all open and above board. It all started simply.

Van made the first move, and he says his best recollection is that he didn't make a second. So far as he can recall, nothing whatever was said when he took Vangie home, about music or the summer festival at Maroon

Meadows. He couldn't have said anything very definite because he hadn't seen a program, didn't know who was playing what. He knew there was an annual festival, and that was all. Vangie invited him in when they got home after the party, and he went in and had another drink or two with her. He may have made a couple of tentative, half-hearted, indefinite passes at her, but actually he was on his guard against her, against himself.

When he was telling me all this, I nodded and said: "After all, she is married."

He replied, "Of course. And besides, Man, I'm ten, fifteen, maybe twenty years older than she is." He fixed a wild eye on me and seemed to place a terrific importance on the barrier of age. He added, "She's young enough, almost, to be my daughter."

I was tempted to say, "Is that bad?" I remembered that his daughter, Elsa, had been quite a cute little number right up to her wedding day, the last time I had seen her, and I was willing to bet she still was. I said nothing.

There's a saying that there's no fool like an old fool, but I don't like it especially. It overlooks how the very stars stray out of their orbit to give an assist against him when a man of dignity and maturity starts to fumble and stumble and gets set to make folly into a fine art.

Van and Vangie laid no plans that June evening. She, probably, was on her guard as well as he. Soon afterward, however, Vangie learned that Wickford would be out of town on business over the Fourth of July, which was on Monday last year. That could have been a blow to her. It could be that she called Van, as Van says. It certainly must have been Vangie who wanted to hear the all-Beethoven program at Maroon Meadows late Sunday afternoon, July 3. The idea of leaving Maroon Meadows after the concert and after dinner and driving all the way back to Sonora Springs that night, two hundred miles over the mountains, and catching up later, on the holiday, with the sleep lost—that idea may have seemed easily possible and quite practical in advance. In any case, they agreed on the adventure.

They started for the alpine fastness of Maroon Meadows Sunday afternoon. It was a grand, beautiful, exhilarating trip. The traffic, at floodtide the day before, Saturday, was negligible now. Vangie was fresh, lively, innocent, attractive—truly a girl on a lark. She exclaimed at everything along the road: the melodies of the meadow lark, the breathtaking, colorful flower-carpet of the pastures, the speck-like cattle lost in the immensity of the valleys, and their mountain backdrop. Had Wickford been holding her prisoner for months in some round tower of their suburban home, Vangie could not have been more pleased with her holiday with Van than she was.

The program in the big tent was lost on Van. He didn't sleep through it, but he dozed. He was alternately too hot and too cold. He was sweetly conscious of Vangie at his side, of her generous flesh, her careless posture, and of those longish legs which seemed always to be getting in her own way. She was carried away by the performance. He could have slept without her noticing it. He was conscious of nothing but her and her perfume, with the swelling waves of music scarcely a distraction. She was intent on the orchestra and the piano soloist and unaware of him. After the concert, they had dinner at a cool, hidden-away dining room. Van kept up a line of cheerful chatter throughout the meal, but, though he didn't mention it, he knew very well he couldn't drive back to Sonora Springs that evening. It was useless even to begin. He was fairly used to day-long driving, but this had been different. He wasn't so much exhausted as suffering from a complete failure of will. That was the way Van put it to me. He wasn't playing a nasty, naughty trick on Vangie at all. He just couldn't drive back. And, of course, her doing so was out of the question.

Vangie sized up the situation herself at dinner, apparently. When they had finished and gone out to the car, she said "Van, darling, it was wonderful of you to do this for me." Tears came to her eyes. He made some awkward, mumbled protestation that it was nothing. She went on, "But we can't just go back again tonight, can we?"

"No, Vangie Sweet, we can't," he said.

They stayed at the Graustark Inn incognito, registered as Mr. and Mrs. John Holmes. When they first went to their suite, they spoke in low tones of suppressed excitement of rising early, before others were stirring, and setting out on their return journey. The plan was perfect, but their execution of it was faulty: that is, human. It was close to noon the next day, the Fourth, when they got ready to leave. It seemed safe, therefore, to Vangie to have breakfast right at the Inn. Van over-ruled that emphatically and hurried through the lobby to the car as soon as he had paid the bill.

He expected to see Vangie already there, ahead of him. She wasn't. He looked back. She was coming, but utterly changed. She looked crushed. Wonderingly, he held the car door open for her. She got in and slumped.

"What's the matter?" he asked.

"Do you want to see something?" she replied in a taut, tense voice. The air with which she said it made him say "No."

She wouldn't be put off. "Go back to the coffee shop, if you want to see something," she said.

"Nothing on earth could make me go back now," he answered.

"You want to know who's having breakfast?" In spite of her restraint, she was screaming. "Wick's in there having breakfast. Do you know who's with him? Your wife from Bolton. Now do you want to go back?"

"No," he said, "I have no wife in Bolton."

She tried to register his denial of a wife as if that were incomprehensible. She said nothing as he started the motor. She was dry-eyed as they pulled out of the Inn's parking space. They were well along their way to Sonora Springs, with her completely oblivious to her surroundings all the while, when she began to weep softly and as one who can't understand what it is she's weeping about. Van felt sorry for her. He took her home; told her he wanted to help her in every way he could; telephoned her various times later in the daytime when he knew Wickford would be at the office to repeat his assurance. She said she appreciated his offers but needed nothing. He hasn't seen her since.

An Afternoon Off

Irwin Edman has made us all aware, of course, that philosophers have holidays. How many know, however, that they also have afternoons off, like maids and fauns? This may seem to be a terribly tiny bit of information, but as we shall see, it has rather unexpected ramifications.

One way of looking at it, the guys are darn lucky, now that summer sessions tread hard on the heels of the regular school year, to have any time at all for loitering, if only a half day. Leastwise, Hornsby Smith, Ph.D. and professor of Advanced Scholastic Philosophy at Cody College, considered himself indeed fortunate to have an entire early summer afternoon that he could call his own. It was his own because his wife didn't know about it and because of an unanticipated leniency on the part of Hornsby's dentist.

The appointment with Dr. Jaquith was at two o'clock, and a few minutes before that time Hornsby was telling the receptionist at the Kirby Dental Clinic that he was there. The mature, poised young woman at the desk was fairly new, but he had never seen her before. She was not pretty or petite, but she was striking, different, arresting, statuesque. She had big green eyes and as he looked into them now the girl asked, "May I say who's calling?"

He told her "Mr. Smith," and as he did his eyes left her face, descended to her firm, brown, thick shoulders and, oh-oh, darted swiftly down to the cream-white breasts which were exposed to his view as the receptionist leaned forward. These were held up, not to say thrust up, by the girl's kindly dark bra, but his glimpse of them was momentary. How did her shoulders get so tanned so early in the season? Here it was only the first of June, and that's early in Sonora Springs. "Yes," the girl was saying, "won't you have a seat, Mr. Smith, and I'll call you when the doctor's ready."

Hornsby took a chair in the waiting room. Was that sudden revelation of the girl's bosom accidental or intentional? He glanced at the receptionist's careful hairdo. Not a strand of her tinted auburn hair was out of place. It was a becoming coiffure, if a trifle too short, too mannish for Hornsby's taste. No, he thought, with that gal nothing happens by chance. By proving her femininity to me, she also proved it to herself, which was the more necessary.

"You can go in now, Mr. Smith." He went down the hall to Dr. Jaquith's office. Hornsby had been having a spot of trouble with one of his eye-teeth. He had just had a root-canal treatment, and now, he supposed, the dentist was going to fill the cavity — put on a crown or an inlay, or whatever. Dr. Jaquith took only a quick look, asked if there were any tenderness in the gum and then shunted his patient to the x-ray room. "That will be all for today," he said. "I want to have the x-ray developed before I do anything." The roentgenologist was through with Hornsby before he had a chance to say Jack Robinson.

The hour or two Hornsby had intended to put at the disposal of his dentist was a sudden windfall. What to do with it—oh yes, the parks must be nice at this time of the year, and Craftwood Park was close by; he'd try that.

He was relaxing comfortably on a park bench and facing directly into the sun when he spied, off to his left, the approach of a young woman in a sun suit with perhaps four or five or a half-dozen tiny tots in front of her, behind her, surrounding her. All evidently were headed for the swings some distance to his right. The little ones, catching sight of their goal, sped past in front of him as fast as their legs could carry them. The bare-foot, bare-legged young woman didn't alter her digni-fied, book-on-head pace.

She was a decided brunette of about twenty years. Her black, black hair had the inevitable, practical bob (darn it). Her face was moist, presumably from perspira-tion or lotion. She paid him no attention whatsoever as she descended into the ravine directly in front of him. He could see the cleft in her breasts from where he sat. She wasn't bosomy, but she was well-built: neither skinny nor fat. Her navy blue suit, so tight-fitting above, had loosely flounced, scalloped legs of a slight straw color. When she passed by him so that he saw her retreating, the frills accentuated the wiggle of the hips in her walk.

Hornsby, now and then, glanced towards the swings. At first, the girl occupied herself with pushing the various children. Then she went over and sat down on the grass, slipped the straps off her shoulder, rubbed herself with oil all over, and like Hornsby, faced into the sun.

Is she the mother of one of the children, Hornsby asked himself. She could be. She's old enough to be the mother of several of them, even. No, she's not the mother but a maid. She's probably better looking than any of the mothers. That's the way it is; maids are always better looking than their employers. Wonder why that is. Besides, only a maid could interfere so little, rock the boat so little, and yet manage to participate in all the high-spirited good fun.

He knew she had noticed his intermittent gaze, for once when she returned from one of her brief tours of duty at the swings, she waggled her flounced rump at him and then, this time, deliberately turned her back on him when she sat down. He didn't care. He had no wish to make love to the maid. Looking down into her eyes would settle none of the profound, philosophical problems that had been perplexing him for so long. He was satisfied to have seen what he had seen, and it was time to move on before he got sunburned. Then, too, he wanted to stop at the dry-cleaners on the way home.

Mrs. Rodriguez was on duty at the Spic-N-Span Cleaners when he arrived. She was a good-natured woman of about his age. He liked her, and she was always glad to see him and enjoyed pronouncing his name. "Mr. Smith," she would say, with a cute accent, on the slightest pretext.

His slacks had been cleaned, "and if you can wait just a minute, Mr. Smith, I'll have them pressed." He could see that she would like to strike up a conversation. "Would you like to sit down, Mr. Smith?" Here she lifted a couple of blankets off a love-seat finished in leatherette from which the color was peeling. He remained standing, and she went back behind the counter. "I thought you wanted the slacks on Thursday, the same as the jacket," she said. "Otherwise, they'd be all set. Sometimes I goof." He nodded and smiled. "We all do," he said.

Their eyes met at this exchange of amiable trivialities. Hers were brown, pleasant, but unsmiling, and she looked at him squarely. His were gray-blue, also unsmiling, and deeply penetrating. He waited, still standing. A belt loop had to be reinforced. He saw or felt or sensed that several times while she was running the needle through the belt loop, Mrs. Rodriguez shot swift glances up at him standing there. Her hands were as big as his own and as ring-less. She is so friendly, she is more than friendly, he thought. Her serious brown eyes not only give out an invitation; they are coaxing.

He looked at her as she went over to hang the slacks on the stand. Her hips were well padded and bulged out around her ample waist. Her neckline V-plunged but revealed nothing. That, of course, did not fool Hornsby's practiced eye. "Don't pay me now, Mr. Smith," she said. "Wait till you come for the jacket." He understood this probably meant the charge would be forgotten, but he assented. Mrs. Rodriguez wanted to make this little gesture, and he would let her. "Okay," he said and took the pants and went out. As he went along the street, he hummed an old rhumba tune he knew. "Ma-ma In-ez, Ma-ma In-ez."

When Hornsby got home, he did not impress Mrs. Smith as his usual, steady, and resigned self, and he certainly did not seem like a guy who had suffered two hours or more in a dentist's chair. His arm lingered around Mrs. Smith's waist, and his lips dallied warmly on hers. "That's the way it is with these philosophers," she said to herself, later. "They're different from other men. That's what comes from always having the mind so high in the sky."

Araby

Once upon a time, during the first administration of President Adams, there lived, in the heavenly city of Sonora Springs, a lawyer by the name of Abner Dulles. Now Ab Dulles, though rich beyond a beggar's dreams and marvelously versed in languages, law and ancient philosophies, was miserably unfortunate. It was all because of his wife, Kela.

In the twenty years in which the Dulleses had been married, there had not been one in which Kela had not threatened, at least a dozen times, to leave the undeserving Abner to his solitary fate and go her way. The unhappy Dulles had become as habituated to his wife's menaces as she had become accustomed to her husband's ways and manners. While he no longer took seriously these oft-repeated threats of his wife, the poor man did do his best to mollify the vixen's temper while she lingered.

Kela reveled in the magic genie of electricity, and Abner indulged her wishes in this respect to the limit. In the evenings he returned from his simple law office to a glorified factory, complete with air conditioning, washer, dryer, hair dryer, humidifier, dehumidifier, etc. One weak and ailing woman, his wife, presided over it all.

Despite the wondrous slaves provided by her genie, Kela worked harder than any of her ancestors ever had done. Sometimes she was so exhausted by the day's activity that she had to lapse into sullen silence; was unable to greet her husband upon his return from work with the customary listing of grievances. Seldom could she muster more than ten words during the evening meal, and frequently she slept as she watched her favorite television program.

Though Kela would not have been able to tell anyone so, the one thing above all which had made life with Ab Dulles tolerable for her all these years had been the shop-talk which her husband brought home from his modest office in the Majestic Building. She would admit, however, and did admit quite freely to all and sundry that Abner discoursed beautifully upon the strange and enchanted world of "short sales" by those having nothing to sell, the purchase of gems having no price but only so many installment payments, income taxes in excess of income, a presumption of the innocence of the one believed guilty, trusts for stray cats, and many, many, other marvels. Thus it was that Kela had remained a dutiful wife.

Abner was delighted that Kela found the content of his armchair and table talk more entrancing than that of the communications and commercials so magically conveyed by television, telephone, and radio. He was, however, no more conscious than his wife of the truly decisive part his stories played in keeping Kela with him as a household partner for the hours before bedtime. For Ab, a world without Kela simply did not exist. Her peevish silences, shrewish complaints, tiredness and nagging were "written" into the constitution of his daily life; had been for years his fate and fare of connubial bliss; and he never even dreamed of a different destiny.

One evening Ab remarked with a degree of self-importance he seldom exhibited, "I took in a new case today. Something quite different. I received a telephone call from the Golden Girl. She is decidedly aged, in her eighties now at least I should say. She asked if I would come out to see her at her home about a will." Kela made no show of interest; did not as much as flicker an eye-lash.

Ab knew his wife was listening, and he continued: "Quite a remarkable woman this client is, in spite of her lurid background. Of course all I know about her past is hearsay, but I understand the Golden Girl of the West once was as popular in her own fashion as the Girl of the Golden West. She worked her way up, I guess; became a notorious madam. She was married once to a guy long since gathered to his fathers—but how she ever got so much wealth I don't know. I do know she now has enough dough to make a bakery jealous.

"She lives beyond the city limits in a modest but modern ranch house; has no close neighbors. Can you imagine—Goldie's all alone except for her dog, a pistol, and a hoard of currency; has her groceries delivered. She told me I had been recommended to her by a friend of long standing; said she would rather not mention his name. She has no relatives at all and wants to will her home and half of her other property to an orphanage. The other half of her hoard is to go to a girl sixteen or seventeen years old who left the orphanage just a few years ago."

Kela waited, without comment, for her husband to go on. He did; "I said I'd be glad to make a will for her, but that I had several suggestions to make. One is that we inventory all this currency you have stashed away on the premises and then put it in a safe-deposit box, so it won't be a temptation to anyone. If you keep it here, I advised her, who can tell, somebody may break in and steal it; maybe kill you doing it.

"Goldie was gruff as all get out. 'Come here,' she said. 'I want to show you something.' We went out the back door. She had taken a pistol from a drawer and asked me to bring a bottle of beer from the kitchen. I did so and set the bottle high up on the limb of a tree as a target, as she wanted it. Do you know, she shot the cap off that bottle of beer at fifty paces without splintering a particle of glass! I drank the beer. 'Do you still think anyone will try to break in and steal from me?' she asked.

"I could see there was no use in insisting upon that particular piece of advice. Besides, I was half-convinced the money was as safe with her as with a bank. So I said that I would like to know something about the orphan to whom she planned to leave so much money.

"'I thought you would,' Goldie said with a chuckle. 'We're having a sort of a family reunion here at lunch. Veva is coming to see me; and two sisters of the orphan-age are joining us. Won't you be one of the party? Then you can see the girl for yourself. Hold your questions till afterward. In fact, by that time, you'll know nearly as much about Veva as I do. Oh, I've known her a number of years, but I never asked her anything about herself; I didn't need to. I've never told her anything either — about the will I mean. That's a little secret between us.' The old gal raised her hand to her mouth in a gesture of pretended secrecy and snickered, 'It's a secret trick on the Grim Reaper. If it works, death will be as sweet as life has been bitter. And it'll work.'

"Do you know, Veva was the prettiest girl I've ever seen! She had a solid wholesomeness about her, like that of a French milkmaid. Her cheeks were rose red. She laughed—yes, laughed, not smiled. She was something to see, I tell you. Her dress was grape or plum colored. I can't say which, but the ripe color, her bursting bosom, her nut brown hair, her dark eyes, her rollicking laughter—and all this in the country air of Goldie's ranch. I tell you it was something like paradise. God forgive me, I thought I could hear the music of pipes and see a satyr dancing!"

Ab had forgotten his audience of one. He had been so enraptured by his recollections that he had almost shouted. Now, lowering his voice to a caress, he went on. "Her skin was not like other people's. It was so soft to the touch; so like a skin should be and never is; so alive and growing; so protective of the flesh beneath; not pale or white but glowing with a gentle ruddiness; smooth; warm....Then her hair! Her hair crowned it all—summarized all the ripe loveliness, yes, the fruitful loveliness of this sweet sixteen. Even more, it was scented with the breezes of the outdoors, of the mountains."

"Stop, stop, stop, you double-dyed, double-crossing, bald-headed, bantam buzzard; you fatuous faun; you addle-pated ass; you grub-worm of a man!" It was now Kela's turn to shout and Ab's to look dazed. If the wife just had caught glimpses of unsuspected flames and fires beneath the ashen complexion of her husband, Abner now learned that Kela long had concealed from him the full extent of her vocabulary. In the end, and still in a frenzy, she grabbed her coat and purse and ran from the house with the unmistakable intention of making good at last the threats she had so often thrown at Ab Dulles.

Ab stared in bewilderment at the door which had been slammed shut with such violence behind the figure of his departing wife. Then he shrugged and uttered a strained laugh. "I'll be damned," he said, thrusting his chest forward and squaring his shoulders, "I never knew it would be like this. Cripes, I feel like I just got the Old Woman of the Sea off my neck. Cripes, I breathe, I live again!" Here he demonstrated his breathing with vigor. "Kee-ripes, if I'd known before it would feel so good to be rid of her, I could have made up a story like that!"

The Black Prince

O nce upon a time, there was an old woman who lived at the edge of a wood. Her name was Mrs. Burr, and she wasn't alone. Charlie lived there, too, and he was about her age and had the same last name, and he might have been her husband. In fact, everybody supposed he was. Be that as it may, he wasn't the father of The Black Prince.

Mrs. Burr wasn't the mother of the Prince either. In fact, nobody knew much about the prince—not even Ethelred, the boy from the neighboring farm who used to spy on the Burrs from his hiding place in the blackberry vines along the line fence. To young Ethelred, though to no one else, the Burrs were a mysterious couple. They didn't have a farm; they didn't have children; and they always carried guns but never went hunting. Mrs. Burr claimed to be a better shot than Charlie, and he didn't deny it. One had as much chance of seeing a witch without a broom stick as of seeing Mrs. Burr go forth from the house without a gun.

It made more sense for Charlie to carry a gun. He was tending a still in a swamp in the heart of the wood, a business which, at that time, required the strictest secrecy. Ethelred knew that as well as everyone else, and he respected Charlie's work-day privacy. It made sense also, because Charlie wasn't the kind of a person who would use a gun, even as a club. Ethelred knew that better than anyone else. He could tell in a hundred different ways which escaped grown-ups. True, Charlie wore a hunting garb instead of farmers' overalls. But he talked in the toneless voice and with all the vacuous solemnity of a judge, and to the innocent eye of the child, Charlie was clearly as ineffectual as the wise, old official whose only strength lives in elections and whose only wisdom is drawn from books.

From time to time, Charlie would be arrested and go away to "do time." Then, Mrs. Burr would be alone in the house with her armory, for The Black Prince lived outdoors, at least at the beginning. It isn't natural for crows to live indoors, and The Black Prince was pretty typical of crows in his age bracket: silky, shiny, raven-black, and debonair; shrewd as shrewd can be and yet with a saving naiveté. The boy and the bird weren't friends—how can such things be—but they tolerated each other and peered at each other with considerable curiosity. The boy's secret hiding place was no secret to the bird.

The Burrs had a garden in which, according to the custom of the time, they grew about every known vegetable, plus sweet corn and popcorn. In the spring-time, The Black Prince and his family would watch the planting activities of the Burrs from a safe distance in the wood. They doubtless marveled, as Ethelred did, that Charlie's own peculiar, private religion permitted him to take part in the seasonal seeding ritual but absolutely forbade him to touch the handle of a hoe in mid-summer. Other meditations of the crows, however, must have been of a more practical nature, for they would congregate near one end of the clearing and caw with the vociferousness of demons possessed. Eventually they would taunt Mrs. Burr into the grove with her gun and then the clever rascals would take turns scratching the seed of the garden patch while Charlie's back was turned.

Ethelred suspected that Charlie was really on the side of the crows and enjoyed their victory over Man, or in this case, Mrs. Burr. Ethelred wondered if beneath Charlie's mask of passive acquiescence in the buffeting of sheriffs and jailers, the guy didn't thrill to the cacophonous battle hymn of the crows. Why shouldn't the guy use his firearm unless he dreamed as it were, of trading guns for wings? Ethelred kept these long, long thoughts to himself, however, and went on watching.

There were a few episodes, indeed, that made Ethelred wonder which side he was on. One ruse of the Burrs, in particular, caused him to desert his observation post in the blackberry vines for several whole days. That was when the Burrs threaded hairs from a horse's tail through some kernels of corn and scattered them at the edge of the plowed plot. Only one, the boldest, oldest, and most brazen of the feathered flock, fell for this trick and carried a kernel off to the underbrush to have his throat cut. Just the same, Ethelred was a witness to the beginning of the end and fled from his nest. For their part, the Burrs saw only the untouched bait and supposed their trick had been completely unsuccessful.

Curiosity brought Ethelred, the wide-eyed, back to carry on. Charlie, in ignorance of the missing victim, seemed happy over the failure of Operation Cutthroat. He may have been pleased as well at the lengths to which he and Mrs. Burr had gone, and would go, to win the war for sweet corn. In a way, it was a point in favor of his real ally. The fat, flappy lady herself was losing no sleep over the waste of horsehair, for she was already busy with other stratagems, foremost, a scarecrow in her image.

The likeness of Mrs. Burr soon stood stiffly at attention between the rows of cabbage bordering the tiny corn field. A couple of men came out from somewhere on the morning of its appearance to get Charlie again to "do time." He said goodbye to Mrs. Burr with a quick brush of cheeks and then took a long, lingering look at her wooden effigy and without a tear got into the car. The crows in the distance maintained a respectful silence until the dust stirred up by the vanishing vehicle had settled to the earth. Afterward, they cawed continuously, for Mrs. Burr's weapon was leaning against her double.

When Mrs. Burr finished hoeing and put the hoe where the gun had been and went into the house to fix dinner, the entire flock descended from the treetops into Mrs. Burr's garden where they strutted around like proprietors on an inspection tour. They had come to visit, not to eat; to laugh and not to prey. Some of the lustier ones perched on the outstretched arms of the statue and burst into song. Art critics admiring a rediscovered Slave Girl couldn't have been more vocal. From his grassy, brushy den at the line fence, Ethelred wondered if there was something in this strange performance he wasn't understanding. If he knew Mrs. Burr, she wasn't the kind of a woman to take anything lying down.

She wasn't either. The next day when the crows came back at dinner time for an encore, three young pinfeathered fledglings stepped into the snares concealed on the sleeves and hat of Mrs. Burr's double. In her anger and vexation, the frenzied woman rushed out of the house to wring the necks of two of her captives and throw their lifeless corpses to the ground. "Let that be a lesson to all of you," she shrieked, shaking her fist at the forest. To the third she said, "I'll clip your wings and keep you for company. Now that Charlie's gone, you'll be my Black Prince."

At that introduction to royalty, Ethelred scampered away as fast as his bare feet could carry him, to fix his gaze later on those high-flying geese which annually migrate from the frozen fastnesses of the north.

The Boss and the Girl

Her boss was an oil man and a big-time operator. It hadn't always been so. There were long years, before she became his secretary, when the boss toiled with his hands in the oil fields, wore dirty, greasy coveralls; and took desperate chances with the meager "working capital" he had been able to scrape together by borrowing from acquaintances and near acquaintances who held down respectable, routine jobs in the banks and warehouses of Denver, Casper, Cheyenne and Salt Lake. The old-timers at the Las Vegas casinos would have shied away from the odds the boss took then. That was quite a while ago, when building a business was the order of the day.

When she went to work for him, Johnny Van Loo, only forty-eight, was president of his own little oil company. It really wasn't so tiny, except by comparison with Phillips Pete, Sinclair Refining, and the dozen or so sprawling giants which owned derricks the world over. Van Loo Oil did its drilling only in the Rocky Mountain states and not all of those. But it sold the produce of its wells at a profit which was the envy of the big boys in other lines of business. Movie moguls on the West Coast and steel barons in Chicago and Pittsburgh had heard about Johnny Van Loo.

Ursula Linden was pink-cheeked, pretty, slender and swayed gracefully, like a willow in the wind, in her high-heeled walk. In addition, she was a good secretary. Van Loo promoted her from secretary to private secretary to assistant to the president; made her manager of the details of the personal side of his business affairs; paid her well; increased her salary whenever an occasion presented itself and sometimes when one didn't. Considering her bonuses, Christmas presents, birthday remembrances and all, Ursula's take-home pay nearly equaled her husband's. Jasper Linden was assistant general manager of an association of casualty insurance companies, and the member companies were not doing so well right then, what with automobile collisions hitting new highs and the breakage of costly wrap-around windshields going on right and left.

The generosity of Ursula's boss was a grand thing, no doubt. Jasper never denied it, or even thought of doing so. He and Ursula were invited out to Johnny's home from time to time on evenings and week-ends. It was evident on the face of things, and without looking closely, that Johnny was in a high income tax bracket and preferred paying handsome salaries to meeting high taxes. Jasper, like Ursula, called Van Loo "Johnny." The latter wanted it, liked it that way. He thought it softened away, somehow, the hard fact that he was a big boss, though others who worked for him found that the evasive tactic of the first name really called attention to his position at the top of the heap. Mrs. Van Loo was content to remain Mrs. Van Loo, and so she remained, at least for the Lindens.

Jasper was under an "underground pressure" that he would not have felt if this slip of a wife of his — she was just thirty and so three years younger than he — had been working for an employer more like his own. It wasn't that Jasper was like Harry Lauder and couldn't give his wife anything but love. He was getting a nice fat check every month and putting a bit aside for a rainy day. He appreciated Johnny's appreciation of Ursula, of course, and, as the husband, was luckier than Johnny. But if Johnny only wasn't so darned demonstrative of his appreciation in solid, tangible, material ways!

Jasper had no idea about Johnny and Ursula that he put into words. There obviously was no affair between the two and nothing to worry about. Nevertheless, he took on a taste and a yen for martinis that was new for him. Besides, he began to notice how efficient his own buxom, bosomy, dark-eyed secretary was. Her willing, incomparable services to the association of insurers were scarcely recognized by the figures following the name Sandra Bender and the magical phrase "pay to the order of." Jasper made her a Christmas gift of a subscription to a fine, arty, expensive magazine. He remembered her birthday with an exquisite bouquet, and, on slight pretext — with Ursula's knowledge — he lavished similar attentions upon his "girl."

Sandra, almost old enough to be Jasper's mother, was nobody's fool. She accepted the tokens of esteem with good grace and kept on about her business as usual. She knew that Jasper wasn't making a play for her. So did Jasper, but what wasn't so clear to him was exactly what he was doing. He was too deep in the forest to see anything but trees.

While this personal web was being woven, the *Wall Street Journal* and *Fortune* and even the regular news weeklies were reporting the mergers of the Chase and Manhattan Banks, of J. P. Morgan and Guaranty Trust, of Signal Oil and Hancock Oil, and of a host of other smaller companies all over the country. No one knew exactly why all these business marriages were going on, but everyone was sure there were very sound, substantial reasons: tax reasons maybe, business reasons surely. It wasn't a simple case of big fishes eating little ones at all, because—well, who'd call either Signal or Hancock little? No; joining forces was as much the fashion of the time as nuptial vows in June.

Another oil company which operated in the midcontinent fields, in the Texas and California fields, under the offshore tidelands of Louisiana, in the Venezuelan jungle, and on the Arabian desert, discovered that it should tap the resources of the Mountain States. It took a shine to Van Loo Oil, and vice versa. They made a deal. Johnny ceased to be president of his own company and became vice president of a bigger one which boasted several similar officers under a president who, in turn, was under a vice chairman and a chairman of the Board of Directors. Inspectors and accountants and management specialists from the main office in Houston began to swarm around the former headquarters of Van Loo Oil, which now had become the Rocky Mountain branch of Tri-Continent Oil.

After the merger, Johnny was forever on the go: at meetings, in conferences, on trips. His business affairs no longer had a personal side. Everything was company business. Ursula became lost in the turmoil of paper work, reports, check-ups, and traveling auditors. With Johnny forced, by his own busyness and by the shortness of his stays at home, to take her for granted, Ursula began to appreciate Jasper to a degree somewhat new and foreign to her experience since going with Van Loo's. Besides, the boss wasn't as much the boss as he had been. The situation at the office wasn't at all the same as it used to be.

"Before the consolidation" seemed to Ursula like the good old days before the fall from paradise. Then she seldom had spoken of the affairs of the work day to her husband except to relay jokes, choice bits of gossip, news of Johnny's latest gesture of grandeur and good will. For quite a while after the merger, though, she would carry home perplexities, vexations, irritations, and complaints.

Jasper made no pretense of easy solutions to the problems which had gotten into his wife's hair. He listened. He was concerned about Ursula's burdens and difficulties. At times, he would try to divert the conversation into more cheerful channels. He always did so when Ursula lamented the consolidation and likened Johnny's deal to an exchange of gold for fool's gold. Jasper seemed to understand not only Ursula's present predicament but also Johnny's preference for shares of stock in a bigger company, shares which had a ready market and could be unloaded quickly, if desired.

If Jasper thought "Johnny's moves are Johnny's affair" or "I'm quite satisfied with the outcome of the big deal," he never said so. He simply and tactfully shifted the gears of the conversation. Ursula, for her part, came around to feeling cozy and at home with this sort of silent treatment, like a cat at a warm fireside.

The sharp edge of disappointment and annoyance wore off gradually. At home now, Ursula sometimes will suddenly remember the events of the day, look up and say, "Johnny came back today from Los Angeles, or Dallas, or New York." It no longer matters especially that the boss wants to be called Johnny. Rather, Jasper is used to thinking of Van Loo that way, and, when it comes to names, Jasper is a creature of habit and absolutely opposed to change. He's also dead set against any form of progress when he's well off, and, what's more, he knows when he's well off. That's not a bad thing for a boss to know.

That Bubble, Trouble

Rudy Sainsot didn't know what to think about his raise under the circumstances. It hadn't come about like any other he'd ever heard of, and there had been a time when business was good and he'd heard from his colleagues quite a few instances of clever word-tennis, tricky verbal fencing, and heroic thrusts of wit, ending with the most satisfying results — year-end bonuses, and what-not. Nowadays, though, the boss was always complaining about the terrific competition for orders, the cost-price squeeze, high taxes, and a million other things. And, despite his wife's prodding, Rudy hadn't even asked or thought of asking for the neat little increase in monthly salary which had become his.

He was musing on the situation as he waited for the bus. He had got through the afternoon to quitting time without any of his fellow workers suspecting what had happened. They had been observing Rudy bending over the papers on his desk with a vacant stare, half asleep, more dopey than usual; and when they, the occupants of the adjoining desks, had heard Miss Slocum come over and say in a low voice, "Mr. Boothroyd wants to see you," they didn't take the message as a forerunner of good news for Mr. Sainsot, not by any means. Consequently, they hadn't fished for details of the interview when Rudy returned. Besides, so far as the latter's face showed upon his return from the corner stronghold of the Old Man, nothing at all out of the ordinary had taken place. Rudy appeared to be in as much of a stupor as before.

The bus stopped and Rudy got on it without any interruption in his train of thought. He was glad the whole damn staff didn't know of his own, private, good fortune. The boss had told him, "Don't let the cat out of the bag," but he knew as well as Old Boothroyd what a clamor that would have caused. It would have begun right away and gone on for months with him in the middle of it. Without a little luck, however, he wouldn't have been able to put his colleagues off the trail at the crucial moment, the instant of his greatest vulnerability to prying curiosity. Not knowing how he looked he didn't realize how much he owed to the unusually heavy, heavy-lidded appearance with which the misadventures of the night before had stamped him.

Now that this workday was over, no one at the office would ever be able to chisel the slightest word out of him. Now, he was their equal. In the morning, he'd be fresh, and he'd be ready for them, and he'd hold them off. He'd tell them nothing. He sighed with the weariness of a successful contestant who has passed through a severe trial, with the relief of an ageing toreador who has just slain the bull. The bus stopped to take on and let off passengers, and Rudy's mind passed on to thoughts of his wife. What would he tell her, if anything? The truth? He knew perfectly well that with her a dramatic face-to-face show-down with Old Boothroyd and a shrewd, long-drawn-out, victorious bargaining for a penny's worth was infinitely to be preferred to verifying his count of the extra dollars at the week's end. The truth was out of the question; was for the pigeons.

He couldn't, however, get any further than that. His mind balked; it resisted contact with his wife's wishes in the matter as stubbornly as an ornery critter evades the corral gate to which the cowboy is constantly crowding it. He gave up, after a little, and dwelt on the incident which had given rise to his meditations, dwelt on it as if he were actually reciting the truth, after all to his wife, with his spouse listening sweetly, patiently and raptly without ever cutting in with "I heard all that this morning; come to the point."

"I've been watching you this afternoon, Rudy. What's the matter? Is anything wrong?"

"Ain't nothing wrong, exactly, Mr. Boothroyd. I'm tired, that's all."

"Vacations will be coming up in another month or two. Do you want to be put at the head of the list, or do you want to take yours right away, maybe, without waiting — go fishing?"

"No... I mean I'm sleepy."

"Insomnia? You?"

"Hell, no. I ain't got insomnia. Ain't nothing I like more than sleeping, far as that goes. That's just it. You see, my kid, my oldest boy, Carl, he wanted to use my car last night, see? Hadda date with a girl at Denver, and his car wasn't good enough. Well, I don't go for that kind of stuff every day, but once in a while is okay. So I said 'sure, sure.' He's a sophomore in college, now, you know.

"Well, that's all right. I saw him drive off, and later on, Bess and I went to bed the same as usual. I sleep so well I didn't even hear the phone as a matter of fact, but Bess shook me, and I half tumbled downstairs trying to get to the phone by the night-light. It was Carl. 'Dad,' he says, 'I'm stuck here at Vaquero. I've run out of gas.'

"'Ran out of gas,' I says, 'Well get some more and come on home. What you calling me in the middle of the night for? You run out of money, too?' I had turned the light on by then and could see it was a quarter of two.

"'No, Dad, it isn't that,' he says. 'I didn't see how low I was on gas till I got out of Denver and was ten miles along, just passing that Happy Canyon side-road. The indicator showed empty, but I made it on a tail-wind and a prayer to Vaquero. But then all the stations were closed. I stopped at that truck diner, Bennie's, and asked Bennie if he'd stake me — sell me — enough gas to make it home. He reminded me of this self-service station down by the tracks; you know, across from the sign for Stratton's Ranch.'

"The kid went there, he tells me over the phone, long-distance, this is. I don't know if you know about these self-service stations, Mr. Boothroyd. I never used one myself. Anyway, you put your money in, and the gas is pumped up into the glass container at the top that holds five gallons. Then you can take down the hose and empty the gas into your tank.

"'Well, then,' I says, 'you got gas.'

"'No,' he says. 'I ain't got gas. When I took the ignition keys off the mantel, I forgot to get the key for the gas-tank lock.'

"'Judas Priest,' I says, or something like that, 'of all the rattle-brained, empty-headed things I've ever heard of a guy doing, that takes the cake.'

"'I know,' he says. 'I know that; but I still ain't got no gas.'

"'Well, find a place to stay. Ask Bennie where you can stay and forget the gas till morning.' That's what I told him.

"'I'll lose the gas I paid for that way,' he says, 'and the cost of staying overnight besides. Somebody will get that gas. Anybody who comes here can get it, if I'm not here.'

"'Then they get it,' I says. 'Five gallons, a dollar and a half. That won't break me.'

"'I was going to get ten gallons. I put money in two pumps,' he says.

"'Blessed be the name of the Lord,' I says, 'I'm coming. Stay there and hold onto the gas.' This was a long-distance, you know, forty miles each way at two in the morning.

"'I lost the best sleeping hours of the night that way. I was doing fairly well this morning, Mr. Boothroyd, but after lunch it seemed like a truck dumped a load of gravel on my head. I declare I've been doing the best I can.'

"Old Boothroyd said, 'I know. Bob locked me out of our car last winter. I was entertaining Kubek from the East—you remember the best damn customer Aladdin De-Greaser's got—and I took him to the hockey game, and Bob too. Kubek's pretty old, you know, and frail, and it was awfully cold and windy that night so, at the end of the first-period of play, it had got pretty chilly inside the arena. I gave Bob the keys to the car and told him to fetch a blanket from the back seat. Bob brought it all right, but when the game was over and we came to go home, we were locked out of the car. The keys were laying there in plain sight on the front seat, but we couldn't get to them. Bob finally got the door open with an old wire coat hanger we found out there on the parking lot, but it was more than a little nippy standing there in the wind, waiting, I'll tell you. And I doubt if Kubek really understood. He's just got daughters, three daughters.'

"Then the Old Man thinks a little and says, 'How long has it been since you had a raise, Mr. Sainsot?'

"'I don't know,' I says.

"He says, 'How would it be if we upped your pay $25 a month?'

"'Okay,' I says.

"'How much would that be a week?' he says...'Six and a quarter? That's not very much, is it? We'll up it $10 a week beginning this week, but, mind you, don't let the cat out of the bag around here, whatever you do. You know how that is. That's all then, Rudy,' he says.

"'Thank you,' I says."

The Bull of the Mountain

Grand Pré Taurus III was a young bull indeed, but he nevertheless had the memories of one incredibly older. It would be difficult to explain why this was so. Perhaps because of the extraordinary emphasis which Pretaurus, for that was his nickname, had always placed on his ancestry. Whatever the explanation, the memories existed. They were as vague and misty as a mirage or a dream, but they were there and not easily banished from mind.

Cows, of course, are known to be uncommonly meditative animals. Reflection goes pretty naturally with time-consuming cud chewing and the comfortable, stretched out and relaxed posture of the *bonnes femmes* during the process. In the bovine family, silent contemplation is a female trait. A healthy, more or, less normal young bull would as soon be caught dead as mulling upon food for thought. Bulls prefer to snort, paw the earth, and roll their eyes restlessly.

Pretaurus wasn't exactly a normal young bull. He had a glossy, short-haired, black coat like all the others on Mr. Smith's ranch, but his hide was shinier, smoother, more beautiful. In addition, Pretaurus was bigger than all the others. According to Mr. Smith, Pretaurus was even more colossal than Grand Pré Taurus II had been, and the latter's size had been the wonder of all who beheld him. Pretaurus' dark horns were short, but they seemed curved in a special, somehow distinctive, manner. And, finally, there were those odd, unaccountable recollections of Pretaurus. Those were decidedly abnormal. In fact, any sense at all of the past is rare among the bovines.

Pretaurus and all the rest of Mr. Smith's valuable Angus cattle were fenced in; and Mr. Smith himself could scarcely recall the time when this was not so. It stuck in the young bull's mind, however, that he had known a time when the ranges of the West were open and free and he himself had roamed them. Pretaurus held no grudges against Mr. Smith. He had no reason to. He had nothing at all to do for his food and lodging and his master, except that now and then, on special occasions, he was given the honor of the acquaintance of some exceptionally treasured cow introduced to him and his pen by Mr. Smith or the foremen. Yet, Pretaurus recalled better days when he dispensed with formal introductions and made his own friends, so to speak.

Millions of people, at rodeos from Madison Square Garden to the deserts of Arizona, have witnessed and forgotten the spectacle of bulls of all colors and sizes tossing riders from their backs with demonic abandon. Pretaurus neither had seen such sights nor forgotten them. Blurred visions and composite pictures of all these and similar events passed across the stage back of his curly forehead and gave way to other dim end vexing visions.

It was late winter, and it had been a long winter. Even the cowboys plodding about their duties in high-heeled boots gave the impression of being weary and burdened. On this particular day, Mr. Smith noticed something different about Pretaurus. He looked at the salt box in the pen. It was empty. "Bring Pretaurus a block of salt," he told his son. Then, being subject to moods himself, he gave no more thought to the problems of his prized possession. Mr. Smith was a fine fellow, but he didn't know the difference between the meaning of Grand Pré and Grand Prix.

As daylight gave way to dusk and dusk to darkness, Pretaurus stamped and shuffled in his pen like an elephant at a zoo. The moon came up — a full moon, yellow and low. It was low enough to jump over, but, of course, not near enough. Later on it would rise in the sky, get paler and much smaller. Pretaurus had never heard of a cow jumping over the moon and wouldn't have believed such a ridiculous story if he had heard it. It wasn't the way of cows to engage in undignified, antic behavior. He hadn't had any notion of that sort himself till now. It wasn't a sensible idea, even in his case, for he never had made the slightest attempt to jump over the fence of his pen, and that wasn't much higher than his front shoulders. He had scratched his neck against the top board when he itched, but jumping the barricade was something else again.

Suddenly, Pretaurus found himself on the outside of his cage. He wasn't sure that he had bounded over it. He must have, because there was the pen back there and here he was, moving toward the old, ramshackle chuck wagon standing by the stacked bales of hay. Beyond that was the yellow, yellow, liquid, low-lying moon. Pretaurus made another leap. He went higher than the rounded roof of the chuck wagon that had been used to take lunches and drinking water to the cowboys. He touched the roof lightly and playfully with a hind hoof. All this was done silently, in pantomime, by moonlight.

He rampaged across the snow-covered fields, now, in the direction of the heavenly candlelight. The snow muffled the sounds. He came upon a meadow with a half-frozen stream running through it. The thin, white ice on the edges of the creek gleamed eerily in the moonlight. Two deer rubbing ears at the water's brink eyed him warily but did not budge. A rabbit scampered away, leaving behind him a trail of triangularly-spaced tracks. Lost now in the immensity of the scene, Pretaurus galloped tirelessly on, as if he were suspended by invisible threads from on high. The vast, looming, grandiose mountains were visibly outlined in front.

The moon got no nearer, but it got higher, as the night careened away. Pretaurus was miles from Mr. Smith's ranch by this time and still miles from the mountains. Then a curious thing happened. The higher he got in the mountains the warmer it became. The snow was becoming shallower instead of deeper; and ahead there were flowers interspersing the crunchy, white carpet. Flowers of all colors, which transcended anything Pretaurus had ever seen on Mr. Smith's ranch, grew so thick as to crowd one another—flowers of dozens of kinds, standing in thin sheets of water, or wide-spreading meadows of spring-green leaves.

Pretaurus did an unusual thing—unusual for him. He lay down, flat on his belly in that wet grass. It wasn't as cold as he had expected. It was even a little warm. He was tired from his long trip. He snorted to clear his nostrils and then, still lying down, he tried, lazily, to drink some of that shallow water. He may have dozed a little. The next thing he knew there were glints of early-morning sunshine on the moist meadow.

He sprang to his feet and snorted and pawed the soft earth beneath the long, tender grass. He caught a glimpse of himself mirrored in the pool at his feet. Or was it himself? It had to be he, but his coat was white, absolutely white. There wasn't even a telltale tip of black on his tail such as the weasel has. He marveled and marveled and slowly and definitely turned his rear end on Mr. Smith's ranch. He would never go back. He couldn't, of course, being white, but he wouldn't, no matter what. That wasn't for him. In fact, he couldn't even remember where he'd come from or anything that had happened. He was home.

By the Numbers

Once upon a time, not so long ago, there lived a hillbilly by the name of Henry Higginbotham. When Henry was a hale and hearty, barefoot teen-ager, he was "hitched" to a cute little neighbor girl who was fond of doing what came naturally. The young married couple had three sons in quick succession, and the chances are they all would have lived happily ever after but for one thing.

Education invaded the hill-country. It reached to every hamlet and hideout, however remote. It knocked at every door with the old-fashioned persistence of the wolf and the revenuer. It spread over the land like one of the weatherman's "cold fronts from the North." Princely palaces and royal retreats were exempt from its visitations, but kings and castles were more scarce in the hills in those days than on the timeless circuit of the Red Death.

So it was that Henry's heirs betook themselves to high school. There, they were the source of great confusion and irritation to all their teachers. They looked so much alike it was almost impossible to tell them apart when they weren't together. Their names—Truman, Lyman and Gahoot—were quite dissimilar, but that didn't help much when one couldn't remember which name went with which.

The brothers may have picked up a bit of learning that they weren't credited with, but, anyway, the principal made it clear to Henry that sex instruction was not on the school curriculum. That was Henry's responsibility; and, true to his trust, the good father organized a series of three lectures, one for each of the three years at the modern senior high school. The first one, Sex Is a Welcome Guest, went off all right. It was the second one that failed to orbit.

It was like this. One morning before the beginning of the fall term, Henry called his three sons together at the garden-patch and in a tone of great solemnity reminded them of the previous lecture, of the third one to be given a year hence on Mating, and of the impending dissertation on Dating. "Before I lay down the law to you on dating," the father said, "suppose each of you tell me what you'd do in this situation: You've got a really special date tonight with a hot number, I mean a cool kid. What preparations are you going to make for the occasion? Truman, you go first."

"Gee, Dad," Truman answered without hesitation, "I'd go to the barbershop. I'd get myself a real close haircut, and I'd have it waxed down as slick as a whistle to smell pretty. While the barber's busy cutting and talking, I'd have the girl in there file my finger-nails and clean 'em up real swell. That's what I'd do. Then I'd be ready for any girl, even Adele."

"Guess you forgot about a pedicure for your toe-nails," Henry said as he turned from his first to his second son. "What you think, Lyman?"

"Yeah, Dad. Guess Truman forgot about his feet, all right, but I didn't. Know what I'd do? I'd take those old

45

parachute boots you brought back from the Service after the war, and I'd hike right over to the shoemaker's and have him shine 'em up, put new heels on 'em, and maybe soles, replace those stiff old rawhide laces with some brown ribbons, and I'd be set to do some high-steppin', yessirree."

"You'd do most of your stompin' inside the shoes. That's my hunch. And how about you, Gahoot?"

"Well, Dad, I been doin' a lot of lookin' at those calendars Cabe's givin' away down there at the fillin' station, and that's the way I like my girls—nekkid. I'd say all I'd do is to take off the clothes I got on right now. That's all the preparation I'd need."

Henry said, "That's it. There ain't gonna be no second lecture. Not so long as you guys remind me of the three Chinese virgins, No Yen-Tu, Too Dum-Tu, and Tu Yung-To. Get your teacher, get Mr. Slocum, to tell you about dating. He's smart. I'd just as soon drive nails into water as to explain such things to the likes of you-all. You can just learn in the school of hard knocks if you wait for me to give you that second lecture. And get him to give you the third one while you're at it. You gotta get all three lectures, but you'll be lucky if I give you even the third one."

Then all the sons were yelling back at the Old Man at once, so there was no telling who said what; but this was the gist of it: "For cryin' out loud, Dad, you've told us a thousand times how you hated it in the army when you had to do things by the numbers. 'By the numbers, bunk! That's for the sparrows,' you said. So why do we have to go by the numbers and take all three?"

Henry's head was bowed. "I reckon you're right, Boys," he said finally. "I'm a fine one to be talkin.' I got my vaccination so late in life, maybe it didn't take."

The Cattleman's Etiquette

People are funny. Some will have it that the Governor appointed me because I am a friend of his. That is a tissue of lies as the politicians say. The time was when we were pals, but friends — friends are the first casualties of high office. I don't expect Alec Hartley has ever said that in so many words, but he knows it. That doesn't mean we don't still make like we're buddies the same as always.

Of course, lots of folks may suppose that I needed the dough, and the appointment tided me over some financial rough spots, and that's what the Governor had in mind. Wrong again. I have a notion that Governor Hartley expected I would be paid for my services and doesn't know that I wasn't. The truth is, though, that no one at the state house ever told me how one went about getting paid for such a deal, and I didn't feel like asking and going through the rigmarole. Had the Treasurer sent me a check, I probably would have cashed it, but something kept me from filling out a lot of papers and asking for money. Don't ask me why.

I wouldn't know, either, why the Governor picked me to advise him whether he should cut the sentence of Gus Runnels down from death to life imprisonment. I wouldn't know why he should pick on anyone: seems to me there ought to be a regular set of officials, a board or committee or something, to do such things. No doubt Alec explained all the whys and wherefores at the time, but I was so dumbfounded at the prospect of visiting Death Row that my ears missed all that.

Up to that time, I'd never faced up to capital punishment. During the war, I knew a colonel overseas who seemed to know whenever there was to be a rapist hanged or a spy shot, and he always was nagging at me to come along with him and witness the business. I wasn't interested. I never even asked if the entertainment was free to the public and with no ticket needed. The proposition didn't appeal to me at all. That was all there was to it.

There was one thing I always did say, though. Or, if I didn't say it, I used to think it. That was this: if we're going to have capital punishment, the judge who hands down the sentence ought to be there for the final fun. The jury, too, maybe, if they have a hand in it. This may seem a little sadistic on my part, but, if you ask me, a guy can only be just so logical in these matters and no more.

It could be that any number of my fellow citizens, voters, and property owners would have given their right hand to have been in my boots when I paid my visit to Death Row. So far as I am concerned, I would have exchanged places with them at a far lesser price. I don't go for profiteering, no how. Not that Gus Runnels is the kind of guy you couldn't possibly enjoy meeting and talking to: but you know!

I don't know whether the Governor gave it to me or not, but I went to see Gus and came away afterward with one fixed idea. The guy's guilt or innocence was none of my business. Somebody else had decided that—Judge Gutknecht, I suppose, or the jury, or the Governor himself. Maybe he's a lawyer, and I don't need to tell you that I'm not. Glad of it, too.

I understood, some way, the Governor couldn't go to Black Canyon himself to see Runnels. It isn't done, too long a trip, and all that. Alec may not have told me all this. He's a busy man. I couldn't have been with him more than ten minutes, and then I was taking up time belonging to the guys waiting in the anteroom of his office. He did say he was appointing me his "alter-ego," and I asked "halter ego, is that good?" and we both laughed at that in spite of everything. I don't know what Alec ever did to deserve a term as Governor. He's too nice a guy for that.

When I left the Governor's office, I got in a word with Jack Morbridge, Alec's first assistant. He straightened me out on that halter-ego stuff. He said, "Forget it; just see Runnels and tell Alec about it, but tell him in writing. Put down what you want to, but Alec wants you to size the guy up for him. Suit yourself about repeating anything he says, but let Alec know what you think of what the guy says, if he says anything. You know enough about government to know that form always counts more than content, so whatever you report, report it in writing." That's ten times as much as I'd got out of Alec, but I don't blame Alec for that.

I came back at Jack about the halter-ego gimmick; told him I couldn't forget; had to be sure Alec wasn't swearing at me. Jack finally caught on that I really didn't savvy. "It's alter ego, and it's Latin," he said. "Means the other self. It's a compliment. See: you're the Governor's other self."

"Well," I said, "if anybody needs a double, it's sure Alec. He's got more irons in the fire than a one-armed window washer in a ladies hotel."

"I'll phone the warden that you're coming. Maybe Jack considered my humor out of place, or maybe he had other things to do for Alec that were waiting. I left. I was halfway down the hall when Jack hollered after me: "Don't forget to make six sets of copies." What a character that fellow is.

Both the *News* and the *Herald* had been filled with stories about Runnels. In fact, their stories were so different, a guy might think poor old Gus had a double, too. Both papers did agree on this, just the same. Gus killed his wife and little daughter, shot them to death with a pistol, and then called the police, telling them to come and get him. The lawyers hollered from here to the moon about insanity, but they couldn't get a single doctor to back them up one-hundred per cent. The guy was due to be electrocuted the day after my talk with Alec; I mean he was due for the gas chamber the next day. That's the way we do it in this state.

I may have overdone it a way back if I let on that Gus was such a terribly tough hombre. But you see what I mean. He did kill two people. What I mean now is that he had been a model citizen up to that time, all his life so far as I know. He wasn't a dentist, but he was the business manager of a dental clinic, and so he had a part, you might say, in helping the sick to health. Alec is pretty sentimental, really, underneath, and this might have got him: Gus's mercy on the sick or distressed.

Before I lit out for Black Canyon, I called the little woman long distance and told her I was going and didn't know when I'd be back. I'd tell her all about it later. She said Henry Hanford had called. I said "Hank

Hanford, D.A.?" She said yes, that she has asked if there was any message, and he had said no. I said, "OK." I knew what Hank wanted. He had prosecuted the Runnels case himself, and he wanted to be darned sure the sentence was carried out and didn't foul up in any way, shape, or manner. I'd as soon have Hank throw lead at me as a law book.

Driving down to the pen at Black Canyon, I remembered the only time I'd been there before. That time, I just happened to be in the neighborhood so I thought I'd go in and have a look-see. I pulled in the driveway up to the stop light. A voice came down to me over the public address system from the control tower: "What do you want?" I told the guy.

The voice rasped back: "Complete the circle and keep going."

I said, "What do you mean?"

The voice responded angrily. "Go around the driveway loop and leave." Well, that was clear enough, but I wouldn't have been surprised if the guard had added: *Allgemeine Zeitung Stalag kaput*. There was no use trying to argue. I scrammed.

That occasion was a good five years ago. This time, I had credentials. I could stay longer without staying too long. The warden was a swell fellow: name of Albert Wellner. I took to him from the start. I told him he reminded me of a good shepherd, and I said "That's a compliment."

He said, "Knowing you're a cattleman, I wondered. But I guess you never met a sheepherder that specializes in black sheep, only black sheep, did you?"

Al didn't say a word to get me off to a good start thinking his way. So far as I could tell, it was all the same to him whether Gus lived or died. That was up to a higher Power, you might say. He took me up to Death Row himself. I had half expected there would be a pretty special look about it that would make an impression on the wife when I described it to her at home. Funny thing: it seemed to me to be just more of the same—either that or I was listening to Al, and things along the way didn't register like they should.

I've seen some pretty cool customers in my day. I don't mean just desperados who carry their courage in a holster. Sure I've lived for all my fifty years on a ranch forty miles from nowhere, but don't kid yourself, nothing ever happens out on the Saddle Horn River. I could tell you some things, believe me; but that's neither here nor now. This Gus Runnels was a cucumber-cool number for anybody's money.

Al introduced me to Gus without adding anything to the real me but without taking anything away, either. Then he skedaddled. There I was with Gus. I'd never figured it that way: in fact, I hadn't figured it any way at all.

I couldn't think what to say, but I heard myself coming out with, "Are you sleeping all right, Gus?"

"Sure, why not?"

"I mean, do you want to sleep?"

He looked at me kinda funny, as if, maybe I had come over from the other state institution down the line a ways. I explained: "Aren't you afraid you're missing just so much of what is left every time you go to sleep?"

"Do you feel that way about sleep?"

"The difference is, Gus, that I'm not under a sentence."

"Ye-es, in a sense."

I tried a new tack. "I suppose you do a lot of reading."

"Not a whole lot. The warden invited me to borrow any book at all that he had in his private library. That was awfully nice of him, and I appreciated it. But, nothing caught my eye except this book here." He held up a volume. The title of it was *Famous Last Words*. I didn't catch the name of the author, but I've never read more than the sports section and the daily livestock market quotations in my life, so one author is the same as another to me.

"It sounds serious," I said. "I mean grim and gray."

"It's a book of humor," he said. "It's so-so."

"Have you been seeing the preacher?" I asked. "This would be as good a time as any, you know."

"Reverend Blaine is peeved at me, but he'll come all right whenever I want to see him."

"Peeved about what?"

"He thinks I should make up for lost time in Bible reading, and I told him that is too big an order under the circumstances."

"Yes."

"He asked me whether I could think of anything better to read. I told him I'd heard tell that the warden has a paper-bound pamphlet with a black border on it that contains all the protocol—fine points, you know—for carrying out death sentences. I said if that's so, I'd like to see that. At that, Reverend Blaine flew off to the warden. That's how come the warden invited me to skim the cream off his personal library. No one would confirm for me, however, whether the book of etiquette exists."

"That's beyond me. I don't know."

"Come and see it tomorrow night, and you'll know. They'll shower me with niceties. They'll smother me with loving care and laughing gas. You'll be there, and then you'll know. What's that expression the French use: *Quelle delicatesse!*"

"I don't know no French," I said. "French and Latin are two languages I don't know."

That was a fool thing to say, because I don't know any languages really except the usual. I don't want to know any or any etiquette, either. That's for sure. That's final.

My feet were stiff from standing. My back was weak, and my legs were tired. There was sweat enough around my loose shirt collar to make it wet and limp and binding, but I was chilled through and through. "Tell me," I said, "whether you'll meet your end like a man."

"What other way is there?"

"I mean without fear and so gain a victory over death."

"To score a victory over death? I've lost you there. Aren't you insisting upon a lie past the point of no return?"

His voice and line of thinking stayed with me like gravel in a boot, but I was no longer listening to his words. I did manage to thank him before I hurried away.

The next morning before I had breakfast, Jack Morbridge was on the phone. It got my Dutch up. I told him he'd get no written report out of me.

"Who cares what you say? Or what language you use, for that matter?" Jack said. "It's Top Secret, but the Governor decided to sign an order of commutation a week or two ago. He wants something in the file from a level-headed, no-nonsense private citizen to back that up come a publicity backfire, a legislative investigation, or something."

Well, boy. I gave Alec that report in billingsgate of my own manufacture, and if Hank Hanford, the newspapers, or the Governor's enemies want to make a fall-guy out of me, let 'em make the most of it. I didn't just do it for Gus. I did it for myself, and I'll stand by it.

Chio

Chio Seal, at eleven, was a charming little blonde of talent and poise and promise. Ricky, the pro at the Sonora Skating Club, recognized this the instant he saw her on skates, and he agreed to give her lessons. Mama had no need to use her powers of persuasion. Of course, Ricky didn't mean that he would give the lessons free. The regular fee for figure-skating instruction would apply. Mama understood that. She knew, as well, that Ricky had few, if any, equals in his profession. It was because of his proficiency that the Club had lured him from his native Switzerland.

After that, Chio became a well-known figure at the Club. She was a born skater, but that is only a good start. She wore her revealing costume with ease and with an innocence that clung to her as she grew older. Her legs were as sharply etched in the mind of every member of the Club as those of Marlene Dietrich in the memory of that lady's most ardent admirer. With the passage of years, the girl's bosom took on the buxom contours the elders of the Club had hoped and waited for. In brief, Chio, a delight to the eye from the beginning, became even more so in her teens.

When she took her skates off, she appeared rather short and heavily geared to the ground, so to speak. With them on, she was a picture—less lightly fair than the Scandinavian star of yesteryear and, if less glamorous, more earthily, wholesomely, healthy. In motion she was grace, strength, speed and abandon, all combined and all personified. She wasn't content to make cute curtsies, to smile prettily and flick her eyelashes. She knew exactly what Ricky expected her to do and, regardless of risks and falls, she tried over and over and over again to do it. She gave her all for the perfection that comes with practice. For Mama and Ricky, she dedicated herself to a routine of repeated repetition.

The Club was proud of Chio. She never had let down Ricky, and she never had let down Mama, who, after all, was footing the bills. We all felt that Chio belonged to us and to the great worldwide guild of figure skaters. We were her Papa. We had seen much of her, often, and felt that we had certain possessory rights. What we had seen we had as good as touched, figuratively. Oh, of course, we yielded, gladly, to her partner, Willis Sloan. He was her age and everything. In our solemn judgment, the two belonged to each other and, after that, to the Club, and finally to the international order of figure skaters.

We knew Chio was going to college now; we saw her chat and chide with schoolmates who belonged to the Club or who came for the simple pleasure of watching her cavort on skates. It may sound silly, but none of us ever had the slightest notion that the girl could have a social life that didn't take place out there on the ice before our very eyes, if we should choose to look. We had homes and work and friends, and, yes, beds, but we overlooked all possibilities of that kind in our acceptance of Chio.

Then the girl up and ran away with an outsider and got married to an artist. We were thunderstruck, amazed, outraged. If anything, Mama, stricken hardest, stood up under the news better than the rest of us. She was just as surprised, but I guess she was a little closer to the fact than we were and couldn't escape facing it. That calmed her down. Ricky cancelled all his appointments for several days. It was a knockout blow to him, not merely that Chio was surely destined to become a famous champion under his tutelage, but that his beloved pupil had snapped her fingers at him, at his instruction, and at his and her kind, had blown everything away by saying "I do" to a guy who called himself an artist, of all things. A sculptor whose marble had vaulted out of the studio window couldn't have been more dumbfounded and benumbed than Ricky.

Well, we figure skaters are a pretty good sort. We play in a crisp, cool, clean atmosphere. We lost our senses, it is true, but only temporarily. It was the sudden shock that threw us. Before long, we began to have glimmerings of understanding; began to wonder it, and hope that, Chio would come back and resume her lessons; started to accumulate and catalogue information about Ambrose LeMay, the man she married. The sum and substance of our intelligences of Ambrose were that he was a good chap and a gifted artist, but he couldn't skate at all.

It wouldn't have confounded us a whole lot if Mama had thrown in the sponge then and there and gone back east to Iowa where she had come from originally. We saw her side of the affair so perfectly we scarcely imagined that there was another. She set us straight about her plans and Chio's: no. Sonora Springs was her home now, and she was going to stay. Chio intended to get a job and do what she could to help Ambrose meet expenses. She was through with skating. "But then, you never can tell," Mama said to me. "I may come in handy if I do no more than stay here on call."

"Let me know if I ever can be of any help," I said, trying to fit my words into the vague pattern of her remarks. She said, "I'll do that. I know how you've always admired Chio."

"Yes," I said. "I always have. So have we all. What a girl." Mama smiled at the warmth of my enthusiasm, I guess. I was conscious, of course, that she had singled me out and set me apart as an unofficial Dutch uncle of Chio's. Mama was as clever as her daughter was pretty; she knew that a bachelor uncle with his detachment and his lack of closely-knit relations has certain knacks a family-man does not. She, a widow, knew that. My respect for the old gal, which had increased considerably since the daughter's defection, warmed into affection.

Still I hadn't met Ambrose. He wasn't even an interested spectator of the sport. Then, one day, six months or a year after the elopement, I received an unexpected invitation to Sunday dinner at Mama Seal's. I still thought of her by that name, though she no longer had occasion to lounge around the rink as a spectator watching the youngsters. "I'm sorry," she said over the phone, "to give such short notice, but you'll understand when you come. Chio and Ambrose will be here."

"That's quite all right," I said. "I'd be delighted to come without any notice."

The dinner went off okay. It was as I anticipated, though. Everything was not all right between Ambrose and Chio. The time was October, and a new season was getting under way at the Club. I surmised that Chio found it hard to resist the magnetism of the lighted, sparkling, blue ice. What once had been a duty for Mama's pleasure had now become a matter of choice for her own. And what a whale of a difference that is.

After dinner, Mama said Chio just had to go show herself to her old neighbor down the street or she'd never be forgiven. Chio was all for it. Inasmuch as Mama went, too, that left me alone with Ambrose.

"You've got a mighty pretty wife, Ambrose," I said. I never was any good at the subtle, indirect approach, and it was too late to change styles then. Anyway, who wants to sneak up on a guy?"

"Yeah, I know," he replied without fervor, almost with boredom.

"Of course, you're an artist," I went on, "and you've probably forgotten more about beauty than I'll ever know."

"Sometimes I think I know all about it where it doesn't count and nothing whatever where it is important," he answered with a vague gloominess.

I sensed a come-on in the reply so I asked, "What do you mean? Aren't you doing all right with your painting?"

"Oh, I'm doing all right with my painting," he said. "It's Chio I can't figure out. You know she did some posing for me before we were married. That's how I met her. She had everything: the body beautiful, a sense of showmanship, a complete lack of false modesty, and guilty, giggling mischievousness. She had everything, but I couldn't make anything of it, no matter how hard or how much I tried."

"So you married her, eh?" I smiled to show I wasn't as cynical or blasé as I sounded, and he went on.

"Ever notice her eyes?" he asked. "They're as perfectly shaped as you could want; of a blue which shades toward a hazelnut color; the iris and the pupil are absolutely, clearly distinct, and the whites are pure white. But," he raised his voice and its pitch, "just try and make those eyes speak and mean something."

He threw a dubious, challenging glance at me and continued. "Yes, I married the girl. I've gone over all this with myself. Yes, I wanted to discover the secret she withheld from me and my brush. Some guys have gone crazy at the mystery of Mona Lisa's smile. Some spend sleepless nights with Goya's Nude Maja, a gal so accessible physically and yet so defiantly, infinitely, indefinitely remote otherwise. If there was madness in my marriage, at least I was mad about a real woman." He glared at me.

"You've come a long way in less than a year, I'd say. I can't see that an artist has any business bothering about scientific secrets and the mysteries of a woman's soul, if any. Surely one who is first a man and second an artist doesn't give a hoot about such things. Besides, doesn't solving a puzzle reduce the very best of them to nothingness?" However, my heart had been thawed a little by his passionate confusions, so I added: "There's as much difference between a trained seal and a real woman as between a portrait on canvas and flesh and blood; and my guess is that Chio also has come a long way since she married you. It takes more than a superfine skater to make a real woman, too. That's what you've just hammered into the ice-block on my shoulders." I grinned, but I was only partly facetious.

"Yeah," he said. "I'm not dead set on her staying off the ice. She just thinks I am, and I was afraid, somehow, to tell her that I'm not."

"Why don't you give skating a whirl yourself?" I asked. He smiled at the invitation and didn't even rule out that possibility. As though our entire conversation up to this point had consisted of the usual insignificant and thread-bare trivialities, we changed the subject by tacit assent. We were laughing at the drollery of the penguins at the zoo when Chio came romping up the steps and burst in the door in advance of Mama.

Cold Day

There's nothing like a cold day to unsettle the routine of an office, especially if it writes finis to a long, unbroken sequence of those bright, warm, dry days which only Colorado can bestow, if Colorado chooses. You'll see what I mean in a minute, but first a word about my sponsor.

I work in one of those plants devoted to the manufacture of a line of electronic specialties, a type of business which seems to choose the Mountain West fairly often. Companies moving to this region from the East commonly say their preference rests on this area's climate and scenery. Not to be too credulous, it is quite possible that the wages and salaries here haven't caught up with those on the East and West Coasts. Maybe, too, there's less pressure on management from labor unions in these parts. In any case, there's no such thing as collective bargaining where I work, call it Yonkel's. Here, as one enters the front lobby, the emblem of the NAM and the Chamber of Commerce are displayed as proudly as that of the Small Business Association.

Normally, our office work on the second floor proceeds as smoothly as the machine tending of our blue-collar brothers on the first floor. We even have our own production quotas. And, while we don't punch a clock, it is a cardinal sin to sign in as much as two minutes late. Then along comes a doozy of a day, and the paradoxical happens: the rigid, frozen discipline melts as miraculously as does an ice cream cone under the August sun.

I live within walking distance of the plant, and hot or cold, I walk to work. The boss, call him the Office Manager for now, as that's more descriptive than our own, official, high falutin' title for him, lives on the same street as I do, only a block or so away. On this day that the mercury suddenly and unexpectedly plunged to twenty-five degrees below zero, he walked. As he stood near my desk explaining to a bunch of fellows how neither his Cadillac nor his Continental would start, I looked down at his feet. The new snow, which had preceded the cold wave and introduced it, was still collected around the edges of the soles of the dignitary's shoes. It was that cold inside.

Mrs. Dewey, one of the stenographers, came hurrying down to the boss with the incredible news that Mr. Hogan, her favorite among us men, would be an hour or so late. Even for us, there seemed to be no reason for the guy to be that late. The dependable Dan Hogan lived but a short six blocks away and wouldn't need to bother with a car.

"Is that so? What's the matter?" Mr. Kornegay asked.

"I asked him what happened, and he said he broke a shoe string."

Mr. Kornegay took the answer seriously but equably. The rest of us looked at each other with a twinkle in the eye, as amused at the boss's naiveté as at Hogan's malarkey. Later, much later, in came Hogan with a pair of those cold-weather, rawhide laced boots that woodsmen wear in the North Woods in winter.

"Got the shoestring fixed all right," someone observed.

"Yeah, that's the first thing I thought of, so that's what I told her," Hogan replied.

"Why didn't you wear spats instead of boots? They keep the ankles just as warm, and they're a lot dressier."

"Because some of you clucks might think I forgot to tuck in my long underwear at the bottom, that's why."

Hank Ross wasn't late, but he came down to the little gathering near my desk, which was trying to warm up before our eight o'clock starting time (that deadline's passing, as it happened, was to go unnoticed), and announced: "First time I've had to ride the bus since I got my new Dodge."

"I have to admire your headgear, Hank," somebody remarked, "but what is it, a hat or a cap?"

"Here he is, for crying out loud, wearing what is undoubtedly the only Hudson Bay cap in the entire state of Colorado, and you ask him what it is."

Hank had put his hand to his head. "Well, I'll be darned. I forgot to take it off," he said. He headed for the coatroom.

Nearly everybody was an hour or so late. Jim Blaine, who lived up the Pass and commuted back and forth twenty miles each way, telephoned to say "My car wouldn't start. The truck won't start. But, I got plenty of firewood." One of the three Bobs, Fat Bob, failed to show until almost noon, and when he finally did arrive, he gave such an excited, protracted, incoherent account of his battle with the elements that his report was allowed to stand, without any attempt to pin point the details, as a valid excuse for his tardiness. Questioning, as Mr. Karnegay knew from experience, would only have made Fat Bob more flustered, voluble, and unintelligible.

When the group around my desk had dispersed and the boss had settled down in his office, Walt Eakins commented in a low voice to those within easy earshot that his car had been heating up by the time he reached the company parking lot. His listeners cautioned him that he ought to make sure his car's radiator hadn't frozen up. Walt, more than ready to act on good advice, promptly vanished from his seat, doubtless to check on the adequacy of his car's antifreeze solution, the operation of its water pump, and the tightness of its hoses. Herb and Ed went out a half hour in advance of lunchtime that I know of so their high-priced machinery would be warmed up when they got ready to drive home for their mid-day snack.

During the forenoon, there was a steady stream of people going down past my desk in the direction of the thermometers which recorded both the outside and the inside temperature. Strangely—and perhaps fortunately, for there was a terrible draft on our backs from the wide expanse of windows—no one seemed to have taken note of the temperature within. All concentrated on King Winter's frigid rage without. Blodgett went past so often to consult the gadget it was a wonder if his hot breath wasn't enough, alone, to make the mercury climb several degrees in its tight, perpendicular cage.

Johnny Boy had no trouble getting to work that morning. His car had started like a charm. Oblivious to the commotion and the conversational tension around him, he hunched over the papers he was shuttling with an abstracted air and a self-satisfied smile all forenoon. Then came lunchtime. I went down the front steps with my shoes encased in rubbers, my neck strangled in a red scarf, and my ears held tightly in place by a pair of tawny muffs, all this for the short sprint to a downtown restaurant. There was Johnny beside me with his overcoat open, both hands in the front pockets of his pants, his elbows pinioned against the coat flaps to hold them open, and his hat at a jaunty angle as if he were about to saunter out for a leisurely stroll through San Rafael Park. His nonchalance was so perfect it was a pity he wasn't aware of it.

Coming back from the Red Crag Inn, I had to face into the north wind. It was terrific; brought tears to my eyes; gave me an increased respect for the power of nature and nature's moods. I hurried in Yonkel's front entrance, gasping. The door took its time in closing after me. The oil in the return machine was so stiff. I grabbed the door and pulled it shut tight. It reopened six to eight inches, and with a deliberation worthy of the Supreme Court, recommenced the laborious operation of pulling-to.

Soon after my return, I asked Haskins in the front office for a lift home. He had offered me a ride the day before, and I had decline, preferring to walk. No, he didn't have his car. I explained that coming to the office wasn't so bad because the wind was at my back. Returning home, I would have to face into that invisible fury. Haskins was sorry. I asked Junell. No, he'd have to hitch a ride himself today. I spoke to Swede Sperling. Swede was glad to accommodate. Mr. Kornegay would be a passenger, too.

During the early afternoon, Mr. Kornegay came to me to inquire whether I had a ride home and to suggest that it would be folly to try to walk so far against that awful wind. I replied that I, also, had made arrangements with Swede. Then I asked, "Where's Johnny Boy?"

"He took his car out to get a sandwich, parked it at a meter, and when he came out again fifteen minutes later he couldn't get the thing started." I remembered, but didn't mention, how Johnny had spun his wheels making a left turn on the snow-slick at the intersection down the street from the plant and had sent me scrambling for safety even as I was struggling to remain upright while navigating the slippery stretch ahead of Johnny's wayward station wagon.

Mr. Kornegay went on, "I sent Biff and Gauger out to see if they could help him; it's only a few blocks away and Biff is so good at car handling, you know; and I thought I could rely on Gauger to use his influence to expedite the project. Now they're all three gone."

It was one thing after another throughout the afternoon. Outside, the temperature, twelve below zero at its highest, slowly lowered until the sun went down below the ridge of the nearby mountains. Then it nose-dived. Inside, by five o'clock, the production schedules so carefully and optimistically devised by a Big Shot in the front office had been smashed and shattered into as many pieces as, in olden days, an earthenware jug flung off a mountain top by a jilted savage tribesman.

Da Orla

Mr. Smith passed for an attorney in the western city in which he lived, Sonora Springs, a well-known provincial metropolis of close to a hundred thousand souls. He was listed that way in the telephone directory. There were very few, however, who had the slightest idea what kind of practice the middle-aged bachelor had. Even his fellow lawyers, incredibly sensitive to news of competition and quick to react to it, were in the dark about Mr. Smith. He didn't belong to the bar association, didn't attend the countless conventions, conferences, and panel discussions of the profession, and maintained no downtown office. The telephone directory gave an office address and a number for it, but callers, such as there were, reached an intercept operator and were given Mr. Smith's home number to call.

The tenants of the apartment building in which Mr. Smith resided were equally at a loss concerning the nature of that gentleman's means of livelihood. There had been a time, long ago, when all these good people had been acutely bothered by the iron curtain which surrounded Mr. Smith's activities. They hadn't dared to put direct questions about his professional operations and rightly surmised that such a move would have been less than useless anyhow. They might have concluded that Mr. Smith was a man of means or a veteran businessman or government lawyer retired on a pension for disability, but his relative busyness, coming and going, receiving callers, mail and telegrams, conversing loudly in the hall, all these things forbade a supposition of idleness or retirement. Whatever Mr. Smith did for clients, whoever they might be, he minded his own business and gave his neighbors no cause for complaint. They ended by accepting the situation as it was—for the time being, that is.

The apartment which Mr. Smith inhabited was a large one, with a vast living room, comfortable bedroom, and a spacious kitchen and study. The study, or office, was cluttered with letters and envelopes, memos, and documents which were spread helter-skelter and layers deep on desk and table. Scarcely a book was in sight, and no day-book whatever for recording appointments. In the jargon of the day, Mr. Smith practiced law by ear. He kept no secretary, which accounts for the unsightly litter of unanswered letters. Now and then, for a few minutes during each day, there would be sounds of a typewriter expertly handled, but no one knew what for, except for Mr. Smith, and he wasn't saying.

All this the neighbors regarded as unduly mysterious, but then who can account for the whys and wherefores of a lawyer's behavior anyway? Besides, these folks had a vague feeling in their bones that the mystery might best be left undisturbed, unexplored.

The newest tenant in the building was not yet adjusted to the set-up. Her apartment was across the hall, but not directly. She had met Mr. Smith by accident, outside the quarters she now occupied, before she moved in, and it was he, in fact, who gave her the name of the right man to talk to in the real-estate concern which managed the building. She was in her grandmotherly seventies, and her first impression of the "young" Mr. Smith had been distinctly favorable. Her opinion hadn't exactly altered, but now she worried unaccountably and terribly when, as sometimes happened, Mr. Smith left his door open but on the chain. She knew he wasn't eavesdropping on her conversations at the door or in the hall; that he wasn't spying on her or keeping her under surveillance in any way whatever. Still, the open door was quite apart from Mr. Smith: ominous, menacing, sinister, portentous, absurdly and awfully frightening. All the more so, because her fears were so unfounded she dared not risk bringing herself into ridicule or disfavor by mentioning them to anyone, leastwise not to anyone in the building, and most certainly not to the manager. Complaining to Mr. Smith was so far out of the question, it never occurred to her as something not to do.

It was fortunate that this Mrs. Hubachek didn't know it, but once in a blue moon Mr. Smith would leave his door partly open without the chain on it. He did so, for example, once right after lunch when he was expecting a life-insurance salesman who was warned to expect no business but who persisted in seeking an appointment so as to be of service to Mr. Smith who was already a policyholder in the company. The salesman, Mr. Draper, rang the doorbell. From the depth of the apartment, Mr. Smith's voice came clearly to the salesman's ears: "Come in." Then, for the first time, Mr. Draper wondered if his coming was a great mistake after all and what "service" he could possibly offer so sophisticated a policyholder as Mr. Smith. Running away was inconceivable at this stage of the game, and Mr. Smith's footsteps could be heard approaching the door.

The two shook hands, and Mr. Draper, an experienced salesman, made the handshake firm enough and long enough to assure the other that the eastern company had a sincere, conscientious, diligent, and effective representative operating out of at least one of its western sales offices. If Mr. Smith was impressed at all by the gesture, he did not show it. He led his caller not to the closed study directly in front of the entrance door but down the dim hall to the living room. He indicated a huge arm-chair for Mr. Draper and seated himself at the near end of the sofa. There was daylight from the windows, but a lighted floor lamp between sofa and chair intensified the faces of both.

"You're an attorney?" Mr. Draper blurted out this well-known fact to break the silence. His training and experience as a salesman suddenly deserted him, leaving him with far less than his usual quota of native resources. Under the circumstances, he wanted, he needed desperately for, his feeling of safety, of well-being, to make the man before him fit into a definite niche in the familiar structure of the business world. Lawyers with their names in gold letters on millions of office doors belonged inescapably to this preconceived pattern in Mr. Draper's mind, but Mr. Smith would escape unless somehow pushed back into place.

Mr. Smith said "Yes" to the question-statement, as if the less said about his being a lawyer the better. He raised his hands and clasped them behind his head and asked abruptly, "What did you have in mind?"

Mr. Draper said, defensively but weakly, "I never assume anyone is in the market for insurance, but the cost of protection is constantly going down and..." He didn't finish the sentence. Mr. Smith had made no sign of interrupting him, but Mr. Draper all at once had forgotten about insurance and had become panicky about the chair he was sitting in. In external appearance, it was just another big, overstuffed piece of green furniture, but in the salesman's racing, twisting, squirming mind, the throne chair he had taken upon entering might be a deadly electric chair. He was now in a hurry to get out of this chair, this trip, out of the room. It wasn't just Mr. Smith that he feared, and it wasn't merely Mr. Smith's presence he wanted to flee. It was the place and the atmosphere. It was everything. That Mr. Smith was waiting for him to go on with his sales spiel, as if there were no reason at all why he shouldn't, didn't make things any easier for the visitor.

Mr. Draper found the presence of mind in some hidden reservoir of strength to pull a circular out of his pocket, hand it to Mr. Smith, and say "This will explain all the new benefits the company is adding to its outstanding policies. Do you want me to put some specific figures in the mail when I get back?"

Mr. Smith took the circular, mumbled "No" to the question, and Mr. Draper, dispensing with handshakes, headed for the door like a man in a state of shock. Before the disappearing back had cleared the doorway, Mr. Smith held the blue goodwill folder which had been thrust upon him over a wastebasket and dropped it.

He had opened the door to the study and was hustling in a businesslike way toward the wash closet just off the room when the phone rang. He lifted the instrument. A woman's voice said, "This is Miss Parsons of the Dupler Dance Studios, and you've just won ten free..." Before she could say anything further, Mr. Smith cut in, "I'll call you back." The remark was so unexpected that it led to an unexpected reply. "Oh, for God's sakes, Mister, don't do that. I didn't mean no harm. I don't know you from Adam, and..."

"All right," Mr. Smith said. "I won't call you back. Then it's settled." He hung up, but not before he heard Miss Parsons sniffling and giggling uncontrollably, at one and the same time.

Mr. Smith resumed the semi-urgent mission to the wash room which Miss Parsons had interrupted. Then he returned to his study, ready to begin the afternoon's business. He placed a couple of long-distance calls, one to Wilmington and the other to New York, and asked the operator to give him time and charges. Both calls were brief. To Joe in New York, he reported that he had run into Gus Langemeyer in the bank that morning and that, contrary to what Gus had told Joe before, their deal was very much "on." That was final; Gus wouldn't change his mind again. A million dollars would be enough to swing it, and all Joe needed to do now was to get in touch with Gus directly and arrange the closing. It took even less time to impart similarly good news to Wilmington. The syndicate which held the desired patents was headed up by local people who were well-known to Mr. Smith and who, of course, would be willing to make a sale of the syndicate's rights for a proper figure. After the calls, he scribbled a few figures onto expense-account forms with a cheap ball-point pen with a fuzzy point. The rest of the afternoon's work seemed to consist of staring into space and shuffling papers.

Though this fact probably was known only to the two of them, seldom a night passed but Mr. Smith called upon a married woman, Mrs. Jim Hudspeth, a college sweetheart who had preferred to marry the other man. After ten or fifteen years of a childless, routine marriage, Jim had lost his mind, perhaps for good, and had been committed to a hospital. The wife had stuck to her husband's name and had been faithful to the memory of their years together. It would not be wrong to say she clung to her marriage to Jim partly to save herself from a renewed courtship by Mr. Smith. She couldn't bring herself to the point of doing without his company, but she grasped, intuitively, that a full-fledged marriage offensive by him would lead her down a dark road to an unimaginable destination.

This evening, Mr. Smith told his friend: "I had a visit from an insurance man — a neat-appearing, well-dressed young fellow — reminded me of Jim. I felt I ought to see him, but, of course, I didn't tell him that all the insurance I'm ever going to buy was bought from Jim."

"You mean he looked the way Jim used to. Oh Seth, I wish you would do something for Jim. I've thought for a long, long time that you could so something for Jim, if you only would. The doctors are so limited by their profession, you know. She hesitated. Mr. Smith's eyebrows had risen, but he said nothing, didn't even answer the implied charge that he had been willfully withholding help from the stricken man. Nor did he as much as intimate in any manner that his expertness was in law, not love, and that Mrs. Hudspeth might be confusing opposites. He just sat there motionless with a quizzical, expectant expression on his face, waiting for her to continue.

"I can't stand it much longer," Mrs. Hudspeth went on. "He thinks the world is in arms against him; that everyone but me is in a giant conspiracy to overthrow him, to ruin him financially and disgrace him personally. Who knows when these delusions or hallucinations will make me, too, one of Jim's persecutors? It's awful to go on and on and on like this." The look which her eyes turned on Mr. Smith was enough to thaw the sting out of an Arctic wind.

"What the doctors call delusions," Mr. Smith replied evenly, coolly, "comes closer in this case to being truth than falsehood. Jim's delusions may err as to details, but there is no doubt they are correct in essentials."

"I don't understand," said Mrs. Hudspeth.

"What I mean, Matilda, is this," said Mr. Smith with restraint. "Jim was born into a nest of enemies, into a camp bristling with fanged foes. If you know his folks and background at all, you know that's the nub of it. So his delusions of conspiracy and malevolence are at least a delayed recognition of the truth, aren't they?" Mrs. Hudspeth shuttered visibly, and Mr. Smith paused for an instant. He resumed: "Jim isn't the first, the last, or by any means the only one to have grown up in the midst of friends and family sworn to the open secret of eternal enmity. He spared himself the knowledge then and took for his own the language in which love and hate are interchangeable, but he knows the truth now. Truth and delusion, one and the same."

Mrs. Hudspeth had let Mr. Smith proceed without interruption. She was powerless to do otherwise. Her usual defense wouldn't work against Mr. Smith, and she knew it. She had learned early in life how to get even with her father for failing to notice her sufficiently or for telling her what she considered offensive, repulsive, revolting. She excommunicated him, as it were; broke off radio contact; stirred up such a static in her brain that nothing her father said reached her at all. She used the trick successfully against others, but not against Mr. Smith. Even the ancient, tall, upright grandfather clock which stood in the hallway of her home forgot to strike the hour sometimes so as to save him from distractions when he was talking to her. She was forced to hear him through.

When Mr. Smith had finished, she cried out, "Oh, my God, I pity Jim. I pity him. Don't you?"

"Pity Jim? Why Jim?"

After Mr. Smith had gone, Mrs. Hudspeth wept. Her bosom shook with sobs which loosened the tightness in her body and flooded and exhausted her. When she could weep no longer, she lay on her knees and elbows and beat her bed with her tiny fists and screamed and shrieked. Until her voice was hoarse and her throat strained, she spat out, hurled out, wailed out, "Da or-la, or-la, or-la!"

The words were from her private vocabulary but better than anything in her mother tongue. They expressed the way she felt. But sleep came, and with it forgetfulness. In the morning, she lived on Spruce Street again, spoke the common idiom, and loved Mr. Smith and her husband and everyone else, as a woman should. Mr. Smith, of course, knew all along it would be this way.

The Denunciation

The telephone rang. "Law offices of Smith, Weedig, Witttich, and Waldstein."

"Is Mr. Smith there?"

"No. Mr. Smith is in court."

"When do you expect him back?"

"Not till about lunchtime."

"Will you make me an appointment with Mr. Smith for this afternoon?"

"I can put you down for two o'clock. Who is this calling?"

"Whatsit matter who's calling? I got troubles."

"I'll put you down as Mr. Trouble, and you can tell Mr. Smith who you are."

"Yeah. Okay."

Mr. Smith returned from court before twelve o'clock in a self-satisfied frame of mind. The court hadn't ruled in his favor yet, but Mr. Smith knew the judge quite as well as he knew the law, and he was supremely confident of the result. The protracted, wearing, wearisome trial of cases Mr. Smith left to others. He argued motions. That is, he pointed out to the courts that his adversary had entered the hall of justice by the wrong door or had winked at the bailiff with the left instead of the right eye and therefore ought to be thrown out of court on his ear. If Mr. Smith failed to win on technicalities, then he turned over to his juniors in the firm the thankless task of relying on the merits of their client's cause.

When Mrs. Vogel explained to Mr. Smith that, in the absence of his secretary, she had made an appointment with an eccentric caller, she asked, "Did I do right?"

"Why certainly, Mrs. Vogel. Did you ever notice that, as a rule, these guys with such terrific troubles have been at pains to make appointments in the first place and ever afterward insist upon keeping them?"

Mrs. Vogel tittered uncertainly." I declare, Mr. Smith, I never thought of it that way before." She reflected that maybe Mr. Smith was as much of a card as she'd heard said.

At five minutes after two, the stranger who had called was ushered into the office of the attorney of his choice. Mr. Smith, without rising and without spoken greeting, motioned his client to a chair.

"I got troubles," the caller began.

Mr. Smith nodded his understanding, and in the silence that followed, inquired the other's name. He picked up a ball-point pen that lay on a big yellow tablet on the desk in preparation for recording his client's answer.

"Woddahell it matters, my name?" the stranger bellowed. He glared at his adviser. Then he added, "You Mistah Smith, but you want me to get particular?"

Mr. Smith remained as poised as if he had gone through all this many times. "I see. You came to see me for advice because you liked my name, is that it?"

"Yas."

"Well, I tell you. I'll just call you Mr. X, will that be all right? Now, what's your trouble, Mr. X?"

"I was playing cards with some guys on a train, see?"

"Friends of yours?"

"I never see 'em before."

"Yes."

"That's the last I remember. After that, I was on the train platform against a steel-beam that supports the roof of the shed. That I was told."

"In the station?"

"In the yard. Outside the main part of the station."

"Would you recognize the guys again?"

"No."

"Were you hurt?"

"I'd been hit hard on the head."

"Your money was gone?"

"Yas."

"But if you have no idea who your assailants were, who are we going to sue?"

"You haven't heard all I have to say. I'm not mad at those guys on the train. Woddahell, when a person falls in with strangers as I did, he falls in with thieves as likely as not. I got no complaint against those guys, the way I figure it."

"Excuse me. I guess I jumped to conclusions."

"Sure. Naw, it's the guys that don't mind their own business who get my dander up. There I was in an unconscious hump against that steel-beam. Why couldn't that bum leave me there? Everybody else did. They passed by on one side or the other. I wasn't in anybody's way. But not this bum, no. He had to help me to his hotel.

"If that bum, and the cabdriver, and the hotel hadn't interfered, the police would've found me. They'd have got me to the city's general hospital. I wouldn't owe anybody a dime.

"Now I owe a hotel bill for a room I was too sick to enjoy. I'm mad at the doctor, too."

"Is the hotel man going to sue you? You want me to defend that suit, is that it?"

"Oh no. I've paid that hotel bill. I'm staying with my sister now for a little while."

"Well, I don't want to jump to conclusions again. Do you want to sue anybody at all?"

"Oh no. I've got nobody to sue. I just want to point out to you, and to everybody else, the no-good meddler who ruined everything for me. Can you give me, or get me, a chance to cry out against that low-down, lousy scum before a justice of peace? That's what I want: to drag that character before a justice of peace and charge him, in front of all the town's drunks and loafers and court hangers on, with meddling in my affairs and with my life."

"Do you know who it was?"

"Who?"

"The man who saved your life."

"Do I know him? That's one fellow I'll never forget."

"What's his name?"

"Mr. Samaritan."

The lawyer paused. "Mr. Samaritan?" He paused again. He seemed startled.

"Whatsit matter? You want to think it over?"

"Mmm, yes."

"Okay. I'll call you in a few days."

"No. Don't call me. I'll call you."

Forenoon of a Farmer

It was snowing fiercely outside—big, wet, smothering, flakes in unlimited quantity—and this annoyed Magnus Peterson more than a little. As a farmer, he had learned the hard way how necessary it is to bow before the decisions of the weatherman. Besides, here it was already the very last of October, and it was impossible to deny that it has a perfect right to snow in Colorado, in case of emergencies, any time after Columbus Day, which, according to the red numerals on the calendar, is October 12. There was, however, a certain hard core of unreasonableness in Magnus's make-up, and he was irritated that he was obliged to declare a holiday, willy-nilly and in spite of himself. He had a trillion things to do, all of them outdoors.

The phone rang. His wife, Dorothy, answered it. "It's for you," she said.

"Who is it?"

"I don't know. A woman, I guess, but she gave me the name of Casey Moore."

"Casey Moore?" He frowned. He couldn't place anybody, man or woman, by that name. He took the phone from his wife's hand. "Ye-e-e-a?" he said gruffly.

"Is this Mr. Magnus Peterson?" It was, indeed, a woman's voice.

"Yes."

"This is Long Distance. Hold on, please; Kansas City, Missouri, calling. Here's your party; go ahead, please."

"Hello, Mr. Peterson. This is Daisy Fulmer of the Earl Shumway Dance Studios, in Kansas City, in K. C., Mo., you know, and you've just won ten free dance lessons, absolutely without charge. Doesn't it sound like good news? Mumble, mumble, and for a very slight additional fee you can get a one-year membership in the Shumway Friendship Club. Does that sound like music to your ears?" The voice was as pleasant as a spring zephyr and positively bubbling over with good cheer.

"Well, Lady, I don't know. Sounds to me like you got the wrong number. I'm Magnus Peterson on Route Two at Rattlesnake Grove, Colorado. I been raising popcorn out here for movie houses for twenty years. Are you sure you were calling me?"

Well, Mr. Peterson, aren't you the one I read about in last week's issue of the *Rattlesnake Grove Gazette*?"

"Who, me? Oh no, you mean whose wife just died? In the obituary column of the *Gazette*? That was Magnus Pearson."

"Then I do have the wrong party, and I'm awfully sorry, Mr. Peterson." She hung up without further ado.

Magnus turned from the phone less aggressively than he had gone to it. Some of his irritation had melted away, too. In its place was a puzzled, baffled, cornered feeling. For one thing, he wasn't used to long-distance calls. As he was about to begin a detailed, word-for-word, round-for-round, explanation to his wife of the bewildering conversation he had just had, he noticed that he and Dorothy were no longer alone. There was a well-dressed stranger in the room, comfortably relaxed in Magnus's own favorite rocking chair. He must have come in while Magnus was on the phone.

Dorothy answered his look of wonder with, "Magnus, this here is Mr. De Goff, come to take a poll, he says."

The stranger rose to shake hands, smiled vaguely, and retreated toward the rocking chair. Magnus remained standing, at a loss where he wanted to sit, not clear about the poll the unfamiliar visitor was taking. Seeing that he had caused some confusion in the Peterson household, the newcomer smiled again and said heartily, "Call me Albert. Quite a storm out there, isn't it?"

"Sure is," Magnus assented.

"Did you want me to leave?" Dorothy asked.

The question startled Magnus. He eyed Albert sternly as he asked, "you with that Dr. Kinsey Sex Interrogation Center, by any chance?"

Albert laughed. "Not at all, not at all. No; no cause for alarm, whatever. No, I just came to ask you folks a few questions about how you're going to vote in the elections."

Both Magnus and Dorothy were relieved—and both, apparently, were a little disappointed. This guy with the slicked hair, fancy name, and rimless glasses seemed like he ought to be on more important business than he said he was. They peered intently at Mr. De Goff to see if he was serious. It didn't seem to make sense that anyone would be driving around on a back-woods, dirt road in such a snowstorm unless on an urgent mission. Just the same, the visitor didn't have the air of a joker.

"Well, the wife she always votes the way I do" Magnus said, regaining some of his normal self-confidence. "And the way I see it, this time I'm gonna vote different. Way I size up the situation, it's the religious issue going to swing the election, and I'm going to swing right with it, you might say, like old Daniel Boone on a grape vine.

"There ain't no telling no how what a guy that's got religion is going to do. That's the way I figure it. This county, Webster County, never had so many unexpected things happening as it did seven, 'leven, fifteen, years ago when that mad missionary monk, name of Schermerhorn, was carrying on in these parts. Folks can talk all they want about the population explosion in India and China and other places. That rip-snorting, self-appointed evangelist caused one right here around Rattlesnake Grove, and like as not he'd be doing it yet if folks hadn't taken up a collection to send him away to convert the heathen.

"And another thing is the money issue. That can't hold a candle to the religious issue the way I figure it, but still and all you got to take it into account—leastwise if you're a farmer, Mr. De Goff.

"Call me Albert," Mr. De Goff said, hoping to use those magic words as a wedge by which to pry himself back into the conversation. Magnus nodded in friendly fashion at Albert's invitation but went right on expanding his ideas about the money issue. "It's not a question of hard money or soft money, of losing gold to foreigners or of tight money and high interest, at all, the way I see it. Not this time. We got a brand new lookout here in this election, and not everybody is on it yet, but they're getting wise. They're getting that way fast.

"The time was when the candidate for one party or the other, usually the same one, always had the dollar sign as a middle initial between his first and last name. In this here particular election, though, both of them's got money as a first name—Jack. It's revolutionary; and I can't say as I like it. But there you are. Looks like the storm's let up quite a lot, Mr. De Goff."

"Ye-e-e-s. It does look that way, all right. Well, it's been nice talking to you, Mr. Peterson, and thank you, very much." Albert left hastily.

Magnus squinted at his wife. "What'd you want to do that for?" she asked reproachfully.

"Well, he asked for it, didn't he? Can't tell yet whether the snow's letting up for good or just waiting till Mr. De Goff gets out of the yard."

"If you hadn't run off at the mouth so much about the religious issue," said Dorothy, "you could pray for this unseasonable storm to cease, same as Johnny did during the Battle of the Bulge. As it is, tain't likely any prayer of yours would do any good."

"Ah, now, Dotty, it was all in fun. You know that. God bless Johnny."

The phone rang again. Magnus started toward it. "I'll answer it," he said. His wife listened.

"Yeah, yeah, Mr. Kline? What TV program did you say? Yeah, yeah. Bermuda? No, I don't want that trip, even for free, fabulous hotel or not. I couldn't afford to pay the tips at that place. Besides, I promised to take the wife to California this winter to visit her sister. Yeah? No, couldn't use a gift of that sort at all, Mr. Kline. Now, if it was a double-suction, free-wheeling, electromagnetic, genuine Mayfair Manure Spreader with three-way action and a monomatic, special process, silver-plated synchromesh transmission, I'd be all for it. Yeah, sure, yeah. Well, that's the way I feel about it, Mr.Kline, and you know where you can go, too."

A Forest Idyll

Once upon a time, long ago, a genie came to light at the edge of a wood just at dusk. He brought with him on his carpet an immense throng, a multitude, of tiny people. To his little charges the genie spoke thus: "You are to pass through this vast, green forest to the other side. You may travel by day or by night as you like. You will find the wherewithal for food and clothing along the way. Take such shelter as you choose. What is on the other side of the wilderness you see before you, I cannot tell you now. Nor is it for me to say anything of the size and shape of the forest or what lies within it." With that, the genie left.

The fine little folks, no taller than a man's hand, looked at each other in bewilderment. There was an animated buzz of conversation, but no one endeavored to make himself heard by all or beyond the immediate circle of companions in which he stood. Yet, there seemed to be a consensus of opinion. The journey should be begun immediately, no matter how many days it might take. The genie would not have put them down at dusk if it was not intended they should begin at once and travel by night and sleep by day. Moreover, their multicolored garments of silken gauze and gossamer were warm enough for the cool nights of the forest only if they were active and moving. Such clothing as they wore was all they had, and it scarcely would be warm enough for sleeping even when the sun was in the heavens, for the heavy foliage of the trees would prevent all but scattered rays of the sun from reaching through to the soft and mossy forest floor.

Thus, the trip of which the genie spoke was begun without delay. The reason for it was unknown. The genie had made no promises of what should happen when it was over. And when would it be over? No one knew.

To traverse a strange wilderness of unknown size in the darkness would not be a simple matter for the giants of the human race, even if attempted by but a few individuals chosen for their knowledge of woodcraft and nature. How much more difficult and terrifying was the task set before this veritable host of elfin folk, men, women and older children, by the genie. None among them knew anything at all about the ways of the wilderness. Still, they all moved forward, as we have said, without a murmur of dissent.

Stumbling, struggling and striving, the huge crowd of gremlins—if we may call them that—went into the wood. A few were joyful, some were grim. Most seemed to be saying to themselves: "Let's wait and see what happens. In time, we'll know whether to laugh or cry." Into this wait-and-see attitude, however, more and more of quiet desperation mixed as the strange pilgrimage continued. But the joyful ones became more joyful, and the grim ones turned grimmer, nettling and vexing each other as well as the great majority which was neither joyful nor despondent.

When the day began to break, first grey, then silver, then pink, the multitude was spread widely. Yet no one was so far apart he could not see, and be seen by, others. As if they all had talked it over and agreed that the first signs of sunrise should be bedtime, this great gathering of tiny folks found places for rest and sleep, under ferns, flowers, mushrooms, seedlings, whatever was nearest and most promising of quietness and comfort or most attractive to the eye. The wind in the branches played a gentle, rustling symphony of sleep. Tiny twigs of the perfumed balsam pillowed their weary heads.

Thus did the days succeed each other. As the last rosy rays of the sunset mingled with the gathering grey, blue and purple shadows of the evening, the peopled circle of the forest teemed with activity as the gremlins picked, plucked, and caught their breakfast of berries, seeds, and meaty insects. A little later, at dusk, the irregular but not disorderly march would begin. As various individuals strayed and straggled, our friends became more and more spread out. The further each became from his fellows, the more desperate, the more needy of help and comfort he felt.

Toward the end of the twelfth night, the throng found itself within a great clearing. All the tall trees had been felled and removed, but many small plants, shrubs, and seedlings remained. As the diminutive wanderers looked at each other as if to read an explanation of the unexpected clearing on the faces of their fellows, the belief arose that this great open space was the kindly work of the genie, a sign or symbol that in time they would find their way out of the wilderness. A few, however, considered the clearing as the end of the forest in a real or at least a figurative sense, and these few resolved to remain.

As the main body left the oasis of openness the next night, they did so with renewed courage, being convinced now that the genie who had set their task before them had not forsaken them. The minority which had determined to make their home in the clearing was equally convinced that their home site actually had been chosen for them by the genie. They set to work, in the daytime rather than at night, to make gardens of varied foodstuffs to justify the genie's kindness and mercy toward them and to provide food, too, for their future needs.

The gardens, which thrived and flourished beyond the wants of the gardeners, were to come in handy. In less than a month, the main body of gremlins which had been wandering in the wilderness stumbled back into the cleared island of space. Unwittingly, they had traveled in a circle and were discouraged and discontented. Their hunger made these returned travelers appreciate in full measure the fresh, garden produce which the fortunate denizens of the clearing offered to them.

It was agreed by all that the minority of the little folks had read the mind and signs of the genie more correctly than their brethren. All now decided to stay in the clearing and to work by day cultivating gardens. Garden plots were so plentiful that no systematic scheme of allotment was necessary. It was apparent, however, that a new, strange, and unhealthy spirit of restlessness and recklessness had grown up among some of those who had taken part in the ill-starred, futile, circular trip. Hadn't they often been weary, ill sheltered, and on short rations?

To live in the clearing for an indefinite time as their good genie evidently wished them to do, some rules were necessary lest the stronger, the stealthier, or the more reckless should abuse their fellows. Since the genie had destined them to inhabit not a great plain but merely a spacious clearing, he must also have destined them for the necessary concomitant of life in close relationship, a subjection to law, good order, and discipline. As the first rules of law came to mind and were adopted for the settlement, they were generously attributed to the good genie. A few laws always showed the way to more rules, and little by little this community of the clearing became more civilized, more limited and restricted by law and the social order. The narrowing, lesser freedom was called freedom under law and recognized as more precious than the greater natural freedom had been, and days were set aside for thanking the good genie for his gift of that foundation stone of civilization, the law.

Indeed, as time went on these people of the inland island prospered, developed, and multiplied. The basic occupation remained gardening, an intimate, commercial communion with nature. There was trade, of course, but it was with each other. As there were no foreigners to contaminate them with the exchange of goods, contraband, and ideas, so there were no outlanders to challenge or resist them in war. The setting was a perfect one for the development of civilization.

There were great poets; sonorous echoes of the people they were called. The artists performed wonders, and all their paintings were so naturally representative of the subjects pictured, they could have been photographs. There were seers and prophets of the highest order, and all proclaimed and praised the marvelous state of civilization and of the arts of peace and friendly commerce.

No privileged classes existed. Everyone specialized in trade, agriculture or one of the arts, and his authority within his particular specialty was recognized. Despite its purity and learning, not even the clergy was exalted. The clergy, too, specialized: one branch in the good and the other in the bad. The results were amazing. As the respective branches of the clergy explained it, their people at least were near and perhaps had arrived at the very pinnacle of civilization.

So well had the clergy done their work that the whole populace knew that all good came from the benevolent genie. Everyone was perfectly satisfied with things that way, for there was no bad in the people either. Their law, a gift of the good patron, showed their banishment of the bad. Individuals might perform an act forbidden by law, but there surely could be no bad in the people as a whole, for, in their wisdom and goodness, they punished such wrongdoers.

To such a height had these sober, orderly cultivators of gardens attained. Devoid of good on the one side and of bad on the other, mediocrity reigned supreme: the golden age of human dreams.

At the moment of their highest achievement, however, these people were removed from the scene of their peaceful conquests. Angry winds swept across the forest, toppling great trees onto the civilized citizens of the clearing and hurtling other trees onto minuscule dwellings. Not a soul was left living. As the final survivor, a wise old clergyman, expired, he murmured with a happy smile on his lips: "Ah, the genie saw we could do no more. We had achieved perfection."

Hamelin, Revisited

Once upon a time, long, long, ago I had visited Hamelin. It was a quaint, quiet, torpid, old-world city picturesquely situated on the banks of the Weser. The moldering stones of the picture-book buildings were covered with ivy. The ginger bread which decorated the structures was so fretted with age it had character if not beauty. The city itself had a colorful, musical, and cultural history stretching back into a misty antiquity. That event which is best known to the world beyond the purlieus of Hamelin pertains to a sort of Pagan successor to St. Patrick known as the Pied Piper and the manner in which he ridded the city of its rats.

Revisiting this distant, obscure, almost forgotten corner of recollection was not exactly of my own choosing. That may sound strange, but the truth is I feared disillusionment. Who could tell what havoc had been wrought by war, what ravages by time, what repairs by progress? If left entirely to myself, I should have followed the superhighway which circles the outer fringes of the town and kept going. Unfortunately I was piqued and prodded by a curiosity foreign to my own nature to revisit these stomping grounds of my youth.

Ah, you'd never know the place, Friends. It has changed so. It is as up-and-coming as one of those mushroom suburbs which sprout up overnight on the edges of Los Angeles, Phoenix, or Denver. It is, too, as large and as populous as one of those suburbs quickly becomes. Moreover, it is as thoroughly modern in outlook; quite as receptive to new ideas as, say, Vacation Village on the outskirts of the metropolis of Sonora Springs. It isn't a company town by any means, and the city fathers, assessors, and tax collectors are glad of every additional industry which locates within the corporate limits. The possibilities of a further reinforcement of the municipality's economic base, by diversification, are always kept in mind, the mayor told me.

Three notable factories have been established there since the last, great war. One plant turns out contact lenses which are renowned the world over for their skillful craftsmanship and the faint, exquisite, roseate hue which they impart to the vision of the wearer. Another manufactures a duplicating machine which proliferates copies of memoranda and documents with such ease and efficiency it is a favorite everywhere, with those few who don't like machines as well as with the many who dislike originality. The third produces a device which catches the human voice, stamps it on a belt which goes around in circles and reproduces it. The gadget is an international sensation.

All this I found very impressive, of course. It was re-assuring to know that these representative voyagers twixt eternities had set their course for the future here-below along firm, clear-cut lines likely to guarantee stability and prosperity so long as peace prevails on Earth and along the Rhine and the Weser. The appearance of the business buildings along Main Street hasn't changed appreciably; a sand-blasting, face-lifting job was found impractical. The faces of the inhabitants are wreathed in smiles, as I remembered them to be in bygone days. The smiles may not be as serene as those of yore, but they are, if anything, broader and toothier. Now and then I had the uneasy feeling, though, that the narrowed eyes which accompanied these ubiquitous grimaces of goodwill and pleasure bespoke agitation, something akin to the latent frenzy or desperation of a prisoner, but I couldn't be sure. I wasn't wearing a pair of contact lenses of the latest, improved design; and, besides, one has to allow for some slight changes — they are inevitable. Finally, the facial expressions weren't frightening at all — just suggestive of the antics of a squirrel on a treadmill.

What amazed me most and unsettled my preconceptions more drastically than anything else was the news that there had been a fairly recent recurrence of the medieval infestation by rats. Trapping, in accordance with familiar styles and principles, was as nothing, I was told, against such numerous, multiplying, swarming, hordes. The newcomers had developed, it seems, a baffling immunity to all the old reliable poisons. The invaders were more than a match for the resources of the Hamelinites, but the wit and ingenuity of the scientists of the central government were equal to the challenge. They came up with a new idea so simple and so effective it was a wonder no one had thought of it before. It was only a variation on trapping; lifted, perhaps from some other, dim, unrecognized context and given application here because of the emergency.

Indeed, it was trapping on a large, systematic scale, but with a difference. The victims were not exterminated. They were transferred to commodious cages and put on a ration calculated to insure healthy growth, firm muscles and well-distributed fatty tissue. There was a pressure, a strain, on cage facilities for a while, but the rate of natural increase began to fall off to a degree which would be incredible if it were not a matter of carefully tabulated, statistical record. The declining fertility was a partial solution to the surplus problem.

For the rest, the scientists set out to prove to the public that the animals are good to eat. This was not easy, so ingrained and inveterate were the prejudices of the populace. "Imagine," they said at first, "cannibalism could not be more loathsome." However, the wise men were able to point out that there was very little resemblance between these, clean, cage-bred, well-fed creatures, whose habitations were in the sunlight, and the scurvy rodents which were wont, from time immemorial, to skulk in alleys and basements, to steal a filthy meal where they could find it, and, unintentionally, to spread the plague. Slowly, little by little, the truth prevailed. Hamelinites revised their prejudices and their diets. At the time of my visit, the local rat contractors were doing a small but gradually increasing export trade.

In Hamelin the seemingly eternal warfare of mankind and rats has come to an end. For the prior relations, which were based on frank, overt, declared, enmity, a substitute adjustment has been found. It rests on scientifically revised principles of prudence, friendship and reciprocity. Men feed the rats, the rats feed them. Everybody's happy. To its macabre legend of yesteryear, Hamelin has added a modern counterpart, an achievement of fabulous proportions.

There ought to be an inspiring moral in all this, but, alas, the gargantuan accomplishments of technical know-how are so much the order of the day everywhere that they tend to be taken for granted. The more's the pity, for the need for inspiration founded on great deeds and good deeds is the one thing the human race probably shall never outgrow. Here, ready-ripened, is a seed to be blown in all directions and, like the cottony lint of the milkweed, given the widest possible currency across all lands and among all contemporaries. Besides, what a wonderful inheritance for succeeding generations if this magic method of mutuality, contract and consideration should be made sovereign and all-pervasive. Ah, yes, what a legacy of love, moonshine, and rainbow for tomorrow's children. The children, but the children!

The Heckler

"I'm Hugh Antill," he said, "and I'm running for Congress: appreciate your vote." He reached for my hand to shake it. With my mouth full of glazed doughnut, I tried to get up from the park beach and brush my hands together to get the goo off. "Don't get up," he said, and he grasped my sticky hand quickly, lightly, limply and let go. Simultaneously, with the other hand, he gave me a brief glimpse of a small card with a printed likeness of himself and then deftly tucked the tiny memento of his name and mottoes into the pocket of my flimsy, old, brown sport shirt.

"Thank you," I mumbled.

He gave me a smile. "Hugh Antill for Congress," he said and moved on. It seemed to me he would like to have lingered for a few pleasant words with me but that the urgent business of meeting many people in a short time forbade dalliance with individuals. He was not a bad looking man, dressed in a dark suit, not tall, plenty of brown hair, greased and combed back. He wasn't, by any means, a dashing or dramatic figure. He was, rather down-to-earth, heavy-set, slow-moving, conservative. I watched him in the sparse crowd in Barksdale Park, in the mountain shadows on the west side of Sonora Springs.

It was Memorial Day, a Sunday. People of all ages were loafing around, talking, laughing, playing horse-shoes with abandon, croquet, pétanque with deadly earnestness, frisbee with a blue platter, catch with red tennis balls; going to and from the wash rooms; taking it easy on benches. Barksdale was like this often in the bright warm weather of early summer. It was on the edge of the shopping district of "Old Town," and not far from a neighborhood of modest, oldish, humble homes. The park was well patronized throughout the year but seldom if ever the scene of organized, scheduled com-memoration services or celebrations.

I had never heard of Hugh Antill. He met people well. He also avoided them with the greatest of ease. I could see that. He had a greeting and a smile and a short-cut message of cheer and savvy for those he sought out. But for those who sought him out, he was always turning away, moving off, preoccupied, in the midst of a group. He wasn't one of us. We didn't wear suits in warm weather (or cold weather, for that matter). He would blend with his surroundings better if he were election-eering along Second Avenue, our local Wall Street. But this was a bank holiday. Maybe even the grocery super markets were closed on Memorial Day, part of the day anyway. That was why Hugh Antill was campaigning at Barksdale Park.

I was surprised, now, to see that four or five young men (in their twenties), dressed in the dark, silky suits of the World of Affairs, had come to the park. Like me, they were keeping their eyes on the candidate. Their interest seemed to exceed my idle curiosity, but they made no move to meet the man of the moment. So far as I could tell, they, like the rest of us, were unknown to Hugh Antill. They listened. They became the nucleus of an intent, little but growing group of listeners. Without any calls of "Speech, speech," and as if before he knew it, Hugh Antill was becoming declamatory. This was something different for Barksdale Park and its easy-going, lounging, drifting, somewhat down-at-the-heel patrons.

"Yes sir. Precisely so; a vote for Hugh Antill is a vote for peace. There is no substitute for experience, believe me. Remember Hugh Antill has years of experience working for peace. Peace here and abroad: labor peace; prosperity, good laws; economy in government. Those are the things Hugh Antill stands for, works for. Yes, and with the help of our Great President and my grand party, Hugh Antill will abolish poverty, cut taxes, raise the prestige of the American flag in every part and every port of the world, plant Old Glory on the Moon in the next ten years, and guarantee peace from here to hereafter."

The brisk young fellows in matching coat and pants who were standing close to the speaker clapped vigorously at the end of his peroration. In this they were joined, though not enthusiastically, by some of the holiday loafers like myself. It seemed that the spontaneous, unscheduled meeting was about to break up with the rosy prospect of everlasting peace on Earth and Outer Space uppermost in mind. Then I observed that a darkly tanned man in a white T-shirt and faded, tight-fitting blue jeans held up his hand for the speaker's attention. His lips were moving, but his voice had not yet come. He was, evidently, a young man of the neighborhood, but his facial appearance was arresting. The glance of his eye seemed to reach out for help or to strike. I couldn't say which.

Finally, the words came. "You said good laws." Hugh Antill nodded.

"What about a tick bite?" the stranger asked.

"What do you mean what about it?" Hugh Antill replied. The tone of his voice was not unkind, but it bespoke his doubt that any good could come out of an exchange of ideas with this sober, somber questioner, with this old young man with tousled blond hair and a trace of a stammer.

"Our little boy was bit by a mountain tick."

"I am sorry; awfully sorry. When was that?"

"Yesterday." The woman at his side corrected him. "It was ten years ago," she murmured softly, more to remind her man, her husband, than to clear up the point for the politician.

"I am sorry." Then to bring the group back into the conversation, he added, "But that's a problem for doctors, for medicine and science. I'm a lawyer, and in public office I've always stood for good laws." He looked around. His audience was waiting, expecting him to say more, to complete his defense, to strengthen his apology, to spell out his innocence in detail. A startled, baffled, hunted look crossed his face. What could he say? The vague questions put to him were certainly unreasonable, irrational, stupidly accusing.

He was about to repeat with variations what he had just said when the heckler resumed. "We had doctors," he said. "We gave him medicines. Nothing helped. It was spotted fever. We lost our boy to tick fever. And you talk about good laws. You come into our park and babble about laws and try to get us to make you our Nimrod to the Tower of Babel." He ended on a note of despair and weariness. Utter chagrin finally had drowned out the bitter accusation which had been implied when, but a few moments before, he first accosted the candidate.

The latter, no doubt realizing that the sooner he withdrew from this odd encounter and this park the less "face," the less stature he would lose, couldn't forbear a parting shot. He hurled a reproachful reminder at the bereaved father. "There's a Higher Will," he said.

"That I know; that is my reliance," the young man responded, ignoring the reproach and innuendo. His answer seemed to come not from his head but from the soles of his feet, the depths of his being. His wife placed her hand lightly on the bare, hard brownness of his upper arm and was looking up into his face. To the office-seeker, this man might be the challenger, but to her he was the champion.

Hugh Antill hustled away. I looked around for the well-dressed clique who had stood the nearest to him and applauded the most loudly at the conclusion of the set little speech. They were nowhere to be seen. They were already gone.

It's Not So Bad

It seems that some folks are incredibly adept at finding opportunities to remind their friends that the first ten years of married life are the hardest. At the drop of a hat, others will deliver a scientific lecture to the effect that we forget the awful difficulties of infancy, but in actuality, all the pathos and tragedy of our later years are fore-shadowed in the trials and tribulations of early child-hood. Yeah, but how many of those wise guys have ever been exposed to "retirement?" So thought Randall Dexter, now sixty-five years old, as he ambled toward the empty park bench.

It was December, but the temperature was in the six-ties. In the early afternoon sun, the crisp, dry air was warm. The snow-covered mountains to the west stood out clearly in a jagged but continuous line. In the fore-ground, down the slope and across the park, was the steel framework of what was to be the new University Hospital, with workmen busily pacing back and forth on the beams. Off to Randall's left, the old buildings had an air of drabness, dilapidation and disuse. No matter, he needn't look that way.

At his right, the growing downtown section of Sonora Springs had taken on new character and beauty in the past five years. Down there, Randall's former colleagues at the Genesee Steel Company would be putting in long-distance calls for Chicago and San Francisco, huddling in conferences, re-confirming airline transportation to the branch office at Kansas City, dictating letters, answering telegrams, quoting prices, meeting competition, keeping records. The girls, now just back from a coffee-break at which they probably took apart the boss's new assistant, would be pert and provocative and yet know their jobs to a T. The recollection of all the office activity and usefulness, the fragrance of cosmetics and perfumes, and the glisten of nylon stockings tightened over secretarial knees made him oblivious of his surroundings for a few minutes. That was the life: movement, goals, achievements.

Then his eyes took note of the morning newspaper which had been left in disarray by one of the previous occupants of the park bench. He seldom read a newspaper any more, though for years his wife had referred to his doing so complainingly, as his morning devotional exercise. They still got the afternoon paper, but he didn't bother with it unless the wife's comments on some local happening, personal incident or social gathering aroused his curiosity. Since retirement, he'd been, somehow, like an automobile engine running without a driver and without its gears engaged: idling the motor.

What was this in the headlines about Bill Hornaday's widow? She had testified before the State Workmen's Compensation Commission that her husband's heart attack had been caused by overwork as dean of the local university's medical school. She was trying to get some kind of a workmen's compensation allowance for herself and her teen-aged son. Her husband had been speaking at a fund-raising dinner for the new University Hospital when he was fatally stricken. The president of the privately-endowed educational institution, according to the reporter, had given testimony in opposition.

This time Randall would have a news item to pass on to the wife. She had no idea what Clara Hornaday was up to, or she'd have mentioned it. Well, it was a brave try on Clara's part, but it would get nowhere. He was certain of that. Sure, that college football player who had been injured had won an award from the Compensation Commission, but that was different. That was football. He couldn't tell Clara so, but she was wasting her time; no doubt about it.

He shuffled the various sections and pages of the newspaper around to put them in order. On page one, there was even more startling news. Raymond Jennings, banker, socialite, political big-wig, had met his death under strange, shocking circumstances. Randall at one time or another had heard quite a bit about Raymond, who was ten or fifteen years younger than he. He had heard so much, indeed, that he felt that the big-shot was a personal friend. Ray, it was true, was given to rough horse-play and crude antics of middle-aged businessmen at a convention, but his conduct on this occasion had been so extreme and the consequences so dreadful that Randall couldn't finish the column.

He had read enough. Ray had been at a stag party the night before with a bunch of the boys from the club. When the bar had closed at two a.m., everybody had gone his own separate way. When last seen by his friends, Ray, not dangerously tipsy apparently, was at the curb waiting for a cab. By some odd, tragic twist of the wheel of fortune, two "girls" in a borrowed Cadillac had gone by and picked him up. He was with these two ugly floozies, mounting the steep, narrow, stairs of a disreputable house when he fell backward and was killed instantly. What a cruel and crushing blow to Ray's wife and children. Randall shuddered at the thought.

He got up and walked over to a waste receptacle and stuffed the newspaper into it and, still shaken, returned to his seat. He lifted his eyes to the hills. Since he had noticed it last, the sun had moved slightly to the west but was not yet by any means directly in front of him. At this season of the year, it would go down behind the snow-caps before it got to that position. The sky was still a perfectly cloudless blue; there wasn't a trace of wind.

He sat motionless until the lower edge of the redden-ing sun was resting on the white shoulder of the moun-tain, and there was a foretaste of the evening's chill. He felt purged: different, dehydrated, drained, purified. The restless dissatisfaction with everything and, more especially, the persistent, constant, envious semicon-sciousness of all those busy, fortunate folks following fixed courses with the color, twirling speed, and bee-line direction of billiard balls careening, colliding, and banking on a green, baize table top—those disturbing emotions were as gone as if they never had existed. He was ready to start afresh.

He rose to leave. What could he tell the wife when he got home? Nothing. She would be curious and puzzled. At her age and after living so many years with the same man, the sudden, surprising acquisition of a new hus-band is no trifling matter, but he would be able to tell her nothing. It might take some time, but she would just have to learn for herself. He smiled as he walked. He hadn't thought of it before, but his wife was ever so much like those dark-eyed little girls, with their hands in Mama's, who used to dart glances of admiration at him, when, after World War I, he would stroll along the streets of Paris in uniform. He had been one of the last of the American heroes to leave France.

Ah yes, retirement; it's not so bad.

Kilgard and Gerow

Some years ago, I had the honor of being host to a distinguished English critic and lecturer. He left my home quite abruptly and unceremoniously, in a state of unusual excitement and without giving any explanation for his change of plans and sudden departure. Later, there was found in the desk in the room he had occupied a manuscript which I long have sought to return to him. All my efforts have been in vain since he disappeared without a trace and not been heard from since.

It is my hope that this publication of the manuscript will come to the attention of the writer, wherever he may be, and will prompt him to make known his whereabouts. Failing in that, the story should intrigue and entertain as much as anything which has flown from the pen of the gifted Englishman. Finally, if any further justification of my action is necessary, I ask the reader if he would have had the heart to keep the story to himself. ****

My lecture tour in America was a great success. I had spoken in all of the great cities of the sprawling republic, and everywhere my criticism of the rough-hewn, materialistic philistinism of the urban melting pots and the prairie provinces had been well received. The favors bestowed upon me personally were positively over-whelming. They included the finest liquors of the Old World and the most generous adulation of the New. It was terrific.

That is, everything was terrific till the end. It would have remained so, if a change had not come over me. The hospitality heaped upon me, as well as the constant travel necessitated by my rigorous schedule, had drained me of the exuberant energy with which I had begun my circuit. This is to put it mildly, for when, at Los Angeles, I finished the last lecture on my list, my exhaustion was complete.

Indeed, I have to confess that the weariness was not entirely physical, not merely lack of sleep, excessive, prolonged exertion, and over indulgence in food and drink. As I journeyed from East to West across the country, the enthusiasm for my message increased, the reception of my criticism became less critical, and my welcome more clamorous. All this—this hero's greet-ing—should have inflated my ego and bolstered my assurance. Oddly enough, the result was precisely the contrary.

I decided to put off my return to London until I had taken a holiday, far from crowds, in these United States. During a day's repose in one of the ghost towns of the Mountain West, I found myself confronting a bewilder-ing, jumbled world upside down. My confidence in the time-tested standards of culture, conduct, and taste already had been undermined, as I have said, by the voracity of my audiences on the tour. Then, on an idle afternoon at an isolated, drab, shabby and deserted city that differed in no essential respect from a dozen which dot the area, an incident happened which caused my faith to give way absolutely.

The friend, Ezekiel Smith, with whom I was staying in Sonora Springs, drove me out to Crazy Horse. He always had wanted, he said, to explore the old gold mine which had been opened to the public as a museum, to visit the crater of the extinct volcano in the vicinity, to rent a horse and jog out to the scene of fossil excavations, and so on. He would leave me strictly alone to follow my own inclinations, which I had given him to understand were distinctly at low ebb, of a solitary tendency and wholly unequal to the vigorous, physical activity my host enjoyed.

When Smith had departed for his gold mine, I managed by dint of considerable effort to climb up the scarred and jagged hillside to a dusty but grassy eminence looming over the remnants of the mining town once so populous and prosperous. There I sat, with the world of vanished splendor at my feet, viewing the gaudy gingerbread on the paintless vestiges of Ma Sloan's boarding house; the ramshackle ruins of Ed's livery stable; the ugly piles of slate-grey stone and earth; the dimming legend of "Madame Minx" on the bold, square, dusty-rose house on a side street.

I was trying to decipher a sign on the second story of the Crazy Horse Bank when my endeavor was interrupted by the approach of a stranger who had emerged from the dilapidated, seemingly vacant house just up the hill. He was friendly. I had trespassed on his front lawn, but he, obviously, did not mind in the least. I, for my part, welcomed his intrusion on my solitude. His browned, weather-beaten face showed a strength and healthiness which contrasted strangely with the surroundings, and, indeed, with his own, nondescript clothing.

"What do you make of it all?" the stranger asked.

"I don't know what to make of it," I answered. "I was just trying to figure out the names of that bank building."

"That's Kilgard and Gerow. You'd have to know it to read it. The words Attorneys-at-Law used to be right below the names, but you'd never guess that now. An odd team they were." Then, taking account of my accent, he added, "But I suppose you have a fair quota of curiosities in your own country."

"I don't know," I said. "We British used to have our queer kettles of fish. I suppose we still have, if one only knew them. My own solicitor is a bear for copyright; probably knows all there is to know about it." To my own surprise, I laughed and added: "Come to think of it, that makes him one for the books, doesn't it? For the life of me, I can't imagine him outside his office, talking to a wife instead of a secretary, or to growing children rather than ageing clients, or sitting on grass in place of a swivel chair. Up to now, I've always taken him for granted, as necessarily and naturally as he is."

My new friend didn't seem the least astonished at my remarks. "Kilgard," he said, "was Danish. He had an accent too, just a trace. Tall he was; distinguished looking. He came to Crazy Horse when there was gold aplenty in these hills. He wanted his share of it, but without digging. He'd have none of that. I don't know if he ever studied law, nor where, nor how much. He wasn't dumb, he was shrewd. His mind was keen but yet not narrow. And he looked every inch a lawyer. It may seem funny, but everybody called him Dr. Kilgard.

"I don't know if that law office was his idea or whether folks talked him into it. The town needed a lawyer, someone who looked the part and could take the part. That Kilgard could, you may be sure. He was all manners, dignity, poise and assurance. Besides, he was slim as an aspen and so faultlessly dressed that one might wonder why he came here without suspecting anything out of the way.

"Folks said they never heard anyone who could speak as well as Dr. Kilgard, said they knew exactly what words were coming before they came. His accent made the most common words seem sweet, they said, and different. I've heard him in private conversation and know that in argument in court, his voice must have been wonderful. It was so deep and rich." The towns-man paused as if it were now his turn to wonder at what he had said or at his excitement in saying it.

The silence lasted several minutes, possibly longer. Then my companion resumed, this time quietly and calmly. "Harry Gerow was as different from Kilgard as night from day. People who didn't know him well called him Gross, because of his looks. His friends, who were many, thought the name Grow fitted his attitude, his nature and his love of life and youth better than Gerow. To Harry, names and epithets were all the same. If he knew anything of etiquette, like as not he came out here to unlearn it. He was a rough-and-ready actor, for sure, but I've never doubted that he learned some law back east. I'm certain, too, that Gerow didn't come west for gold, like Dr. Kilgard. He could have had as much as the more lucky miners if he chose. He didn't choose.

"Harry was rude and uncouth in everything. In court, he didn't shrink from skinning a man on occasion, whether the guy were the opposing counsel or a crafty witness; it made no difference. It was rumored that some clients sought the quick justice of Harry's fists rather than the harsh but slower persuasion of is expletives and eloquence, but of that I can't be sure. He seldom went to a saloon. Drink could hardly have made his speech less refined, for his language was that of the camp at all times. I never overheard a conversation between Kilgard and Harry, but I surely wish I had. It would have been an experience to remember.

"They're both dead now. Gerow's buried here in Crazy Horse. He died long, long ago, in a cave-in when he was trying to get some miners who were trapped. He just carried the pitcher to the well too often folks used to say. He had the hairy strength of an ape and seemed to itch to go on rescue missions. I've never known anybody like him. There's the cemetery over there. His grave is not marked, but those who knew the man remember him and what he did. With him, impulses came first and rules and laws afterwards, as my mother used to say. He did a lot for my mother and me no one knew about."

"How about Kilgard?" I asked. "Is he in that cemetery, too?"

The question remained unanswered for so long that I feared that I had wounded the feelings of my friendly informant in some manner. Finally, he took note of my inquiry. "No," he said slowly. "Kilgard left Crazy Horse later on, not long after Gerow's death, when the gold was petering out, and the miners, the girls, and the gamblers all were pulling stakes. He quit the practice of law and moved to Denver. He didn't need to work anymore, even though he lived into his nineties. He cultivated his few friends and many admirers, but his funeral in Denver was a showy affair, with lots of flowers, according to the papers. His will directed that his entire fortune, after funeral expenses, should be spent on a monument to him. I expect it's a mighty big one, but, to tell the truth, I've never seen it.

My friend moved as if to leave. I rose, in order to detain him for a minute and to express my appreciation of his courtesy. "What a story," I said. "It bowls me over to think that the fantastic reality seen by these grim, ghastly and unsightly ruins rivals the most imaginative romances of my country's comfortable capital. I came expecting Crazy Horse to be but a monument to your countrymen's insensate prostitution for gold. You have given me a glimpse of a legion of troubled, toiling, hiding, refuge-seeking individuals differing from one another as greatly as Dr. Kilgard and Mr. Gerow."

I could see that the floridity of my remarks puzzled my companion, although he was pleased by their complimentary tenor. I hastened to add, "I'm Geoffrey Blake, a writer, and I thank you sincerely for your kind introduction to your home town."

"I enjoyed a chance to tell a bit," he said, simply. "I have no legal right to the name, but I've always been called Kilgard." With that, he quickly turned and went back uphill.

Lady or Tigress

God knows I needed the money at the time, even so little as the job would bring in, but, just the same, I couldn't forbear a little curiosity. What in the world could possibly impel a guy with enough sense to be going to college to give up the pleasant prospect of taking private lessons with Madame Daisy Ravenel and to engage me as a tutor in French? In addition to Daisy's almost legendary charm, she is French-born and has an accent which puts my own to shame.

I put the question to Charles Dimwiddie frankly and without beating around the bush. "What's wrong with Daisy that you want to quit? What you got against her, son? Folks tell me she speaks as if she just left Paris last week and looks it, too."

Then he told me how it was, with many pauses and hesitations and liberally sprinkling his explanation with "I mean," "You know," and "See?" I hadn't a doubt he was telling the truth.

His professor in French at Custer College was Wilma Hexman, one of the best. Charles was an average student in his other subjects, maybe a trifle above average, but, for some unaccountable reason, the French tongue completely baffled him. When the first-quarter grades were figured out, Professor Hexman decided to have a talk with Charles. He was a nice boy, she thought, a little older and more serious than those who had managed to have their military training postponed.

After reviewing the situation with Charles and after many declarations of concern, Wilma recommended some individual instruction on the side. Could Charles afford the time and money to do that twice a week? "Well, that's good, then. You go see Daisy Ravenel. I've already called her, and she'll be willing to have you come. You couldn't have a prettier teacher or a better one. Of course, she's old enough to be your mother, so you won't be getting any romantic ideas, I expect. Anyway, she's as good as engaged to a guy she knew long before she and her ex-husband came to a parting of the ways. You may have heard of him, Butch Masterson, a retired sea-captain."

That's the way it started. Daisy made Charles feel at home right away. She had plenty of time for lively chit-chat before and after they concentrated on verbs and vocabulary. The lessons were more like a game than serious business. Besides, Daisy definitely was cute — dark-eyed, plump, and infinitely magnetic. She told him that Daisy stood for Desiree. She was born Desiree Duval. Charles was tempted to ask if Ravenel stood for ravishing, but he thought better of it.

It may be that Daisy bent over backward to make Charles feel at ease. She confided, on her pupil's first or second visit, that she was as fond as any coed of the current football favorite, Bradford Bullock. "I could just put my arms around heem and hug heem when he makes a play like that," she said. Charles said, "I know him well. He's in Trig with me." Then he told her, "I'm on the wrestling team. It's not at all like what you've seen on television. I mean it's a real sport. I've lost forty pounds since I've been in training."

Daisy was vastly impressed by the weight-reducing possibilities of wrestling. "Forty pounds! Forty pounds! Is there any chance for me doing a little of that wrestling? I'd sure like to slim-up in such a fine way." Charles didn't know exactly what to make of such an unexpected remark. He couldn't express his enthusiasm for having her on the wrestling squad, and he couldn't tell her what a perfectly gorgeous figure she had already. He paused to let her pass to another subject.

He was amazed at the possibilities for double meanings each lesson had — the sex agreement of adjective and noun, the conjugation of verbs, and the copulative something or other, for example. But he couldn't make out whether Daisy was as aware of this as he. Then the way she illustrated the use of the *tutoiement* or intimate, second-person pronoun made him wonder if she really meant she held him in intimate regard and was encouraging him to put his questions to her in the second person singular. However, he couldn't even summon the nerve to call her Desiree, much as he liked that name. Daisy, which he used, was commonplace as an old shoe, but Desiree was a name to conjure with: Desiree...Desiree.

There is a certain degree of intimacy in the simple, ordinary, relationship of tutor and pupil that is capable of enhancement. Once Daisy called him to make some inquiry about or some rearrangement of the time of their next "rendezvous." She made it sound like a tryst. The place always was in her quiet, comfortable, secluded, one-bedroom apartment. Once he chanced to glance in the bedroom from where he sat opposite Daisy in the living-room. What he glimpsed was a kind of a billowy, frilly dream. Aside from the chic dressing table and chair, which were more or less distinct, the rest of the corner that he saw was enveloped in mist. Trying later to recall what he had seen, he could only remember a screen decorated with blue-powdered flesh and pink rosebuds in languorous scenes like those so dear to Boucher, Rouais, and Boucher again.

He was able to recall the screen because she undressed behind that. That is, he figured out that Daisy dressed behind that and so, no doubt, undressed there, too. One time when he had come for his lesson, Daisy hadn't come to the door at his knock but had called to him, "It's unlocked. Come in. I'll be with you in a moment."

When she emerged to greet him a little later, she added, "I was dressing." Her voice had come from the corner the screen was in. The top button of her blouse had been missed in her hurry not to keep Charles waiting. She didn't always wear a blouse. That is, she might have on an incredibly stunning robin-egg blue smock with Chinese lettering in bold, crude black — the kind that ties around the waist and doesn't have any buttons at all. You know what I mean! Her semi-swarthy skin and dark eyes against that delicate blue — you know her, don't you? Or maybe she used a bright red sweater for contrast with her skin and hair and gave the effect of bulging the buttons off the scanty knit wrapper.

Her hair is more black than white, but the colors don't mix to look grey. Maybe she dyes her hair, and maybe she doesn't. How would she get that effect, if she did?

One time when Charles was leaving, Daisy explained, quite apologetically and with a trace of exasperation in her voice that she had a date at a hen-party, one of those women's doings, and she asked if he would run her by the home of the hostess. Of course, he would and did. Charles would have gone on and on with details and incidents like this, I guess, if I hadn't broken in finally and asked him, "Well, what brought the matter to a head? How do you happen to come to see me now?"

He kind of skittered with fright at the question, startled. It seems they were standing at the door enjoying the sweet sorrow of parting as had become their custom. Charles didn't know exactly what was being said or who was saying it. Daisy was near, near, near, and warm, and perfumed, don't you know, and looking up at him and smiling and—and, and—and there was a loud, harsh, jangling at the door-knocker. It was Butch Masterson, Captain Masterson, the ugly, misbegotten, son of a sea-cook. Charles left immediately, but not before he formed a thoroughly bad impression of the older man.

"So that's why you've come," I said. "You want no truck with Butch?"

"It's not that," he said. "I ain't afraid of that old goat, no-how. But what I can't figure out, sir, is this: Is Desiree a lady or a tigress? That's what I want to know."

"Well, son, I'm just an old, broken-down retired schoolmaster, but I'll be an optimist till the day I die, and I'll give you odds she's a tigress. I would, I mean, if we could settle it that way. But, boy, if you have to ask, you'll never find out. Yeah, and if you're ready for a go at the irregular verbs, I'll take you on right now."

Landing Party

The trouble with history is that it's always written after the event. If as a people, we have been smart enough to devise press releases that purvey the news of accidents still going somewhere to happen, I don't know why we can't do the same with history. That's what Dad says, and he ought to know. I like it when he gets going on the War between the States and tells how General Beauregard said Robert E. Lee was a pretty good guy and things like that, but then that's neither here nor there.

The earliest voyage of discovery around the moon was made by a cow and was chronicled by Mother Goose. The Russian historians freely admit this, because, you see, the Russians invented the cow. Some of their bearded researchers even claim "a first" with respect to Paul Bunyan's blue ox, but that's a disputed point. There's also a war of words going on about who put the first man on the moon. It rages as fiercely between poets and scientists as between Soviets and Americans. Dad says "Who gives a darn? It's like those early discoveries of Columbus." He's right. All that matters is that the first permanent colonists on the moon were from the good old USA.

Dad says that under the circumstances I ought to get busy and put the whole thing down on paper. "Think of it," Dad says, "if De Gaulle's joker-journalists beat you to it, they'll make a hullabaloo over the number of telephones that the official tables of equipment allotted to each member of the official landing party. *'C'est de la blague,'* and all that." Dad's right. It's up to me to set the record straight before it gets fouled up in funny foreign words beyond all untangling.

You sure can't accuse general headquarters of faulty planning for the trip. The guys in charge had read the past like a prologue; had learned from experience; and they observed the rules of Noah's ark to the T. There were fifteen men and fifteen women, all unmarried, in the pioneer expedition; and one of the men, Reverend Holton, was a member of the clergy. The latter's profession didn't create any imbalance in the situation, though, because reverend Holton wasn't one of those clerics sworn to eternal bachelorhood. I still say the planners didn't make any mistakes, and that reminds me of a little ditty that Dad sings:

"And if you're too chaste, Sir
To share my point of view
Each one to his own taste, Sir
Chacun à son goût."

You've heard it said, no doubt, that when Greek meets Greek, they start a restaurant. According to Dad, whenever two Yanks come together from their homeland, they hold an election and provide for the rotation of offices. Dad's right, too, because that's just what these lunar colonists did right at the very beginning. Of course, the first English settlers on American soil had a different procedure. As soon as they set foot on dry land, they got down on their knees and thanked Divine

Providence for bringing them safely to shore. That's all right. Times change. *Mutatis mutandis*, as my Latin teacher says. Yes, and *E Pluribus Unum*. I'm not so dumb. My father says so himself.

It wasn't any fault of general headquarters and the experts that no ballot box had been provided. It was wisely forgotten that a few things have to be left to improvisation and the ingenuity of the landing party. And I might say these fifteen men and fifteen women rose to the occasion gloriously. You see there were two waste baskets per person included in the table of equipment, and every one of them had arrived on schedule. A hat could have served as a ballot box quite as well as a waste basket, perhaps, but passing a hat around seemed a great deal less dignified than having each voter come up to the improvised receptacle on his own two legs to exercise his sovereign prerogative as a citizen with a passport to high adventure and a rendezvous with destiny.

Far be it from me to leave the impression that all these preliminary organizational arrangements went off without a hitch by general consent and unanimous acclamation. No, there was a fair amount of parleying and hemming and hawing preceding the balloting. Even so, there was no formal campaign with opposing parties, platforms, and promises. No, there was just a good-natured exchange of views, as the diplomats announce. For example, Dr. Asa Plotkin suggested a voice vote and reminded everyone how General Washington had created a sensation in the early days when he rode up on horseback and declared in a ringing voice "I vote for Light Horse Harry." Somebody then asked Dr. Plotkin, "Who do you think you are, George Washington?" Another demanded "Maybe you think you're Light

Horse Harry?" A more raucous heckler chipped in, "You look more like Light Fingered Louie to me."

There was a little high-spirited horseplay, too, over the office to be filled. "Who are we going to elect?" Max Kaiser wanted to know. At that everybody snorted. "Spoken like a German," one of the party threw at him. "You know Major Littlejohn's our leader," said another. "Whaddya want us to do, vote *Ja* to confirm him?" Max smiled sheepishly, but he had a comeback. "You couldn't vote *nyet*," he said. "That's reserved for vetoes in the Security Council."

Jimmy Littlejohn was weary of all this banter about a proposition so obviously subject to no difference of opinion. "Students!" he called out. He got a perfect chorus of replies "Treasurer." Jimmy smiled beatifically. "Of course," he said. "Our first need is a Treasurer." Everyone beamed happily over this clear-cut demonstration of group unity of purpose.

"Who's running?" somebody shouted.

"Leslie Snodgrass," the reply came back out of the crowd. "He's running."

There was a hubbub. "Yes, Leslie to be sure. Where's Les? Snodgrass for Treasurer. Certainly, a perfect candidate. A felicitous suggestion, by Jove. I say, where is he? Where's Les? Where's Les, the ideal man for the ideal office?"

The voice that had mentioned Snodgrass in the first place cut in above the din: "I mean he's running with the GIs. He's out there somewhere, I expect." The speaker gestured vaguely toward the new horizon.

There was a blank look on many of the faces. Gloria giggled. "The GIs. I say, what a quaint expression. Amongst ourselves, we girls call 'em the—uh—the diarrhea."

A shout went up, "Who cares about such stuff and guff. We want Les. Get more with Les. That's the slogan. Let's put him in office by acclamation." A few voices echoed the cry. "Get more with Les. We want Les. We want Les."

"Whoa there. Hold on. Hold on," Jimmy Littlejohn hollered. "Conrad Hooligan wants to be heard." There was a silence. "Whaddya say, Conrad?" Jimmy asked. Conrad made as if he would like nothing better than to sneak off the job and only spoke because Jimmy had put him on the spot. "Well, I don't know," he ventured timidly, "isn't Les pretty old for such an active office?" He smiled craftily as he went on more boldly, "I've heard said that Snodgrass is a sexagenarian."

The electorate was stunned by the charge and labored to understand it. Nadine was the first to regain presence of mind. "It's a dirty lie," she said vehemently. "I mean about his being a sexagenarian, octogenarian, vegetarian, or whatever the bum said. Les is a fine man, as really swell a guy as there is on this whole damn expedition, and believe me, I know. So there!" She glared at Conrad. And then, as she shifted her gaze to meet that of Reverend Holton, she blushed, suddenly realizing how far her vigorous defense of Les might have committed her in the minds of some. She couldn't know it, but Reverend Holton already foresaw himself performing a marriage ceremony.

"I'll go along with Hooligan this far," said Spike Smith. "We've got the ballot boxes, and we ought to use them. The secret ballot has been an American tradition ever since the Australians introduced it to a waiting world. I don't go for this acclamation stuff any more than Hooligan. Let's cast an old-fashioned secret ballot while we can. In a few years, the frontier will be gone, and we'll probably be using voting machines. Let's cherish our ancient, precious privileges while we're new up here and can do so."

Milton Middlemist spoke up to second the motion. "As far as I'm concerned," he blurted out, "this acclamation business is a foreign conspiracy. From what I hear this guy Les Snodgrass is an Anglophile. Where is he now? I'd like to hear him answer that, if he can, before I vote for him. Who really knows where he is now?"

"Shut up, Muddlehead."

"No McCarthyism for us, you crackpot."

"Go take a flying flip at the moon."

"Middlesex go home."

"Why shouldn't he be an Anglophile? We're all refugees, aren't we, or we wouldn't be here."

"We'll make a Martian of him before his term is over, you drizzle-puss."

"Yeah, if not a martyr."

Jimmy Littlefoot ruled that further discussion was out of order. Tiny slips of white paper were distributed to each colonist, marked by the respective voters, and dropped one by one in a couple of waste baskets picked from the ample supply there on the moon. There was a little bickering after that whether a committee of one was sufficient to tally the final results. Jimmy had appointed Horace Pettigrew to that task. In the end, Jimmy's decision was upheld, vive voce, and Les Snodgrass was declared duly elected during his enforced absence from the meeting.

Thus it was that Landing Party AV (A for Able, and V for Volunteers) elected a Treasurer and established a beachhead on the moon.

The Last Frontier

It looked like a remnant of the wilderness of his forefathers as he stood there at its edge. It wasn't vast, but it was thick and green. Beyond its shadows, the sun beat down fiercely, so far as the eye could see, on fallowed fields. Even weeds had to fight desperately for a toehold on those sizzling arid stretches.

His name was Slim Tandy. He proposed to make a journey into the forest. His reasons were not clear. He was prodded by instinct. If he had anything in mind at all, it was exploration, not exploitation. He paused now, gathering strength before he plunged forward. He removed his hat.

A nutshell fell on his head. He felt something hit, and he saw a shell tumble on the ground. It was midsummer, not fall. It was not yet the season of harvests, mists and mellow fruitfulness. He picked up the evidence at his feet and examined it. It was a shell, but he was unable to assimilate it to any variety of nut known to his experience.

Another tidbit made itself felt through the thickness of hat and hair. He didn't see where it landed. He looked up. He saw nothing and heard nothing except the movement of the branches and their soughing sound in the breeze. A tiny hailstorm of shells pelted around him. "What ho," he said, "am I not welcome here where I stand — or, maybe, not wanted at all in these parts?" Some more refuse dripped from above.

He walked along the border of the woodland, keeping in its shade. "I might have been so close to a nest of young squirrels," he said to himself, "as to worry the parents." He paused, still bracing himself for his trip into the shadowed recesses of the giant grove. This time, a shower of shells slapped his face and cuffed his ears. He decided to look into the matter.

In his youth, Slim had bought peanuts to feed to the squirrels that fattened in the parks of his hometown. He knew their cleverness, their timidity, their greed; but insolence was something else again, at least this kind of impudence. Red squirrels, of course, will scold like a jay, vociferously and at length, but they aren't sly and covert and — let's face it — they aren't intelligent.

Without losing sight of the blazing light which held the fields in thrall, he stepped off, experimentally, a short distance into the forest. He surveyed, as well as he could, the tops of the circumambient trees, hardwoods of various species. While he was looking up, a shell conked him in the eye before he could turn away. The speed of its descent exceeded that of gravity. It was as if it had been thrown by an invisible monkey. If this stoning were the work of squirrels, the creatures were either numerous or well-organized, or both.

He wasn't by any means, panic-stricken, or even especially fearful. He had faced real dangers with courage and could do it again. The point was that he had been challenged at the very outset of his mission into the interior. He had to meet that challenge before he did another thing. The threat to his safety might be negligible or nonexistent, but he needed information so that he could evaluate the situation. Reconnaissance was called for.

He gathered together a few stumps which he managed to kick out of the earth. Then he took up a position beneath a huge maple in a cluster of maples. He tossed his heavy missiles on the far side of neighboring trees while he scanned about him for the quick motions of squirrels in the process of putting a trunk or a limb between themselves and the noise of the thrown stumps. It was like a mass movement. The woods were alive with squirrels! He was reminded of the current war and its tides of displaced persons. Only that is pathetic; and in this swift, silent rearrangement there was a suggestion of the sinister and ill-disposed.

He half-expected a volley of shells to sprinkle on him and around him. Instead, he received a single, bouncing, blow which served notice with rude emphasis that the previous use of bits of shells had been dictated, partly at least, by a desire to conserve ammunition. He glanced at the latest pellet as it rolled into the dark, earthy, leaf-mold. It resembled, in its color and its corrugations, a black walnut—perhaps one which was so thick-skulled as to have no room for a meat inside. Still, he couldn't swear it was a black walnut—only that a resemblance existed.

Now he saw that the strangers were emboldened. There were dozens visible on the near side of the trunks, heads down but thrust away from the tree so as to mark him and measure him better. They were gray, mostly—but wait! What a tail! There were a few tan or tawny hairs in head and body, but the tails were golden. Even in the dim rays of sunlight which managed to penetrate the dense foliage, these tails shone like spun gold. And they thrust stiffly outward from the squirrels' posteriors, outward and downward toward the head, for all the world like so many deadly arrows, down-turned thumbs, or inverted phallic symbols.

To see these curious creatures poised so, in the stereotyped alertness of a military formation, was enough to make Slim hesitate. These were the familiar gray squirrels in a familiar pose, but there was a difference which he needed time to reflect upon. The squirrels he had known had been acquisitive and conservative, but not organized, aggressive, and unfriendly. They had treasuries, not armories. Those bushy, golden tails were more expressive than anything else, but of what? Some pitiful regression—some rabid possession within? The whole spectacle, indeed, was more disgusting, somehow, than frightening; more vaguely disturbing than disgusting.

He might still go forward as he had planned; he might well do so. The forest was big enough for both himself and its oddly hellish denizens. Coexistence was one of the alternatives, certainly; but he had anticipated something different—if not friendship, at least a benevolent neutrality or indifference. He had some thinking to do. For the time being, he would just withdraw. The squirrels proceeded to do likewise, vanishing instantly. Slim's retreating steps made no visible or audible impression on the soft, moist, cushioning, forest floor. Not an owl blinked to see him go. Not a canary chirped to call him back. The sustained hush left the next move squarely up to the departing man.

Lawn Party

"All the world's a stage, and all the men and women merely players." Some parts we play better than others. According to the boss, I never turned in such an abominable performance in my life as last night.

The boss's name is G. W. Joab, and he's the editor of the *Sonora Evening Tribune*. Everybody called him Old Joab because he had been around Sonora since the days when they called it Sonora City. He says himself that he was the first west-bound passenger on the Kansas City-Senora City Railroad, now a part of the Mountain Western Line, but, of course, that's only a joke. Old Joab isn't a lot older than I am. The only difference is that he made good in a big way as an editor, and I work for him as a reporter.

Old Joab sure applied the lash to me this morning for my piece on the Swigert's lawn party. I suppose I asked for it. You see, I've reported almost everything for the *Sonora Trib* except society. I wanted to round out my career a bit by doing at least one stint some time on the high-living set. Hilda Blair, who runs the Social Section, couldn't make the Swigert party, and all her regular helpers were on vacation—this was August—so it was understood that my chance had come.

Old Joab was as riled as the waters of Crystal Creek during the spring runoff. "A cub would have been ashamed to turn in such copy," he said. "You should have been studying, not just reading, what Hilda Blair grinds out day after day. You think a dash of realism is in order, or a trace of humor, maybe? Well, you're wrong. I tell you there's no place for humor. There's no need for improvement, either. The secret of reporting play is to approach it with deadly seriousness. Why do you suppose you were transferred from city news to sports to financial? Promoted? Yeah, like a guy kicked upstairs. Get hep to yourself, Quincy."

The little woman had given me a hint of what to expect from Old Joab. I showed Sarah what I had written at breakfast time, and I saw her wince. "If you go ahead with that story," she said, "I'll have the druggist cut off your supply of tranquillizer pills. You seem to forget that culture has come to Sonora. It's not the sleepy little village you persist in keeping in your mind." My wife is by no means my friendliest critic, however, and I laughed off her indignation without even asking for details. She usually praises my blunders and howls with pain at my best efforts. I knew that if she was right this time, it was sheer accident.

It isn't so easy to dismiss what the boss told me. He and I are good friends, and I use rough language to him at times, too. Most probably he stubbed his toe getting out of bed, or his flighty daughter eloped with that hillbilly guitarist from Ogden, or Hilda Blair tore into him just to keep up the pretense that there's a peculiar witchcraft about the doings in her shop. Phooey!

The boss hurt me the most when he struck out along the line the little woman had taken. "You wanta give the town a bad name? Throw obstacles in the path of progress? This isn't Sonora City any more but Boom Town. Don't forget it. We're in a neck-to-neck race with Phoenix for the fastest rate of growth. And you hand in an odoriferous screed like that. Take it home and burn it before witnesses. That's my advice. I ought to speak to the government about reducing the Social Security payments you'll get in your old age. Remember the motto of the *Trib* still is what it always has been: Don't knock — boost. Now leave me, Quincy. Leave me."

I could have told Old Joab a thing or two. Give the town a bad rep? As though that guy has a monopoly on love for Sonora. Him and Hilda Blair. Why last year, when the Civic Crusaders were planning to give their award of the Young Man of the Year to a real pink-shirt square for the fifth time in five years straight running, I invited the president of the organization to the press club for a few drinks and read him the riot act. I got him to see Sonora would be better off going alone as a cow town than by becoming known as a city of geldings and that the standards of the Crusaders needed revision.

I did that: and where were Old Joab and Hilda Blair then? I ask you. Yeah, I ask you, Folks. What's more, while I'm at it, I'll put the previous question, as they say in Congress: Do you think my story about the Swigerts is way off base?

Last night's lawn party at the Swigerts undoubtedly will go down in history as the biggest event of the August social calendar in Sonora. Six hundred invitations went out. There were no police estimates of the size of the crowd, but a quick count by your reporter around seven o'clock p.m. showed that approximately 598 persons were present for the Grand Gala at the home of Sonora's leading socialites, Mr. and Mrs. J. Owens Swigert.

The Swigert lawn can boast of having been trampled into shreds by the fairest, fastest, richest, and smartest of the city's settled set. The fairest of the fair was not a blonde but a brunette, not a lady but your reporter's wife. She was the buxom babe in a red dress with white shoes and an ever-so-wispy green scarf held in the hand. The tall, statuesque, sleek female in a yellow sheath with tiny crescent moons the color of tiger-lilies also rated more than first, second, and third glances. She is the healthy, athletic wife of one of Sonora's top-notch businessmen, Mr. O. B. Grinnells. Her husband, who is much older than she, wasn't with her — presumably being out of town on business.

The owner of Madame De Spano's Fashion Shop was there. Despite her years, this blonde, fair fixture of the Sonora social scene exhaled the fragrance and elegance of a late-blooming rose from which the petals have begun to flutter and scatter. Her young-looking husband, the oil man whose drillings at Wyandotte made him famous, was the only man present who wore a figured shirt and a Centennial tie. I overheard Madame De Spano giggling about the way her sharp heels drilled into the turf. The oil man smiled faintly, said nothing, and clanked the silver dollars he had in his pocket.

The son and scion of the fabulous Frothingham family was there. He has grown a beard and looks different that way. The son of Frosty Forrest is no youngster and no longer is feared and admired by the matrons of Sonora. I saw several ladies playfully testing the texture of Frothingham's facial adornment and heard them pronouncing it soft and silky and every way remarkable. Usually the dames can't spare a kind word for these stiff, bristly hairdos so far beyond their own power to produce, but Frothingham's seemed to be different—a silvering testimonial of better days and, as such, praiseworthy.

Frothingham sometimes says his best days were B.C. His friends all know he isn't using B.C. in a historical sense, but, of course, they give him the come-on one way or another so he can explain. Then he says, "Yeah, Before Canada." It's understood this refers to his starring role on the Custer College hockey team way back before the routine of filling the squad quota with Canadians.

Two artists lent the glamor of their presence to the gathering of the elite. One was Rodney Burrus, the fashionable portraitist, and the other was Gilbert Osborne, the local leader of the Aspen Tree Cult of Painting, so known from its profitable predilection for depicting the fall costume of the high altitude forests. I was flattered, but a little uneasy, at the way Sir Rodney, as everyone calls him, kept eyeing my own lady in red.

Blanche Crochetti was conspicuously present and strikingly pretty, but so far as Sir Rodney was concerned, the gal might have been on a mountain top. Blanche, of course, suffers from two serious handicaps: ill health and intelligence. She was the only old maid at the party, but her very eligibility for attention (not to mention her intelligence) would be a disqualification in the eyes of that perennial Romeo, Rodney.

Thanks to Blanche, the theater needed no representation at the Swigert's. Her tall, gaunt figure and those dark, black eyes set in the rouged pink oval of her face, proclaimed eloquently, though falsely, the possessor's liaison with the stage. If Blanche ever had a liaison, it has been so long ago as to be forgotten by the city's older inhabitants, perhaps even by her. On this occasion, she was unescorted, but in the company of her friends, the Christoffersons. To her belongs the honor, if it be an honor, of keeping this lawn party from perfect observance of the rule-of-twos laid down in Noah's time.

The wife isn't as fond of Blanche as your reporter, but I think she appreciated Blanche's remark that Donald Frothingham, with his whiskers, reminded her of a painting by El Greco. I suppose El Greco is some sort of relative of Michelangelo's, but thank goodness this reporter and his lawfully wedded spouse were spared a lot of prattle, gabble, and babble about Michelangelo. From Blanche a mention of such things is okay, she isn't just sounding off, but deliver me from the usual drivel of the dame who puts on culture with a powder puff.

I heard one roly-poly gal who was transferring a sizeable portion of cold baked salmon from the buffet to her plate say something to the wife about Bake-oven. Thinking she and Sarah were hashing over items of culinary art, of which I know nothing, I paid no attention. On the way home, Sarah spilled the beans. The gal with the low-cut dress and peasant shoulders had been talking about Beethoven. Still, it wasn't an arty crowd. You could tell that by the way they fingered their canapés: with their fists, I mean. It was a good all-around bunch, the kind I like.

Howie Scarborough was there, and a number of other lawyers and their better halves: Louie Devious; Ronald Gordon, the angel of the visiting operas; Smith Sashmire III. My wife had a long chat with Smith's wife. The latter is very civic-minded and interests herself especially in the affairs of a home for unwed mothers. My wife said afterwards she never had any idea how fascinating charity could be: more so than club work.

Speaking of club work, that's my wife's long suit. Playing cards, I mean. I was dead set against her going into that at first, but she won out. I used to tell her that my father always called cards an invention of the devil. She threw at me that her daddy never said anything like that, and I had no come-back. Now I'm glad the argument turned out as it did. I know what my wife is doing when she isn't home, and if you have a good-looking wife as I have, that's a welcome comfort, believe me. Of course, this is by the way, a page from experience, you might say.

I picked up several items of incidental intelligence myself. Guys with cauliflower ears don't go to such shindigs. I didn't spy anyone of my acquaintances of the prize ring there. Another funny thing: no one wore a hearing aid. This may have been the first time Oswald Hackberry left the privacy of his home without that handy gadget of his, but there was Ozzie razzle-dazzling around this lawn party with a pleasant smile, a roving eye, and a ready reply for every bit of cocktail chit-chat which came his way. A guy never knows to what heights he can rise till he tries.

I'll say this, though. If Ozzie heard the strolling violinists above the hubbub of voices, then I'm the one who is hard of hearing, not Ozzie.

Another interesting oddity: Scotch and water isn't nearly as good as Scotch and soda. I made the discovery the hard way. The roaming waiter who gave me my first drink handed me the wrong mixture. That way I found out the importance of soda.

Just before Sarah and I left, we had a talk with our host, Owens Swigert. He told us about the pool which tinkled so musically to the fall of running water and gave an illusion of coolness to this corner of the lawn, despite the blazing torches which lined the garden wall and helped illuminate the throng. "It used to be a wading pool," Owens said, "but we converted it into this fountain setup last year."

Owens is a banker, first, last, and always. He knows my wife has her own little portfolio that her first husband left her, and he said: "I know I shouldn't be talking business at my own party, Sarah, but did you ever open up a savings account with us? Ten dollars a month wouldn't be much, $120 a year, but there's nothing like systematic saving. You should put away a little every month."

"I know," said Sarah.

At that, we took our leave from the wonderful party. The invitation said from six to nine, and it was now about five to nine already. However, the crowd was still enjoying itself immensely and evidently had no more thought of going home than a Roman army of occupation.

Legend of Flim-Flam Inn

The year the winter Olympics were played at Squaw Valley, California, there were several grand surprises. In the first place, the United States hockey team defeated both the defending champions, the Soviets, and the outstanding contenders, the Canadians. Even more astounding to those who had an eye for the aftermath as well as the contests, was the spirit with which our Northern neighbors accepted the results. To lose with good grace is, of course, a cardinal requirement of good sportsmanship, but the Canadians, players and spectators alike, seemed to fix their eyes above and beyond traditional duties and obligations, and to regard their loss as a victory.

If you'll pardon me, I think there's an old legend that has a lot to do with this seeming indifference to scores, this incredible example of playing the game for all that it's worth and letting the winged victory-bird perch where it will. To be sure, you're not likely to hear this legend from the lips of the Canadians. With them, it's a case of think of it always, speak of it never; perhaps because they regard it as an actual happening. I was born and brought up in Minnesota so close to the border, shared so fully the consuming fanaticism for the past-time, as a child played so often with Canadian boys—yes, with, not against—that I absorbed the story as if it were an inseparable part of this fast-paced, crazy carnival on ice known as hockey.

Once upon a time, at the beginning of the modern revival of the Olympic games, not all winter sports were played at the same spot. The ski competition might take place in Colorado, for example, the figure-skating razzle-dazzle in Switzerland, and hockey still somewhere else. There wasn't enough money in those days for the building of a grandiose complex of buildings in the wilderness as was done at Squaw Valley. It was hard, way back then, to finagle the various governments into picking up a tiny tab. In Canada, if anything, the government was even more economical than elsewhere, for two of the world's sturdiest traditions of thrift existed there side by side, the French and the Scotch.

In this rather remote, indefinite, time there had developed in the wide-open spaces of Western Canada, at the relatively little town of Flim-Flam, a remarkable aggregation of stick-handlers. There were just six of them and they played the whole game without substitutions or first lines and second lines. All were whizzes on skates and wizards with the puck. Their system, if it was a system, was to create a scene of bewildering confusion in their opponent's section of the ice and then, when the situation clarified, it would be discovered that the puck had come to rest, in some strange, inexplicable fashion, in the net around which the skirmishing had taken place.

It was natural, under the circumstances, that the Olympic committee in charge of selecting a site for the great, quadrennial, international, competition should give the nod to Flim-Flam. The budget of that town's team was as small as its fame was great. Thus it came to pass in the time we're speaking of that Flim-Flam was scheduled to become a sort of winter capital of the world for one hectic week in February; and it goes without saying that Canada was to be represented at the spectacular meet by the team hitherto known simply as the Flim-Flam Sextet.

Now on this sixsome of hardy Flim-Flammers was a young man known as Willie Bloch. In this tiny constellation of stars, he, if possible, outshone all the others, including the goalie. The demands on the Flim-Flam nettender, after all, were comparatively few and far between. The wings, center, and defensemen saw to that. They might not windup the game with a basketball score, but, so far, they never had failed to manage it so that the game was played almost entirely on their opponents' half of the blue-lined, red-lined ice.

Willie had been born in Germany but had been brought to Canada by his parents in early childhood. All the Blochs had become, as often happens with immigrants, more Canadian than the Canadians. Erick Bloch, the father, kept the town's only regular, permanent inn, the Flim-Flam Inn. The mother, Minnie, was forever on the go around the hostelry doing whatever needed to be done, which was plenty even when the spectators and officials were not converging on Flim-Flam from far-flung corners of the globe.

As nearly everyone knows, it was the custom in the old days for hockey to be played outdoors. The mammoth arenas and ice palaces of the present time were unknown. Lakeside shelters, indeed, were rare. Huge open fires might roar along the shores of the lakes for the convenience of spectators, but the hockey players themselves kept warm at their sport. Until the round of games in question, benches on which to sit while putting on skates were an unknown luxury at this outpost of progress originally founded by the Hudson Bay Company.

As far north as Flim-Flam, "skating on thin ice" was then, as it is now, practically a meaningless expression. The surface of Flim-Flam Lake usually froze to a depth of two or three feet early in November and stayed that way till the middle of May. During the late, great war, the impression may have gotten around that the cold Russian winter is something unique. That's a mistake, as almost any resident of Canada, not to mention Vermont or Alaska, can tell the doubting Thomases. There is such a thing as a "January thaw," almost as regular as clockwork, but that's just the exception that proves the rule.

It remains a mystery, therefore, how Willie Bloch went through a hole in the ice while he was skating around and warming up for a practice session with his friends and team mates. He may, as some guessed, have got too close to the point where fast-flowing Moosehead River empties into the lake. In any event, down he went, and he had to be hauled out of the freezing waters by a "human chain" formed by his fellows at great risk to themselves.

It was the last word in tragedy, for Willie had lost his life—and on the very eve of his expected triumphs against the best competition this world could put on a rink! The townspeople did what they could to soften the blow, but Willie's parents were inconsolable. The family's grief was so overwhelming that everyone felt obliged to respect the request made for absolutely private funeral and burial services. It was too late, however, to switch the site of the tournament to a less ill-favored location. The games had to go on as planned.

Before the foreign visitors began to arrive, the members of the Canadian Olympic team came into town from their cattle ranches and wheat farms around the countryside and, at the invitation of Erick Bloch, were put up in grand style in the finest rooms of the Flim-Flam Inn. Besides, the men on whom the country's athletic glory depended must have a dining room to themselves alone. Erick Bloch insisted on that; and positively everything was free of charge.

During the days just preceding the crucial tests of skill and speed, the local team was on a pretty steady diet of wiener-schnitzel, according to the menu. The heroes grumbled among themselves at the consistent fare of wiener-schnitzel, wiener-schnitzel, wiener-schnitzel, but they hadn't the heart to complain to their sorrow-stricken, generous hosts at the lack of variety in their meals. The all-important games came, were played, were won.

Only if you can remember how American hearts palpitated when our great Indian athlete, Jim Thorpe, was shorn of his medals and awards, can you have the slightest conception of how Canadians felt at what happened next. The chairman of a special, Olympic Committee of Investigation demanded to see the portion of the Flim-Flam Inn occupied by the newly crowned champions. In a closet of the room of the team's captain was found a fresh, bare-bone skeleton exactly the size of Willie Bloch.

The Lion That Squeaks

L eo Mason and Mortimer Mallory had been members of New York's exclusive San Marco Club for a long time, but they nevertheless were no more than speaking acquaintances. Indeed, as the head of the house known as Peebles-Rexoid Publishing Company, Leo felt he had a certain right to look down on Mort who was president of an insurance company which went by the common-place, home-folks, solid-granite name of Rock of Ages Assurance Society. Selling insurance, according to Leo's lights, was a very ordinary business, and publishing books was an aristocratic, risky, arty, decidedly unbusi-ness-like business, and success, when it came, meant more.

On this particular occasion, though, Leo was willing to swallow his pride; what was left of it. He was glad to see someone in the club dining room he didn't know too well, for he had a lot to say, and he would rather empty his heart into the ear of a stranger than to take his chances with a friend. He didn't want his friends to know that he, the mighty patron of arts and authors, had been nettled and stung by a two-bit writer who merely chanced to have a book on the best-seller list—a gross fellow so crude as to violate the common decency by offending unintentionally, for it was certain that Hyde had had no idea his bumbling remarks would be disturbing to the president of his publishing company.

Leo hesitated by Mort's table. "Just beginning?" he asked. "Yeah, just sat down. Have a chair; glad to see you. How's business?"

"Oh, it's all right; can't complain. Never can tell about the publishing game, though; only settle one problem to bring forth a new one."

By this time, Mort had sensed that it wasn't one of the everyday problems of profit-and-loss that Leo had on his mind, but he remained poker-faced as he replied "Yeah, same in my business; insurance, you know."

"I know," Leo replied. The waiter interrupted by placing a highball in front of Mort.

"Have a drink with me?" the latter asked.

"No, thanks. I had a stiff bourbon, straight, before I left the office. I'll just wait till you finish yours. The publishing business is a damn unbusiness-like business, you know, and…"

"Yeah; so I've heard" Mort murmured.

"And I had this guy Hyde on my hands this afternoon—a real screwball from St. Louis or St. Paul, a suburb, he said, of one or the other; I can' t recall which. Well, this guy's book just happens to be a best-seller, and we got it out for him, and so he's in New York, and he calls on one of the editors, and Halpern brings him in to meet me. To be a good Joe, I offer to show Hyde around our little shop, you know."

"I know," said Mort. "We do things like that for the visiting members of our Million-Dollar Club."

"But this fellow got there by luck, not work. He's not a salesman at all. I haven't read his book, of course, but I understand that it's filled with the kind of rough-house, country-boy comedy that's riding so high these days. Shaggy-dog humor, it's called."

"Oh, yeah. Yes, I know what you mean—the shaggy kind— yeah, wacky. I like that kind; crazy about it. Never heard of Hyde, though. What's his book?"

"*Look Homeward, Screwball.*"

"Boy, what a title. Sounds terrific. I'll have to remember that; never could remember a joke, on my life. Who'd you say wrote the book?"

"Hyde."

"Hyde? What a name for an author. I begin to see what you're getting at. Yeah, a name like Dingelhoofer or Feibleman or Vandervelt, yes, but Hyde? I see what you mean. A wolf in sheep's clothing, you might say."

"A Wolfe in sheep's clothing. Ha ha. But that's only part of it. I haven't got to all of it yet."

"A Jeckel in a man's hide yet."

Leo, who was beginning to be a bit annoyed by Mort's appreciation of Hyde, was delighted to see the waiter hurrying up with their mixed-grill dinners.

"Hyde's not satisfied with being wacky, as you say. He's got all the answers. You'd think he could run a publishing house better than those who make it their business."

"Yeah, I know how it is. We got an employees' suggestion box ourselves."

"But this was different. Here I was taking Hyde around to meet all our head editors, and he sounds off like it's all old stuff. Doesn't just wisecrack, which would be all right, or anyhow not so bad. He sounds off like he's telling me; like he's boss and I'm just a flash-in-the-pan."

"Yeah—and really the lightning just struck him."

"Exactly. I mean I wish it had."

"I know."

Leo noted with satisfaction that at last Mort was showing signs of a sincere interest, a sincere sympathy.

"I introduced him to Mrs. Eustace, our juvenile editor; not first, but right after he'd shaken hands with the folks in the detective division. Well, with the mystery gang he just got off the usual worn-out gags, about crime does, too, pay, for detective editors, and such stuff. But with Mrs. Eustace...

"I didn't like his way with Mrs. Eustace at all. She's a lady, you know, a perfect lady; and here's this guy Hyde with his crinkled collar and over-sized tie-knot and long hair, not combed since last year, and dry, and off-brown, and stringy, and he says to Mrs. Eustace, 'Call me Larry.' I should have said his first name's Lawrence.

"Then, this guy Hyde turns to me and he says 'I'll bet this is where you make money, in the Juvenile Department.' He looks at Mrs. Eustace like he's scored a great victory. She smiles ever so little without saying yes or no. I say 'Per book, yes; but not over all.'"

"'You get out more detective books,' he says, like he's suddenly detecting something himself. I say 'yes.' 'You know what I'd do if I were you' he says." Leo glanced to see if Mort had been following. Now, Mort was coming over to his side; he could see that.

"Well, this guy Hyde goes on. 'Tell you what I'd do' he says. 'I'd combine the two—Detectives and Juveniles—I'd put the big money-makers together, right together.' I was hoping Mrs. Eustace would up and slap his face, but she's a lady as I was saying, and there she is just smiling as faintly as Mona Lisa and all the time wondering what's cooking the goose.

"We're a well-rounded house, you know, with lots of departments. I mean we get out a balanced list of books year after year. We don't specialize at all; not really, I mean. Not like some houses do. Well, wherever we went, this guy Hyde goofs off, gushes forth with bird-cage asphalt. In the trade department, for example, Mr. Scroggins has got a pronounced New England accent."

"I know," said Mort. "I'm originally from Massachusetts myself, and for years we had our home office in Connecticut before we moved it here."

"But Connecticut isn't at all the same," Leo said. "This guy Hyde asks Scroggins 'You from Vermont?' and Scroggins has to say 'Yes' and Hyde says 'I didn't know anybody ever came from there or went there.' Well, Scroggins has seen these writers come and go, and he just grins wide like it's a brand new joke, but personally I didn't like it."

"I know. Like come to Unspoiled Vermont and help spoil it."

"But what teed me off, especially, was when the guy comes darn close to getting sacrilegious, not just for a laugh, mind you, and not for any dough, either. Well, we'd been through the How-to Division and the Do-It-Yourself Division, and we're in the Science Division when we came to the desk of Mr. Hornblower. Well, after we'd met Mr. Hornblower and exchanged a few words and were continuing on back toward my own office, this guy Hyde stops in his tracks. 'You know,' he says, 'that gentleman is a misfit where you got him.' 'Who?' I says. 'Hornblower,' he says. 'I'd transfer him to the Religious Division.'

"Before I can get my breath, he changes the subject. 'And you got altogether too many technical departments. I'd merge the How-to and the Do-It-Yourself Divisions into the Science Division so as to have just one great Science Division. And while you're doing all the reorganizing of your departments and all the rationalizing of your processes and procedures,' he says, talking like a lawyer or an efficiency expert, 'I'd merge, I'd simply fuse, the business office with and into the Religious Division, or vice versa, in the interests of simplicity. There's nothing like a little fusion to prevent confusion.'"

"God, I'd a killed the bastard," said Mort. "Exactly," said Leo.

"What a nerve," said Mort. "Beats anything I've ever heard of. It's colossal."

"You know it," said Leo.

"A guy like that is a one-shot success," said Mort. "You'll see. The lightning never strikes the same place twice."

"I know," said Leo. "I've always heard that, but this guy Hyde said the trip through the plant had given him a red-hot idea for his next book. 'What's this?' I says. 'Will it be fiction or non-fiction?'

"'That's just it' he says. 'It'll be tremendous. I'll write it for true, and you can sell it for fiction. It'll outsell *Look Homeward*. It'll play on Broadway; and it'll outstrip the current favorite, *Love, Love, Love*. It'll outstrip it, Man. I'm telling you.'

"'What's the title?' I says. '*The Lion that Squeaks*' he says."

"Well what do you know."

"That's what I say," said Leo. He grabbed for the chit the waiter had left. "I'll get this. It's been great talking to you, Mort. I'll be seeing you around. I gotta get home."

"Sure thing," said Mort." Enjoyed it. I think I'll stop at the bar and wet my whistle before I go. I live right in town, you know."

"I know," said Leo.

Live, Love, and Learn

In all the annals of doctor and patient, there probably never was a more bizarre relation than that between Dr. John Bishop and Clarissa Carter. The former, a young psychiatrist, had never been married. The latter, less young, had been accepted as a patient shortly after her ten-year marriage, already stale, had foundered on the rocks of divorce.

At the time of her first consultation with the sturdily built Dr. Bishop, Clarissa no longer was what one would call a crazy, mixed-up kid. She looked mature, thirtyish. She was a strikingly tall brunette, with dark eyes, jet-black hair, a thin face, and a nose ever so slightly tapered. She favored broad-brimmed hats, no matter what the fashion of the moment might be. Her dresses ran to black relieved by white, never red. She had had her fill of red, maroon, and orange as a child, she said. Her parents never had dressed her in anything else.

Clarissa, in fact, took a pretty dim view of about everything her parents had done for her. Her father, for example, had fastened on her the name of Davis, and there were some who thought Hubert Carter's main attraction for Clarissa must have been his last name. It went so well with Clarissa: Clarissa Carter. For his part,

Hubert, in time, teased Clarissa, not entirely in malicious jest, that he had fallen for her figure without fully realizing that everything she had was really "standard equipment."

She and her husband had had no terrific rows, Clarissa had confided to her doctor. After her father died, however, she just tired of Hubert. He seemed so unable to do any more than give her a name that she began to despise—Carter—as much as she had Davis. The more she wanted from Hubert, the more he failed her: no child, for instance. Her figure having palled on him, and his name having lost its magic for her, the two turned to trading insults. The divorce put an end to that, but Clarissa kept Hubert's name for whatever it might be worth.

Dr. Bishop had made no comment on this bit of personal history. Clarissa thought he could have reciprocated by telling her a little of himself. She had waited expectantly. Nothing was forthcoming. Dr. Bishop apparently assumed she would go on. She did: "I like your name," she said. "Do you mind if I call you John?" Dr. Bishop had smiled faintly, perhaps wearily, but had not forbidden her to use his first name. She didn't call him Dr. John, but after that, just John.

Dr. Bishop was both pleased and displeased by Clarissa's yen for his first name. It had been given to him, and he liked it—all the more that it fascinated his patient. Just the same, Dr. John would have been a more respectful handle than John, if still less respectful than Dr. Bishop. Oh well....

Dr. Bishop's office near downtown Sonora Springs was in a big, old home which had been converted into doctors' offices. Soon after Clarissa had appropriated the doctor's first name for use, she noticed that the familiar couch had been removed from the consultation room. She had felt there was a subtle dig in this but decided against making a point of it at the time. It was an insulting gesture on John's part to imply that she might want to give up the chair from which she faced him over a coffee-table and to lie on the couch. It was exasperating, but she realized he would have a ready-made answer for any protests: none of his patients ever used it. She didn't want to hear that or to think about him having other patients besides her.

They had begun by having three consultations a week. By the time Dr. Bishop decided that twice a week would be enough, Clarissa had made up her mind that John was a pretty remarkable fellow in every respect save one. He didn't appreciate her sufficiently, or, at least, he didn't give her enough evidences of his regard. She considered him her doctor, but he persisted in having other patients. Of course, the guy had to make a living, and he had a profession to practice, but there was a way out somehow, if John willed it. And he ought to do without any prompting from her. In time he would.

Dr. Bishop still called his patient Mrs. Carter. On impulse one day, she called the doctor's attention to her possession of a first name, and then, getting angrier as she went on, she demanded, "Don't you think it's pretty anachronistic for you to be calling me Mrs. Carter when I call you John?"

"You make it sound bad by calling it 'anachronistic,' Clarissa. But you wanted to call me John, if you'll remember. Clarissa is a nice name, though, and I'll call you that, if I may. It goes awfully well with Carter, as you told me long ago."

Clarissa, taking account of her profit later, wasn't sure how much she had gained. She had given the doctor the use of her first name, insisted upon giving it, and what had he given her? It wasn't like her to give something for nothing. One of the things she had learned at her mother's knee was the broad, general principle of tit for tat. Now, here she was, actually pushing John to use her first name without strings attached. She was puzzled. Maybe John would see to reversing the gift somehow. That was probably it.

Dr. Bishop, however, never gave her anything to speak of except his time. His remarks were so few that Clarissa asked him once if he begrudged her a few kind words. Then, of course, he had had to compliment her, but he had been pretty left-handed and clumsy about that. Hubert, for goodness sake, had raved about her buxom bosom long after it had ceased to seem at all unique; had praised her hour-glass figure even after his feelings had been bruised in their wrangling over the divorce settlement. The most John could do was to say she was getting along fine. "One of these days you'll be well, as the doctors always say," he ended. This conclusion so completely confused Clarissa she couldn't think of a reply until it was too late. Afterwards, she thought: John never gives one thing without taking two.

As if to prove the absolute correctness of Clarissa's sad reflection on his character, Dr. Bishop proposed, at their next confab, that in the future they should meet but once a week. She was furious that one of whom she was so fond could place so little time at her disposal. She told him as much, using the word "fond." He had pacified her then by saying, "Don't think I'm not fond of you, Clarissa. I am fond of you. We've had a lot of fun together — learning."

The pacification lasted to the end of that particular interview. For her next consultation with Dr. Bishop a week later, Clarissa appeared in war paint and decked out in the complete panoply of battle. She had taken special pains with her make-up. Her neckline, if not more revealing, was at least more plunging and more promising of revelation than usual. Her stockings had been selected with care. She struck the cross-legged pose of a not-so-dizzy blonde on the witness stand before an elderly judge and an all-male jury. She didn't expect any comment, but she was alert to the direction of John's glances and watched whether his defenses could withstand this full-fledged offensive on her part. Warfare was less her forte than bargaining, but this was war, not merely a calculated display of her assets and trading cards. She was mad and desperate.

He surprised her by saying "You're pretty dressed up today, aren't you? Does that mean you've got it in for me?" He diverted her from her scheme, thus, and blunted her attack. At his chiding, she lost much of her ardor for dazzling him by the flashing wings of her darkened eyelashes, the thrust of her up-lifted bust, the casual carefulness with which her skirt fell short of covering the knees. She granted his defenses equality with her pretenses for just this once, counting, however, on the long-range possibilities of reaching her goal by maneuvers less militant and more in keeping with her accustomed shrewdness, her woman's wiles.

The infrequency of their meetings under the new schedule played tricks on Clarissa. By the time the succeeding week rolled around, she had forgotten not only the campaign she had begun so recently, but also the occasion for it. Fighting was foreign to her nature and, besides, there were other fish to fry. For example, there was the matter of the doctor's fee. She was far from pinched by it, but there was a principle at stake. If John was fond of her as he said he was, then why the charge? She was sure, moreover, that the charge made to her was as stiff as those he made to other patients of whom, presumably, he was less fond. She would have a favorable chance to play this ace if she kept her eyes open.

Perhaps she could have waited for just the right occasion if she had been patient, but it wasn't worth the effort. She had a bone to pick with John, and she wanted to pick it and have that behind her. It wasn't long, therefore, before she began one of her visits by saying, without any pretext whatsoever, "John, are you thinking of cutting down again on my time with you?"

He replied: "Aren't you crying before you're hurt?"

"Well, I just want to know."

"Do you think we should?"

"Well," she flared back, still in an accusatorial tone, "I was just thinking that you really aren't giving me any time at all. Did you ever think of it that way? You aren't giving me any time. You're selling it. I'm paying for it. You've never given me anything, anything at all, not since we first met."

"When you first came to see me, you liked a bargain, above just about everything else. At least you gave me to understand that you always managed to get more than your share that way. And 'why be a dope?' Maybe you never really cared for the system, though."

"No! I was just trying to deceive you, as I had myself. I always have wanted something without fighting for it and without trading for it. And I have no patience with price tags, measuring cups, hesitations and second thoughts in my own make-up, either. I especially hate friendship on a business basis. I mean I hate it absolutely, deep-down, through-and-through, even more than stealing. If we're fond of each other, why can't we be real friends?" She smiled through her tears.

"We can, from this very minute on. I knew we'd call a halt to this scheduled, time-table rigmarole one fine day and be pals, but it came sooner than I expected." He rang for his secretary. "Lucy," he said, "Will you bring us a couple of cups of coffee?" At this, as though on a code signal understood only by the three of them, they all smiled, and Lucy left for the coffee.

The Long Engagement

Elsa Bennett awakened that morning with a great sense of relief. She had finally broken off her engagement to marry Philip: not that she had regarded marriage as an impending disaster, a sword of Damocles hanging over her head and likely to over-strain its cord at any moment and to fall upon her. Goodness no, she had been engaged to Philip too long for the marital state to loom before her like the iceberg in the course of the Titanic.

Nor was her new-found serenity terribly troubled by the easy realization that she was confronted with certain new problems. Her engagement was a sort of public property, like the few remaining herds of the almost-extinct American bison. She would have to exercise all her ingenuity and tact in explaining the sudden rupture in diplomatic relations between herself and Philip. Otherwise, her colleagues at the office, the first persons she'd be seeing, would place her in the same category as that catastrophic storm last fall which broke so many limbs off the noble elms in Sonora Springs' grandest park. She took all this as a matter of course requiring attention but not worry.

Silence was not one of the alternatives. Philip usually drove by the office and picked her up after work, and his failure to do so would be noticed in no time at all. It would be best to "leak her story" before anyone observed a change in her routine and questioned her about it. She could make it appear that Philip, the cad, had disappointed her expectations after all these years. Yeah, he was the one responsible for all the damage to the trees on Civic Center Mall, the unseen Public Enemy Number 1. But her pride was an obstacle to that way out; she didn't want to be pitied nor consoled as a poor girl who hadn't sense enough to pick out a dependable man. After all, she'd been through the marriage and divorce mill before some of her would-be sympathizers had finished their second year in kindergarten. She wanted none of their tears.

Truth, of course, was not one of her alternatives, though it would have been a comfort to her to know it, to know it really. The exact opposite might make a tremendous hit as an explanation of last night's red-letter event.

As she dressed in the only bedroom of the little apartment which had been her home ever since Bob, her ex-husband, had walked out on her, Elsa mused on the situation. She had been dating Philip for more than ten years. His proposal had been made and accepted so long ago that both had pretty completely forgotten the exact circumstances of it. Their engagement had become taken for granted by themselves and by many others, quite as a marriage often is. The only ones who had come close to an open, vocal, questioning of the finality of the existing arrangement between Elsa and Philip were a few girl-friends of Elsa who, when most disillusioned with the length and finality of their own life-sentence to happiness, would seek to make Elsa jealous and to find consolation in that.

These friends (and their remarks) were not entirely without effect. They generally failed, it is true, to excite Elsa's envy. She'd been around too long and knew their game too well for that. But there was something about Philip that fired Elsa's anger at times and which always stood ready to trigger her temper. She wasn't clear exactly what that something about him was, but she was certain that it was there, that it existed. Elsa's friends furnished a good strong peg on which to hang this anger of otherwise doubtful paternity. Thanks to them, she had for years been able to say to herself and to imply to others that her sudden rages at the guy were simply because he kept stringing her along instead of marching her forcefully to the altar.

The honest-to-goodness truth that Elsa came right to the very verge of divining every now and then was that she could get madder because Philip didn't change his own first name than because he didn't change her own last one. That idea would slip right up to a window in her mind and then, as she started to look, would run away and disappear down a dark alley as quickly as it had come. As it was, she had been as embarrassed at her fiancé's name as if it had been Roy or Leroy or Ray. It smacked of royal pretension almost as much. Wasn't Philip the name of the Prince Consort of the Queen of England? Yes, and there were a good dozen of Philips who had been kings here and there along the chariot-route of recollection: Philip the Fearless, Philip the Handsome, Philip the Second, and so on ad nauseum. It really was nauseating, when it wasn't maddening.

The odd, the paradoxical thing about her calling the whole thing off just when she did was that she was becoming less and less concerned about Philip's name. She no longer needed to remind herself that his parents had given their son the prefix he wore and that he himself had had no voice and no choice in the matter. She hadn't drummed on this theme so often that she had ended by being taken in by it. No. On the contrary, she had begun to fall prey to the curious, inexplicable notion that her ordinary, bear-like, bristly, blundering fiancé did possess certain subtle attributes of majesty. She couldn't force the sly and foxy notion to jibe with what she saw when she looked at Phil, but that didn't alter the crazy idea's hold on her in the least—or her growing disposition to feel at home with it.

Elsa was in no mood this morning to make her own breakfast as she usually did. She had one important fish to fry: to cook up a perfectly air-tight alibi, so to speak, for her rash action; not an apology or a defense but a flattering vindication. She would have to get a roll or cereal at the cafe across from the business building downtown. She was taking longer than she should with her make-up, and she knew it: she was dabbing and patting and smoothing in helter-skelter fashion and squinting at the atrocious, slap-dash results with unseeing eyes.

If she just kept her mind on the subject long enough, she was bound to get a line on a good, respectable angle on the scandal. Ah, there it was, off in the distance, I spy: Philip had never given her any reason for his prolonged delay about fixing a wedding date. He simply seemed satisfied, wholly and completely, with things as they were. She never called point-blank for a show-down. There was her pride, to be sure, but to come down to brass tacks, she was pretty content herself. Then, besides, there were those fits of anger with the guy which shaded into spasms of doubt whether the marriage ever would work, whether she was good enough for him, whether the customary vows would add anything but constraint to their comfortable understanding, and so on. She, therefore, had let the affair drag on as it had with only a vague, half-hearted suggestion of impatience now and then. Those nudges Phil chose not to understand.

There was, however, one fairly open secret which had unlimited possibilities as an accounting to her public, which at these particular moments of thought consisted only of her well-wishers at the office. Nothing was half-way as credible with the folks at Holbrook and Scales as the financial slant. Now it was common knowledge that Phil was a mighty fine fellow but an indifferent businessman. Just recently, as it happened, he had picked up a couple of fine commissions that were quite unexpected and out of the ordinary. One thing he had done right afterward was to trade in the old clunk he had been driving for a shiny, showy, new job from Detroit. "I want you to ride in style, Queenie," he told her. None but the two of them knew about the commissions, but practically everybody knew about the car.

Here, right at hand, were the markings of her pitch to the girls at the coffee break. The latter would invent any necessary or becoming ornamentation. All she'd need to do was hint: "Yes, Phil came into quite a lot of money lately, with more in the offing. I don't want to stand in the way, to be mercenary, don't you know? I told him he was free, free as the wind. It isn't as if we were married, after all." The girls wouldn't ask what he said then, but if they did, why she'd have an answer of some sort. Well, it was time for her to go, and pronto, if she were to have any time for even a coed's breakfast.

Her hand was on the doorknob when the telephone rang. It was Phil. "Would you like a lift downtown, Babe?" he asked, as if nothing at all special had happened the night before.

"Oh, that would be wonderful," she said. "I'm running late and haven't even had my morning coffee. It's awfully nice of you to offer, Phil, after…"

"Look for me in that coral Cadillac of ours, Els. I'll be with you in two jerks." He hung up without saying goodbye.

The Lost Sweetheart

None of us guys knew much about the business office of the *Rocky Mountain Oil News* except that Leona worked there and every day she'd slip unobtrusively into our office, the editorial sanctum, with the personal mail that happened to be addressed to us at the *News* by mistake. She was cute, cute, cute! It's hard to say whether she ventured amongst us guys bravely or fearfully. Maybe it was both.

She didn't come into our den with a rat-a-tat-tat or a click-click-click of high heels. There was no sauntering swagger of the hips; no flaunting, taunting, challenging swish of the skirt. She came in with her bosom held high, but she tread softly without touching her heels to the floor as if she feared attention more than she craved it. Her lips were taut and tight as she headed straight for Mrs. Runkel, the middle-aged clerk-typist who served us all. There, Leona would drop off a few letters and scoot on her rounds to the other departments.

Little was said about Leona. She was probably a teenager, seventeen, eighteen or nineteen, on her first job. A guy didn't get to be an editor and come out of the fields to stay in the all-weather comfort of the *News* office until he was at least thirty, and most of us were older than that, with wives and children and grandchildren. We noticed her and watched for her daily appearances, and, with the judgment which went with our experience in the world, approved the colorful, thin-striped, glistening, clinging dresses which slenderized her figure without, thank goodness, slenderizing it too much. We liked her habit of fixing her youthful, long-bobbed tresses in old-fashioned hair-dos. We admired what a skirt and a short-sleeved blouse did for her waist, hips, and butt. We wondered about her unknown voice, about her unseen smile.

This went on for months with nary a word coming to my ears about Leona. I was relatively new to the staff and was intrigued by this curious, incredible, seeming "conspiracy of silence," unbelievable under any circumstances, but especially so in the case of that gang of gabbers. Man for man, those colleagues of mine on the *News* can talk longer and say less about nothing with more eloquence than any legislative body known to history. I'd even be willing to bet they could out-blab the Russian members of a Geneva disarmament conference.

We were positively, pathetically, desperately hungry for subjects of chit-chat which had practically inexhaustible potentialities. The annual fall classic of baseball was wonderful, but it never exceeded seven games. Political campaigns were so-so but came around too infrequently. A visit to the United Nations Headquarters by Khrushchev would keep tongues wagging for the duration, but no sojourn of his was in fact as interminable as it seemed. Yet Joe stuck to writing the trivialities of industry gossip for which he was paid; Hank reluctantly heeded the call of duty and recorded the latest in tax gimmicks, loopholes, and fancy formulae for escaping the government dragnet; and Barney heralded new drilling inventions, gadgets, and devices to a world weary with waiting — all this rather than open the floodgates of conversation by mentioning this very special woman who was as close as the office across the hall and as far away as the moon.

My situation was a little different. It wasn't for a newcomer like me to break the spell. One day, however, there wasn't even a particle of junk mail to be carried beyond our office to the newsprint warehouse or to the print shop. Having left her slight burden with Mrs. Runkel, Leona retraced her course past the desks of Joe, Hank, Barney, Fatso Skinner, Clancy, Wes Wesselink. In a low voice but with such an intensity that I was sure Joe must have heard her, Mrs. Runkel said to me, "Get a load of Mr. Brenimer. He hasn't taken his eyes off that girl since she came in." I replied, "Why don't you tell him to put his eyes back in his head?" I could see Joe's ears and neck taking on the color of Concord grape juice.

At noon, Joe asked me to take lunch with him at the Yucca Club. We often went out together for a mid-day snack, but I knew this was different.

"The Yucca Club," I said. "And how. Cocktails, maybe?" Joe grinned feebly and cryptically, without saying aye, yes or no. The *News* is a weekly trade journal, one of the best, but it is by no means as broad-minded and tolerant as the regular news dailies when it comes to a snifter or two or three or more at lunch. Joe had been known to break over the traces more than once without his work suffering in the least, but he wasn't the kind to tip off the management in advance. At the Yucca Club, he didn't so much as tell me what he had in mind or ask me to join him in a quickie. He merely said, "Catch a table, and I'll be with you in a jiffy." He headed in the direction of the bar.

Joe wasn't gone long. As soon as he sat down across from me, he said, "If you think I'm sizing up that girl with the notion of making a pass at her, you don't know me at all. Nothing is further from my mind. I'm not such an ass as you guys at the office may think. I'm old enough to be her father. Sure, that doesn't guarantee she's immune to a pinch in the right place. I know there's no fool like an old fool.

"Trouble is, you guys hear me talking about how Updike made a fast fortune at Casper and the way Guptill took Ponsford when the Rangely Field was first opened, and you think I don't know anything else. Just like Hank. He figures no guy is nothing but a taxpayer, a taxpayer, a taxpayer till he's sick to the stomach and dead in the head. Well, it ain't necessarily so, as the Bible says. It ain't necessarily, ain't necessarily so." He fixed me with a bellicose eye.

"Sure," I said. "It figgers."

"No, it don't figger by a damn sight," he said, "but I'm telling you. I'm telling you, see?"

''I know," I said.

"And I know, too," he said. "I know a helluva lot more than I get paid for knowing. I know a helluva lot more than that the revenooers have been hot on Paul Dalzell's trail ever since the safecrackers made away with all that cash and currency and furnished free clues to tax evasion. I wasn't born yesterday. I've done a lotta living that don't go down on no company time sheets."

"Of course you have. We all have. We all…" I was going to say we all were for him, but he didn't give me a chance. He was like a rodeo bronco that has lowered its jaws to its shoulders and is resisting the bit between its teeth.

"We all, hell. You all ain't, either, known another girl like Leona. You all been trying to tell me that right along by your goddam unnatural silence. I'm onto your game, and it ain't so. You ain't, either, all of you, left a girl like that behind you. It couldn't be that you all have. Maybe you think you have. Maybe you dream you have or imagine you have, but you haven't. It ain't in the cards for you all to have a lost sweetheart, let alone one like Leona. But I really have." His words were emphatic, but he was becoming less rambunctious, more quiet, even as he uttered them.

"Okay," I said. "You really have. Did you ever hear the one about the guy from Urelia who'd been away a long time, and…?"

"Yeah, Urelia, 'You're a liah; you really ah…' Yeah, yeah, it's old as the hills."

"Okay," I said, "Okay, okay, okay. Well, I don't know about Hank and Barney and the rest, but speaking simply for myself, I do know a double for Leona. If Leona only wore glasses, she'd be the spittin' image of Grandma."

"You're nuts," said Joe with finality. "This girl I'm talking about even had a name like Leona. It was Lana, Lana Shanahan. She looked more Irish than Leona. I'd say Leona is a little on the German side, wouldn't you? And she hasn't any expression at all. Have you ever noticed that? Leona is as expressionless as the seafaring men in Winslow Homer's paintings. You've seen that? She isn't unique at all. She could be any woman." His voice trailed off, died away.

"I mean she isn't just Leona. She's Lana Shanahan, or could be. Did you ever hear of Leona having a last name? Did you ever hear her speak? For all we know, she's a deaf-mute and can't even smile. For all we know, but I know better because I knew Lana Shanahan."

"How is that?" I asked.

"I was going to college at the time and working a four hour shift at night in the installation and repair department of an electric refrigerator concern. That was way back when ice-boxes were giving way slowly before these new electric gizmos."

"I remember that," I said. "That wasn't so long ago."

"It was plenty long ago," Joe said. "You could even see horses pulling milk wagons now and then on the streets. That's how long ago it was. It was a different world entirely, then."

"Oh, I don't know," I said. "But what's all this got to do with Leona. I mean Lana?"

"Everything. Lana had come in from the farm country, the same as I had. She worked for General Refrigerator in the daytime, same as I did at night."

"A pretty cool set-up, wasn't it?"

Joe ignored my remark. "She was a stenographer, and I answered the telephone when our users called to report their machine had gone wrong at night. You'd be surprised how many of those newfangled affairs went haywire at night."

"Like people," I said.

"Like some people," Joe assented. "But if you'd a known Lana, you wouldn't say things like that. She made everything seem right. She was the original, and Leona's the carbon copy. That's how alike they are. There's an incredible resemblance. Lana had great big blue-grey eyes, a rose-petal complexion, and hair the color of a raven's wing. She was taller and slimmer than Leona but built exactly the same."

I was tempted to ask how she could be taller and slimmer than Leona and still have the same build. Or how she could have blue-grey eyes and jet-black hair and still be a dead-ringer for our own little cutie, but I let that pass.

"What happened?" I asked. "Did you marry the girl or did somebody beat your time, or what?"

"Nobody beat my time," Joe said. "There was a joker, a jerk, a snake-in-the-grass, by the name of Bud Christgau who used to date her once in a while, but he didn't know a real pearl from a false one. He dropped her for a dizzy blonde waitress he met one time when he was fixing the compressor in an ice-cream cabinet at the New Canton Café."

"But what about you? How did you lose her?"

"I didn't lose her. She never was for me. She wanted marriage and kiddies, and I was still a freshman in college and working my way through. I didn't have a chance. I was majoring in geology and, what with that and my job, I hardly ever had a spare moment."

"So busy with geology you had no time for anatomy, eh?"

"It wasn't that. She clearly wasn't for me. She was an angel in disguise. She left General Refrigerator. A strange geek chased her one evening as she was passing Pantages Park on the way home. He didn't catch her; he gave up the chase when she screamed, and he ducked back into the crowd in the park. But he scared her half to death. She quit her job after that and went back to Onamia, Nebraska, where she came from. I never saw her again; never heard a word since. That's all I know."

"I see," I said.

"So you see there isn't the slightest danger that a guy as old as I am, a guy who has really lived, would ever make a fool of himself over Leona, don't you?"

"I ain't worried at all about Leona," I said, "but don't you ever make a pass at Lana, Joe. You got too much to lose — a wife, grown kids. But let's get to hell out of this Yucca fire-trap and get back to work."

"Rog-er," he said, signing the tab the waitress had left on the table. "Let's look back."

I was already on my feet and set to leave. "Look back, hell," I said. "Let's look forward. Leona'll marry that lame-brain, Higby, in the print-shop, and live happily ever after. You wait and see."

My comment brought a grimace of concern to Joe's face, but he offered no argument.

Love Is a Triangle

"My psychiatrist says I love you." That was all the card said, and it may have been a joke, but it was to disturb the even tenor of his ways terribly. It was signed clearly and in a feminine hand, Clotilde. He had no idea who Clotilde was. No other mail was in the box at the apartment-house entrance.

There was no special occasion for anyone to send Bert Smith such a card unless it was that he would be on his annual summer vacation on Monday. This was Friday. It was the first time the company had given him two whole weeks, because he hadn't been with it long enough before this. As it was, he had had to work like a dog until late in the evening to clear his desk of problems and papers. Being an actuarial trainee for a life insurance company, even a small case is no snap these days.

The girls at the office had kidded the guy about always going home to Mama for his vacation. One of them could have signed the name Clotilde to cover her own identity and sent the card to him in a spirit of horseplay. Sure, that was it. Girls always resented a guy's mother — all girls, not just wives. He put aside the evening paper and got up to look at the postmark. He couldn't make it out but was sure it wasn't local. That scotched the theory that one of the office jokers mailed the message.

There was very little packing to do. He was going to a small town just a hundred miles distant from Sonora Springs. Several pairs of old slacks, a few sport shirts, and so forth would be all he needed. He got a suitcase out of a closet, opened it and threw in some things and then went back to the newspaper.

He had had a long, hard day. On second thought, a drink was in order. He usually had beer when he was home and alone in his compact, furnished, buffet apartment, but the occasion called for a high-ball, whatever the occasion was. Oh yeah, his vacation. He took a few quick gulps. They hit the spot. Next thing was to raise the windows and let a little air in. He had forgotten to do that as soon as he entered.

He wouldn't mind if that cute blonde at the office with a voice like a bird call had sent that thing. She's awfully good-looking—cuddly too, probably. She fancied him, maybe--or would if he made a play for her. He hadn't thought of doing so till now. When he got back from vacation, he'd have to see what kind of time he could make with her. Her name is Matilde. Matilde: most likely she sent that card and changed her name ever so little just not to be too brazen; not to appear to be chasing him. But no, he came back to the fact that it didn't have a Sonora Springs postmark.

He knew a little about doctors generally from his work and from personal experience. Psychiatrists—well, they were something else again; they were strange, unfamiliar, incalculable phantom figures, yet not without authority. He had a mental image of a whiskered guy in a white coat with an old-style, short, full beard and maybe even a test-tube in his hand. No, not that;

test-tubes were for chemists. Psychiatrists used couches, but he couldn't imagine how or why. He was pretty hazy on psychoanalysis.

He would have felt better about Clotilde if she hadn't dragged somebody else, her whiskered psychiatrist, into the affair. Why couldn't she have left Whiskers out of it, for crying out loud? He took a terrific draught on his highball and then decided to finish it off, get it out of the way and pour another. He had some concentrating to do. It seemed he was playing second fiddle to Whiskers.

It was not till he sat down again with his drink that it came to him with a flash and a shock that his father had been dead for over three years. He had been planning to visit his folks; his father as well as his mother. How he loved him. This made his impatience at taking a back seat to Whiskers all the worse: unkindly; uncalled for. It was quite wrong to think — yes, even to think — ill of the defenseless deceased.

When the girls were teasing him about going home to Mama for his vacation, he was nettled enough once to be tempted to answer them by saying he was going home to Papa, as well. How could he have forgotten his father's departure? He had loved Dad so; him and his poorly-shaven, stubbly, grizzly-grey whiskers; his rough-feeling corduroy shirts; and the smell of tobacco smoke which seemed to permeate and envelope the Old Man. Huh, but the era of corduroy shirts — that wasn't just yesterday.

Clotilde didn't say she loved him, Bert Smith, and he couldn't be sure she did — if she wasn't sure herself, whoever she was. She made it all depend on Whiskers. She hid behind the doctor's white coat the way he, Bert, as a tiny tot used to hide behind his mother's skirt at the approach of strangers. That was decidedly a long time ago, over twenty years, and that's a big percentage of anyone's life span. It doesn't take a full-fledged actuary to know that.

Furthermore, if he were to leave Whiskers out of Clotilde's declaration, what kind of a love was it that she had for him? One that she dared not declare on her own or in person? What kind would that be? A pretty name, Clotilde. Unusual. A bit like his mother's name, Claudine—as much like Claudine as Matilde. An old-fashioned sort of name that somehow belonged to long-vanished Arcadia almost as much as Evangeline. His mother was Claudine for others, but not for him.

A flush spread over his face, and his lips quivered. He got up to inspect the postmark again. His eyes blurred a bit. His fingers trembled. He let the envelope fall with relief. It hadn't been mailed in his old home town of Custer City. He was pretty sure; sure enough. It was foolish to have supposed any such thing anyway. Foolish and wrong; especially wrong. He shouldn't have had the second drink. Beer was for him.

He set the tall glass down on the table. Then, experimenting with the phrase and with his eyes glassy and staring off into space in a trance, he whispered, hoarsely, "I love you, Clotilde. I love you. I love you."

He went over to the bathroom and looked in the mirror. He had a faint, unfamiliar smile of pleasure and satisfaction on his face. The sight of himself snapped him out of the mood he had been in. He chuckled and declared out loud: "It's pretty nice to be loved by a stranger. Probably nobody but a Smith could have such a lucky break. A case of mistaken identity is all right once in a while. Gets a guy out of himself."

He turned his back on the mirror and, gesturing for emphasis at the half-empty, staring suitcase on the living-room floor, he added: "I'd like to know that gal Clotilde. She might put a spell on me again, but I'll bet you this much. I'd take her away from that psychiatrist."

Mr. Merriwell's Ordeal

Mr. Merriwell is not the kind of man one would expect to get in trouble while his wife was away for a week or two. That, however, is what happened this spring when Mrs. Merriwell went to Omaha to be with their expectant daughter while the baby was born. Oh, the dignified gentleman didn't take advantage of his wife's absence to sample his secretary's lipstick, to rumple the clothing of the church soprano, or to compromise the virtue of his neighbor's pert little wife. The "facts of life" which he savored to his sorrow were of a different kind.

Richard Merriwell and his wife, Nancy, had already celebrated their silver wedding anniversary and were grandparents twice over when their only daughter, Gwen, was married. That was a year ago this spring. The two of them took a trip of their own while the young folks were honeymooning. Their children, son and daughter, were grown. Both were married, and one already had youngsters of his own, with another one in the oven. The Merriwells felt well rewarded for the hustle and bustle at office, home, and playground which kept the sheriff and truant officer from the door. They sold the house and moved into an apartment within walking distance to downtown Sonora Springs.

They were just beginning to feel more or less accustomed to their new situation when Mrs. Merriwell was called to Omaha; the baby was coming any day now. Mr. Merriwell didn't see that he could be of any help at all in welcoming the newcomer to the world. He stayed behind to keep the files of papers moving through his office in City Hall, but he had no sooner put his wife on the overnight train for Omaha that Sunday evening than he began to have chills. He awoke the next day with a honey of a spring cold.

He was having a late breakfast in the kitchen, clad in his bathrobe, when the doorbell rang. He went to the door. There stood, or rather huddled, a strange woman: middle-aged, no make-up, a complexion that matched the vapid beige of her dress. Her hands were clutched over her flat chest in distress. She said "Can I come in?" He said "But I don't know you. Are you Mrs. Hanadan?" The woman nodded in the affirmative, and he motioned for her to come in. Mrs. Hanadan was the caretaker's wife. She made quickly for the big arm chair in the living room and plopped into that. She said "I fell down the stairs." He noticed a huge black and blue spot beside one eye. She complained of pains in her back.

From the beginning, Mr. Merriwell doubted that Mrs. Hanadan's pains and bruises were occasioned by a fall. The caretaker was new to the building, and Mr. Merriwell had seen him but once. That once, behind the building where the tenants park their cars, was enough to give an impression of shocking brutality. The man's stance was not that of a purposeful and busy workman but shrieked doubt whether to lunge forward or run away. The eyes glared up from the puffy, downcast face as if this man were the one who might be called upon, without warning, to head off an all-out attack. On top of all that, and as the sum of it, was that appearance of brutality.

Still, impressions can be wrong, and Mr. Merriwell didn't know what happened. It would have been possible for anyone, especially this visitor, to have fallen. She sat erect on the front of the chair with her hands clasped so tightly together that he had the feeling one hand might go right through the other. One so tense as that might have fallen, surely.

He wondered a bit whether the woman had been drinking. He didn't know much about such things but eliminated that possibility. She said, "I'm so sick at times the doctor says I'll end up at the state hospital if I'm not careful." She burst into tears, gasped for breath, and said, "I don't want to do that." She cried briefly into a crumpled handkerchief held with both hands so as to muffle all but weak sounds of sniffling.

"Would you like an aspirin?" he asked. She nodded, and he went for the pills and a glass of water. He returned to find her with her chin on the arm of the chair, almost asleep. He didn't know what to make of that. He put the aspirin and the glass on the other arm of the chair.

She looked at him. "You know how I got to the hospital the other day?" she asked. "I called the police, and they took me. If they thought I was drunk, they'd have taken me to jail."

He replied, crediting the police with more savvy than himself, "Well, they know the difference between the drunk and the sick." She liked the answer. She swayed slowly back and forth from the waist as she swallowed the aspirin with a drink of water. Then she lapsed back into drowsiness. He went for a bottle of cleansing ammonia his wife kept in the kitchen and came back and gave Mrs. Hanadan a sniff of that. She perked up, and, telling her to be sure to hold onto the railing and to be sure to call a doctor, he held her by the arm as they went down the backstairs to the basement. She seemed much improved, and he left. He was glad none of the neighbors had seen him in his bathrobe leaving her apartment.

He put on some clothes and went out, just a block, for a morning newspaper. Some of Mrs. Hanadan's tension had rubbed off on him. He felt jittery. He read a story or two, not too carefully, of new instances of juvenile delinquency: a purse snatched from an elderly woman, an old man slugged by two teenagers, the same old stuff. The thick head which went with his cold was no help to his understanding of the stepped-up war of youth on age. The mayor, Mr. Merriwell's boss a few rungs removed, had come out for public flogging of the culprits "under official supervision." The newspaper carried an editorial endorsing the suggestion and adding a recommendation of work camps.

Mr. Merriwell found himself doing something he had never done before: writing a letter to the editor. When he had finished, he inspected his handiwork with satisfaction. It was a masterpiece of satire, he thought. Especially good was the declaration: "The perfect partner, the finishing touch for flogging and work camps is extermination camps." Then, another effective thrust was the sentence: "Flogging and work camps are simple answers, but no simpler than extermination camps. And only the last of these has the merit of being a final solution, a really permanent liquidation of the problem." To sign his own name to such a caustic criticism of local politics might endanger his job. He toyed with the pen names Dow Jones and Davey Jones but settled upon David Jones. He put the epistle in the mail. Without bothering for lunch, he doctored his cold and went back to bed.

The next day at breakfast time, Mr. Merriwell was interrupted again, this time by the telephone. A friend of his from California was on the line. The friend and his wife were in Sonora Springs for just a few days, visiting. Mr. Merriwell invited the two of them over. Only Ernie could come. Laura had engagements, but Ernie would be over in a half hour. He was as good as his word.

Ernie had been a professor of psychology at the state university not far from Sonora Springs, but he had left several years ago for a position as a clinical psychologist in a well-endowed psychiatric hospital on the West Coast. In the meantime, they had not corresponded. They were both from Missouri, shared a delight in banter, got along well conversationally, but had never been best friends. Anyhow, when they were in a firm and comfortable agreement about such satisfying subjects as Truman's superiority to Eisenhower, the excellence of Napa Valley wines, and the exciting qualities of red-haired women, why should they bother to discover and explore possible differences of basic outlook? So they had felt and left it at that.

He greeted Ernie heartily as a heaven-sent messenger of personal tidings and bearer of a special balm for that stay-at-home loneliness which had become as depressing as his cold. Ernie had news, plenty of it. He had so much news that he had no time at all to listen to Mr. Merriwell. At first, the gossip consisted exclusively of troubles: overwork, working conditions, ignorant unappreciative superiors. The asylum, it seemed, would be better off run by inmates. Ernie was a doctor of philosophy in psychology, but that counted for nothing with the doctors of medicine who were in charge of everything around the hospital. The only kind of trouble Ernie didn't have was the marital kind. He and Laura were getting along famously as they always had.

The restaurants around San Francisco were terrific: such foods, such wines, such merchandising genius. One shrewd operator, recognizing the propensity of customers to write on the walls of washrooms, installed a blackboard in each for the convenience of his patrons. One wag took advantage of the opportunity to record the following: "The Constitution guarantees every citizen the right to revolt, so if I want to be revoltin', man, that's my business." None of the first-rate places advertised. The local yokels just had to discover them the hard way. Ernie and Laura had had the good fortune to run across one busy little dining room which had models demonstrating lingerie, the sheerest of sheer lingerie, during the lunch hour. That was right downtown. The places in obscure, out-of-the-way locations were every bit as up-and-coming and clever. For example, one had converted the basement into a theater and, as an after-dinner treat, exhibited the finest pornographic films.

Mr. Merriwell gathered that, once released from the boredom of the sedate college town near Sonora Springs, Ernie and Laura had discovered themselves while exploring for eating-places in the gastronomic capital of the country. He told Ernie that one can't have everything here-below. "You are lucky," he said. "Your marital harmony must offset, and more than offset, all the stupidity you run up against on the job. After all, it's love that makes the world go round."

Ernie agreed. "I know," he said. "I ought to know." He grimaced. "Of course, sometimes I think it's hate that makes the world go round." He winked at Mr. Merriwell as if he were only kidding, but he was suddenly in a hurry to go. No, there wouldn't be time for another meeting or to bring Laura over. They had to get on the road and head home. On the mountain passes the spring snows are the worst ones. "Got a job to do, you know," Ernie said. "And Laura is crazy to get back to her parakeets." For both it was a sad parting, so much so that Mr. Merriwell forgot he had had no chance to say anything.

Ernie's abrupt departure left Mr. Merriwell up in the air. The cold, which had seemed better earlier, had worsened. His breathing was as labored as the navigation of an ocean liner in a wind-blown drizzle. He wasn't hungry but decided that the thick split pea soup that Mrs. Merriwell had prepared for him before she left would, if eaten good and hot, relieve the congestion in his head. He thinned the soup stock with butter and cream as he had been instructed. It was delicious: a meal in itself.

There was no use going to work, the way he felt. Maybe he could sleep again this afternoon. It was worth a try. The steaming lunch had been calming. He probably wasn't up to, wasn't equal to, enjoying those fine Italian dinners which were ashamed of spaghetti. Funny — to remember those lines of verse he had learned as a child: Won't you walk into my parlor said the spider to the fly, tis the prettiest little parlor that ever you did spy. He fell asleep.

It was a good thing the rest of the tenants had all gone off to work or market, or the worthy Mr. Merriwell might have been arrested for disturbing the peace. His snoring resounded through the building, but he slept on, blissfully unaware. He dreamed.

In his dream, he was on a sailing ship, a ghost ship, all gray, including the sails. It had been stricken from the royal registry of good Queen Bess for piracy on the high seas. It no longer hoisted the Jolly Roger and levied toll but forever sailed and drifted through constant mist and fog, a gray ship on a gray, gray sea. That was her destiny till some unknown event should free her from this fixed and fated routine.

It was understood on board that a change might occur. That change, however, was feared, not hoped for. His own arrival on the ship had caused grave concern among the crew lest it should be the signal that some variation in their schedule was impending. Even the cadaverous captain was worried and had Mr. Merriwell brought before him. The latter stood mute, however, unable to speak, and the dream was over.

When Mr. Merriwell awakened, it was Wednesday. He may have established a new long-distance sleeping record, but he had to get plenty of rest if he was to be well when Nancy got back to complete the cycle. Already Wednesday! Good grief, a week in Sonora Springs would be a "cycle in Cathay." Whatever it might be that makes the world go around, it goes faster than it used to.

He seldom read the morning paper, but he wanted some company for brunch. Besides, he was feeling well enough to wonder whether the editor of the *News* had dared to print his letter. He went out for a copy of the paper. As soon as he was back in the apartment, he opened to the editorial page. His letter wasn't there. Just as he thought: the editor didn't dare. There was, however, a letter that looked ever so much like a point-for-point answer to his own message. It was, strangely enough, signed A. Lincoln.

He let the paper slide onto the floor beside the kitchen table and stepped on it as he got up to look into the possibilities of a home lunch, or rather, brunch. No eggs, no bacon, no cereal. There was bread, so he could have toast. There was beer for "hot beer on toast, hot beer on toast." Ah, back to business again, there was still some roast beef left from Sunday dinner. That plus beer and toast would be it. The therapeutic qualities of such a lunch might not be guaranteed, but a cook has to work within the framework of the possible, the same as a politician, or else go out to eat.

If he felt better it would be different. He would go out for groceries. And if Nancy were home, she'd cook them. He and Nancy never had compared notes on the blackboard witticisms to be found in the respective restrooms of the better metropolitan restaurants. Their marriage had never known such a culmination of harmony but had been no less satisfactory on that account. He missed Nancy but had no yearning for the mystic, sophisticated joy that goes with a cultivated taste for caviar.

He wondered if perchance Nancy had written since she had got to Omaha. He hadn't checked the mailbox at the building entrance for days, close to a week. He went down to see. No, nothing but a lot of advertising junk and an invitation of some sort in a small envelope that had almost escaped his attention in the midst of the bulk and so gone into the waste basket with the rest of the haul. He and his wife were invited to attend the cocktail party and own-your-own preview at the art museum. These were annual affairs, and he had taken Nancy to them several times.

It would look funny if he were too sick to go to work in the daytime but well enough to attend a cocktail party in the evening. Still, he might see something Nancy would like: not a painting, but a vase, a flower pot, or something of that sort. Going would be better than staying at home alone to sleep, to dream, or not to sleep, to twist and squirm. He decided to rest that afternoon and afterwards to make use of the invitation.

The Marsden Mutual Fund was the sponsor of the affair this year and was footing the liquor bill, paying the bar tender, matching the invitations presented against the list of invitees. A uniformed flunkey held the door open for Mr. Merriwell, took the invitation, bestowed a smile, and then as he passed the card to the two girls hovering over a desk he asked, "What's the name?" Mr. Merriwell, with the air of a man whose identity is well known and speaks for itself, headed for the cloak-room. "Smith," he called back over his shoulder as the girls rushed through the pages of their list. That was that.

There were no textile exhibits this year and fewer ceramics than in the past. He saw nothing at all that appealed to him as a gift. The preview undoubtedly was well-attended, and many of the ceramic exhibits already had red "sold" cards affixed to them. He turned to inspect a collection of metallic objects. In so doing he bumped against a woman with a highball in hand, causing her to rock her glass so violently that some of its contents spilled over. He apologized. "No harm done," she said indulgently. "It all went on the floor." She motioned at one of the wire contraptions. "Isn't it wonderful?" she asked

"It's form," she said. "It's balance."

"I don't know about such things," he confessed, "They're new, aren't they?"

"In a way," she agreed. "They're just coming into their own. I think balance is a wonderful thing, don't you? I mean the struggle for balance, the artistic creation of balance. Nothing is so important, nowadays, as balance."

"Ye-es. I know." He moved toward the bar. The Marsden people were dispensing good scotch. They could afford to. Anyone with enough dough to be in the market for art was a potential investor in mutual funds. He elbowed and shouldered his way along the array of paintings. Two well-known young men about town, partners of a sort, were explaining one of the paintings to the crowd circled around. Mr. Merriwell noticed his own friends, the Hokansons, in the charmed circle.

Florence Hokanson spoke up, addressing the young-ish man who seemed to be the senior partner in the interpretation team. "If you divide paintings between daubs and smears," she said with the beatific smile of a woman sure of her perception and taste, "this would be a daub, wouldn't it?" The interpreter was grateful for such knowingness, and his smile showed it, but he didn't precisely confirm his questioner's pronounce-ment.

"I'm thinking of getting this for Howie," he said, nodding at the junior partner who was gazing at the blob on canvas in open-mouthed ecstasy.

Mr. Merriwell avoided the Hokansons' eyes lest he should be called upon to descant upon the peculiar excellence of daubs as contrasted with smears. He couldn't, however, manage to get an unobstructed view of anything. He didn't know why. The bright-eyed dwarf, only four feet tall and almost as wide, shuttled through the throng with the greatest of ease and ap-peared to be enjoying herself immensely. Indeed, no one else seemed to be having any difficulties or to be conscious of any distraction. The group-judgment of admiration was given voice in the same raucousness as the contented gabble of a poultry yard on a perfect summer day. Only this was louder, much louder. Mr. Merriwell fled the scene like a dog with his tail between his legs.

On Thursday morning, Mr.Merriwell was at his office bright and early. His colleagues were pleased to see him back. They all agreed he looked like a ghost but couldn't forbear giving him the old razzberry "What's the matta?" Chris said "Can't stand your own cookin'?" He didn't stay for an answer. "Remember, you're not gonna be the Papa," Joe said, "just the Grandpa." Mr. Merriwell took it all good naturedly. He was glad to be back on the job.

His secretary, an older woman with civil servant status, tenure, and veterans' preference galore, said, "Should think you'd be glad when the old lady's gone. From what I hear, she always has the last word..."

"Yeah. She always has the last word because I let her have the last word. We both like it that way."

"Not bad," his secretary assented.

He was relieved when the day ended. His cold had virtually disappeared, but it had left him weak. He bought a paper and read it at the table as he had dinner downtown. There it was, in black and white, with names and numbers. G. W. Hanadan was being held by police on suspicion of manslaughter. Mrs. Ruby Hanadan was dead. The husband disclaimed any responsibility for her death, but violence was obvious. No charges would be made until after the autopsy.

At the office the next day, a hubbub developed spontaneously around Mr. Merriwell's desk over Mrs. Hanadan's death. He volunteered nothing about the victim's visit to his apartment on Monday but spoke as one who was as much of a stranger to the misfortune and as much surprised by it all as his fellow workers. Indeed, he was as much surprised by it.

On Saturday morning, Mr. Merriwell's cold was a thing of the past. So were the early spring showers and clouds that had dominated the weather all week. It was cool, but the sun was bright and cheerful and glorious. He had breakfast close to his apartment and took a walk.

When he got back home there were two solicitors going up and down the apartment hall ringing doorbells He left his own door open. He didn't have long to wait. The two of them, the boy and the girl, were primly, not to say grimly, dressed. The girl, eighteen to twenty, was pretty plain of face as well. The boy, possibly younger than the girl, had a shrewd gleam in his eye, Mr Merriwell thought. "Excuse me, Sir," the boy said. "We're collecting money for the heathen."

"Who are they?" Mr Merriwell asked.

"In darkest Africa, you know," the girl replied

"According to the Book, charity begins at home," Mr. Merriwell countered.

"We're not asking for charity according to the letter," the boy cut in, "but according to your heart and your means. Unless you give in accordance with your heart, your charity is not genuine."

"And there is a great need," the girl said.

"Are you two, by any chance, heathen?" Mr. Merriwell asked.

The boy didn't bat an eyelash. The girl, his sister or his sweetheart, was deeply hurt, humiliated, ashamed. The lad came back quickly with "Yes, Sir, we are." There were tears in the girl's eyes.

"Well, then, here's a half dollar. Don't spend it all in one place." The lad didn't take it but permitted the girl to drag him away by the arm. "Thanks all the more, Sir," he shouted back. Mr. Merriwell closed the door.

Later on that day the telegram came. It read, "It's a boy. All fine. Congratulations, Grandpa! See you soon. Love, Nancy."

With the telegram still in his hand he sprawled in the chair Mrs. Hanadan had used. Love, Nancy. He knew Nancy agreed with him, and together they could stand off Ernie's notion that it might be hate which makes the world go round. Then, as he lounged there only half awake, it came to him. It isn't either-or. It's both. And the doggone world doesn't go round just one way like a boy's top. It alternates, first a dozen times one way and then a dozen whirls or so the other. It resembles that toy he used to make as a kid by threading a three foot piece of string through both eyes of a big button and then tying the ends.

The muscles of his wrists relived that sensation, that tension and rhythm of stretching out the string and letting up, pulling taut and relaxing. He could hear again that whirring or buzzing of the big button as it spun madly forward till the string was wound tight, reversed itself and went the other way as long as it could. Z-z-z, love and hate, Z-z-z.

The telegram slowly descended from his hand and settled upon the thick carpeting beside his chair. The ordeal was over. He slept.

Murder for Money

My most humiliating experience happened quite a few years ago, at a time when I was at the height of my career as a lawyer. Yet I have never told anyone about it. It certainly isn't the sort of thing one tells at a party. There is an element of the macabre in it: something which I am sure would freeze the bubbling current of conversation at any social gathering. It isn't, you see, a simple tale of my most embarrassing moment, of which I have one to fit nearly every occasion. I get as much kick out of telling about my various most embarrassing moments — when, for a brief instant, I looked ridiculous in the eyes of the jury, the judge, or friends — as anyone.

But now, I am going to recall something rare, strange and extremely humiliating: a dazzling flash of time when I seemed ridiculous in my own sight; when I suddenly had my self-respect shattered to bits; when I felt a rug pulled from under me and when my tight, little world wobbled on its axis. It was over quickly, yes. But it isn't over yet. It lingers in my memory like a vivid, fantastic dream; like the adventures of Coleridge's Ancient Mariner. You'll see what I mean soon enough.

I haven't even told this story to my wife. She would say "I told you so," or "It serves you right," or something like that. Indeed, I decided to take the case which caused my mortification in a spirit of contrariety toward my wife as well as in a mood of benevolence toward the son of a deceased friend. God knows I could see no hope of winning a verdict, for the judgment had been pronounced already in the pages of the most influential daily newspaper of the nearest city. The case was in that class of outrageous occurrences, fortunately small but unfortunately larger than commonly supposed, when a jury is convened, like the old Russian duma, to ratify and give due form to the prior decision of the ultimate authority, in this case, the respectable readers of the *Morning Gazette*.

At breakfast, my wife was in a dither. She was horrified by the awful crime, the murder of that nice, universally loved Mrs. Singleton who, as everybody knew, had lived on Xavier Street for years. I scarcely could read the *Gazette*. I hardly needed to, for its columns recounted the ghastly details as my wife and with the same frenzy and overtones. I was but vaguely irritated by all this, by the excessive acidity of my fruit juice and by the tepidity of my coffee, when I learned the name of the confessed killer, Glenn Mayhew. That did it.

At the mention of Mayhew, I knew I had to take the case if he would have me, which was a question, for I had long since earned the right to concentrate on civil suits and to refer criminal cases to the younger members of the bar who were less established in the profession but also less rusty in the defense of criminal prosecutions. Young Mayhew was the son of an old friend of mine who had died many years before. Glenn must have been under ten years of age when his father, a preacher with a burning missionary zeal, had "cashed in his chips," as they used to say in taverns of our beloved, rough-and-ready, gold-mining town of Pembroke, about a hundred twisty, windy miles west of Sonora Springs.

Glenn's widowed mother had moved shortly after her husband's death. She made a good living, in one way or another, for herself and her only child, Glenn. That I knew, but not first hand, for in the past decade I had not seen Mrs. Mayhew to talk to. She was utterly unlike Fightin' Bob, as we called her husband. She knew how to get along in a way Bob never did. She calculated, where he fulminated. He used to joke about it in the old days.

I knew Glenn had been in the army for a while. I heard about it when he left and when he came back. I saw him once after he returned to Pembroke. With a weary smile on his face, he said he had been a clerk in Headquarters Company, but he didn't seem inclined to say any more. I thought at the time, "Well, he'll feel better about things when he gets his feet on the ground back here in Pembroke." After that, I didn't see him. He worked at the bank as a bookkeeper, lived quietly, never got in trouble.

I was thunderstruck to learn that Glenn had confessed to killing Mrs. Singleton. It didn't add up. If he actually did it, he must have been insane. For his father's sake, at least, I would have to help Glenn if he would let me. It was an inevitable decision. My wife's barrage of words was intended to head me off from such a hopeless, perhaps thankless, undertaking. But I had no choice, really.

Glenn had been jailed on the strength of his confession. I turned the details of the violence over in my mind as I walked to the county jail. According to my wife who had read all about it in the *Gazette*, it was a clear case of murder for money. "What is the world coming to anyway," my wife had asked, "when such a smart boy as

Glenn Mayhew would do such a thing? He stood almost at the top of his high school class without half trying, Mr. Somers, the principal, said. Then, not so long ago, that good-looking young Kramer fellow drove over his own father with a car simply to get the insurance money. Something has to be done to put a stop to such things," my wife had concluded with vehemence.

The childless, ageing Mrs. Singleton was known to have a yen for coins all her life. A fortunate marriage in her youth, followed by a quick divorce, had given her the means to do more hoarding than was customary in the community, and she took advantage of the opportunity. It had pained her a good deal when, in the early days of Roosevelt's New Deal, the government required everyone to turn in their gold currency. However, the woman had refused the paper notes which the bank had offered in exchange for her gold. She had been content to become a depositor.

The silver coins which had remained in the hoard after the exchange of the gold were not collector's items, neatly segregated according to size and kept in cardboard or leather folders. The conglomerate collection simply had been half-hidden around the house in vases, sacks, corners: in brief, put wherever opportunity and security converged or were thought to do so. When Mrs. Singleton's strangled body was found, soon after the crime, many of these shiny, minted discs lay around her on the floor. A nylon stocking still was wrapped and twisted around the victim's neck.

The officer at the gate to the jail obviously was surprised at my request to see young Mayhew, but he gave me an entrance pass without protest or delay. After the screeching falsetto of the *Gazette*'s headlines and columns, the excited voice of my wife, and my own whirling thoughts and hurried steps, the jail seemed an island of calm. When young Mayhew emerged from his cell to face me in the booth made for such consultations, he seemed, somehow, to heighten this effect of tranquility.

I say "somehow" for he was not really calm. His face, indeed, had the quiet pallor of a mask, but that was all. His hair was tousled and his clothing rumpled (but they scarcely commanded attention). In his eyes, in his manner, and in his speech and gestures, I was astounded to see jubilation and triumph. Yet the air of victory was restrained. It must have been the self-containment, the self-control, which gave the effect of alert repose to the person of young Mayhew and contributed somehow to the general atmosphere. There was, too, an observable element of resignation mingled with the exultation, as if the sense of victory in him was overshadowed and becalmed by a simultaneous sense of defeat.

I began by asking the prisoner a few questions of personal history; by mentioning my friendship for, and treasured recollection of, his father; by requesting little items of information relating to himself and his mother during the years just passed. All the time I was looking for an answer to the question: is he sane? Glenn's answers were brief and to the point. His mother, he said, had moved away from Pembroke during his tour of service in the army and now made her home in a neighboring state. He had not heard from her lately. Probably she hadn't received the latest, tragic news of him. I thought his voice trembled a little as he spoke of his mother.

I wouldn't want to give all the minutia of this interview, even if I could. My humiliation lay in that tiny fraction of it when we were discussing a motive for the homicide. Glenn insisted that Mrs. Singleton had reminded him of his mother. He knew she hoarded money but had no idea how much or how little. He lived nearby and had seen her quite often. He always thought he liked her more than any other elderly woman because she seemed so like his mother. Then this last evening when he visited her and saw her fondling the coins she had poured on the table from her nylon stocking, he knew he hated her more than anyone else and more than he could put up with. On a sudden fierce impulse, he seized the stocking from its place beside the piled silver and strangled the woman to death. After he had grabbed the hapless woman and until the body was limp and lifeless in his grasp, he thought the victim was his mother. Then she became Mrs. Singleton for him again.

"Ah," I said, "that's all very well; but the coins were not merely scattered over the floor of the dining room, but along the path which leads to the sidewalk. But for that, the murder of Mrs. Singleton might be the act of a madman. But for that, we could plead insanity. Those tell-tale coins which you lost in your flight will scream murder for money, and who would believe such a crime was committed in a fit of insanity?"

He managed the same weary smile I had seen on him before. "You're like the rest," he said. "You're all alike," he continued, as I flinched and almost fainted from the humiliation or what-have-you that I saw on the way. "I knew it all along. What you call my savage outrage was the sanest thing I ever did, whatever else it might have been. A plea of insanity would be more than I can stomach. I had to prevent that. I just can't live with the insane, no matter how I try. That's clear at last, even to me. That's why I scooped up coins from the table and scattered them along the path I left."

The rest is incidental, and you can almost guess it. Though Glenn understood the purpose of his trial perfectly, he chose to regard it as in effect a scientific experiment in which certain hypotheses of his own were, by fortunate chance, being verified. Moreover, he seemed completely satisfied with the results of the test and his own conviction of committing murder with the eminently sane, understandable motive of acquiring the victim's money. When the wing of victory was shifted to the other sandal, so to speak, and Glenn was sent to the gas chamber in the state penitentiary, he said farewell to me with an unforced and cheerful smile, as if he were leaving a foreign country for home, finding at last a different, truer asylum. I can't forget it.

The Necklace

It's funny how it came about; it's the sort of thing one doesn't expect to happen and can't satisfactorily explain after it has happened. It was just accident, really, that after twenty-five years of happy married life in Sonora Springs, the Fiddlers agreed that Rusty should take a vacation that winter on his own. He wanted to go to Mexico. Lorna didn't. They could go to Europe for the same price and to Hawaii for less.

If Rusty had proposed a visit to the Mexican mainland, Lorna might have been halfway interested. She could see herself, at least through a glass darkly, strolling with her husband along the capital's Paseo de la Reforma; looking world-weary and sophisticated, with her ageing husband at her side, at a lakeside bar at Chapala; or having her fling and doing her thing with a bikini on the sands at Acapulco. But no, his mind was unaccountably set upon soaking up sunshine at the unheard-of city of La Paz on Baja California. If he wanted to go to that isolated, uninhabited backwash of civilization, he could go alone. She'd do her part by praying he escaped dysentery.

In truth, Rusty needed a vacation, and Lorna didn't. The Colorado winters were so mild, compared to those of her childhood in Duluth, they were her favorite among the seasons—to be enjoyed and not escaped. He was ten years older than Lorna, and he worked like a demon every day in his office at the Sonora Springs *Citizen*. He was tired, tired, tired.

"Don't bring me anything," Lorna said when they were talking about it.

"Well, of course, I will," he said. "I've already been thinking about it. Probably not a handbag, although they might have them made from the iguana."

"You always get me heavy things. I want light things. After all these years you don't know what I like."

"I might get you a necklace. Somewhere I've heard La Paz is noted for pearls, especially the dark ones."

"Ah, those are rare and expensive, the black ones. They'll swindle you at any ordinary shop. Don't buy anything anywhere except at a department store."

"I'll know where to go and what you like. I expect it to be expensive. I want it to be."

"The only thing, don't come back with syphilis. That's not the word I want. What is that sickness?"

"Dysentery."

"Oh yes."

Thus, to his own surprise, Rusty went off alone— unwilling this time to give up his own preferred spot for the great advantage of his wife's company. As for Lorna, she was unable to understand her own willingness to let this man of hers go off on a solo flight without a final "Oh, I guess I could go for some of that South Sea sunshine myself." She kissed him goodbye at the airport at seven-thirty in the morning, and they both stood up admirably, without tears on her part or "There, there, now," on his. He simply said, "Next time, by God, you're going with me!"

"I certainly am."

Rusty's first days at La Paz were one prolonged siesta. In his room he dozed. He had taken along *Berlitz Spanish for Travelers* but couldn't focus on it. D. H. Lawrence's *Plumed Serpent*, which he thought might be appropriate reading for a Mexican holiday, was simply a jumble of printed words—the alphabet arranged by a print-shop explosion rather than by a gifted novelist. On the beach he dozed, indifferent to his own appearance and that of the others. He carried sand back to his room with him in the hair of his legs and chest and shed it on the furniture and carpet before showering for lunch. Fastidious as he generally was, he didn't mind.

He walked from hotel to beach in a pair of white-rubber, Japanese-made locker-room sandals that he'd had for years. The old, gray swim trunks he'd worn out at home by use and by carrying them around in the car trunk were disgracing his figure here. The waist was loose and hung low on his belly, making him look far more pendulous than he actually was.

The chambermaid and the bellboy weren't drumming up business for their employer when they asked, one in Spanish and the other in stiff-jointed English, how he liked the bar at La Mision. The bar was at a different hotel. They were interested in him and were encouraging him to snap out of his lethargy. He guessed, without effort, there would be other Americans at the bar, but he had come to soak up sunshine not alcohol. Later he might exchange trivia with his fellows at the bar.

One day he made a brief excursion along one of the shopping streets. He purchased a pair of leather sandals, put them on then and there and signified to the merchant that the latter was to throw away the locker-room white-rubber junk. He felt better treading the sidewalk in leather sandals—the first pair he'd ever owned or worn. At home, sandals were principally the prerogative of the hippies, but he had only a faint realization of this and was not in the least disturbed by the dim notion. He had sent his wife some cards but not yet a letter. Now, he'd have something to write her about, his leather sandals.

The next day he sought out the Rufo Department Store. His guidebook recommended it as a safe place to buy pearls, but he first wanted to see if he could get a new pair of swimming trunks for himself. The clerk, who had a smattering of English, produced a pair of maroon trunks and held them against Rusty's waist. "They look a fit," said Rusty.

"Sexsational!" the clerk replied with a smile, eyeing his customer to see how he'd take the description.

"You couldn't have said it better," Rusty replied. He added with a show of bravado, "Cuanto es?"

"Cincuenta pesos."

"How much, again?"

"Fifty pesos."

"Okay, I'll take 'em."

Without showing any intent to become a customer then or later, he went past the jewelry counter and display on an inspection tour. He would save handling and pricing for the next day because he wanted to come back again—and wanted something specific to do mañana.

At the hotel, the clerks, bellboys, and the chambermaid took note, happily, that Señor Fiddler was looking better—more rested, more relaxed, more alive. The stocky thirtyish chambermaid spoke cheerily to him in Spanish. He didn't understand the words, but he got the idea. The bellboy approved the sandals and swimming trunks in English but was puzzled when Rusty repeated the sales clerk's description of the trunks as sexsational. The desk clerk looked more alive at seeing Rusty more so. This was his silent way of complimenting the señor from Colorado.

Rusty hadn't been thrilled by his cursory inspection of the jewelry department at Rufo's. The clerks looked competent and trustworthy. It looked like a sensible place to buy jewelry, yes — but he was looking for a different kind of place — less sensible, even less trustworthy, more — more something or other. Maybe more adventurous, more romantic. Nevertheless he went back to Rufo's and bought a pearl necklace for each of his two daughters-in-law.

He didn't see any black pearls, and he didn't ask. By now he was determined to hunt elsewhere for a necklace for Lorna. He was half-afraid Rufo's would tell him black pearls didn't exist. He'd heard of dark ones from someone, but until Lorna mentioned black ones, he'd never heard of those. Sometimes he'd been surprised at the extent of Lorna's knowledge of such esoteric, feminine subjects as jewelry, but he never was sure she wasn't bluffing. He knew she had a weakness — or call it a talent for bluffing, for pretending to know more than she did.

While he doubted Lorna, he trusted himself to learn and to be a match or master for any swindler he encountered. He was already in the second and last week of his stay at La Paz when he began his search, without inquiries of anyone, for a shop which might have a necklace suitable for Lorna — suitable for her to wear and suitable for him to give her as a gift.

A tinkling bell announced his arrival at Dulcinea de Mexico. It was a shop like several others he had been in:

dusky, small. The shop owner in this place as in the others was dark-skinned, dark-eyed, slow-moving. She let him scrutinize through the glass-topped counters a while before she came over. "Can I help you?" she asked in soft, accented English.

He met her eyes. She was pretty. "Are you Dulcinea?" he asked.

"Yes."

"I don't see any black pearls."

"There aren't any. I mean I haven't any in stock. Does it have to be black pearls?"

"Yes."

"I think I could get some for you. You want a necklace?"

"Yes."

"A single strand?"

"Yes. Not too tight, not too loose, not too small pearls."

"I'll see what I can get. Can you come back tomorrow or in a day or two?"

"Yes."

"You're Señor?"

"Fiddler."

"All right, Mr. Fiddler. Mañana."

Rusty felt excited when he left—so much so he tried to account for it to himself. It seemed to be everything but nothing in particular. The search and the possibility of success, yes, they were part of it. Dulcinea? Yes, she excited him too in some vague fashion, because she seemed to be excited, with him, about the search for the right pearls, the right necklace. He compared her appearance to Lorna's, and Dulcinea lost on every count. Lorna still resembled, to Rusty's eyes, Renoir's Gabrielle stepped out of the canvas and full of life—more cool and collected, as American women are, but still fulsomely beautiful. Dulcinea was not a picture come to life but a piece of dark, molded or roughly-sculptured living clay poised for an uncertain move. He decided the two couldn't be compared but wasn't satisfied with the final decision.

"At least," he comforted himself, "I'm not forgetting Lorna." He didn't wonder whether Lorna had forgotten him. When, on his next visit to Dulcinea's, he found her busy with a couple as obviously American tourists as he was, Dulcinea excused herself momentarily to tell him, "I don't have it. Can you come again tomorrow?"

"Yes, but tomorrow is my last day. I'm leaving by the early morning plane the day after tomorrow."

"I'll have it for you tomorrow." Then, as he hesitated about leaving, she repeated gently but finally, "mañana," and turned back to her customers.

Though Rusty was certain Dulcinea would come forth with the necklace he wanted, he didn't like being put off. He could wait, but he wasn't good at that, never had been. He would like to have met Dulcinea at the shop in the morning when she opened the doors for the day's business, but he sensed that was unseemly, was not the right thing to do. He tarried at the beach, marked time there enjoying the sunshine and sea air but with the urge to hurry to meet the important events that were calling him, demanding his presence and his decisions. He prolonged his wait so long, indeed, that he then wondered, as he walked over to the shop, if he would be in time.

He wondered too, as he walked, at his growing yen to know Dulcinea better this last day at La Paz. He marveled at his strong impulses, but, at the same time, was sure he could never put a proposal to her in words. It wasn't that he feared a rebuff, but that he couldn't bring himself to suggest something so contrary to his in-grained habits and accustomed grooves of thought, anything so inconsistent with countless editorials written for the Sonora Springs *Citizen*. As the male it was for him to take the initiative or suffer the consequences. He knew that and knew this was his last chance; it was now or never. Yet he felt helpless, so much a prisoner of his past that he even considered abandoning the project, getting a necklace, any necklace, from Rufo's and going home without the very special one for Lorna that he had dreamed about and schemed for. His feet continued, just the same, to take him to Dulcinea's.

She was alone in the store this time, and she had a string of black beads around her neck. Beneath the necklace her dress dived to display, ever so slightly, the curving contours of her dark-brown breasts. "You're ravishing!"

"Do you like it?"

"Ever so much. I adore them."

"Okay. You can have it."

"Okay. I'll take it."

"You'd pay any price I asked, wouldn't you, onyx or pearls?"

"Yes."

"It's for your wife?"

"Yes."

"You wouldn't accept the necklace as a gift?"

"No."

"Well, it isn't for sale for a price. It is mine, personal-ly, not the shop's. It was given to me. It's not new. I shouldn't sell it at all. I wouldn't sell it to anyone else; but you're different. At first glance you look like all the others, like the man you saw in here yesterday with his wife, but even before the first glance is over a new image is forming. You're not just one of the crowd, not just another tourist."

"But what can I give you? What can I do for you?"

"You expected to get your wife an expensive present, didn't you, when you came here to La Paz?"

"Yes."

"You brought the money with you for that purpose?"

"Travelers checks."

"That's okay. Have you paid your last hotel bill yet?"

"Not yet."

"But you know how much you need for that and the incidental expenses of your return trip?"

"Yes."

"For the necklace, I'll just take the rest—what you don't need for the hotel and incidentals—whatever that rest may be."

Rusty took out of his pocket a folder of travelers checks. He kept two and ripped off three, signed them and passed them over to Dulcinea.

"Does that leave you plenty?"

"Yes."

She took the checks; folded the necklace caressingly as she put it into a small deluxe box; gave him the packet; and then she slowly closed the door and flicked off the lights.

"Closing for siesta," she said.

"Do you live back of the shop?"

"Yes."

"Could I see your apartment?"

"Oh yes; please come in." She stepped over to the doorway and held the drapes aside for him to go through. He did, surprised with himself but exultant.

She followed, letting the stiffly-starched drapes plunge into place after her.

The New Man

One couldn't blame Maury Sogard for taking the first job that came along. He had been out of work for months when he received a telephone call from Mr. Gast at the Micromatic Division. There was very little industry in the mountain town of Sonora Springs, and, the situation being what it was, a guy couldn't afford to pass up anything at all. Micromatic's wages were minimal, but there were fringe benefits: grocery checkers who got to know one's employer unconsciously forgot to add in certain charges, such as bottle deposits; laundry clerks saw to it that elbow holes were sewn-up free; things like that.

As the Hollis-Henlein Company, Micromatic had been going downhill fast. Then, the Rudy Robot Stoker Company, which wanted to diversify its manufacturing and take on a few products with a different market from that of coal- stokers for home furnaces, had decided to take over Hollis-Henlein and its government contracts and operate the business in Sonora Springs as a division of Rudy Robot Stoker. This merger of Hollis-Henlein into the bigger Milwaukee outfit gave the Sonora Springs satellite a financial shot in the arm, and, as it turned out, gave Maury Sogard a job.

Mr. Gast introduced Maury to Mr. Wilcox, who was the foreman in charge of "civilian commercial production," a minor phase of Micromatic's "output" or "product line," as they called it. "You got pretty good eyes, I guess?" Mr. Wilcox asked.

"I guess," Maury said. "I passed the test."

"Well, come with me, then. You can work here at this bench. Remember, your number is 27, right between Mr. Slocum and Mr. Carver." Bringing Mr. Slocum into the conversation now, Mr. Wilcox said, "Frank, this is one of our new men. Will you see that he gets what he needs and keep an eye on his work till he gets the hang of it?"

"Sure will, Oscar."

"Okay. Introduce him around a little. Get Earl to help you with instruction if necessary."

"Sure thing, Oscar," Frank chirped to the chief who was now going back to his battered desk in the corner of the plant.

Turning to Maury as if the two, being alone, could slough off pretense and talk sense, Frank said, "How much did Willie tell you?"

"Willie?"

"Yeah, Wilcox."

"Oh. Oh, nothing at all."

"Well, then I might as well begin anywhere. Here are some time cards. The company keeps a strict count on how much you do in a day, a week, a month, but that will come later, when you're 'on production.' In the meantime, you can just disregard this column, number of units, and write in there 'Training.'"

At this point, Maury's attention was distracted by the sight of Wilcox barreling down the aisle between the workbenches at a terrific speed. His head was thrust forward so as to add to the momentum achieved by his pistoning feet. Every soft, bulging, muscle on the fore-man's body seemed to ripple and bounce and quiver with effort. His face was flushed to an apoplectic red and managed, somehow, to suggest all the timeless, tragic, woes and miseries of the world. In his hands the frenzied foreman clutched a bundle of papers, some white, some yellow, some blue, some pink. Whatever the papers were — letters, orders, contracts, time-cards, blank forms — they were held high on the chest, tightly, to signify the great value the holder attached to them.

The two watched the guy disappear into a cubby-hole office at the far end of the shop. Then Frank explained: "You'll get used to that. That's just Willie training for a heart attack. You'll see that performance twenty times a day, every day. That office down there is Mr. Carr's. We call him Jitney. He's the vice-president in charge of production. When he crooks his little finger, Willie starts running. There's no intercom system between the two offices. Willie knows by instinct when he has to start sprinting for Jitney's office. You can pity the poor fellow, if you want to. At home his wife uses him as a door mat. But he's the guy we get our orders from, and that's that. Maybe he's heard the crack of the starting gun again." They watched Willie race off in another direction.

"Looks like he's suffering from the GIs, a bit," Maury commented. "Yeah. As I said, you'll get used to that. Willie's not a bad sort, really — only got no backbone. He's been with the company, though, for years and got seniority galore. The company sent him out here from Milwaukee. He's a real company man. He'll never retire. He'll die on the job, have a heart attack right here one of these days, right in this very aisle. Some of us will carry him out.

"You know what the company's retirement plan is?"

"No. Mr. Cast didn't say. Said something about insurance after being here long enough."

"They got a plan: those steps right out in front. The guys all call those our planned retirement. At this altitude, climbing those steps is sure to get you in the long run. Then your beneficiaries will collect the insurance. Ha ha!" He seemed to think it was one whale of a joke.

"Won't you run behind with your work if you don't finish explaining what I'm to do and get back to your own bench?" Maury asked.

"Not that I don't enjoy talking, but I'm just wondering."

"Don't worry about me, Fella. What's your name, again?"

"Maury."

"Well, don't worry about me, Maury. I can take credit for training on my time-card, too. This is a gravy assignment for us both, trainer and trainee, while it lasts, and we'd better make the most of it. We'll be on production soon enough, and then there's no rest for the wicked."

"Tell me: Does our pay depend on results? I mean, on how much we turn out in a day?"

"Listen. How many units did they tell you they expected? Did they say?"

"I'm not sure. I think Mr. Gast said something about fifteen an hour."

"Fifteen an hour! You do fifteen an hour, and they'll want twenty; do twenty, and they'll come at you because you're not doing twenty-five. I actually think they'd ride you to do more if your rate of production was a hundred an hour. Your best bet is to keep 'em complaining. You're a fool to be over-conscientious. You know that, I guess. You weren't born yesterday. I'm only telling you because you're a new man."

As Frank talked, he had been giving Maury a demonstration of the work to be done: slip the little mica disc into the slotted shell this way, then hold the hair-spring taut and insert the set screw, so. Maury, in turn, had started to copy the technique of his instructor.

"That's good, Maury. That's it, exactly. Your fingers are naturally nimble; and you have no idea how they'll improve as you go along. Just spare your eyes. Make as much use of that glass there as you can. When you've really got the knack of it, you'll be able to recite the box score of the last game of every team in the major leagues as you go along; and you'd better talk it up or you'll go mad, stark-raving mad. Why does a hockey goalie talk it up during a close game? Same principle.

"Another thing. You'll never do more than a part of a part, but don't let that get you down. The company itself simply makes a sub-assembly of a sub-assembly of a sub-assembly. Get it?"

Earl Carver had come over from his bench to look on. "I'd say he's well on his way to micromagnetic migraine, wouldn't you, Earl?"

"Gosh, yes. I've never seen any guy pick it up as fast as you have, uh, uh...."

"Maury Sogard."

"You carry on with him, Earl," Frank said. "I gotta go you know where."

"Maury's for Maurice, I suppose," Earl said. Maury nodded. "The other guy that began this morning was late the very first day," Earl went on genially, apropos of nothing in particular. "You ever been analyzed, Maury?"

"No. Do you mean circumcised?"

"No. Analyzed, psychoanalyzed?"

"For crying out loud, whatever gave you such an idea?"

"Oh, I don't know. I gotta nephew, says it's wonderful; thought you might have tried it, being as you're a young man. Got a family?"

"Gotta wife and two kids. They're both in school. Wife works at the Moonbeam Film Company. Secretary to one of the big shots."

"I wouldn't have thought you were old enough to have kids in school."

"Oldest will be in junior high next year. With a little luck, we'll see him educated. There's nothing like an education for the young people."

"Yeah? Some say that, all right."

"It's taken some doing, I'll tell you."

"I'll bet. You ain't seen the boss yet, I guess. The big boss? He's just back from Arizona; spends the winter there; comes back here in the spring when it gets too hot for him there. The company's got a division down there, too."

"You mean the vice president in charge of production, Mr. Carr?"

"No. I mean Mr. Stamwhite, the big boss from Milwaukee; originally from Milwaukee. You'll see him around if you stay here long enough. He doesn't come into the shop very often. He has more allergies than he has dough. We've got a saying the reason he visits the shop is to check and see if the exit lights are on. You like it okay?"

"Of course, I like it. I need a job. Maybe my wife can quit after a while."

"That would be nice, wouldn't it? By the way, have you been saved?"

"You mean at church?"

Earl was reaching into the pocket of his plaid western sport shirt, fumbling to get his fingers on something and twisting his whole body around like a corkscrew to help his fingers. He brought forth a circular with blue printing on cream-colored paper. "Read that," he said, as he unfolded the tract and put it before Maury. As Maury took it, he saw the warning in bold letters at the top: "Unless ye be born again...."

"Thank you," he said. "I'll read it tonight at home. Do you want it back?"

"I can get more," Earl said, "at the Blessed Fury Tabernacle. That's my church."

"I'll take it home with me," Maury repeated.

When things had quieted down that evening — dinner over, dishes washed, kids at their homework — Maury's wife asked, "Did it really go all right today, Maury?"

"Why, certainly, Sue, Sweet. It's a great place. I feel like an old man."

"You said 'old man,' darling."

"Did I? I was absent-minded, I guess. I mean I feel like a new man. New faces, new opportunities, new products, and the same little woman, which counts most of all." He went over, put his arm firmly around her, and, with his eyes closed, gave her a lingering kiss low on the cheek. She yielded, partly, automatically, to the embrace, but with her eyes meanwhile staring over her husband's shoulder into space. Then she, too, closed her eyes, put a hand on his shoulder and cuddled to him. There they were standing, silently, when Dennis and little Arleta looked up from their books in wonder at the complete hush which had come over the household.

A Night on Knob Mountain

The patron saint of, the watchful guardian of the all pervasive influence over the growing city of Sonora Springs is Knob Mountain. All the inhabitants of the city, young and old, know that their fate, for good or ill, is determined by the smiles, storms, and unpredictable whims of the great and massive knob which towers over the city into the clouds.

The knob is the head. The forested shoulders of the mountain stretch for miles, lengthwise and crosswise. Criss-crossing the broad shoulders, like a system of veins and arteries, is a network of dirt roads and trails built by the Forest Service and, during the Depression, by the CCC and other alphabetical agencies of the Government. These rude routes, carved out of the wilderness at the cost of such prodigious effort, are open in summer to the public, to travellers. In that brief season, they offer views of breathtaking grandeur and beauty: wide meadows of multicolored flowers, distant plains bathed in sunlight, a picturesque village tucked snugly below in a tight little green valley.

Winter is a different story. Herb and Rickie knew that when they set out on their rabbit-hunting expedition on a Saturday at the end of January. They both were seventeen years old and more than once had discussed the plight of motorists attempting to make a short winter trip on one of the roads on Knob Mountain. Herb could remember the peculiar hush in his father's voice when the latter reluctantly yielded to requests to tell about the excursion he had taken once, all alone, years before in late spring or early summer: too early in the summer, too late in the afternoon.

The two boys knew, but they nevertheless went on their rabbit hunt. They had a rugged car with four-wheel drive, a Jeep which was well-nigh invincible. The day was warm and bright, so they wore only light jackets. Rickie's father and mother were at work. Herb's father was out of town. His mother did not think to caution him against the possible but improbable. Nor did Danny, the nineteen-year old neighbor boy with whom the two had often hunted.

They had an early lunch and set out on the paved highway which follows a gentle pass across and gradually over a drooping shoulder of Knob Mountain. After twenty miles, they turned off the well-travelled paved highway onto the Random Hills Road, a dirt road winding north. They continued along its twists and turns, ups and downs for ten miles. Then they turned east onto a trail sometimes called the Greg Gulch Trail.

The highway had been dry. The snow on the dirt road had been a foot deep but had given no trouble. On the trail, which led through a narrowing ravine to a dead end at Greg Gulch, the snow was deeper. It was evident to the two boys that they couldn't go far, but they saw no place where they could turn around without grave risks of getting stuck. Finally, the truck-like vehicle could go no further.

They jumped out and tried to shovel enough snow away from the wheels to gain traction. They worked furiously, mindless of time, but to no avail. They began to sense the seriousness of their situation. The sun had not gone down but had given way to clouds, and it was already dark, or, at least, twilight. They had taken off their light jackets while they were shoveling. Now they put them back on but were cold just the same.

Further shoveling was useless. Trying to walk back to the highway with night so near would be foolhardy. The few flakes in the air were a portent of more to come. Their heater in the Jeep wasn't working, but the cab would offer some protection from the moisture, the cold, and the increasing wind. They had no food and no blankets, but there was no sensible alternative to getting in the car and waiting out the night.

They both realized their danger but did not speak of it, much less dwell upon it. Indeed, their realization was mixed with incredulity. How could they, so innocently, have blundered into a predicament with such deadly potential? They spoke of other things. They savored the greatest redeeming factor in their ordeal — their comradeship.

"Have you ever been to Manfried Lake?" Herb asked.

"Have I ever! Many times have we built a fire in that shelter in the fall and roasted hot dogs on a stick."

"Isn't that a beautiful lake?"

"Yes; and the view of the Knob from there! It's Mom and Pop's favorite picnic spot, even in summer when it's crowded. I guess my favorite spot is Trout Creek. Do you know that?"

"I'll never forget it. I learned to fish there. Everywhere else my brother would catch fish, and I couldn't. It made me feel as low as a snake's track. Then, one time Father took my brother and me and Danny to Trout Creek. I don't know what I did different, but I caught eight trout. My brother didn't catch any, and Danny only caught one. Gee! Then I knew I could fish."

"Your Dad takes you all kinds of places, doesn't he?"

"Yes. He used to. With the Jeep, though, I can go places myself."

"I know."

They listened to the wind's muffled howl as it drove snow around and over the Jeep. They huddled together for warmth, to feel less cold. They peered out in the vague, vain, half-formed hope the moon might be trying to make her appearance over the Knob. From time to time they wiggled their numbing toes and fingers.

"Where is your Dad, Herb?"

"In Kansas. He might be back tomorrow. He will be back if he hears on the radio we're missing."

"On the radio?"

"Yes. Pa listens to the radio while he's driving."

"I expect my Mom and Pop will be pretty worried about us."

"Gosh, yes, Ma will! She'll try to call Pa if she knows where he is. She generally has a pretty good idea. Do you know where we are, Rickie?"

"Yeh, in a way."

"We're about on a line with Penmam Lake. You know that's where the rain storms and blizzards go when they can't think of any place else to go."

"I know. That's where they burn the Yule log every Christmas. I'd like to be standing around that fire right now. I'd cook a hamburger."

"If we had one to cook."

"Yes."

"That's why Penman Lake never grew as much as other places, I guess. Too much weather."

"Yeah, I guess so."

"It's sure a pretty place, though."

"Yeah, it is in summer."

As they talked and writhed and wriggled, the night passed. They didn't try to sleep, and neither of them even drowsed off. Time didn't rush by, and yet it didn't drag at a snail's pace. It wasn't a dreadful, anguished night. Yet, in that night, as in a draftee's first months in the army, the world seemed to change in a mysterious manner. The world? Yes, not to shrink down to the limits of the Jeep's cab, but to change in some immense, incalculable, indescribable way. It was as if they stood outside the regular, ordinary, everyday world of home and school, of street and city, and viewed it from such a distance that they could make out no details except their own position outside.

The restless, worried, anguished night was that of their parents, except for Herb's father somewhere in Kansas. He felt sick and had "holed" up in a motel. When he felt better, he'd call home. Rickie's folks had called the sheriff's office, and the sheriff had called other sheriffs and the Four-Wheel Drive Club and other rescue organizations. Captains of search parties had definite promises of volunteers to be ready to set out from Sonora Springs early Sunday morning.

Ken Matson, the deputy sheriff who knew the Random Hill area best, had Herb's neighbor Danny on his team. Ken was a veteran of rescue operations and was familiar with tragedy in its various forms and degrees. In this case, he was hopeful. He had to hope, to be sure. He knew Herb and his parents, and he felt as if misfortune would hurt him almost as much as the parents.

In the morning, Herb and Rickie knew they might have to try for Random Hills Road and the main highway. Still, they put off the high-risk gamble. The effort required appeared so gigantic. The snow was about five feet deep and was still coming, still driven by a fierce wind. The visibility was so low that they scarcely could make out the pines which marked the edge of the trail. At eleven o'clock, Herb said to Rickie, "It's now or never. Are you game?"

"Yes, I'll go. I'll try."

"Okay." He pushed open the snow-blocked door of the Jeep. The ill-clad pair worked rather than walked through the snow, away from the car, between the forests on either side, toward the Random Hills Road. They had gone half the distance to the Random Hills Road—about a mile—when they suddenly bumped into Ken Matson and Danny whom they hadn't seen. Ken and Danny had dimly seen the dark blobs six or eight feet away and had leaped from their Jeep to meet the marooned hunters.

"Am I glad to see you guys!" Ken said when they were within the protection of the closed Jeep. The two walkers managed a weak smile through their frigid faces, but they didn't speak. They loved Danny when he said "I figured you'd be here," but they made no reply.

Ken's search party of four Jeeps had to leap-frog their way (as they had coming in) till they got back on the Random Hills Road. Then they were able to roll slowly and continuously one after another. The boys were on their way to the Matson's and to a good midday breakfast of toast and coffee and scrambled eggs and bacon. They were on the way to a reunion with their parents, to warmth, words of comfort, medical attention.

While temporarily disabled by frostbitten feet and legs, exposure, and fatigue, neither Herb nor Rickie suffered any permanent physical injury from the stormy night on Knob Mountain. They both, however, carried an incredible recollection of the experience and their rescue. Even Herb's father, who was unaware of the whole thing till it was over, would never forget those whistling winds and pelting snows faced by his son and his son's comrade.

In late May, but not before, the garage men at Pinecrest, up the Pass, was able to get to Greg Gulch Trail with a tow truck and bring back the Jeep. After a few minor repairs and adjustments, the car was back in good running condition.

Knob Mountain, of course, is still there, but it's not just standing there. It's watching and waiting. It's presiding, as always, over the winds — and over human life, death, and destiny.

The Order of the Garter

What I don't know about the Order of the Garter would fill one of those thick paperback books, fine print and all. On my first trip to London, years ago, Dad told me all about the ancient knightly honor. The trouble is that afterwards we went to the theater and saw the leading lady swinging back and forth on a crescent moon high above the stage and peeling red garters off her legs, one after another, and flinging them, helter-skelter, to the excited, grasping, gasping bald-headed guys in the front rows. Since that, so help me, I've confused order with scramble and considered a garter as more of an accessory worn under a woman's skirt than a decoration for a man's lapel.

Now, my old friend, Dale Wendel, has just been awarded some kind of a foreign decoration. I don't know the name of it. As I said, I'm pretty confused about such things. It entitles Dale to stick some kind of a ribbon in his lapel like a flower. If he were a soldier, I guess, he would wear it on his chest. I don't know. It's for sure this ribbon isn't the sort made for holding up a man's sock. That's for darn sure.

I've always liked Dale. Many of my friends are older than I am, not just Dale. He used to drop in at my office every now and then, and I'm sure he'll continue to do so. Sometimes he was soliciting for one of his favorite charities, sometimes he just wanted to talk or to have coffee with me. He used to say that he once had trouble paying his bills, and now he has trouble paying his taxes; used to relay gossip of high finance and the local street we've all nicknamed Cold Cash Canyon—things like that, nothing serious.

The first time I met his wife, Charlayne, was when we all were going from Sonora Springs to Chicago on the same plane. I noticed Charlayne before I saw Dale. She was reading *The Wall Street Journal*. When Dale saw me, he introduced the little woman and explained that since his promotion to the presidency of the contracting company, his wife had to keep up with the trends of the money market. "They put more rocks in the wagon now, you know," he said.

"Yes," I said. "I know." His wife wasn't bad looking—not pretty, but not dowdy.

Dale complained about taxes, but he knew all kinds of ways to keep them down. He knew just lots of ways, honest ways. One time, I remember that he and his partner had a chance to sell a piece of business property at double its cost to them. It was a pretty tempting offer, and Dale didn't want to cheat his partner out of a nice profit. He said, "Instead of selling it, I bought him out at the other guy's figure so my partner had his profit and I saved income taxes." When the time comes, Dale will have a way to get around inheritance taxes. I'll bet on it. As he would say, just postponing them is something.

Over the years, Dale has talked to me plenty (and Charlayne has, too, a little) about their only daughter, Emily; and Dale used to get terribly worked-up about Emily's ex-husband. The so-and-so, he said, was a no-good chaser. He hadn't been married more than six months—and, if the truth were known, probably not more than one month—before he began "chasing." The first time I heard Dale running down his former son-in-law, I tried to kid him out of it. I said, "Oh, ninety per cent of those chasers are no more harmful than a dog that runs after cars." Dale didn't like my remark at all. It didn't set well with him. He kept right on worrying about the subject of chasers like a dog shaking a small snake.

At other times it was hard to forbear interrupting these ill-tempered tongue-lashings of the little man no longer there (in the family circle) by exclaiming: "Dolls or dollars: don't we all chase one or the other?" But forbear I did. Dale is a good guy.

I never have met Emily. To tell the truth, for a while I saw to it that I shouldn't. Dale and Charlayne might have expected something to come from such a meeting, and I strongly suspected that Emily wasn't especially feminine and attractive. Besides, I had my gal, and I was well off, and I knew it. In the meantime, Emily has remarried, to a kind of fuddy-duddy, I hear, a fellow with a pile of dough and a stable of horses much older than she. I mean Bill Moroney is older than Emily, not his thoroughbreds. Still, her parents will feel better now that their girl has come in out of the cold. Everybody pities a spinster's folks as much as the spinster, even if the gal has lost her amateur status as such by marriage and divorce.

Fumy thing, I've known Dale for a good many years, as I've said, and it wasn't till he won that foreign decoration that I learned he has a woman who doesn't care a flicker of a painted eyelash about the financial page of the newspaper. He has "another woman," as they say. I got to talking at the honor-award ceremony with the wonderful Mrs. Lano who used to be Dale's secretary before she left the company to get married. "Oh yes," she said, "Mr. Wendel wouldn't get rid of Madge for all the tea in China. He's had her too long."

The news made the whole Wendel jigsaw fit together perfectly, but it was unexpected, and I was slow in assimilating it. Not to let Mrs. Lano know how slow my mind works sometimes, I quipped, "Madge is his badge."

"Yes, of nightly glory." I could see the twinkle in her blue eyes changing to moisture. I was moved myself. I sympathized with Dale in his triumph.

A Page of History

For a long time it used to bother me — I mean it puzzled me, I didn't get headaches over it or lose sleep — that all the important things had happened before I was born: like the Civil War, the Stock Market Crash, Jesse James' robberies, John Brown's raid, and the Fall of France in forty. Besides that, it seemed mighty peculiar that anything really big always, almost always, went somewhere else to happen. You know?

That was before I got my job with Sonora Springs' Peak National Bank, working with Mr. Moss, the head of the Advertising Department, and with his secretary, Miss Cogswell; and, especially, before the Horneday Finance Company went broke in an apparent Ponzi scheme. Maybe you'd call me the office boy. I asked Mr. Moss my title, and he didn't specify. He said, "In England you'd be called a junior clerk, but as long as you're paid well, it doesn't matter, does it?" He wasn't kidding about the pay. In a way, I'm not doing so bad. It just costs me, the same as everybody else here, every morning when I look at the early sun lighting up Snow Peak.

Mr. Moss didn't like Bill Horneday or his company. Bill paid more interest than the Bank, lots more, even, than the building and loan people. He was his own advertising manager, and he didn't play around with signs on buses, free ball-point pens with the company's name on them, news pictures and blurbs in windows of empty buildings, and rigmarole like that. He went on television himself, instead of sending some stooge with a phony moustache and a trumped-up English accent to do the job. He got business.

The Bank couldn't do such things. It wasn't dignified. It wasn't done, Mr. Moss said. I heard him say it. "Bosh," one customer replied: "You bankers used to say 'no' in seventeen different languages, didn't you? And now you say 'yes' in as many languages plus umpteen dialects! It could be done."

"It shouldn't be," Mr. Moss said. Mr. Moss could say yes all right, but he was still a "no" man at heart. He'd agree to that, I'm sure. He liked to put his foot down and say that this or that or whatever was a matter of principle. How he ever landed in advertising I don't know— same way I did I guess. He was told "You're in advertising," and forthwith he was.

Mr. Moss has explained to me about his promotion to advertising—at least, I've overheard the recitations he has given to lots of others. Each story is different except for one point. Mr. Steptoe, the President of the Bank, told him to "keep down costs." I'll have to think my way around that one if I ever want to get a raise. In the meantime, I'm keeping my ears open in case anybody else has a formula for sidestepping that obstacle: costs.

I don't know exactly when the court signed the order closing up the Horneday Finance Company. It must have done it over the weekend, but I didn't hear about it till Monday morning from Miss Cogswell. When Mr. Moss got to the office, he said, "There's a crowd collecting over there, Ellis, over at Horneday's. You go see what's going on, what's going to take place. Let me know before it happens."

Mine was not to ask why. Besides, I was anxious to get on the scene and see for myself. Mr. Moss had made it seem as if a mob of angry depositors, lenders, creditors or whatever you want to call 'em, were going to storm Bill Horneday's new, one-story, cinder-block Bastille. I hurried right over, past the Y.M.C.A., the Appliance Village, the supermarket, the revival tabernacle with its sign, "Jesus Saves." Next door was Horneday's, nicely set back from the street, with the spring grass beginning to green between sidewalk and building.

There was a mob there, all right, and it was doing a lot of damage to Bill Horneday's lawn with its scuffling and trampling. Anger there was none. This was no siege of Bill's Bastille. I was one of the youngest members of the group. These were oldsters, mostly men with a tiny sprinkling of women. They stood around in twos and threes, talking together in low, dull voices, shifting their weight from one foot to the other. They weren't excited or surprised. Their look was one of bewilderment and betrayal, more that than inquisitive. Their shoulders hunched, and there was a sag in the lines of their backs. There wasn't even a policeman to keep order when I first arrived. Actually, none was needed in the slightest.

I talked with one woman, or, rather, she talked to me. "Did you lose a lot?" she asked.

"No," I said, "you?"

"Forty dollars."

I shook my head sympathetically, and she continued, "It was just about all I had." Again I shook my head. I didn't know what to say. She was so thin and humped and wasted. And then, apropos of nothing at all, I remembered how an old maid isn't married nor nothing.

This poor gal before me was an old maid nearing the end of the trail all alone.

She went on "My husband says…." I missed the rest. I can't savvy women. I can tell when they're pretty pregnant, but I sure can't read their minds. I made no response about the husband. I just shook my head again, this time a little more vaguely. The woman moved away.

Two men near my elbow, at the sidewalk's edge, evidently had just finished their preliminary greetings. "Were you rooked, too, Irv?" one asked the other.

Irv repelled that idea scornfully with an explosion of breath. "No-o-h-h. That eight and nine per cent scared me. I'm surprised you did, Joe, you're so conservative. I hope it works out all right for you, for everybody."

Joe was silent, hurt, but he didn't fight back. Irv carried on. "My investments on the stock market have turned out wonderful. My Magna Champa just hit a new high. The whole list is advancing: rails, utilities, industrials. Even rails! Probably some new mergers in the wind we don't know about yet out here. Motors. My Chrysler has gone way up since I got it. Well, good luck, Joe. See you." He plodded away.

I could see Joe was indignant as he watched Irv departing. For my benefit he made a face at Irv's back and said "Oink, oink."

"What's the matter?" I asked.

"Did you hear that guy? You know Irv Graybill?"

"No, I don't. He could be Bob Barefoot for all I know."

"You hear him say he passed up Horneday? If he hadn't seen me or someone else he knew in this crowd, he'd been right here where I am now. Trouble with that guy, he just can't admit he ever made a mistake. He bought Chrysler, yeah, when he could have bought

American Rambler shares for five and been on Easy Street by now, if he sold right."

"He sounded like a BTO, though," I said.

"He sounded like it yes...Whaddya mean, BTO?"

"Big Time Operator — a wheeler and dealer."

"Him? J. P. Morgan, Defender of the Faith, Bulwark of Business! Why, I'll bet you Irv Graybill doesn't have as many as a hundred shares of any stock. Him and his utilities and rails and retails. I'll bet he's hard put to pay his brokerage fees, if he ever has any. I seriously doubt if he has a flush toilet, that guy."

"I'm sorry," I said.

"That's all right, Boy," he said. "You were only talking appearances; I know."

We both noticed at the same moment that Paddy Horneday, Bill's daughter, had come around from the parking lot in back. She always looks like a case of mixed hormones, and that effect was accentuated this morning by the man's blazer she was wearing open over her dress. She had a bundle of papers in her hand, and I saw now that she was going to pass out these mimeographed sheets for her Old Man. I took one.

"Dear Friends,

I have been ordered to close my doors to business for the time being.

If I'm given a chance, every investor in Horneday's Finance will be repaid dollar for dollar, with interest.

If there have been any violations of law involved in our operations, as the SEC claims, I am confident they will turn out to be technical only.

I do know this, our own auditors and those of the State Banking Department have gone over our books regularly, year after year, without reporting a single instance of interest being paid out of depositors' capital."

When I finished reading, I saw that my Dad had come along. He's an editor of the *Sonora Springs Town Crier*. I offered him the copy of Bill's apology. Dad waved it away. "I know what's in it," he said.

"How'd you know?" I asked.

"They're all the same," he said. "They follow the old-time script: 'If the government hadn't interfered, everything would have been all right; not a single investor would have lost a penny.'"

"Gosh, that's close," I said. We started off. Lots of others were doing the same. I could see the line in the *Town Crier*, "The gathering dispersed before noon."

"What was it like?" Dad asked.

I told him how gloomily quiet it had been, but added, "Just the same, I feel like I saw a battle. Funny thing, though, I don't know what it was about or who won. It's right there, almost, ready to be told, but I can't get it out." Dad nodded but didn't comment.

"Was it people against property?" I asked, fumbling.

"Oh, I don't know," Dad replied. "I expect some people lost and some other people won."

"People won? Who won?"

"Dan Dinkle, for one. He'll be the Receiver. It's in the script. He'll hire a slew of lawyers, accountants, auditors, investigators, and so find a use for what remains of Bill's assets. It'll keep the staffs of the SEC and the Banking Department going for years. Judges, too, and scores of bailiffs and clerks, all as busy and important as High Commissioners."

"Those people in the crowd, though. They lost, didn't they? There's no doubt about that?"

"Yes, they lost. But they took a chance. They knew but maybe forgot that in such affairs, as in gambling, everybody loses a little, nobody wins much."

I was helpless in the face of heresy, and I didn't like it, even if the heretic was Dad, and I'd known beforehand, in a general way, what he thought. "But," I argued, "a few, at least, do win a great deal. Not Dan Dinkle in this, but the real Big Shots."

"For Dinkle, it's not the money he'll win; there won't be all that much left over after his elaborate expenses. It's a chance to shine in the public eye, and you can bet he'll make the most of it. In business and politics and public life, there are many glittering, dazzling, impressive prizes of publicity, colored balloons, and shekels, and I won't say they're fake," Dad said. "But they're consolation prizes. Booby prizes for the Booboisie. What's worthwhile is strictly, purely personal; so private, sometimes, it is secret, and people wonder 'What's his secret?' It doesn't make news for the *Town Crier*, a success like this, the only success, but it's there and it's real!"

"In the meantime," I retorted feebly, "Dan Dinkle's position in Sonora Springs is strengthened, and he will redouble his attacks on Custer College, its liberalism, and its left-wing professors and beatnik students, by which he means all professors and students."

"I wouldn't worry about Dan Dinkle or Custer College. Dan wants to look out on the world and see Dan Dinkle. He wants to look at Custer College and see himself. A guy that has to look in the mirror all the time, do you think we have cause to fear him or envy him? Maybe he needs to be reinforced a little by a receivership here and some political pap there."

"Yeah," I assented, but holding up my inflection of the word so Dad wouldn't get the idea he had bowled me over completely, once and for all.

"How's Herb?" Dad asked.

"Herb? Who's he?"

"Herb Moss, for crying out loud."

"Oh, Mr. Moss. I've got to get back to the Bank before lunch."

"Where do you think we are now, at the Bastille?"

"Oh," I said. He had me there.

Passion in the Desert

"Well, what do you think of my old friend?" Bill Smith asked as Rufus left us still at the table on the excuse he had to get back to "the salt mines."

I was surprised at the question, but I laughed and came back with "He's your friend, isn't he?" The fact was that Rufus Tyndall had made a pretty definite impression on me, although I had seen him for scarcely more than fifteen minutes. He had chanced by our luncheon table at Club 11 on his way back to the office just as Bill and I were ordering our pie and ice cream.

Bill persuaded him to join us for dessert. Club 11, I might say, is named for the floor of the Mountain National Bank Building on which it is located, and it's sort of a "captive club" which the building management organized for its tenants.

"I'm as close to being a friend as anybody, I think," Bill replied, "but speak as frankly as you want. I have my reasons."

I took Bill at his word. I'd known him for years, and ever since I had opened my law office in the growing, thriving city of Sonora Springs, Bill had found ways, from his point of vantage downtown, to swing business to me; and, in time, I had been able to reciprocate for Bill and the Bank's trust department.

"I'd say Rufus is the salt of the earth," I said. Bill laughed. "But?" he said.

"Yes," I replied, "but!"

"But what?"

I hesitated. Bill's persistence was picking away at hidden faults in my reasoning, and I knew it. Still, I had gained a clear-cut, not wholly complimentary estimate of Rufus, and I might as well confess it as fairly as I could.

"It would be going too far to say your friend, Rufus, is screwball," I said, "or even a little screwball. Just the same, well, I mean, I damn near had to laugh when he said he'd been a member of the Socialist Club at Princeton and then asked, 'Aren't you scared?'"

"I noticed that," Bill answered. "I noticed he was willing to clown a little in front of you. He rarely does anything like that. I have no doubt he's never told anyone at the Bank he once belonged to a socialist club."

"That's what I mean," I said.

"What?"

I flushed a little. "You're not a banker," I said defensively, apologetically. "In the trust department, that's different. Besides, you never were or would have been a typical banker, a flawless example."

"You said that as if you meant a perfect specimen—a dried butterfly mounted on a board."

"You're on the trail. Yes. I guess that's what I'm trying to say. The guy is a pattern, a just-so gentleman, too perfect. You know, that gray suit, that pinkish-white soupçon of moustache, that straight-edged, geometrical design on the blue field of his tie. He's the consummation of our tradition. I almost said that he's the prototype, the granddaddy of us all, that we follow where he leads, copy what he does."

I stopped, a little breathless. I had exaggerated, I knew. I meant what I said and yet had a suspicion that Bill had led me astray, so far astray that I had made an ass of myself.

Bill was silent, thoughtful. I went on. "If you'll pardon such a remark about a friend of yours," I said, "Rufus is an ass, a nonentity, a gray blank, an egregious, ineffectual nincompoop. I mean the bastard's so educated and cultivated and refined, he has no more character than granulated sugar. Than brown sugar, for Chris' sake!" I glared at Bill and challenged him to correct me. At the same time, I felt as guilty as if I had painted an unvarnished sketch of Bill, my companion and client, instead of the absent stranger, Rufus Tyndall.

"That's strong language for Club 11," Bill said, "and I agree with you one hundred per cent."

I was dumbfounded by Bill's lame reply and completely dissatisfied as well. "Then why in hell—yes, hell—did you bring all this up?"

"I agree with you one hundred per cent, even though you're absolutely wrong," Bill said.

I had been irritated with Bill for questioning me about Rufus, displeased with myself for rising to the bait, and now the S.O.B., this old-time friend was playing me for a sucker in the way that a shrewd shyster makes a goof of an uncomplicated Joe who is trying to tell the truth on the witness stand. I was grasping the table edge as if it were a life raft on a storm-tossed sea and waiting.

"Rufus did go to Princeton," Bill said. "Whether he was ever a member of the Socialist Club there, I don't know. He might have been kidding about that. It's the first time I've heard that mentioned. He's a member of this club, Club 11, for business reasons. The Bank pays the bill for us. He's fairly active in the Knights of Sirocco, a kind of charitable, do-good, semi-religious association. It's not a church fraternity, you know; not a service club, either, but a cross between the two.

"Rufus comes from a good family: the only son, only child. His father died when Rufe was only ten or twelve. I may be the only who knows all these things about Rufus. He really is a wonderful fellow. I wish I could do something for him." Bill spread his hands helplessly. "I mean he's lonely. He has lots of colleagues but no friends. None, I'd say."

"His father was a war casualty?" I asked.

"No, not exactly. His father was president of a soft drink company that made a beverage called Gingerette. You may have heard of it. They had plenty of competition. On one side was a giant company urging everybody to pause and relax and take it easy and eat a white-bread sandwich with its sparkling dark concoction. Another behemoth was pushing from the opposite direction to make everybody friendly and sociable and sophisticated by the use of its product. Rufus's old man originated the sales theme 'For those on the go' and then followed it up with 'For those on the make—Gingerette!' He might have held his own with the Goliaths if he hadn't had a heart attack. That finished him, and his business fizzled out, more or less, after that and was sold.

"Rufus never married. He lives with his mother in the old home on the edge of Belden Park.

"But what I wanted to tell you, and I know we got business to do, but what I wanted to tell you is something nobody else knows. It's a kind of secret, a burning secret, and I've got to get rid of it. As a lawyer, you're used to such things. I'm not. Trust assets are my line.

"Rufus is in the Commercial Department. Before he got to be an officer, he had a desk out there in the open, on the edge of the lobby, where the depositors mill around the tall writing stands. It was like working in a goldfish bowl. Strangers by the hundreds every day would come in, look over the people at their desks as the employees talked on the phone, rummaged through customers' files, dictated letters into recording machines.

"Rufus always appeared poised, cool as a cucumber, in his element. In front of him and one space to his left in these rows of desks on the fringes of the banking lobby sat Mrs. Peppard. I know her well, at least by sight. Time I'm speaking of, her husband had some sort of job with an armored truck company, security officer he was called, really a guard. Mrs. Peppard, Opal, is as heavy-set as Rufus is slight and nearly as tall as Rufe.

"There is a certain attractiveness about the woman, though it would tax your intelligence to the limit to figure out the source of it. You've heard of legs like whisky kegs? She has 'em. She's still at the Bank, you know; still happily married, still at the same desk, so to speak. She has a lumbering walk which makes an elephant seem as spry, nimble, and graceful as a gazelle by comparison. I remember when she used to traipse around, ignoring the gaze of customers and swinging her hands together in front in a carefree, childlike, elfin manner that was out of this world.

"She isn't in the least mannish, but neither is she a feminine siren. She isn't fat, but she is heavy-heavy-legged, heavy-armed, stolid-faced, unseeing eyes. Her bosom is held high, but she's not especially buxom. My guess is she has far more dresses than any other woman at the Bank, but her taste runs to subdued plaids, almost exclusively. Perfume I've never noticed. You get the picture? Oh, yes, a blank, full face, a nasal voice with a babyish, wheedling quality. That's the gal; not youthful when this happened, which seems like yesterday but surely wasn't.

"A hypnotic magnetism sprung up between Rufus and Opal. Sitting where she did, she was always in his range of vision, and she was aware of his constant awareness of her slightest move. No one else, however, seems to have noticed the glances the guy darted at the gal. It was as if a thick, silent fog of smoky, mad impulses was isolating them from the gaping, changing crowd of outsiders and their own numerous colleagues. This confused huddle bothered her more than him, and she tried to clear the atmosphere in several ways before the two of them got tangled up, more mixed up, more indifferent to all but the flood of desire.

"For example, she would go over to his desk in the morning before the Bank opened, and at odd moments during the day and try to talk about business, about her success or lack of it at bingo the evening before, about anything at all to give this growing, overpowering obsession of theirs a chance to drain off and get lost in the desert sands of business and social small-talk. Rufus was tongue-tied. He couldn't rise to the occasion. He saw she was trying to break the spell; he realized her method would work if he cooperated; he knew the danger of letting things drift; he wasn't equal to the effort. As far as that goes, none of the men at the Bank managed, either before or after, in getting Rufus involved in a conversation beyond the immediate business of the moment. He seems unable to throw himself into the job beyond the absolutely essential.

"Another thing she did was to persuade her husband to come to work for the Bank, so as to impress Rufus with her ties, her status, her anchorage, and perhaps, to shift her own responsibility. How much the gal told her husband of her fears and temptations I couldn't say. The man had his mate's unseeing eyes, the same plodding step. He was a masculine version of his wife, you might say. He didn't stay with the Bank long: went back to his old job. Rufus doubtless seemed to him more like a paralyzed jack rabbit than a dangerous rival. Anyway, hubby left.

"It wouldn't surprise me if Opal resorted to other diversionary schemes that missed fire and that were so subtle that Rufus was blind to them. You can foresee what happened. They came together. Then, for months, for over a year, these two reluctant, middle-aged lovers savored a grand passion such as damn few young sweethearts and honeymooners ever come close to, let alone experience. The opportunities were catch-as-catch-can, not to say humiliating: stolen hours and evenings in cars, parks, motels. The emotional costs must have been terrific; the term was bound to be short. The high flame burned low more suddenly than it had started but none too soon at that, given the circumstances."

"I'd never have guessed it," I said. "I had no idea he had it in him."

"And the contrast in the two." Bill said. "Senator and slave-girl."

"I suppose that was at the heart of it," I mused. "I suppose the key to a grand passion is some immense obstacle, some towering roadblock, some inescapable difference in age or in race; an existing, well-mated marriage on one side or both—something of that nature."

"It beats me," Bill said.

"Me too. I'm just talking."

"I know," Bill said. "Same with me. I had to talk to someone about it."

"Rufus, Rufus, Rufus. It must seem that everything before was preparation and everything since has been unnecessary."

"It beats me," Bill said.

The waitress came up with the tab. "You gentlemen were so wrapped up in your business, I didn't dare disturb you," she said. Bill signed the chit. I looked at my watch. It was later than we thought.

The Quill Pen

Abraham Shunoff, general manager of Sonora Springs' great Gold Seal Department Store, was deep in the heart of a mid-morning lull, but he didn't know it. He was too busy studying the hodge-podge of figures on his desk. The girls in the outer office were there, as usual, but unaccountably quiet. The silence was broken by the angry voice of a woman.

"Where can a furious customer go to make a complaint—and I don't mean no complaint department!"

Mr. Shunoff descended from the rarefied realm of accounts, reports, and merchandising data with the suddenness of an astronaut re-entering the Earth's atmosphere. This wasn't his automatic reaction to all complaints—only to this one. The stranger's voice wasn't especially feminine, a trifle too husky for that. It wasn't entirely the faint, quaint, cute French accent that caused him to hurry out to meet the customer before his efficient secretaries gave her the routine brush-off. It was partly that and partly something else akin to what used to be described vaguely as "the call of the wild."

"Can I help you, Madam?" He beat the girls to it. He saw a brown-haired, dark-eyed woman of medium height. She was not young, but she had one of those charming, curvaceous, mature figures that made Mr. Shunoff glad of it. She was dressed in a becoming navy-blue suit which showed the white frills of her blouse at the neck. He liked her face, those eyes.

The woman sensed, or knew, that she was talking to the general manager himself; and before his open, obvious admiration of the picture she presented, all her fury evaporated. She was flattered; and left only with the need to carry on, more or less as an act, the beginning she had made in all sincerity.

"What would you say this pen sells for?" She held it, the plumed pen, up high before her bosom for him to see.

"I don't know. You put me on the spot. I'm not a merchandising man." This was a bare-faced lie but not one intended to deceive, because he knew that she knew that merchandising was his line.

"Would you say a dollar, two dollars?"

"Yes; maybe. Isn't the price on it?"

"The price isn't on any of them. The clerk told me three ninety-five and refused to check on it for me. I was furious, but don't let her tell you that I was rude. I let her make out the ticket. It's a charge." She had continued holding the unwrapped, buff-colored quill pen up in front of her all this time, and now she produced the sales slip. Mr. Shunoff reached for it.

"You're Mrs. Marcelle Kehoe," he said.

"Yes."

"You want the pen?"

"Yes."

"I'll give it to you."

"Oh, no. I mean at the right price."

"You can take the pen with you. I'll see that the charge is corrected."

"Okay, thank you very much." She left.

Without watching her depart and without exchanging glances and smiles with his girls, Mr. Shunoff went back into his office. Before his eyes was a persistent image of the upraised quill pen and below that, as in a foreign film, subtitles, only the subtitles weren't wholly in English: *La plume de ma tante*, the feather in Mother's hat, and the pen *de mon père*. He had even forgotten that *père* had meant father years ago in French I at school, but there was the word just the same, mysteriously resurrected. His father, as it happened, had passed away long since.

"I'm seeing things," he muttered, trying to banish the senseless subtitles from his mind and get back to his study of the different foreign language which Mrs. Kehoe had interrupted.

Three days later, a hundred miles away, Cletis Ball was dozing over a manuscript of the "how-to" variety in which Shamhart Press specialized. His mind had come to rest an hour or so ago on the words "Now slip a noose over the moose and…" He became aware, he knew not how, that his fellow editors were engaged in a lively conversation. The morning mail had just arrived, bringing a number of them an advertisement. The makers of the Magic-matic Copier offered to give every prospect on its mailing list who sent for a booklet on the advantage of Magic-matic a "free gift" of a quill pen.

"I'd like the quill pen," Joe was saying, "but I wouldn't care a damn for the booklet."

"Tell 'em just to send you the pen."

"Tell 'em you know the advantages of the Numismatic Copier."

"It's Magic-matic; numismatic is money. Or is it stamps?"

"Hell, ain't money magic?"

"What could a guy do with a quill pen? Pick his teeth?"

What a gang, Cletis thought to himself. They'd take any subject whatever, any at all, and worry it to death—absolutely exhaust it—leave the lifeless corpse by the wayside like a porcupine struck by a car at night. The discussion was still going on.

"Are you old enough, for crying out loud, to remember quill toothpicks? Maybe you can tell us, then, if this claim is right. Says here it took a week to copy the Declaration of Independence with a quill pen. You must have been around along about then..."

"Maybe they mean a week of coffee breaks."

"Yeah, or Sundays. No copying on Sundays."

"Yeah; and now you can copy your income-tax return with Magic-matic in one simple operation, in the twinkling of an eye."

"Yes," Cletis cut in with a vehemence which surprised himself as much as the others. "You can copy the Declaration of Independence, but can you make one with your magic-antics? You can copy Thomas Jefferson, but can you do anything with all your gadgets and gewgaws that your sons will want to copy?"

"Well! Clete's all steamed up this morning."

"We can declare our dependence on money-magic. That's one thing we can do."

"If you're too damned original to do any copying, Clete, how about this? Guy's got the title, *How to Prepare Your Income Tax Return.* No imagination. No zip. What'd you say? *How to Prepare Returns for Refunds?*"

"I'm not so damn smart, you guys. I only meant that copy work is the lowliest job those old guys did with a pen — the least we can do with one. I was talking about pens."

"Yeah, you can't squirm out of it that way, Clete."

"We heard you compare yourself to Tom Jefferson."

"Tommy, he said."

"Oh yes, him and Tommy."

"He comes before Tommy because he can make sense out of nonsense."

He could indeed. He could see that the noose slipped over the moose was really a rope looped over a joist. Of course, there still was plenty of nonsense left — in that part about heave ho and a rafter is up and a house is taking shape before your very eyes. Saleable copy, though.

It was Clete's custom on Sundays to drive to Denver to see his sweetheart, Marcelle. He had been doing this for years, and she was not yet his fiancée. To tell the truth, he had never formally proposed marriage. He could see that it would be futile. Marcelle, a widow, was too comfortable in Denver, more so than the two of them could be in his hometown on his peanut salary. Besides, she was a "city gal;" could no more get along without the cultural advantages of the big town than spare mushrooms from her diet. He didn't argue the point. What good would it do to tell her that she didn't know mushrooms from toadstools? In time she would weaken.

On this visit, one of the first things Clete saw as he entered the house was a new quill pen in the familiar glass inkwell on the small, dark, old-fashioned desk in the living room. "Oh," he said, taking the tip of the feather between his two fingers, "something new has been added."

"I wondered if you'd notice it."

"Notice it! I'm kind of surprised."

"There always used to be one there, long ago. I don't know what became of it. I never thought of getting another exactly. It's just an ornament, really. I mean, isn't it?"

"Maybe—I guess—I don't know; but you miss it if it isn't there, I suppose. Seems like it's always been there now. One gets used to it quick."

"Yes, but I wanted to tell you. I was in the Gold Seal, and I spied this pen; and I strangely got the idea I couldn't buy it; I'd have to fight for it or steal it. I was ready to do either. Did you ever hear of such nonsense?"

"Oh, I don't know, there are things…"

"But not pens. And there were so many of them, really. What got me, I guess, is that there was no price sticker on them. And, then, there was one of those advertising pictures of an ancient *philosophe* with a quill in his hand and an impish grin on his face. He looked for all the world as if he were mocking me. I got panicky for a minute."

"I'd like to have seen that." Cletis burst into laughter.

"Oh, you quit laughing at me. It wasn't funny. It was like momentary madness or whatever they call it, temporary sanity."

He had put his arm around her waist. "Madness without method is the best kind," he said, and then he forestalled a reply by tightening his grasp around her waist and drawing her to him.

Rip of the Mountain West

Lester Wood was walking around the lake with his new-found friend, Big Bill Benton. He had met Big Bill on the golf-course that morning. They had had lunch together afterward on the terrace, and now they were taking a tour around the tiny, man-made lake for the somewhat futile purpose of getting better acquainted. They discovered they both had arrived at the grand, Sonora Springs mountain-resort hotel about the same time a few days before.

The early afternoon sun this August day was bright and warming, but thanks to the altitude, the air was comfortably cool. The rim of the sparkling, blue-brown lake was a riot of color from the carefully-tended zinnias, morning glories, and other garden flowers. On the left side of the walk, and separated from it by a high, closely-woven fence, was the golf-course on which the two had had their game. An abundance of rainfall, which was unusual at any time and especially so this late in the summer, had kept the course looking fresh, and the greens were even greener than they had been earlier in the season. In front of them as they walked were the mottled mountains, reddish, dark, and multifarious shades of green.

After their morning competition and their lunch, the two were in no mood for energetic exercise. They were strolling now for want of something better to do. As they plodded ahead dully, they both watched the strokes and strides of the group of ambitious, younger folks beginning their rounds. Big Bill was eyeing the figure and commenting on the stance of one of the women players when Les noticed, with a thumping heart-beat of recognition, the weather-beaten face and firm step of Ed Norden, a classmate at Yale, the class of 1940.Was Ed, on the walk and now directly in front, in work clothes? He was not in the buff livery of a bellboy nor in the blue work uniform of the hotel's laboring staff, but most certainly he was not in the deliberately-chosen casual wear of the ordinary hotel guest.

Les had not yet been recognized by the approaching Ed. The latter, once gaunt and consumptive but now a veritable picture of health and serenity, was looking attentively at the flower beds bordering the lake. Les stopped. Big Bill, still intent on the buxom, young amazon in golf shorts, kept ambling forward, unmindful that he had lost his companion. Les put a hand on Ed's arm as they were passing. "Ed", he said, "Ed." In quick recognition, Ed grasped for Les's hand and shook it vigorously. "Lucky Les Wood. I'm sure glad you're here. A second honeymoon?"

"No, Ed. Hester died suddenly, just six weeks ago. I'll tell you about it later. What are you doing? When can I see you? Perhaps tonight?" Les could see that Big Bill, just out of earshot, was waiting for him and was slightly curious about Les's conversation with one who resembled a workman more than a guest of the hotel.

"Sure, tonight," said Ed. "Any time after work. I own the greenhouse over there. It's named after the hotel, but it's mine. We do work for the hotel on contract. Meet me there at five, if you can."

"Okay. At five then." Les rejoined Big Bill. "I wanted to compliment him on these flower beds," he said casually.

"Uh, yeah. The hotel does a good job on them, all right," Big Bill acknowledged.

They continued their circuit of the lake with ponderous gaits which suggested the waddle of the ducks which came out of the water from time to time. As the two idled along, they exchanged bits of personal history. Neither was used to vacationing at all, let alone without the wife or family. Big Bill explained that his wife had taken their two teenage kids to Cape Cod for a couple of months. He had attended a trade convention here at the Primrose Park Hotel and had lingered a little afterward; he soon would have to leave and spend a week or two with the family in the East before returning to Chicago. "Then," he said briskly and with joyful anticipation, "back to the steel business." He added, "Nine-tenths of all patented articles are made of steel. Look it up sometime."

Les was more reticent than Big Bill. He was a patent lawyer in Kansas City. He just had lost his wife. He could have divulged, had he chosen to do so, that those who knew him best liked to chide him with the well-worn remark that he himself had a patent on making money. He enjoyed being teased that way and had developed an invariable jibing answer which amused everyone. "Yes," he used to say, "and if Dale Carnegie hadn't given away his formula for making friends, I could have got him a patent on that, taking a majority interest in it as a fee, of course. Then I'd have had friends, too."

Les couldn't bring himself to tell Big Bill about the circumstances surrounding the loss of his wife. Maybe he could speak of that to Ed. He had been stunned, as anyone would be, by his wife's sudden death in an airplane accident. But that wasn't the hardest part. Hester had not told him in advance she was going on a trip. He got the news from a note she had left. In that, she had explained that she was leaving him for good and had asked that he should not endeavor to locate her. Her departure was her own impulsive idea, and she hadn't disclosed it to anyone. She did not plan an immediate divorce, but that might come later. At present she just wanted to think things through for herself without help or hindrance. Les had made no mention of the message. Then, after the crash, when the condolences were pouring in, what could he do?

The marriage of Les and Hester had not been based on a grand passion, even at first. That it was "a natural," however, was agreed on by all sides. Les, though fresh from school, already was a man of manifest destiny in his profession. Hester looked like a movie star and could have been one. The union which had been the talk of the town settled quickly into accepted, proper routines which Les found so satisfactory that he had taken his matrimonial success for granted. Wasn't he Lucky Les Wood? From Hester's note he learned for the first time that she had not been as completely and perfectly content with their childless, respectable married life as he had supposed, as she had let him suppose.

After the funeral, Les had expected for a while, to carry on as usual, or, rather to carry on. The once-loved humdrum of office activity with its applications, complaints, answers, and briefs failed to hold his attention, however. He had known a few others in his circle who had become irked and annoyed with their domestic ties when, upon reaching retirement age, the manacles of daily employment were abruptly stricken from their hands. Something like this had happened to him. With his feet accidently freed from matrimonial fetters, so to speak, he chafed for the first time at the work-a-day shackles on his hands. Accordingly, he decided that he, also, needed to think things through for himself. Instead of making his customary annual vacation sojourn to the cottage in Michigan, Les had sought the refuge of a setting which would have fewer memories for him.

In parting, after their walk, Big Bill and Les made a golf date for the next morning. "Maybe I can round up some feminine company," Big Bill had said jovially. "We both need it, and I've seen some gals on the course who sure looked good to me." They had left it at that.

Les went up to his room. Till then, the mountains, despite their massive, towering immensity, had failed to impress themselves upon him. Now he stared at them in fascination. He stood up after a while to view once more the walk, the lake, and the spot at which he had met his old chum, Ed Norden. Then he sprawled back in his armchair. He saw the tops and branches of the pine and spruce gently moving in the breeze and could imagine the whispered confidences of the wind. He wasn't sure whether he sensed the pure, refreshing, cleansing odor of pine through the open windows or merely thought he did. One rugged rock on the hillside took on the aspect of a full-faced man with a ruddy complexion. The Man of the Mountains winked at him as if to confide that there were unearthed, unmined hidden secrets in his mountains. Sleep stole up on tip toe and silently overpowered Les.

He dreamt that Ed was showing him some flowers grown in the open air behind the greenhouses which, like the hotel, nestled at the base of the mountains. The blooms were large, waxy, and more orange-red than wild poppies; they were blood-red. The stems were tall, slender, swaying. He had never seen such flowers and didn't know the name of them. Without taking his eyes from the spread blanket of color, Les asked, "Did you come out to this arid country for your health, Ed, soon after you got out of Yale?"

Ed nodded. "Yes; and for my life," he answered in a slightly Scandinavian accent. "It was later that I got out of yail. But this arid country is not desert, Les. The Great American Desert is not a geographical area. That exists in the humid, steaming jungles of buildings in the East, as well: wherever junk accumulates and men worship the idols of the marketplace; wherever people take in each other's laundry but never clean themselves with fresh air and sun; wherever they scratch each other's back but never scratch the soil. But you ought to know that. Weren't you the one who patented the Great Deception that the fertile and fruitful, the hopeful and happy valleys and coasts could be made more so by dim, dismal taverns; by blazing and blinking neon lights; by the cluttered squalor of traffic, television sets and a million and one patented medicines, cosmetics and metal contrivances?"

Before Les could answer, the Man of the Mountains frowned down at him and said "I'll put a bug in your ear that's not humbug." Simultaneously, Les felt a sharp rap on the ear as a huge insect settled into it. While still bewildered by the curious occurrence, he saw a honey bee rise from one of the desert-like flowers and fly toward him. It was heavily laden with sweet nectar and dusty pollen, but it seemed so determined about its mission that Les feared an attack. With a vocal expressiveness unequalled since Aesop, the bee said "I'll put a buzz in your bonnet," and managed in a miraculous fashion to light under his sport cap, where, instead of buzzing in the approved manner of bees, it insisted "Be, be, be."

Les turned to Ed. "I've got to go," he said. "I have an appointment to play golf with a big steel man from Chicago. Besides, I am being hit by volleys from the right and thunder from the left as if I were five hundred guys in the Valley of Death. You seem to forget that I'm Lucky Les from Kansas City."

Ed laughed at him. "You're a fool and a fraud," he replied. "You don't even know who you are or what you are, and you don't recognize others for what they are. You're play-acting Lucky Les according to the humdrum script written by humbugs for dunces. You were born Lucky Lester, back in Georgia on Tobacco Road, but you've become plain, old Jeeter Lester of Country Club Road in Kansas City.

"You didn't even pay attention to the Man of the Mountains. He'd have told you something if you'd been at all receptive. He doesn't even speak to most. At least you were lucky enough to be noticed by him.

"Didn't you understand the plain meaning of the honey bee? The bee transforms beauty without destroying it. That's not so dumb, is it? Can the same be said for you? Is your head so thick that it can't be pierced by either stingers or simple sense? Do you only comprehend the double-talk of the country club and the tedious verbosity and repetition of Whereases, Wherefores, and Valuable Consideration?

"You've strayed further from Lucky Les than the Prodigal Son wandered from his father. You're less lucky and less Lester than when you started. The bee in your cap has told you often enough to be yourself. Even you should see that, without having to hold your eyes open. Do you listen with your eyes?" As Ed spoke, Les had felt so sleepy and overwhelmed that he had put his hands to his face to hold his eyes open. By this time, he had begun to like the warm, cozy feeling of the bug in his ear.

Ed went on. "And Big Bill isn't a steel man. He's a stealing man: a pirate. He's not Big Bill, either. He's Big Bluff. Forget your stupid appointment with him. It's not today anyway, but tomorrow. Remember the rendez-vous you have today; yes, and tomorrow and the next day as well."

"What appointment is that?" asked Les wonderingly. "With myself?" But Ed was gone.

Les awakened with a start. "Good grief," he ex-claimed, "I'll miss my date with Ed if I don't hurry, and I haven't seen him for years. I must have slept a long time. And how! I must have slept for years and years, like Rip Van Winkle."

The Salesman

Once upon a time, not so long ago, there lived on the shore of Lake Grizzly, about 100 miles to the north and east of Sonora Springs, two brothers, Chris and Earnest Ashburton. They were bachelors, neither one any longer young. The small, old, brown-painted clapboard house in which they dwelt had been the home of their parents until long ago when those good folks had passed on to their heavenly reward.

The brothers did not live in town, and they had no close neighbors, but there wasn't much to know about Chris and Earnest that wasn't public knowledge. They had been born in the very house which they now inhabited, had gone to school nearby, and were known to everyone for miles around by their first names or as "the Ashburton boys." There was, however, one little detail which was a secret between the brothers; and maybe there'll be no harm in revealing their secret now since it fits in with the rest of the story.

On their little lake-shore property with a stream running by, the brothers had a well. So far as they knew, it had always been there. From it they took their drinking water, as their parents had done. In the early days of the New Deal Era, they had yielded to the pressures and promises of the local rural cooperative and installed electric lights and a pump, but their ill-swept, well-repaired house still remained completely devoid of modern plumbing. Behind a loose brick in the pit encircling the upper portion of the well, three feet or so down from ground-level, was a nice little cash hoard that no one else knew about and which they themselves hadn't inspected for several years or more. The spot was hard to get at.

Had the federal income-tax collector had any idea the Ashburton boys were so well-heeled, he might have insisted that the odd jobs which they performed, on request, on frequent but haphazard occasions, were far more profitable than was actually the case. Had the county-assessor known about this hidden wealth, he probably wouldn't have cared, any more than others, whether it had been earned or inherited. It had, in fact, come down to the boys from their father who had been so miserly and so surly that the tramps and peddlers who used to pass along the rutted old road from time to time, in days gone by, had avoided the place like the plague.

The boys were quite different from their father in this respect, so that salesmen and wayfarers who had no hope whatsoever of profiting thereby sometimes would stop in for a chat. By no stretch of the imagination of the most optimistic passerby could these old fogeys be called "prospects," but then there was always the off-chance of being the first to interest the eccentrics in one of the current fads of the marketplace. The brothers were at least "suspects," for that is a term which takes in a lot of territory.

One hot summer afternoon as Chris and Earnest were taking their ease on the front porch, a car drove into their yard and stopped. They waited silently and patiently for the driver to put in his appearance at the door. Chris kept his seat. So did Earnest, who was whittling on a willow stick he had brought up from the shore. They could hear the stranger's footsteps as he approached, even before he turned the corner of the porch and came into sight.

"Howdy, Folks," the visitor greeted them. "I'm Mr. Otis Satin; nickname of Skeeter."

They both nodded, looking him over. He was wearing a pair of bib overalls of the cut so popular with the farmers and railroad men of the countryside. There wasn't any question of Mr. Satin being either a farmer or a railroad man, however. His overalls weren't the familiar blue denim and never had been. They were made from a gray material of a sort the brothers had seen before but not often, and they couldn't recall quite where. On this man, for some unaccountable reason--not simply the amplitude of his belly—the conventional work outfit seemed tight-fitting.

"I got a proposition to make that I reckon will knock you over," Mr. Satin went on.

To his brother, but for the benefit of Mr. Satin as well, Chris said, "Seeing as you're busy, Ernie, we'll go out here under the oak tree by ourselves and talk it over." Earnest signified his assent by a token gesture of his head.

Chris led the way to the shade of his favorite tree and sat down on the acorn-strewn grass in an attitude of receptive nonchalance, obviously quite willing to listen. Mr. Satin remained on his feet but squatted low so as to be face-to-face. He let his arms hang between his knees so his fingertips rested on the ground to balance his precarious stance.

"I got a proposition that'll knock you right out of your chair. It's as new as tomorrow, and I'll bet you any amount you care to name you've never heard of a deal remotely like it as long as you've lived." Mr. Satin looked at Chris challengingly.

"Haven't lived so long as I hope to."

"It hooks right up to your water system. What kind of current you got here, AC or DC?"

"I'm not sure."

"Well, it doesn't matter a bit in any case 'cause this works with both AC and DC. Just shoots either kind of electrical impulse right into the pipes of your water system with effects you wouldn't believe possible if they weren't true. What do you think of that?"

"Tell me about it," Chris said.

"You've heard about this sleep conditioning? Just about the newest thing out and around till my company came along with its Impulse Charger. We weren't satisfied with something that would only work while you slept. We wanted something as up-to-date as K.C., Mo. By the way, did I tell you I'm from Kansas City?"

"Yes, I know," said Chris.

"You know?" said Mr. Satin. "How did you know that? How did you know I wasn't from Memphis? Kansas City people are so up-and-coming, I guess."

"Memphis people are up-and-coming, too," Chris said.

"And we weren't going to be satisfied with a product that pepped you up for a while so you made friends all over the place and then lost them as soon as the effect wore off. We wanted a process as cheap as a memory course or a series of pep talks, but with a daily boost, a continual re-charge. We hit upon the idea of sparking the water system so you get a revival every time you take a drink. You might say we weren't content to go around with our eyes on the ground looking for the Fountain of Youth. We set about inventing it.

"It'll add years to your life, Brother. It'll do wonders for your health. It'll give you a wholly new outlook: zest, vigor, bounce, and I mean bounce. You can't possibly afford to be without it. Can you imagine going to Europe without Baedeker? Can you imagine..." Mr. Satin saw Chris had something to say, and he wanted to encourage the latter (within limits) to speak up, so he stilled his tongue momentarily.

"I can't imagine going to Europe."

"You will, Brother; you will. You wait and see. A Baedeker is indispensable; as well try to savor the sauternes of the Rhone and the rieslings of the Rhine without the Wine Bibbers Bible; as well try to practice law without Sunegan's Skip-Tracer."

"Skip-Tracer?"

"Sure. Tracks down rules of law the way a magnetic missile seeks out an atomic warhead in this direction. Scientific. You can no more live without this Impulse Charger than you can play the stock-market without Hickenlooper's Wall Street Index. You've heard how all the nations in the world have given top priority to finding a good way to remove the salt from seawater? That's nothing compared to our Impulse Charger. We don't take the slightest particle out of water. We add to it. No more buying ginger ale and soda. With this, Brother, you got it made!"

"How much is it?"

"Fifty dollars."

"Fifty dollars? Ho-ho, then, no!"

"The price is nothing," Mr. Satin asserted, trying hard to sound positive and unimpressed by the objection; but his ears already were reddening angrily, and he had the sensation of a hand having a tight grip on his abdomen.

"The price is everything," said Chris, and he said it with such quiet, immoveable finality that Mr. Satin left without ceremony so he could explode in fury all the sooner and all alone. He couldn't trust himself to erupt then and there.

"Who was it?" Earnest asked when Chris was back on the porch.

"A salesman," said Chris.

"He sure fooled me at first," said Earnest. "I thought he was an engineer." Earnest ceased whittling an instant to reflect on the marvel of it.

As the two sat there, Chris wondered how it was he had forgotten, when he was talking to Mr. Satin, that he and Ernie didn't pipe their drinking water into the house anyway, but he didn't bother to mention either the conversation or this little lapse of memory on his own part to Earnest. Before many minutes had dribbled away, Mr. Satin was just the latest in the long procession of similar strangers who had come and gone from the Ashburton door.

School in the Sky

When I left the school, I left in disgrace and, in fact, was permitted to leave solely on condition that I should hold my tongue. I was sworn to silence for ten years. The agreed time so solemnly agreed upon in writing has elapsed long since. Something akin to amnesia, something more powerful than any stipulation in the lawyer's arsenal, must have kept me quiet all these years, for up to here, my mind has balked absolutely at any recall of those school days. And now, for reasons beyond me, I am no freer than the Ancient Mariner; I must speak!

I have called it the School in the Sky, but it has a different name. In accordance with the custom which prevailed then as now, the official title of the institution was so dignified and austerely conservative as to be in fact high-sounding: Alpine Institute of Civic Leadership. I say "official" title because I have no doubt that a secret connection existed between the government and this select conclave of gifted students and dedicated doctors of philosophy. Of proof on this point I have none, but of conviction plenty; and that will have to suffice for the present.

The student body was recruited in a peculiar way from young men who, at the close of World War II, had just been discharged from the various branches of military service. It appears that all who were considered eligible for the special, experimental instruction in store were sent to Fort Roper for the purpose of demobilization. In any case, in a tavern just off the military reservation the school officials were able to sign up as many guinea pigs as suited their purpose. There is no denying we all were persuaded; not impressed against the will in the heavy-handed manner which the British Admiralty used with American seamen in playing the 1812 Overture. The Alpine Institute's offer sounded like a good one at the time: no tuition, no red tape, no Veterans Administration. So we signed up. We bought a pig in a poke.

I may have been gullible, but, if so, I did not lack company. Speaking for myself alone, for the sales pitch varied according to the vulnerability of the victim, I was softened up and made receptive to the alleged advantages of the Shangri-La by flattery. Boyd, the school's representative, confided to me, with that unctuous regard for another's welfare which was his trademark, that only those with phenomenal ratings in the military intelligence tests were being considered for this first class at the newly-established academy. I had such a rating, he said. Besides, I was the right age and hadn't yet been contaminated by attendance at any other college. That guy, Boyd, he might have been an honor graduate of Dale Carnegie's; but our destination was a school of a different sort.

I'll give the fellow his due. There was no misrepresentation about the physical site of the school. Mr. Boyd was a little coy when I asked about the location of the school, saying, "That's one of the things I can't tell you, Mr.

Worth. I can say this much, though: it has a setting which rivals that of Shangri-La. I judge from your record that you know a lot about mountain country, but I'm willing to wager that you've never seen grandeur and splendor to compare with what you'll see at the school." Well, he was right about that. I have no kick coming on that score. I want to be fair, as fair as one in my circumstances can be. Give or take a few brain cells, and I'm as average as my neighbor. I'm human.

I was the only student who failed to be satisfied with the course of instruction; and, as I've said, I didn't quit on my own initiative. There may have been others who were expelled as I was, and on similar terms. If so, it happened after my departure. There is the possibility, too, that a few others were skeptical of the value of the teachings but were unwilling to throw in the sponge and say farewell to what was surely one of the most luxurious educational setups in existence. Perhaps we were experimental guinea-pigs and no more, but we were just as well-fed, well-clothed, and well-sheltered as we were tailless. Don't forget that.

To say that I wasn't satisfied with the instruction may be claiming credit which really isn't due me. After all, I by no means foreshadowed those foreign students of the present day who topple cabinets and ministries and who, while ranting and rioting in the streets, still have the presence of mind for the delicate task of advising members of parliament how to conduct the affairs of government. I was intellectually humble in the best American tradition. I was well disciplined up to a point; but I'm putting myself ahead of my story. I'm sorry. I don't count; and the story does.

There were exactly fifty of us accepted for training, all discharges from Fort Roper. We went to our destination in three chartered DC-3s, those good old oxen of the post-war airplanes. However, we went by night, and we cruised so high we could see nothing. We travelled for seven hours, whereas almost any point in the Rocky Mountains certainly should have been within a maximum of three hours flying time from Fort Roper. To be sure, no one in position to know ever confirmed our speculation that the school was in the Rockies, but where else could it have been and still been in this country? Looking west, one could see tier after tier of up-thrust humps outlined in purple haze. On the clear days of early fall as many as a dozen snow-streaked peaks were visible.

Whenever fifty young men are assembled together, someone is bound to stand up in front of them and give a spiel and tell them he never in his life had seen fifty finer fellows in one place at one time. At the first formation upon our arrival at the school, it was the Dean of Studies who greeted us and told us that. We had arrived at dawn, and the reception assembly was held that evening in a plush-seated auditorium the size of those cozy convention halls the newer hotels have. In the meantime, we had slept, eaten, and inspected in a preliminary, incredulous way the scenic magnificence which surrounded us. We were overwhelmed. The Swiss Alps could hardly compare.

The buildings, all three, were relatively small but brand new and in a class by themselves. True, they were not homey. Marble halls never are. Nor were they shrine-like. For one thing, they weren't white. Here, at the school, the designers had tried something new in exteriors—the prodigal use of polished black marble. On bright days the stone's reflections were a sort of weird midnight sun. The interiors of the study halls were replete with rich, dark mahogany. The high-ceilinged lounges, disproportionately large for the buildings, were hung with huge, thick tapestries depicting buffalo hunts, exchanges of furs for merchandise at trading posts, and so on. Yet, inside as well as out, there was a chill in the air for which the architects were not responsible and which had nothing to do with altitude, temperature, or weather. I feel this in retrospect, even now.

There was no indication in the size of the lay-out that more than one class would ever be there during the same term. The Dean of Studies told us in his speech that persons of our caliber were expected to complete the equivalent of a four-year college course in one year. There were, of course, to be no distractions, no lives beyond the campus, no travel, no coeds, no schedule of intercollegiate sports. This information was pretty ominous: grim, forbidding, and foreboding—and not to me alone.

As it turned out, the fall months, September, October, November, passed very agreeably at the school, with little sense of strictness or tension. There was a minimum of friction among the students; and yet no hint of order imposed from above as in a military setting. Everything clicked off so smoothly, efficiently, and swiftly that I, in common with the rest, was congratulating myself on my good fortune in being picked for the party.

At one of the class assemblies, the professor in charge at the time read from a little slip handed him by the dean's secretary that Ellis Worth was requested to report to the office of the Dean of Studies. I took off at once. The professor nodded perfunctorily to signify my dismissal from the room. The dean's office in the administration wing of the building was less than a block away. Through the glass partition, the dean noted my arrival in his reception room, which was empty at the moment, and he signaled me to come in.

The dean greeted me without a smile and waved me to a chair. "It didn't take you long to get here, Mr. Worth," he said. "Did you run?"

"No," I replied. "I walked."

"You're out of breath," he said.

"It's the altitude, I suppose," I said.

"Do you have an idea what I want to talk to you about?" he asked.

"Is it some news?" I mumbled.

"Yes. Some bad news, some very bad news for you and for us, for the school."

I waited for him to continue. For what seemed a long while he hesitated, at an impasse, uncertain of the right starting point. Then he looked sternly at me and proceeded. "No one here has denounced you. No one at all. Nor do I have any accusation to make. All I want to do is to announce an irrevocable decision of the Faculty Council. It's not just my decision. It's a group judgment, and you may as well know, the vote was unanimous." He looked at me to see if I understood, if I followed the drift of, his remarks.

"What vote was that?" I asked. What the dean had just finished saying had caused every watch wheel in my brain to spin at full speed in uncoordinated confusion, but I could feel in my bones a single meaning as cold and numbing and saturating as a fog from an arctic sea.

"The vote for your expulsion." That's the way he put it, without mincing words, cutting it short, without going on right away to explain. I would have felt better if he had not told me in advance that the vote had been unanimous. Indeed, I had the feeling that it hadn't been, that this very man couldn't be telling me the news so cruelly if he himself had been against me.

He showed no sign of going on. I had the impression he thought he had done his duty; conveyed the order for my expulsion; and that nothing remained to be done now but to inform me to have my belongings packed and be ready for the plane's departure at such and such an hour that evening. I just sat there. Had he told me "Be set to go at six," I probably wouldn't have questioned him but would have let it go at that. It was he, finally, who figured a word or two of explanation might be in order.

"The school is as disappointed as you are," he said. "We know your record." Here he tapped a file to signify the extent of his data. The French couldn't have had a thicker dossier on Dreyfus. "What I shall never understand," he said, lapsing from his impersonal reserve momentarily, "is how one who knows as much of the anguish and agonies of war as you do could answer as you did that question whether World War II was the last and final war." This remark of the dean may seem odd now when the cold war threatens, like a volcano, to erupt from some mysterious inner stress, if not in Viet Nam, then in the Congo or at some obscure new Danzig in Europe. But I understood. The second great war to end wars had just been won, and it was the official doctrine of the school that the objectives of the victors had been achieved.

"No wonder you couldn't appreciate the solid truths and the serviceable ideals the school aims to impart." Now, as the dean's diatribe was gaining momentum, he was striking a pose of self-righteous indignation such as, in 1940, the isolationist assumed when lecturing the internationalist, and vice versa. "The cornerstone, yes the entire foundation of American civilization, is the rule of law. And what kind of an answer did you give in Professor Hobbs' class? A flippant plug for the alternative of the reign of love." The dean frowned in the fashion of a lawyer browbeating a witness. "In this religious nation, Mr. Worth, we have a separation of church and state, and in this school we have no place for the frivolities of the feather-brained who would dilute the purity of the secular state and the single mindedness of commercial activity with religious nonsense. In this day and age, life is too practical for pap."

I knew I couldn't have said anything so terribly bad— anyway, words are but words—but the dignified, gray-templed dean no longer resembled the smug winner of a service club's Man of the Year award. He looked absolutely outraged. He shot at me, "It's in the Constitution. Religion, yes. But we separate it from the State and Business. Everything has its separate time and place. Get that?"

He paused to give his militant wisdom an opportunity to wash me off my feet like a tidal wave or to bowl me over as a well-directed ball scatters and shatters a flock of duck-pins. This gave me an opening. "It wasn't as serious as all that, Dean Bradford," I said. "I merely told Professor Hobbs 'Curse on all laws but those which love has made.' It was just a poetic quotation. Nothing was further from my mind than tingeing anyone's politics or daily pursuits with poetry or religion. I was speaking only for myself, just sounding off, really."

My defense sounded weak even to me, but that's what I said. That's all I could think of right then. Humor might have worked, but none came. My brain was as torpid as an alligator in an ice bath.

"You defend your heresy by repeating it," the dean retorted, "just as they all said you would at the Faculty Council. You taint whatever you touch, young man. And the pattern of your errors touches everything held dear at some point or other. You have no faith in the continuance of peace because you despise the rule of law which alone can establish peace. Only the rule of law, backed by force, can save us from extermination by war. But law can do it. We must have faith in force. I mean law. Where there is no faith, the people perish."

He beat his desk with his fist, but not to overcome me with his arguments so much as to beat himself into submission. His eyes were closed, and a smile played uncertainly on his lips as if, just this once, he were having difficulty bringing into focus a mystic vision of peace enforced by the sword of justice. He looked at me closely for a minute to see if I, too, had caught a glimpse of the spiritual splendor he had been seeking to focus and to describe. I wondered if he were playing a game with me and with his colleagues on the Faculty Council. What a triumph for him if he should be able to announce my conversion to his way of thinking and to appeal to the Council to revoke its irrevocable decision and vote for my reinstatement.

"Where is the Heavenly City, Mr. Worth?" I didn't know what he meant. I didn't know what to answer. I didn't know if he expected me to answer. Evidently the question was rhetorical, for he went on. "Not up, Mr. Worth; not up. That's the great mistake that students in the ordinary colleges make, but it's a mistake we can't tolerate here at the school. Don't look up; look down. The lowest common denominator is the holy grail. Emerson's over-soul is really under foot." He was talking more to himself than to me, and it was a matter of indifference to me what he meant for I knew my fate was sealed. No doubt, the dean would be willing to champion my cause to the Faculty Council as vehemently as he had just spelled out the standards of the Faculty Council to me. I was certain of that by then, but I was sure, too, that his terms were unconditional surrender; and I'd see him in hell first.

The dean saw how it was, but he had another bargain to propose. "You don't know where you are, do you?"

"I know up from down," I said.

"That's at least something," he admitted. "We are in the midst of a vast wilderness area," he said. "There are no roads and no trails. To attempt to reach a settlement on foot, with Old Man Winter getting ready to close in on us, would verge on suicidal. Plane transportation can be arranged, as you know, but there is no other means of coming or going. Do you see what I'm getting at?"

"I'm listening," I said.

"I'll make a deal with you," he said. "If you keep mum for ten years about everything concerning the school and in particular about our conversation just now, you can leave by plane within twenty-four hours."

"I give you my word of honor."

"Thank you," he said, "but, of course, we'll have to have it in writing, for the record and for a contract, and tit-for-tat and the rule of law." The bantering manner he suddenly had assumed was a cover for his agitation. He meant what he said. He wanted an agreement in writing, all right. He wanted it legal.

"I understand," I said.

That's the way it was. Until that meeting with the dean, I idolized the crazy place, the sybaritic paradise. After what he spelled out for me, or for himself, he didn't need to expel me. I was ready to go on his terms or any terms. And now, after all these years, a travel agent who knows the secret of the school's location (if any agent does) could not give me an all-expense-paid sightseeing ticket to the place. That's the way it is. It's all behind me, for good.

Sex as War and Peace

There were a lot of red-letter days on the calendar the year the society for barber-shop quartets met in Sonora Springs. I'll never forget last spring's bowling congress, either. The convention that topped them all for me, though, was the regional get-together of the amateur association of parlor-pool players two years ago. Maybe a guy pops more vest buttons with laughter at the miners' annual sow-belly dinner, but I'm not talking about just laughs and professional clowns. I'm thinking of the kicks one can get out of the way his own buddies will hoist a tale on top of a chuckle when they're winding up the semi-finals and got practically their whole mind on a tight game of pool.

Going great guns that fall were Judge Cluny, who is from Denver himself and just had been elected to office; Red Hopper from I don't remember where, maybe Salt Lake; Cliff Stickney, who won the title; a couple of oilmen from Casper, lousy with dough; and bankers and insurance men and ranchers from all over a seven-state spread. I don't claim these characters know a bit more about women than the rest of us, but it was more fun than a barrel of monkeys to hear all the special angles. Love may be the morning and the evening star, like the preacher says, but I'll be bamboozled if sex isn't war and peace.

I suppose I'm fine one to let you in on it all when I can't even remember a joke long enough to take it home, but I'll do the best I can. There isn't anybody who can take the place of Jeffrey Chaser, who was our club secretary from the beginning, but he passed away since the meet, and somebody has to carry on. If you know the gang at all, you can guess that he told this one.

You Don't Say

When Joe Blount telephoned me long distance and told me, in his sober, dead-earnest manner, that he had been served with notice he was going to be prosecuted for wife beating, you could have knocked me over with a feather. In the first place, people who live in Colorado, and particularly in those wide open spaces known as the Eastern Plains, don't beat their wives, and when they do the whole affair is hushed up. It may be brooded over, but it is brooded over in silence. In all my years as a lawyer in Sonora Springs, I had never heard of such a prosecution.

In the second place, it was surprising that Joe shouldn't have gone to a local lawyer who would know everyone concerned, including the prosecutor and the judge, and be in position to conciliate husband and wife and to still the tongue of gossips by delay while he arranged one of those deals in the interests of community respectability. Finally, I'm a tax lawyer, and what I don't know about the technicalities of crimes of violence would fill as many books as line the shelves of my office.

I pointed these things out to Joe in a few well-chosen, emphatic words, but he was entirely unimpressed. "I don't care whether you know any law or not" he said. "I want you. Besides, your knowing a lot of law wasn't what helped last time, and it would be worse than useless now." Of course, a lawyer with any sense would have turned Joe down flat. I think maybe my mother dropped me on my head sometime or other when I was a baby because every once in a while I do a damn fool thing such as taking a case like Joe's. I told Joe I'd be on my way out to see him the next morning.

The trip was two hundred miles or so, but I had become well acquainted with the highway three or four years earlier when I had ironed out a misunderstanding between Joe and the federal revenue agents. The revenuers had absolutely no evidence of tax evasion (there wasn't any), but Joe had ordered them off his ranch, and that had made them both suspicious and vengeful. Naturally, I had had no qualms about charging Joe a good stiff fee for my services in straightening out that little mess, but that was business, and this was something quite different. You can't soak a guy who is having woman trouble even if the woman is his wife.

My curiosity worked overtime all the way out to Joe's ranch at Pitchfork. I had stayed overnight at the place several times and knew Zelda almost as well as her husband. She was the daughter of a rancher in an adjoining county. After she had finished high school, she had spent several years at home helping her mother with the housework during the day and sizing up various young men of the countryside at night. She hadn't met a suitor that fitted her mental specifications for a husband until Joe came along.

Joe had quit high school early in his sophomore year when his father died. He then had taken over as boss of all the outdoor operations on the ranch. Like Zelda, he was an only child. By the time the boy had reached his late teens, he was treating his mother in the same stern, taciturn, forceful way his father had. He took no interest in the young ladies of the community, although his mother did what she could to promote a match with certain favorites of hers whom she could have bent to her will had she found herself sharing the dwelling with a daughter-in-law.

Not until his mother died when he was past twenty-five years old and almost a confirmed bachelor by the standards of that rather remote rural area, did Joe appreciate the need for a wife. He courted Zelda and before long was more successful than his more experienced predecessors had been. Zelda moved into the ranch home, which had been renovated in honor of the occasion, according to her whims.

The couple got along fine from the beginning. Zelda understood everything Joe had to say about cattle and crops far better than the average housewife follows her husband's comments on office politics, the fluctuations of the stock market, the danger to the domestic steel business from imports of foreign cars, and all the rest. Joe was by no means the talkative type, but it made conversation easier for him to have a wife who was so well aware of differences in the kinds and qualities of hay, ground-up cattle feeds, and chemical fertilizers.

At the time of the tax case there had been two children, a boy and a girl. Zelda had declared to me in Joe's presence that two was enough. It sounded as if she meant more than enough. I had noticed, too, that she seemed to consider talking to me about tax troubles something in the nature of a theatrical performance, and she was anxious to have as much time on the stage as her husband. She had added tiny details to his account of that muddle as if she were supplying the really important facts which her husband had overlooked. Or, at times, she restated what he just had said as if, of course, the city lawyer would have difficulty in understanding anything not expressed in the King's English of a high school graduate. Well, there's no end of wives who can do everything their husbands do and do it better, so I hadn't paid too much attention to all this at the time. And, I'd been too wrapped up in figures and fine points of law to see if Joe gave any signs of displeasure at his wife's bumptiousness.

When I arrived at the ranch, it was about noon. Joe came out to meet me. "Come on in," he said. "Zelda will have dinner on the table in a few minutes." I hesitated a little. "Oh, she's not hurt so bad she can't work," he said. "It's not as bad as all that."

"But I'm your lawyer," I said. "You sure she won't put poison in my soup?"

He laughed. "You mean you're her lawyer," he said. "She got herself into this, and she'll have to get herself out. I did all I'm going to do when I called you. Come on. Let's go in."

We went in. Zelda, bustling about in the kitchen, greeted me without enthusiasm but without rancor. Her busyness apparently gave her a welcome pretext for turning from me. She was a bit embarrassed by the incident which brought me there. There were no visible bruises, but she favored her left hip when she walked.

The lunch went off all right. There were just the three of us. The children were at school. Joe was his usual self except that he exerted himself to keep the conversation from lagging. At that, I had to do the same. Zelda was not sullen, but she took no part in the table talk.

When the dishes had been cleared away, we all remained at our places. Zelda spoke up. "I wanted you," she said. "I didn't want these gabby lawyers around here to be able to say they learned this or that firsthand from me. What I want to know," she went on, "is can they get anywhere with this case if I deny anything happened?"

"What do you mean?" I asked. "Didn't you make a complaint? Don't you want a prosecution?"

"What do you think I am?" she answered. "My father stopped by just as we were having a little family argument and jumped to the conclusion I was being abused, and he signed the paper. I don't know what I may have said then, but Joe didn't give me anything I didn't have coming. He flared up because I kept hammering at him that according to everything I'd been reading in the papers, he should have held onto some steers and not sold them when he did. Who is to decide when to sell and not to sell if it isn't Joe?" she asked. She was smoothing her left hip with her hand as if it carried a tenderness that she especially prized.

"Well, what do you know?" I thought. "Joe has made her proud of him. It isn't every husband who gets such splendid results from a swift kick. And it isn't every woman who has such forceful reasons for being proud of her husband."

Needless to say, the case against Joe fizzled out like a wet firecracker. Zelda's father had a change of heart, the prosecutor was relieved of a painful duty, and a solemn peace settled over the wheat and cattle country of the Eastern Plains.

But here's the strange thing. I suppose I have told this story to friends around the fireside at home as many as a half-dozen times. Up to now the response has been invariable: "You don't say!"

"Wait a minute," said one of the ranchers. "That story doesn't make any sense. Where I come from, we don't disrespect women like that guy Joe did. They're too precious. After all, when my kin first settled here in Colorado, there weren't many women, so each one of them was a treasure. A valued treasure to be respected and protected."

"Y'all took the words out of my mouth," said Cliff. He's from Texas, I think.

"Aw, who cares. Now it's my turn," said one of the oilmen from Casper.

The Boss and the Girl

Her boss was an oil man and a big-time operator. It hadn't always been so. There were long years, before she became his secretary, when the boss toiled with his hands in the oil fields, wore dirty, greasy coveralls; and took desperate chances with the meager "working capital" he had been able to scrape together by borrowing from acquaintances and near acquaintances who held down respectable, routine jobs in the banks and warehouses of Denver, Casper, Cheyenne, and Salt Lake. The old-timers at the Las Vegas casinos would have shied away from the odds the boss took then. That was quite a while ago, when building a business was the order of the day.

When she went to work for him, Johnny Van Loo, only forty-eight, was president of his own little oil company. It really wasn't so tiny, except by comparison with Phillips Pete, Sinclair Refining, and the dozen or so sprawling giants which owned derricks the world over. Van Loo Oil did its drilling only in the Rocky Mountain states and not all of those. But it sold the produce of its wells at a profit which was the envy of the big boys in other lines of business. Movie moguls on the West Coast and steel barons in Chicago and Pittsburgh had heard about Johnny Van Loo.

Ursula Linden was pink-cheeked, pretty, slender, and swayed gracefully, like a willow in the wind in her high-heeled walk. In addition, she was a good secretary. Van Loo promoted her from secretary to private secretary to assistant to the president; made her manager of the details of the personal side of his business affairs; paid her well; increased her salary whenever an occasion presented itself and sometimes when one didn't. Considering her bonuses, Christmas presents, birthday remembrances and all, Ursula's take-home pay nearly equaled her husband's. Jasper Linden was assistant general manager of an association of casualty insurance companies, and the member companies were not doing so well right then, what with automobile collisions hitting new highs and the breakage of costly wrap-around windshields going on right and left.

The generosity of Ursula's boss was a grand thing, no doubt. Jasper never denied it, or even thought of doing so. He and Ursula were invited out to Johnny's home from time to time on evenings and weekends. It was evident on the face of things, and without looking closely, that Johnny was in a high income tax bracket and preferred paying handsome salaries to meeting high taxes. Jasper, like Ursula, called Van Loo "Johnny." The latter wanted it, liked it that way. He thought it softened away, somehow, the hard fact that he was a big boss, though others who worked for him found that the evasive tactic of the first name really called attention to his position at the top of the heap. Mrs. Van Loo was content to remain Mrs. Van Loo, and so she remained, at least for the Lindens.

Jasper was under an "underground pressure" that he would not have felt if this slip of a wife of his—she was just thirty and so three years younger than he—had been working for an employer more like his own. It wasn't that Jasper was like Harry Lauder and couldn't give his wife anything but love. He was getting a nice fat check every month and putting a bit aside for a rainy day. He respected Johnny's appreciation of Ursula, of course, and as the husband, was luckier than Johnny. But if Johnny only wasn't so darned demonstrative of his appreciation in solid, tangible, material ways!

Jasper had no idea about Johnny and Ursula that he put into words. There obviously was no affair between the two and nothing to worry about. Nevertheless, he took on a taste and a yen for martinis that was new for him. Besides, he began to notice how efficient his own buxom, bosomy, dark-eyed secretary was. Her willing, incomparable services to the association of insurers were scarcely recognized by the figures following the name Sandra Bender and the magical phrase "pay to the order of." Jasper made her a Christmas gift of a subscription to a fine, arty, expensive magazine. He remembered her birthday with an exquisite bouquet, and, on slight pretext—with Ursula's knowledge—he lavished similar attentions upon his "girl."

Sandra, almost old enough to be Jasper's mother, was nobody's fool. She accepted the tokens of esteem with good grace and kept on about her business as usual. She knew that Jasper wasn't making a play for her. So did Jasper, but what wasn't so clear to him was exactly what he was doing. He was too deep in the forest to see anything but trees.

While this personal web was being woven, *The Wall Street Journal* and *Fortune* and even the regular news weeklies were reporting the mergers of the Chase and Manhattan Banks, of J. P. Morgan and Guaranty Trust, of Signal Oil and Hancock Oil, and of a host of other smaller companies all over the country. No one knew exactly why all these business marriages were going on, but everyone was sure there were very sound, substantial reasons: tax reasons maybe, business reasons surely. It wasn't a simple case of big fishes eating little ones at all, because — well, who'd call either Signal or Hancock little? No; joining forces was as much the fashion of the time as nuptial vows in June.

Another oil company which operated in the midcontinent fields, in the Texas and California fields, under the offshore tidelands of Louisiana, in the Venezuelan jungle, and on the Arabian desert, discovered that it should tap the resources of the Mountain States. It took a shine to Van Loo Oil, and vice versa. They made a deal. Johnny ceased to be president of his own company and became vice president of a bigger one which boasted several similar officers under a president who, in turn, was under a vice chairman and a chairman of the Board of Directors. Inspectors and accountants and management specialists from the main office in Houston began to swarm around the former headquarters of Van Loo Oil, which now had become the Rocky Mountain branch of Tri-Continent Oil.

After the merger, Johnny was forever on the go: at meetings, in conferences, on trips. His business affairs no longer had a personal side. Everything was company business. Ursula became lost in the turmoil of paper work, reports, check-ups, and traveling auditors. With Johnny forced, by his own busyness and by the shortness of his stays at home, to take her for granted, Ursula began to appreciate Jasper to a degree somewhat new and foreign to her experience since going with Van Loo's. Besides, the boss wasn't as much the boss as he had been. The situation at the office wasn't at all the same as it used to be.

"Before the consolidation" seemed to Ursula like the good old days before the fall from paradise. Then she seldom had spoken of the affairs of the work day to her husband except to relay jokes, choice bits of gossip, news of Johnny's latest gesture of grandeur and good will. For quite a while after the merger, though, she would carry home perplexities, vexations, irritations, and complaints.

Jasper made no pretense of easy solutions to the problems which had gotten into his wife's hair. He listened. He was concerned about Ursula's burdens and difficulties. At times, he would try to divert the conversation into more cheerful channels. He always did so when Ursula lamented the consolidation and likened Johnny's deal to an exchange of gold for fool's gold. Jasper seemed to understand not only Ursula's present predicament but also Johnny's preference for shares of stock in a bigger company, shares which had a ready market and could be unloaded quickly, if desired.

If Jasper thought "Johnny's moves are Johnny's affair" or "I'm quite satisfied with the outcome of the big deal," he never said so. He simply and tactfully shifted the gears of the conversation. Ursula, for her part, came around to feeling cozy and at home with this sort of silent treatment, like a cat at a warm fireside.

The sharp edge of disappointment and annoyance wore off gradually. At home now, Ursula sometimes will suddenly remember the events of the day, look up and say, "Johnny came back today from Los Angeles, or

Dallas, or New York." It no longer matters especially that the boss wants to be called Johnny. Rather, Jasper is used to thinking of Van Loo that way, and when it comes to names, Jasper is a creature of habit and absolutely opposed to change. He's also dead set against any form of progress when he's well off, and, what's more, he knows when he's well off. That's not a bad thing for a boss to know.

The oilman paused, as if the story had come to an end. "Is that all?" asked one of the ranchers. "Is that the end of the story?"

"Well yes," replied the oilman, smiling. "I tell's it like I see's it."

"That reminds me," said the well-dressed dude in a banker-grey suit. The two guys from Casper winked at each other, and the dude took over.

Travel Is Broadening

Travel is broadening, and especially so for those, like Adrian De Vries, who are inveterate stay-at-homes. Adrian had gone along in the same old rut for years, and then, pop, something happened which suddenly opened his eyes, and, as the travel circulars put it, "broadened" him.

He wasn't doing any traveling at the time. It was Adrian's old friend and war-time comrade, Matt Conover, who was in a "travel status," as they say, at the time of the incident. Matt's business kept him in airplanes much of the time, on trips to inspect branch offices, to pep up local managers, and so forth, all over the country. Every once in a while, maybe once or twice a year, Adrian's telephone would ring, and he would hear his friend's voice on the other end of the line, announcing that he was making a brief stop-over in town on the way to St. Louis or somewhere, just long enough for an Old Fashioned, maybe lunch, and a chat.

This sort of thing is always happening to Sonorans and most inhabitants of the city have been forced, in self-defense, to tell their callers over the phone how truly wonderful it would be to see the visitor, but, unfortunately, they have to present an important guest speaker to the banker's convention within the hour or they were at that very moment leaving for Aunt Sophie's funeral. Adrian, however, always made an exception to the rule in favor of Matt. He had been Matt's adjutant during the war, and in the meantime, he had failed to make a mark in the business world the way Matt had. He was one of six or seven vice presidents of a medium-sized bank, and Matt was president of a huge insurance company on the Coast, on the executive committee of a bank in Arizona, and a director of several big companies in Texas. Besides all that, Adrian was young enough to be Matt's son and had a healthy respect for gray hairs. He looked up to Matt.

Matt seldom stayed long; never long enough to suit Adrian, who hungered for a rehash of those hectic days in Normandy in the summer and in the Ardennes in the winter. As for the bank at which he worked, it was quite willing for its newest vice president to be away from business and to spend as much time as he saw fit with the wheeler and dealer from California. On one of Matt's longer stays, Adrian had driven him down towards Canyon Springs to see the showplace Hereford ranch with its magnificent picture-window view across the meadows, hills, herds of white-faced red cattle and beyond to the towering Front Range of the Rockies.

On another occasion, there had been time for Adrian to take his friend over to one of the state tax offices and introduce him to Millie McGuire, a dried-up, hairy-lipped, coarse-featured old maid who supervised a horde of civil servants of various ages and who, it turned out, shared Matt's enthusiasm and passion for office equipment and could tell exactly which make of machine was right for what operation. These wonders of science and invention left Adrian cold. If he had any feeling whatever about punch-card systems and the marvelous machinery for writing checks and stuffing envelopes, it was an icy hatred. He was glad, however, that Matt and Millie got such a kick out of the devices. It fitted in with their business; and his own, thank goodness, was different. He wondered if Millie's aged mother, who lived with her, enjoyed hearing about the mechanized operations of the state tax office. And what about Matt's light-hearted, bubbling, frivolous wife, Sukie: did her eyes widen and brighten at the prospect of the eventual automation of office procedures? He doubted it.

So far as Adrian knew, however, Matt never had spent as much as two consecutive days in Sonora Springs. Matt would say he liked being "on the go" too much to make a stay of any duration, even in the "climate capital of the world." It was paradoxical that it was the older, rather than the younger, man who should relish hopping from airport to airport. Matt had a wife at home, and his youngest child had not yet flown the nest, whereas Adrian had lived the lonely life of a childless bachelor since his post-war bride succumbed to "quick cancer" three years ago.

It hardly could be said that either of them was a lady killer, chaser, or Don Juan. Girls temporarily had lost their thrilling, irresistible magnetism, so far as Adrian was concerned. He liked to admire them, observe their eyes and points of beauty. He was fascinated by their smiles, wiles, and tricks of manner, but in that curious, semi-detached attitude of bird-watchers looking upon the antics of chickadees. Even in their days together in the army, after the end of the war, Matt had not taken up with the *frauleins*, as so many, including Adrian himself, had done to relieve the monotony of military life abroad. He had had platonic friendships with American nurses but scarcely could wait for the orders which would send him back to his charming wife and adoring family in the States.

This time Matt's phone call got Adrian out of bed on a Sunday morning. He had been skiing, for a change, the day before and was tired, stiff, and lame. Still half asleep, though the hour was not early, he quickly promised to meet Matt at Barron's Motel for lunch and to drive him to the airport to catch the three o'clock plane.

Matt was in the process of packing when Adrian arrived at the motel. He took time off from the chore for a hearty, cheerful greeting and the kind of exchange of flitting chit-chat which precedes the more quiet conversation which comes after the mind has had an opportunity to fit new impressions of the old acquaintance into the existing, familiar pattern of recollections. He was on the way to Chicago in connection with some unspecified business for the Arizona bank and was relatively taciturn, something out of the ordinary for him. He breathed a bit heavily, wearily, Adrian thought. Just the altitude, probably and, come to think of it, Matt was not getting any younger.

They decided that the best arrangement was to have a martini and their lunch at the airport. Then they'd be there when the plane was ready for the take-off. As Matt was waiting in line at the motel's check-out counter, Adrian wandered off to a spot nearby where he could observe the quick motions of the pretty switchboard operator as well as Matt's progress in the lineup of departing guests. He had no thought whatever of eavesdropping on the remarks of the clerks behind the counter, but he had an eye for color, for motion, for people, and he wanted to be where he could survey the scene.

As he stood so, dreamily, vaguely, sweetly conscious of the situation in the office and in the peopled lobby, he heard the girl at the information desk say over the phone: "Miss Millie McGuire? No, she's not here. Yes, Mrs. McGuire, she has been here, but she checked out, say an hour ago. Yes, I know her and her car, and I saw her leave myself. I'm sorry; but she'll probably be home soon. She told one of the girls here that a night away from the cares of home does wonders for her. She said it does you good, too, to have the house to yourself once in a while. All right, Mrs. McGuire. Good bye."

At the airport, no cocktails were available. They had forgotten about it being Sunday. As they had their lunch, Adrian now was as absent-minded as Matt. By sheerest chance, he had overheard what he did. Pure coincidence also might account for the two friends having been at Barron's the same night. He had an open mind on the subject, but he was ashamed that he had; rueful that he couldn't forget his ill-gotten, unimportant information altogether. Why should he be thrown off stride, so to speak, at possibilities of no consequence to him personally at all? But if only Matt were less moody, more like his usual self. It was sudden doubt, not revelation that bothered and broadened, him.

A guy in cowboy boots interrupted the dude, saying "I second the motion." He was as a rancher from Ouray.

"What motion?" said the dude.

"There never was a good war or a bad peace," the rancher replied.

"You got something there, but let me finish the story," says the dude. All of a sudden, though, he realized that his listeners were watching the rancher who was having a run of luck, and it looked like he could clear the table if he didn't miscue. Everyone seemed to brighten up as their attention shifted to the pool table, effectively bringing the dude's unfinished story to an end.

Shave and a Haircut

The customer had his doubts about the barber and waited till the dark, dumpy, suave-looking fellow was pretty nearly through with the haircut before ordering a shave. He guessed, rightly, that very few of the local yokels went to Jim's shop for a shave. Still, he needed his facial foliage trimmed, and what's more, he felt like having it done right then. So he took a chance.

With the smile of one highly pleased with himself and his world, and supremely sure of his ground, so to speak, Jim's pudgy assistant tilted his customer back to a position of prostrate helplessness. With grave deliberation, he held a heavy towel under the hot-water faucet and then brought it to rest on the soft reddish countenance which faced upward, eyes closed.

"You're a stranger, I see," the barber said, stropping his razor rhythmically. "We get plenty of 'em during tourist season, but boy, this town rolls up its sidewalks every evening at nine o'clock after Labor Day. There ain't nothing to do from then until Memorial Day again. Oh, a few of the guys get away to the hills for fishing in September and hunting in October, but what I mean is that it's quiet in this burg from now on out till come next June."

He took off the towel and, with his fingers as a trowel, began smearing his customer's face with lather, after which he applied another Turkish-type towel. "The place is too small, you know, for the usual amusements and high jinks. Everybody just exists here at the foot of the mountain, waiting for warm weather. Sure, you can get a beer or go to a movie over at Sonora Springs, but it's dead there, too, in winter." He stopped talking to step back, take a drag on a cigarette, and peer at his customer as if he could see through the thick coat of white foam.

"Last year, just about this time of year, the winter closed in on us early, and there was a guy with a gag over in Sonora everybody was talking about and trying to guess who it was. He called himself the Oracle of Daffy or something like that—a kind of a man fortune-teller. I mean he was a man, not all his comers. Jim lined up a little group of our customers, mostly guys who work at the mine over at Redstone, to go over right after we closed the shop at five, and he says to me 'You come along.' Jim thinks I got a good ear for a voice, and I can tell who it is pulling the public's leg. Jim thought maybe it was Clem Ahroon, the ninth-grade gym teacher, earning a little dough after hours.

"Well, we all went, and I swear it was the funniest thing I ever seen. The Oracle had rented that space over the Davis drugstore on San Miguel Street where Blessing and Barley used to have their Temple of Yeawohl, and he had a waiting room and a studio what-you-call-it. It was partitioned with thick drapes, and you couldn't hear very well what was going on inside unless you listened hard. Jim and the other guys said they couldn't hear at all. Of course, I knew I shouldn't listen, but I was curious.

"They got a statue, you know, in Sonora Springs of a guy on horseback: a general or somebody. I knew once who it is, but I've forgotten. It's on one of the main drags, the statue is. I mean it's in the center of the divided street where the grass is, and last fall there was a lot of fuss about what happened to it, and this woman was giving that a going-over with the Oracle.

"'It's right in front of our apartment,' she said, and I knew right away who it was. I mean who the woman was. The Oracle I didn't know. It wasn't Clem Ahroon. That was for sure.

"'Did they paint the horse all over?' the Oracle asked.

"'No,' she said. 'It's not really a horse, you know, but a stallion.'

"'You mean—'

"'Yes,' she said.

"'Just there?' he asked.

"'Yes.'

"'This happened during the football season, just after a game maybe?'

"'Yes.'

"'Tell me what color was the paint they used: green, or gold maybe?'

"'Gilt.'

"'Come again?'

"'Gilt paint, gilt like guilty.'

"'Oh yes,' he said like he'd been knocked back on his heels. 'I getcha.'

"'Why would anyone do a thing like that? That's what I want to know. That's why I've come here.'

"You could of knocked me over with a feather, fella, to hear her ask that. It just wasn't like Mrs. Borland at all, and I've known her since she was little Sally Jones, and we went to Longfellow School together.

"'Football prank, Madam. One of those guilt-motivated pranks the young folks play when their team loses a game, and their feelings get the best of them. Now, if that answers the question you had, you can leave right this way, Madam, by the side door. I'll give you a little light.'

"'You fool!' she said so loud that even Jim heard her. Then she went on more quiet. 'I gelded that general, that horse, nobody but I did it because I got tired seeing him that way every time I looked out the window. Football, my foot!' and I heard her slam the side-door.

"The Oracle came into the waiting room in a minute or two with a pink and black silk mask on, and he didn't want to have anything to do with us. 'It's dinner time,' he said. 'Come back in the evening. Come at eight.' When we told him we didn't live right in Sonora, though, he said he'd take time to help one of us for five bucks, and Jim's customers talked it over between them, and Riley went in.

"To make a long story short, I wasn't surprised at what I heard Riley lead into. He says 'I know a big exec.'

"'Big exec?' the Oracle says.

"'Yeah. What's funny about that? A big exec. A big shot.'

"'Oh yes. Go on.'

"'Well, you know, on Halloween somebody put sugar in the gas tank of his Cadillac. Now, why would anybody play a dirty trick like that?'

"'Where was the car at the time?'

"'In front of his house. It was in the papers, all about it, the next day or so.'

"'How well did you know him? I mean by that, is he your boss or something? Do you work for him?'

"'Yes. Well, no, I don't work for him, exactly. He's the big boss; he's over my boss.'

"'Is he a pretty good Joe? Would you say?'

"'I don't know. His name is Womrath. The guys all call him Wormrath. To tell the truth, he isn't my boss. He's my buddy's boss, my friend out there in the waiting room.'

"'Do you know if this big exec is a strong man?'

"'He's a company man. He's sold his soul to the company store, if you know what I mean. He sells us down the river, too, to get ahead.'

"'Oh, yes. Well, it isn't for us know, to meddle. After all, that's a pretty crude way to tell some guy that he has treacle in his trickle or lacks spine in his brine, isn't it?'

"'I don't get you,' Riley said.

"'I'm speaking of the worm, of Wormrath,' the Oracle said.

"'I still don't follow you,' Riley said.

"'That'll take another visit and another five dollars, then, the Oracle said."

The barber was massaging a perfumed oil into the customer's clean-shaven, tender face with both hands, in a gentle, rolling motion. "We never did go back," he said. "Pretty damn clever, these oracles: clam up when they get to the payoff. Ain't that the way of it, though?" He tilted the chair back to the upright position. "There wasn't another darn thing happened all the rest of the winter. What brings you to these parts, anyway, Mister?"

"I'm trying to figure out whether that shooting up the Pass on Saturday was accident, suicide, or murder. Know anything about it?"

"You're with the Government or something?"

"The CID."

"No, I sure don't, Mister; not about that. There's no set price on shaves, sir. I'll just make that a dollar. That'll be two-seventy-five in all."

The stranger parted with three ones. "Keep the change," he said.

"Thank you, sir. Goodbye."

"Goodbye," Jim said to show he'd been listening all the time and was going to join his assistant for the finale.

"Goodbye," the stranger said and walked out.

Short and Sweet

I had known Stella Keane for several years, even more, but had seen her only at intervals. Two successive summers she had come to Sonora Springs for a vacation and to work on *The Citizen* for me, for me indirectly. I needed help at the time and, as I told her once or twice, she was the best damn re-write man I'd ever seen. I spoke to her like that—in a jocular vein but with a real appreciation of her extraordinary capability with words and phrases. She played with words as a juggler does with balls, lovingly, dexterously, with showmanship.

Stella was good-looking, yes. Her dark eyes made one look twice and then held one's gaze. Her short figure was not bad, but not remarkable; her hips were too broadly assertive. I had met her husband and two children on a few random occasions, which made me wonder if Stella were a good deal older than she looked, to have a daughter almost grown and a husband with the appearance of a man in the upper range of middle age. He made a fair living, I guessed, as the Kansas City representative of a big New York book publisher. I didn't ask if representative meant salesman, but I understood Herb travelled a lot.

Well, after those summers I didn't see Stella for a while. Once a friend of hers called to ask me to join a group assembling to meet Stella, who was on a brief visit to the Springs for lunch. I was happy to do so. At table there was much bright, glad talk, except by me. I was my usual quiet self. Even so, I had the curious feeling that my coming was somehow a special event for Stella and that nearly everyone knew it, sensed it as I did. I wasn't exactly flattered. I wondered that it should be so.

I spoke of the lunch at home in a guarded way. I told Ardis, "That gal, though married, is looking for a flame who is a writer, an artist, a creative Bohemian."

Ardis replied sententiously, "I gathered she is on the make."

So we dismissed Stella from our conversation. Not for an instant at that time did I think of myself as the light around which a moth would flutter. I knew very well, in fact, that I was not, am not, another Tom Wolfe or Hemingway. I've written a little poetry for magazine publication in recent years, yes, but little. I'm too busy for more and, as for great novels, they simply do not well up in me and demand to be told. It isn't just that my wife tells me this. I know it to be true. I'm more businessman than writer, even more businessman than editor, despite my title. I'm that realistic, I think.

When I've received a Christmas card from Stella, I've sent one, without keeping her address. Last year, none came. However, in the first part of January, I received a beautiful, arty New Year's card: no news, just that. I responded with a similar card with some short-hand personal news and the comment "Maybe we'll see you this summer."

Bang, I received a short note at the office: "Can't make it there this summer as you suggest, but could we have a visit right soon, not there at the Springs, but at Yucca City, which is big enough these days for the two of us to get lost? You can answer freely because Herb definitely will be away, out of town, for six weeks. Better yet, phone me."

The conspiratorial tone of Stella's reply did not come to me as a complete surprise. Even so, I felt as though, without intending to do so, I was travelling in disguise, under false pretenses. She took me not for a Romeo but for some sort of an imaginative, writing demigod I most certainly am not. Without pointing out her mistake, and also without reinforcing it in the least, I called her, and we made arrangements to meet.

Ever since I made it to the editorial top at *The Citizen*, eight years ago, I generally have taken a winter vacation the last two weeks in February. I enjoy it more when Ardis comes along, but I get along if, as happens more often than not, she tells me to shove off on my own.

When I called Stella long distance, I told her, truthfully, I already had plane reservations to and from Mexico City. "This time, I'm staying at Hotel Florida, but you come a day later and I'll meet your plane and have a room for you at the Hotel Texcoco nearby. It's better that way. I know I can get you in there, and I know you'll love it there. Call me back at the office after five about your flight."

At first glance, it may seem that I was planning a pretty underhanded trick on my wife and Stella's husband; and right now I'm sorry I'm relating this in the first person. According to the world's pretensions, my innocent Mexican holiday had taken on an evil aspect, but the world's pretensions are one thing and its practices are another. The former I despise; and to the latter I conform with respect. Believe me, I know the ways of the world. I ought to; and I do. However, if you are in position to judge me and sternly insist on doing so, go ahead. But wait till I finish my story.

We met in Mexico, as planned. It was fun. The weather was spring like. Stella looked good to me, well-dressed in a woolly brown skirt and a silky rust-colored blouse, bright-eyed, alert. We spoke of what we saw at the airport, what we glimpsed on the way to the hotel and of people and places we remembered in Sonora Springs. For the first time, I was dimly conscious that we were only acquaintances who, with slight preparation, had set out to be friends, friends away from home. I anticipated showing Stella around, guiding her—I almost said chaperoning her. She was mine; she had placed herself in my keeping.

I left her to unpack and to unwind after the flight by herself. Afterwards, I took her to dinner at the dining room of the Hotel Texcoco. It was different: entirely lit by candles in candelabras hung from the ceiling and thrust up from the walls. Each table, too, had its candle surrounded by thick handmade colored glass. The table-linen was in subdued color. The place plates were huge, not of china at all but of gold-colored metal with impressed decorations around the rim. I requested California's best champagne, and we got it. The soup was delicious, from a vegetable never heard of in the States. The steak wouldn't have been recognized as such by the Stockyards Inn back home, but more power to the originators. We both agreed on that.

Between the dining room and the hotel's inner court-yard, there was a small dance floor. Now and then a couple would dance the rhumba to the insistent music beat out by the pianist and his accomplice on the drums. Neither of us cared to dance, but we were fascinated by the efforts of the others and by the Latin flavor imparted to what we always had supposed was American music. The waitresses raced to and from the inconveniently-distant kitchen as if the music had got into their bloodstream as the champagne into ours. It all was wonderful. Though Stella was to express reservations later, she certainly had none whatever at the time. We surrendered to the situation. Finally, I said, "You know what I'd like? A little quiet. If you'd like more champagne, I can have it brought to your room."

"I'd like some quiet, too. Let's go."

The next morning, after a light breakfast, we went to church. Going was Stella's idea. She ruled out the great cathedral downtown and insisted upon an English-speaking service. I knew of a small church on the fringe of the Zona Rosa. We arrived late and left early but saw no one we knew (which was a minimal risk, anyway, I thought).

"What would you like to do now?" Stella asked.

"Oh," I said, "what about a stroll in Chapultepec Park?"

"OK, but I warn you I didn't come down here to go native."

"You don't need to warn me. Neither did I."

"I'm not so sure. You seem to go for all this stuff more than for things at home."

"I go for it, yes, but I was born *norteamericano*, and I'll die *norteamericano*."

"See what I mean? *Norteamericano*."

"Why, Darling, you're serious." I could have said she was on the verge of tears, for she was.

We meandered leisurely, with abandon, joyfully in the Park, not hand in hand but with her hand on my arm. It was sunny and warm. The walks were crowded with carefree, native families, some self-consciously dressed up and straight from mass and others in clothes that looked as if they had been slept in. The dark-skinned children broke their rule of sobriety with smiles which highlighted their white teeth. It was like City Park in Sonora Springs on a sunny summer afternoon, only better with its beautiful Castle museum, which we toured in our lazy, rambling way.

We went back to Stella's hotel for a rest and for our afternoon meal. Stella's gaiety had left her. I was getting the impression it almost always cost her some effort and couldn't be sustained for long. She held up a glass, "You like the glassware?"

"Yes. Don't you?"

"I like light things, lightness. Look how heavy this is in weight and color; and look at the chimneys around the candles. Heavy, heavy, hangeth over thy head."

"Ye-es." I learned long ago the best argument against a woman is silence. The only proposition a dame will invariably agree with is that she is beautiful, wonderful, perfect.

"Did you like the church service this morning?"

"Yes, pretty well. I went for the hymns the most."

"But the hymns were commonplace revivalist types, ordinary gospel songs of the Salvation Army on skid row and of the working-class tabernacle and the uneducated youth's summer camp meeting."

"I know. That's the kind I like: direct from the movie of *Elmer Gantry*; the more ignorant the better."

"I'd fume at D. H. Lawrence himself for ever saying anything like that. I want music, preferably sung by a choir in Latin, accompanied by the sonorous roll of an organ. How can you pretend to be a prophet with such uncultivated tastes?"

"Pretend to be a prophet? If we were latter-day saints, Sweet, we wouldn't be here together."

"At home, you're a poet, a prophet, a man of distinction. Here, you're just a sex-obsessed beachcomber. I know I shouldn't say such things, but there." She bit her lip tremulously.

"That's OK. It's quite all right; except that I'm no model of a modern major general back home, either."

"You could at least act like a gentleman."

"Would you believe me if I did? I've heard about the will to believe."

"Yes; and there's also a will to disbelieve, and I've got it. I guess I've got both, first one and then the other. I'm sorry. I'm sorry if I'm spoiling your trip with my tantrums."

I half-stood at the table to lean over and kiss her forehead in a conciliatory gesture, but I knew I never again would be her high and mighty Great Man of Letters. I could no more be a hero for her now than I could be one for a valet if I had such a fellow. I couldn't if I tried, and I didn't feel like trying.

"Why don't we go down to Acapulco," she said, "and raise hell in the sun and on the beach and in the bars and forget about all the pyramids and ruins and museums you have in mind, ready to spring on me."

"I don't have anything of the sort in mind. What I was going to spring on you was a bus ride to Vera Cruz. I've been to Acapulco. I'd feel like a phony going again. That's one of the places, like Vegas, that is not for me."

"OK, OK. I'm going, and not by bus. You go east and I'll go west."

"And never the twain shall meet."

In spite of our disagreement, we stayed together, clung together, a bit beaten down to be sure, until I saw her off the next day for Cuernavaca and Acapulco under the auspices of American Express. I had no deep regrets. After all, the hare-brained adventure was better than none at all.

A Simple Case

Eric Dudley had liked his client from the start. Her face was pretty but not strikingly so. It still showed the effect of weeping and grief. Her appeal for him was more than a matter of a trim ankle, a slim waist, and the right curves at the right places. She was his kind of woman, and he knew how to talk to her. That was it.

He saw that Mrs. Thornley was a lady, carefully brought up. She loved the well-worn paths of life: the quiet pleasures of the home; the measured merriment of dignified social gatherings; the controlled emotions of placid domesticity. The mere idea of a sudden, violent action or of an extraordinary thought or feeling would be shocking to one of such delicate sensibilities. The lawyer had sensed all this at the beginning of the brief consultation. He had spoken to her accordingly, and she had engaged him as her attorney.

It was a perfectly simple case. The insurance company would pay up without hesitation or delay—the more readily because the refined widow was neither in need nor greedily interested in the supposed money equivalent of her husband's life. She wanted to do the proper thing. Making a claim, like carrying insurance on one's self, was the obviously correct thing to do after a decent interval of time. The lawyer had not been the first to tell the widow that. No one else, however, had impressed upon her, as Mr. Dudley had, that her husband's death, though a grievous, inacceptable loss, at least had occurred under ordinary and acceptable circumstances.

Mrs. Spencer Thornley felt greatly comforted as she left the lawyer's office. Not since her husband's untimely, accidental death six months before had she felt the same calm, the same peace of mind which went beyond resignation and verged on contentment. It wasn't merely that Mr. Dudley had reassured her about the outcome of her case against the insurance company. She had been certain of that before, had taken it for granted since she first thought of seeing her legal adviser.

The words which Mr. Dudley had used with the effect of a benediction ran through her mind in various arrangements and combinations. "I understand your feeling perfectly, Mrs. Thornley," he had said. "You are shocked and grieved by this accident. Naturally. But these cases happen every day, really. Your husband died a perfectly normal death. An automobile accident nowadays is as much in the order of nature as heart attacks. As time goes on, your misfortune will seem less special. Take it easy, and you will see your case is an ordinary one. Legally, it is a simple case. It is a simple case, a very simple case."

Spencer Thornley had been driving alone when the accident occurred. He was returning home in a contented mood from Cadiz, just thirty miles away, by the Oak Creek Canyon Road. There had been a light four o'clock shower, but the hot, thirsty pavement had absorbed the moisture so quickly the road was already bone dry. Spencer could see the brilliant western sun in his rearview mirror. He turned the gadget slightly to avoid the reflection of the sun's glare. A few minutes later he met the fatal car.

The oncoming vehicle came swiftly around a curve. It was in Spencer Thornley's lane. He swerved abruptly to avoid a collision. Either he swerved too far or else the gravel shoulder of the roadway gave away. The next instant his car was rolling down the bank to the floor of the canyon, near the creek.

Mr. Thornley was terribly shaken up but was thrown clear of the car. He lay perfectly still. He felt no pain but was sure he was badly hurt. His body was numb. He could feel, however, a warm trickle of blood flowing down his forehead, over his right eye and across part of his cheek. This confirmed his diagnosis of serious injury and, without precisely alarming him, raised the question: Are my wounds so severe that I am dead?

He heard the sound of a siren. It was that of an ambulance approaching. How welcome. It meant help if he still needed it. Moreover, he would soon have the answer to the question which was becoming insistent and a bit disturbing. If the attendant who put him on a stretcher pulled the sheet up over him only so far as his neck, he was still alive. If the sheet were drawn over his face, it was curtains for sure already. He knew that, and he waited silently, breathlessly.

There were two attendants. They were ever so gentle. It was a comfort to realize they knew their job. But they certainly took their time as they eased the athletic frame onto the stretcher. He could hear the dull rustle of a sheet as it was unfolded. An attendant tucked one end of the sheet under Spencer's feet. As the latter waited for the ultimate verdict with bursting impatience, the attendant slowly drew the hem up to Spencer Thornley's chin and then, after the briefest of pauses, extended the cover quietly but quickly over the face.

"It's strange,"said the one attendant to the other, "I could have sworn I saw him wink at me just then. That's what made me pause."

"You know that couldn't be," replied the other. "It is as simple as that."

"Yes, of course. That's why I hurried afterwards."

The Sinner

Sometime I'm gonna tell you about the way I almost got to be a famous criminal—one of those awful tax dodgers you read about in the papers. But that was when the trial came up and all. This time I just want to talk about the way I missed an appointment with my lawyer.

Of course, it all started the same way it was when the revenue agent showed me a big book that said Internal Revenue Code on it and said he was gonna throw the book at me. I know he wasn't kiddin'. The book was big as the old Sears Roebuck catalogue we used to have in the privy, but I knew "throwing the book" was only a manner of speakn'. I'm not so dumb; my only trouble is musin', as my wife says.

You see, I own an orchard, and she says I never get my work done 'cause I'm forever musin'. Well, crickets, you know how it is when you can see the mountains any time you look up and the Arkansas River and all the cherry and apple trees and things.

But I was gonna tell you how I missed an appointment with my lawyer in Sonora Springs. I say he's my lawyer, but he really isn't. He's a kind of young fellow. My real, regular lawyer lives right here in Piñon Cañon.

But he says, "You go see this fellow Brooks in Sonora Springs. I don't want to get messed up at all with those tax men."

That's how I got my appointment with Brooks. Walsh made it for me. He says "You see Brooks. You ain't done nothin' wrong. We know that, but you need somebody to explain it to those revenue agents. I don't know what they mean by 294 B and 294 D penalties, and I don't want to find out. I just don't want to, not even for you, Tony." That's the way it was. He made the first appointment for me.

It wasn't the first appointment that I missed; it was the second. I called Brooks right after lunch; that's when I was supposed to see him. He was out to lunch, then, so you see it wasn't really my fault I missed him.

If one of Brooks' girls had said "call back at 2," I wouldn't have gone to musin'. I'm almost positive I wouldn't. But his secretary didn't answer. Brooks did. I don't mean Brooks himself, but his voice. It was almost scary to hear it say "This is Brooks speaking by recording. I'm lunching with the Indian Club. Will be back about 2. Leave a message, and it will be recorded." Well, Sir, I couldn't think fast enough to leave a message right then, and afterward I fell to musin,' all right. I admit it, but it wasn't all my fault.

Somehow that recording business made me think of different things. As long as a guy can get one or those recorders, Mr. Brooks would have one, I expect. The girls in his office sure are real business-like, sittin' at their typewriters, even the pretty one. And that pretty girl fits into her nylon clothes like a watch into a gold case. She sure does.

It was just a week ago that I had my first appointment with Mr. Brooks and went to the Indian Club with him for lunch. Mr. Brooks was real proud that the club meets every Monday noon as regular as clockwork. Those people I had never seen before clapped for me and played the piano and sang "Welcome, welcome, sweet stranger." Guess they liked me so much because they liked Mr. Brooks. Gollee, yes, they all talked like Mr. Brooks, and even the ones as old as I am seemed to look like him. Like apples off the same tree. Funny thing, ain't it?

I can hear them yet. The stock market has been wonderful lately. Yep. Yes sir, no doubt about it. What this country needs to keep the machine runnin' smooth is a good conservative president who won't have a heart attack. Yes sir. Ha ha! A sound ticker, one like a Heyer pump. You're right, Joe, a good conservative president who can keep those socialist labor lords in line and keep tickin'. Yeah, that's for sure. You're not just woofin'. That's what this country needs, a solid business administration without heart trouble.

When lunch was over that time, Mr. Brooks certainly impressed me. That guy knows more about taxes and 294 penalties, I bet, than Admiral Byrd knows about penguins. You'd never guess there was so much to know. I told my wife about it.

I kind of thought she would ask if Brooks knows anything else besides taxes and penalties, but she didn't. She just said "There ain't no use for him to know about apples and cherries and cider. The government don't care about that. It wants taxes and penalties. It's good that Brooks knows about those."

Sometime I'll tell you what a fine job Brooks did for me. He sure knocked down the book the revenue agent threw at me. But that was later, at the trial.

I'm not denyin' Brooks is a good man. I can't understand what he says, but I guess he has to use a different language. He never seems to care a bit about the orchards and the river and the way things look around Cañon in the spring.

But I was tellin' you how I missed my appointment. Course I know that with recorders and things talkin' and getting' like people and with men and women gettin' more like machines there can't be no place for musin'. But there you are. That's the way I forgot to keep my appointment.

Soup 'n' Sandwich

He was a bank clerk in middle life. Although he was without family responsibilities, he no longer could afford to take his lunch at the Chinese Pheasant or even, for that matter, at the Longhorn Café. Until he had finished making the payments on his new car, he would be obliged to give his patronage to the Chuck Wagon, situated diagonally across the intersection from the nice little state bank at which he worked.

He had no idea how long the waitress at the back counter had been there when he started going to the Chuck Wagon. Maybe she had been there for months or maybe she, too, was new. He didn't even know her name. He could see, however, that she was a cute little number with large dark eyes that contrasted prettily with her healthy, ruddy skin and with her white uniform. She had all the other girls, whether they served the counters or had the good fortune to wait on the brown-stained booths, beat by a long ways.

She was on the plump side, and he liked that, even if he would have preferred to see a waist which pinched thin enough to accent the bulges above and below a wee bit more. (It could be that one so generously proportioned at twenty-five or thirty would be fat at forty.) Her black hair was cut too short in back to suit his fancy; it was a mannish affectation, he thought, but then, he wasn't looking for a sweetheart at this convenient café, just the soup 'n' sandwich special at seventy-five cents.

The first time he had taken his place at the counter, the pert little miss had spotted him. He may have impressed her as a swell; he didn't know. His sport jacket and slacks were not new, but they were natty, and he wore them with an air: casually, jauntily. Besides, he didn't team up with his fellows at the bank who came over in twos and threes. There was something different about him. Anyone could tell that.

Leastwise, on his very first visit, the girl muttered ironically, "Don't mind me." What could he reply? He wasn't going to say he had noticed her. So, he ignored the remark and maintained the absent-minded, abstracted look he had seen the president of the bank wear at times.

Then began a curious little battle over a tip. It was part of his plan in coming to the Chuck Wagon and sitting at the counter to escape the tipping which had added to the expense of having lunch at the Golden Lantern and the Pheasant, where they had no counter or booths, only tables with white linen. She didn't know about this aim of his, and, of course, he couldn't tell her.

After a few visits, she would ask him if he would have coffee to drink and then put off bringing it till he had about finished the sandwich. After his first week of visits, he went without the second cup freely poured out for the other customers. He might get his soup promptly and have to wait for the sandwich, or it might be just the other way around. The delays and forgetfulness were all pretty pointed, but they stopped short of giving a clear cause for complaint. He could have made an issue of the second cup of coffee, perhaps, but refrained from doing so.

For his part, he tried staying away now and then. This wasn't too satisfactory. It was hard to beat the soup 'n' sandwich special. At Joe's Hamburg Inn, he felt terribly conspicuous among the mechanics and deliverymen; and, besides, the food was dry and tasteless unless you so doped it with raw onion slices that he carried the odor back to the bank. When they weren't so busy, the girls in the tellers' cages tried to account for the new aroma and speculated vocally whether their customers had gone in for a new onions-in-the-diet fad. The Wing Ding Dairy Bar was handy, but he was as hungry when he left that bacon-and-tomato place as he had been on arrival.

Fortunately for him, time was on his side. One day, he overheard the head waitress ask the girl if she would prefer the front booths. He didn't catch the reply, but evidently it was no, for the girl continued to wait on him at the same old counter, blinking her painted lashes like a bird beating its wings; smiling broadly or a la Mona Lisa; stammering a bit on purpose to get attention; forgetting to forget; refilling his coffee cup without comment and without a signal or request on his part.

He looked her squarely in the eyes in the grave, un-smiling way befitting a banker. He tried to let her know by some means not too obvious, like always sitting at her station, that in his reserved manner he had a friendly interest in her. It never occurred to him, however, until later that having overcome her finagling, he might relax the strictness of his economy in her favor.

Then one day she wasn't there; nor the next; nor the next. He knew about the terrific turnover of labor at restaurants and that he wouldn't see her again. He felt a little like the general of an army which had won a battle and lost the war. He would miss her; he would miss her. The soup 'n' sandwich special would lose a lot of its savor, no denying that.

The Suicide Club

As I look back upon it, one of the most peculiar things I ever did was to join a suicide club. It was such a strange thing for me to do. I prefer to think of it not as an experience which I had but, rather, as one which befell me without any choice on my part. It happened on my only visit to Oklahoma City — or was it Tulsa — about five years ago. I'll tell you about it.

I was in the government civil service at the time. The bureau for which I worked had just established a new office in Sonora Springs. The announcement of my promotion to head up the Bureau's newly created branch caused much vexation to those political manipulators all over the country who had hoped to secure the plum for themselves or for their favorite. My colleagues in the Cincinnati office had overwhelmed me with congratulations, good wishes, and farewell parties. There were well-organized plans to welcome me to Sonora Springs.

Then a wintry blizzard had forced my plane down in Oklahoma City. The airline gave me a ticket entitling me to a single room for the night in one of the best hotels downtown. Unfortunately, there were no cabs or limousines at the airport at this late hour, and I, like other stranded passengers, would have to stay where I was until some dauntless driver considered the probable fares awaiting him as more than equal to the hardship of making the trip in the storm from the central hotel district to the airport on the city's outer edge.

The first floor waiting rooms which normally would have been dimmed and quiet after midnight were the scene of an unusual amount of aimless activity and confusion. Some passengers were sleepily lounging about relating their stormy adventures in the air to one another. A few sprawled in chairs for the night; still others were making futile attempts to wangle a commitment, or even a guess, about the next day's plane departures from the patient employee behind the counter.

I went upstairs. There was a large, low, round table in the small lobby outside the main dining room, which, as usual at this hour, was dark. The lobby itself was decidedly dim. I sat down at the table opposite a middle-aged nun. From the erectness and tension of her posture, I could tell that the sister was wide awake. As my eyes became accustomed to the gloom, I could see fairly well, but it was my sixth sense, not my vision, which registered that the nun was blind. If she had the customary white walking stick, it was not visible from where I sat.

I had entered the government service from Sonora Springs years ago when I was in my twenties. This return should have been a triumphant homecoming. The honor of my high appointment had come unsought. My associates at Cincinnati had exulted at my good fortune and, quite naturally, they had assumed that in my quiet way I rejoiced even more than they. In truth, I did not; but I took pains not to shock anyone by revealing the true state of my mind. Now that the bustle of leave-taking was over and I was at the very summit of my career, I was crushed beneath a stupendous burden, an insupportable feeing of failure.

What difference was there between me, as I was transferred about the country from station to station, and the wooden, lifeless pawns which are shifted around a chessboard in a silly, solemn game? The pistol in the holster under my arm felt warm to the touch, familiar, full of promise, more promising than my new job. I withdrew my hand from the comforting steel as my glance took in Sister Nicole. How alert, intense, alive that woman looked. Yet she was sightless and, I gasped at the thought, perhaps jobless in the ordinary sense. I shifted my gaze to the window. The drifting, driving snow outside made me think of the white-faced, red cattle huddled against the storm in Oklahoma's open, level fields. I dozed.

When I opened my eyes again, no more than minutes later, I am sure, two more men had taken places at the table. They were facing each other. Still across from me, still wide awake, was the nun. Then I noted, with an astonishment I had difficulty in suppressing, that both of the newcomers were toying with pistols in the semi-darkness. There was in their actions, however, no hint whatever of sudden gunplay. The tentative, experimental quality of the restless motions of their hands was apparent to me: the two were testing out whether they actually could point their weapons at each other in a serious and determined way.

Shifting my weight in my chair to serve notice that I was awake, I spoke to the nun. "Have you traveled far, Sister?" I asked.

"You can't imagine how far," she replied. "From the darkness of blind despair to the light of hope, without ever moving from this chair."

"You speak cryptically," I said. "Nevertheless, I understand what you mean and can almost anticipate what is coming next."

"I am Sister Nicole, and everyone expects me to believe in the miracles by which God manifests his goodness and glory. I expect it of myself. It was easy for me to live up to my name and nature when I only needed to look out a window and behold the miracle of the sun going down behind a mountain and infusing, as it does, the distant clouds with light and color; or when I had but to glance across my desk in a classroom to marvel at the love and wonder on the faces of children.

"Later, when I looked at the familiar things and faces without recognizing and, afterward, without seeing, it was not easy to credit stories of miracles, even rare ones. To believe as a matter of words is not impossible, but I could never be content with that. Could you? When faith falters, one has to hold off the most awful, blighting, devastating doubts. I came up here to be alone and to protect myself from fatal, stabbing questions. It is a good thing I was not left alone. What I have seen here in the dark has helped restore the faith by which I can see."

One of the newcomers was a large, soldierly-looking man. He was clad in a warm, gray top coat, which doubtless was a memento of his military service a few years earlier. He now spoke up. "You must have seen what my friend and I were trying desperately to make out," he said. "In spite of the dusk, we realized, somehow, that you were blind. But we didn't know that you could see." He spread his hands apologetically.

"I'm not in the habit of speaking in riddles. My name is Rotenwald. I am a Jew. I was in the American army in World War II when I met my friend here, Major Dietrich. He wasn't my friend then or any time till this moment.

Up to now, he was for me a German officer; and I owed my life to him. What kind of life do you suppose that could be, one which I owed to my country's enemy, my own enemy, and that enemy a hated Nazi. You have no idea how a proud man can suffer under so humiliating an obligation. It was worse than death."

He was silent a few instants, struggling to control himself. The he continued. "It all happened this way. Dietrich and I met on the battlefield in the closing days of the war in Europe. We were near the Czech border at a time when the Russians were approaching from the east, and the disorganized Germans, caught in a pincers, were surrendering to our troops in droves. There was a temptation to consider the krauts harmless. I, for one, was careless. Dietrich surprised me alone in a wood. He had the drop on me with a pistol. He could have killed me without the slightest risk to himself. With the military situation what it was, he could have taken me prisoner. Any other kraut would have taken my life one second and forgotten about it the next. This man threw his Mauser automatic to me and, in English, asked me to use it on him. My men arrived in a few minutes, and we captured Major Dietrich.

Dietrich nodded. "Imagine. Me a prisoner of war after all I had gone through. I did not consider myself lucky as did many. How could I? Hitlerism had never appealed to me in any way whatever, but I was German and therefore a legitimate prisoner of that wicked, political movement. When the war came, the army drew me to it. I fought its battles as best I could without faith either in its cause or in its ultimate victory. Long, long before the war's end, I was drained completely of all my strength. Only habit kept me going.

"Captain Rotenwald is wrong in one respect. I did not surrender to him. The American army didn't capture me. The Nazis took me without a struggle, overwhelmed me without killing me physically. I still walked around, wore a uniform, gave orders, signed papers; but, all the time, I hoped for a Russian or an American Rotenwald to put an end to my miserable pretense of existence. A man who has surrendered his soul as I had, a fellow without faith in the present or hope for the future is not a man, is not living, but is, rather, a mere animated puppet of flesh and blood.

"Ever since I got out of the prisoner of war camp, I have schemed and worked to find Rotenwald. He had told me he lived in Oklahoma. Yesterday, I located him. We agreed that both we and the world would be better off if we took each other's life simultaneously. That agreement was distasteful to each of us, naturally, but it was a compromise. We were going to fly back to the Czech frontier and reenact the scene of 1945 — this time in a way which would satisfy us both."

"That is true," said Rotenwald. "However, as I fingered my pistol here in the presence of Dietrich, I realized, as you saw, Sister, that neither my pistol nor hatred of my enemy could nerve me to carry out the bargain I'd agreed upon. I began to like that guy Dietrich."

"Me too," blubbered Dietrich. "Same with me. It's a bad bargain. I want none of it. Rotenwald is my friend. Always has been."

Sister Nicole smiled. I had tears in my eyes as I tried to be nonchalant. "Never have I heard, never felt, such close harmony as in this chance meeting of old fellows of the Oklahoma Suicide Club," I quipped in my best humorous imitation of an English accent. "You don't mind being called an 'old fellow,' in the English sense, do you Sister Nicole?"

Summer Capital

Time was when my home town of Sonora Springs was only the climate capital of the world. Things weren't so bad then. Things were actually pretty good. Now and then the monotony of provincial life and day after day of perfect sunshine and night mountain breezes would be broken by the visit of somebody from "outer space" with personal views of politics in Washington, the gossip of Hollywood, and the low-down on the integration of schools in the border states. From time to time, there would be a welcome guest to entertain, but not often. As a rule — though quite by chance, I assure you — the friend or relative timed his stay to coincide with "unusual weather": got marooned on Mt. Jonah on the Fourth of July or blanketed under a September snowstorm that made him vow never to return, ever.

In the meantime, all that has changed. Sonora Springs has become the summer capital of the nation. I'm not quite sure how the change was brought about, just why it happened, or what it's supposed to mean. Several summer sojourns by the President started it off; a centennial celebration continued it, I guess. I don't know. All I know is that it came to pass. Progress has a way with it, you know; and here we are, the summer capital.

Joe Blow arrives unannounced from Hoboken and wants to see exactly at what point in the stream the President stood when he snagged that two-pound or five-pound native brook trout; to trot around the golf links immortalized by the low scores of Bob Hope; to tread the ground made sacred by the first discovery of gold in the days of fifty-nine; or to retrace that stretch of highway which induced T.R.'s remark that its scenery bankrupts the English language. As soon as Joe leaves, Tom Jones wings it in by personal plane from Detroit with a wholly different set of interests. And so on, and so on.

Yesterday was a red-letter day. The telephone rang at two-thirty a.m., and when I answered it, who do you think it was? Yes sir, none other than my old army pal, Bill Windhorst from Akron, Ohio. He'd been in Las Vegas, Nevada, all on his lonesome and having a wonderful time but couldn't pass through Sonora Springs on his way home without saying hello. No sir. How about meeting him for breakfast, about nine? He's staying at the Prospector's Manor. Okay, okay. The wife said later she didn't sleep a wink after that, and I was bothered by a dream that somebody mistook my leg for a slot-machine lever and kept tugging and straining at it.

I made it to breakfast with Bill, all right. He wasn't up yet when I got there at nine, but I sat around while he showered, shaved, and dressed. While I was waiting, I called the office and explained that I'd be in by coffee time; I was going to have breakfast with Judge Windhorst. Bill had told me that he had become a judge, a justice of the peace or something, so I wasn't making things up this time.

I did get to the office about lunch time. Bill had wanted to give me a blow-by-blow description of his adventures at Las Vegas before I left the Prospector's Manor, but I told him that he could do that at dinnertime. We'd have dinner together, of course, and hoist a few for old times' sake. My assistant, Frieda, gave me a message to call the wife and added, verbally, that the boss was in a bit of a huff. He had had to see the rich, old, oil man, Mr. Gaspard, and his lawyer in my place and to sign the papers without knowing all the background. The lawyer kept telling the boss that everything was all right, that I had double-checked everything and gone over it with a fine-tooth comb and all that. And those repeated assurances had only made the boss more uneasy about the deal and more furious about my absence. Well, I knew enough not to try to explain the situation until a certain "cooling period" had elapsed. Anyway, Frieda confided that the boss had left for home already with a headache, so my excuses would have to hold over till the next day at least. The deal was a perfectly good one. I could show the boss that.

When I called the wife, she'd like to take my head off. She had a headache, too, and I made the mistake of suggesting that an aspirin or two would fix that up in a jiffy. Hold 'er Newt, did that remark rub her the wrong way! "You know very well," she reminded me forcefully, "that aspirin disagrees with me the worst way; makes me sick to my stomach." I was sorry and said so. "I'd feel better if your so-called friends would just leave us alone," she said. "That would do me more good than aspirin, that would." That's when I broke the news about Bill Windhorst being a judge now. She said, "I'm not talking about Bill Windhorst. I'm talking about Craig Aspinwell."

I said, "Craig Aspinwell? Where'd you ever pick that name out of a hat? Who's he?"

"Who's he? That's what I'd like to know. He telephoned as soon as you got out of the house this morning and told me how you were old friends from way back, how you two worked out a settlement with the BMG people in Sweden when the engineering on that job went wrong. Turned old Goteborg or Gutenberg, or whatever it is, upside down together, not to mention that quick side trip to Helsingfors that you didn't tell anybody about."

"Well, I'll be darned," I said. "Is Craig in town?"

"He got me out of bed this morning to tell you he is in town," the little woman said pointedly.

"Well, I'll be darned," I said.

"I invited him to dinner," the wife went on.

"That's good. That's fine," I said. "Bill is coming, too. I invited him."

"That's just great," said Sara. "That's just wonderful. I've been wanting to have dinner on the town for quite some time. Will you make the reservations, or do you want me to?"

"Leave that to me," I said. Things were going a little too fast, and I wanted to slow them down a bit. I wasn't born yesterday, and I learned long ago that a dinner and drinks on the town invariably is a dinner and drinks on me. I said to myself that there ought to be some other way out this time. Could it be that Craig was on an expense account? Bill, I knew, wasn't. I'd have to play the game for the breaks, like that old Michigan football team, and, with Sara in her present mood, I couldn't be sure of her cooperation.

I was late getting away from the office. When I got home, Craig Aspinwell was already there, talking with Sara in the living room. Craig was a lot younger than me the short time we'd been together on that milling machinery job in Sweden that Craig's company had sold and mine had financed. He was practically a kid then. To tell the truth, I couldn't be sure from the sight of him now that this guy was Craig. I didn't doubt it, but I couldn't perform the mental operation of stripping fifteen years off this fellow and seeing him as the Craig Aspinwell I'd known. I tried to slide over the awkwardness of it with an effort at cordiality and joviality. Sara did her part then drifted away to dress while I carried the ball. I explained to Craig that Bill was due anytime and that we were going out to dinner.

Before Bill arrived, I excused myself to Craig and slipped into the bedroom where Sara was dressing. I couldn't have timed that trick better if I'd tried. Sara grabbed for her robe in haste. I took two twenties out of my billfold and waved them in the air and looked about the room for her purse. "What in the world are you looking for with that money in your hand and that wild stare in your eye?" Sara said.

"Did I scare you?" I laughed. "I just wanted to put these two bills in your purse for emergency use," I said. "That way I won't have enough with me to foot the bill tonight. I just want to be prepared to 'let George do it,' but if that doesn't work, I don't care to wash dishes."

Sara winked at me. "It might be more dramatic," she said, "if I put the stuff in my bosom. Then when the manager gets threatening and things look the blackest, I'll come forth triumphantly with the green magic."

"You would create a still greater sensation if, with everybody looking on and pressing in angrily around our table, you bent over and pulled a roll of bills out of your stocking. Only trouble is I'd have to stake you to a roll of bills, and I don't want to go that far to see some stuffy manager doubly paid."

"Go on with your doubly paid! My legs aren't that good looking. You're just saying that."

"I'm just saying that because it's true." Then, as Sara was standing there in her modesty, partially and precariously screened by the robe which she held up to her neck with both hands, I kissed her lightly on the cheek and again on the ruddy flesh of her firmly rounded shoulder and went back to the living room.

Bill was late, but it was just as well. Sara was taking her time getting ready: painting her toe nails, shading her eyes, missing nothing. Craig wasn't on an expense account. He was in the process of what he called "relocating." He was moving from Butte to Dallas; still in engineering, he was going to start a new job with a company that tied in somehow with the government's missile program. With metal prices so depressed, business had been slow the past couple years on the mining and milling machinery side of his company.

When Bill finally came, I rattled off the names of a half-dozen restaurants in town. "Where do you want to go, Bill?" I asked. "You name it, and we're all agreeable." I looked at Sara and Craig for confirmation. They both nodded.

Bill seemed to be in a state of excitement. He may have had a drink or two before he came. I couldn't say, but he was more agitated and wound-up than high. He didn't seem to grasp the question or be interested at all in going to dinner. I had to repeat that we all were hungry and all left to him the choice of an eating place. He forced himself to make the decision. "The Chalet," he said. Sara then picked up the phone and called Maurice, told him we'd be over in fifteen minutes, and asked him if he would roast a chicken big enough for four. "Sure," he said.

I did the driving. Bill sat in front with me. He had little to say, but it was evident that a Niagara of talk was pressing on its dam. In the back seat, Craig was telling Sara in detail about engineering, machinery, and the prospects in the missile field. Sara would ask questions which showed she'd fallen off the sled at the first turn in the conversation, and then Craig would go way back there and patch up the misunderstanding and start all over again at that point. Presumably, Sara had exhausted the family chit-chat with Craig before I had got home. There was nothing for her to do now but learn about missiles.

At the Chalet, we were seated immediately. There was a delay, however, in serving us. Bill, who had absorbed the idea that he was the host on this occasion, took a dim view of the delay. He grumbled to the waiter, who explained "It takes quite a while to roast a chicken." Bill took issue with that. "Twenty-five minutes," he said. "Call the captain." The latter already was hurrying up. "What's happened to our dinner?" Bill demanded. "It's being roasted," the captain said. "That takes forty-five minutes." Bill groaned his disagreement: "A half-hour, easy, infra-red." The captain shrugged his shoulders and left.

"What about gambling in Las Vegas, Bill?" I asked. After that came the deluge. He had won fantastic sums. At what? At keno, craps, roulette, and twenty-one, mostly; but it was clear that Bill regarded my pin-pointing questions and interruptions as a nuisance. What I needed to know were the vague, dream-like details of his misty maneuvers to court Lady Luck and the fabu-lous manner in which that dame had showered him with her favors. He would bet with two-hundred in chips at one hand and with five-hundred at the other, at one and the same time. "I bet big," he said. "The guy standing next to me thought I was a magician. 'How come you pull it off like that over and over again?' the neighbor had asked."

Suddenly Bill remembered he wanted to call his wife in Akron. He got up abruptly and disappeared in the direction of the check-room. While he was away, the waiter pushed the cart with the chicken on it alongside our table. The golden-brown fowl looked positively delicious, bursting with luscious juices. The ends of the two drumsticks were decorated with curlicues of wispy, light-green paper. The waiter took his time carving. He feasted his eyes on the food. So did we. The paying customer wasn't there.

"Let's begin," I said. "We can take it slow, but let's begin. The way Bill is wound up tonight, I'll miss my guess if he doesn't talk over long-distance as if home were next door." We all lit into that appetizing chicken and its trimmings.

"Would you like a wine with your dinner?" the waiter asked. "Why that would be nice, wouldn't it?" said Sara, "a good white wine." She turned her big dark eyes on Craig. He smiled in spite of himself.

"How about that, Craig," I said, "still as crazy about wine with the meal as you were in the old days?"

"I don't know about that," Craig answered, "but there's no better time than now. What would you folks like?" He looked at Sara.

She asked the waiter, "Do you have a white Bordeaux?"

"We have a splendid Grave. Or would you prefer a Grave Superieur, maybe?"

"Oh, Grave Superieur is one of my favorites," Sara declared with a gasp of rapture and a glance at Craig.

"That'll be it, then," said Craig.

When the waiter returned with the wine, Bill was still away. He put one of those covers with a hole at the top over Bill's plate. "It's too bad," sighed Sara, "but he doesn't eat much anyway." The waiter looked as if he understood that remark better than I did. We were tackling our food more slowly now so as not to finish it before our host's return.

"Do you suppose Bill's really coming back?" asked Craig. "He'll be back, all right," I said.

"He surely couldn't be talking that long over the long-distance phone," said Craig, doubtfully.

"Never fear," I replied. "He hasn't had any dinner yet. He'll be back." Then I remembered something encouraging. "He was a regular chow-hound in the army; couldn't fill him up."

As if to prove the accuracy of my description of him, Bill reappeared. He began to talk before he was seated and as if he had been gone but a minute. "My wife," he began. "My wife mmm mm mmm." He had stuffed a generous slab of breast of chicken in his mouth, and one couldn't make out what it was about the wife. He did what he could to improve his speech with a hearty swig of Grave Superieur. "My wife mmm mm mmm," and again he became incomprehensible.

"We're way ahead of you, Bill," I said, "so wait until you catch up and then give us the news." To tell the truth, I had begun to suspect that the news might be embarrassing to Bill, and, therefore, just as well delayed; or, better yet, put off altogether.

Sara had the same idea as I did, I knew, but she was more curious. "Did you say you had been at Reno or at Las Vegas, Bill?" she asked.

"Both," Bill replied. "They're both good towns. Akron isn't a bad place, though, you know. It stays with you better on the long haul. Reno I'm going to forget, and Las Vegas is too rich for my blood. A little of it goes a long way. I'm ready to go home." He sighed. His eyes had a faraway look. He had spent his supply of words, apparently, and was ready to listen. He was more like his old self: no longer tremendous and magical and no longer Fortune's favorite, but understandable, likeable, and down to earth. With a gulp, he finished off the last of the wine. "That roast chicken was a good idea," he told Sara, "makes a guy feel more human, doesn't it?"

After coffee and dessert, Bill paid the dinner check cheerfully. Craig grabbed the wine tab and repurchased our hats at the checkroom. I told everybody to wait and made a bee-line for my car which was parked at a garage a half-block away and across the street. It was raining furiously now.

When I returned to the Chalet, Sara got into the car alone. "They're inside calling cabs," said Sara. "I told them I knew you'd be delighted to drop them off at their hotels if it weren't raining, but that you didn't like driving in the rain at night anymore. It turned out they're staying at opposite ends of town. It was their idea to take cabs. They're both leaving in the morning and said to tell you good-bye till next time. Craig said '*Auf Wiedersehen*,' to be exact." She laughed.

I laughed too. "Sara, you're wonderful," I said. "You're grand. You play every card just right."

"Do I get to share in the swag, then?" she asked.

"What swag?" I wondered.

"The swag you put in my purse," she replied. She took out the two twenties.

"Well, I suppose we should split it," I said.

She crammed the bills into my pocket. "What you've said is all I want. The dough is yours. You're pretty grand, yourself, you know."

"Yeah, I know," I said, keeping my hands on the wheel and my eyes on the wet streets, but appreciative just the same. "It was a pretty nice evening, after all, wasn't it?"

"It was nice, all right, but believe me I'm ready for bed."

"So'm I," I said, "but we'll be home in two jerks." The rain, one of those sudden showers of late summer, had disappeared; the clouds were moving rapidly to the side, and, as I drove along, I could see the stars coming out from under wraps ahead.

Vacations a la Mode

When Honey O'Brien caught sight of her husband, Tom, driving up the street, she knew instantly that a domestic storm was likely to hit as soon as he arrived. The hunch of his shoulders and the thrust of his head toward the steering wheel are as eloquent in their way, she thought, as is a violent wind in the tress across the street. She figured the most she could do was to prevent the erratic lightning of Tom's anger from striking her. She met him at the door with a quick, wifely peck on the cheek and "Gosh. It's nice to have you home early, Tom."

He gave her a perfunctory embrace. "It's good to be home," he said. "What a day at the office. I couldn't take many days like this one. That's for sure." Tom was the manager of a large law office, or factory, in downtown Sonora Springs. Others looked up the law, dictated documents, and typed letters. It was Tom's job to find those others to do the leg work, the brain work, the typing; to keep them happy doing it; and to wheedle them into accomplishments which surprised both him and them. Honey knew enough about the affairs of Reynolds, Wolf, and Walton to appreciate that Tom had ample cause for a headache now and then.

"Get some olives for me, will you, Hon?" By this time, Tom had assembled some bottles on the kitchen table and was holding an ice tray under the cold water faucet at the sink. Honey was on the way to the refrigerator when he spoke. "Coming up," she replied cheerfully. "Put two olives in my martini this time, Tom. I feel like having two in my drink tonight."

Tom handed Honey her martini and took a generous sip from his own as the strolled onto the back terrace. "Three guys got back from their vacation this morning. I've learned more about fishing, flirting, and gambling than I ever wanted to know. First, I had to listen to one, then the other, all day. It was terrible. I wished they had stayed away permanently, or that August lasted another sixty days. They made me absolutely exhausted. Besides, they left us, Honey, with no place whatsoever to go on our holiday."

"What do you mean by that?" asked Honey, spearing one of the olives out of her drink with a toothpick.

"If you'd have heard those fellas griping and grieving by the hour as I did, you'd know all right. The Towners went to the desert; Rudy Feldman took his family to the mountains; Don Brooks went to the seashore. Where else could we go unless we went to the moon?"

"Who had the best time?"

Tom snorted. "Who had the best time? Nobody did. Here we sweat it out in Sonora Springs through all this heat, and these three goofs get the best month of the year off and come back with nothing but bellyaches. It's the limit; it's a crying shame, it is." He poured himself another martini and looked at Honey's glass, which was more than half full yet.

"Yes. Judge Towner came into see me first. I really believe that old duffer has begun to slip. Anyway, he and Nancy went to the desert, Nevada, somewhere near Reno. Only name I seem to remember is Monument Valley. After all I've gone through today, it could be Death Valley. He spent all his time there gambling. Russian roulette is the only game he didn't try out. I felt like telling him that's precisely the one he should have finished up with."

"Did Nancy gamble all the time, too?"

"Oh, I don't know. He didn't say. I don't see how he could have lost so much dough as he did without help. Nancy didn't come back with him, though."

"She didn't come back? What in the world does the judge have in mind, leaving Nancy out there in the desert alone. I've never been a judge, but I'd know better than that."

"She wanted to stay. She met a joker from Reno who just got unhitched. Nancy's gone to Reno herself; says she wants a divorce. Maybe she's just miffed with the judge, and it will blow over. But one never knows. Nancy's not out of the fateful fifties, you know. Still, the Towners have a daughter in California, and I have a hunch Nancy pulled out of Reno for San Francisco as soon as the judge left for Sonora Springs. We'll see."

"That's their problem, Tom. You can't take everybody's cares onto your shoulders. The Towners are old enough to know what they're doing. Nancy's at least fifteen years older than I am. Besides, their children are all grown. Pour me another with two olives."

"Yes, yes. I know all that. But how about the Feldmans? Their baby isn't grown by any means."

"For goodness sake, what about the Feldmans? Surely nothing happened to them."

"I don't know. They don't tell me everything. Rudy went away with his family and came back without it. That's all I know, you might say."

"You might say that, and you might say you know a sight more, Tom O'Brien."

Tom smiled for the first time since he had been home. "Well, they drove up to Montana on a fishing trip, somewhere in the mountains. Took their two-year-old baby with them and rented a cottage at the edge of a fishing stream, fifty miles from the nearest two-by-four village. At the end of the first week, Rudy had caught three trout and lost a wife and baby, for a net gain of one, you might say."

"Tom O'Brien! How dare you sit there and joke about other people's sorrows with your net gains and you-might-says. I think it's shameful."

"Well, Sara left a note saying she'd caught a ride to Denver and was going home to Mama in Dallas, with the baby, and never coming back, never. She was sick and tired of getting away from home only to vegetate in the backwoods, and Rudy was a mighty poor fisherman as far as she was concerned. That's just about it."

"Does Rudy think she will come back?"

"What would you do, if you sweltered a goodly part of August in Dallas? Of course, she'll return. After she had gone, Rudy went further into the mountain wilderness to show how many trout he could catch when he wasn't hampered by women and children and could get far enough away from civilization. Sara was tickled pink to hear from him, you bet, when he finally called her long distance. She's coming to Sonora Springs by plane tomorrow or the next day. Silence is golden, and Rudy proved it by leaving telephones, telegrams, and the daily post far behind him for a week. Of course, the Texas heat contributed its part to his victory over misfortune." Tom poured himself another drink.

"Yes, and you can be sure all those fish he caught helped reestablish him in Sara's mind. A woman's gotta respect a man before she's willing to come back to him."

"What fish are you talking about, gal? I didn't say Rudy got any trout in the next week."

"You mean he didn't have any luck fishin' after she left?"

"I mean he didn't catch a single thing except those three measly trout the first week. No fish gets hungry enough to take bait in August unless he's artificially starved."

"Well, I declare, the Feldmans have had a time, haven't they?" Relieved at the prospect of a happy ending of the Feldman spat, Honey laughed. So did Tom.

"I didn't think I'd ever laugh again after I heard about all those vacations. You know what Justice Holmes said 'Three generations of imbeciles is enough.' I guess the sky hasn't fallen after all. Maybe what I need is to get away from everything for a while. What about some food? I'm as hungry as a Montana trout in early spring."

"After this drink....But, didn't you say that that handsome Don Brooks got back from his vacation today, too? You've only condemned two generations of imbeciles, my Master, the older and the younger. How about our own?"

"No, I didn't so much as refer to Don Brooks, Mistress Mine. It just happens that he did return to the office today, though. And you just happened to remember his due date, didn't you? For a guy of his age, of his maturity, he's as asinine as he is good looking. Either he's too big a fool to forget his ex-wife, or he fancies his middle name is Juan. From what he says and what he doesn't say, I gather he's making an earnest, diligent, hardworking effort to improve on Don Juan's techniques and to break that guy's record with women.

"Lady-killer, my eye. I'll bet he looks nearer death than any of those ladies of easy virtue he razzle-dazzled with at that Atlantic beach. After weeks at the shore, he has less sun tan than we've picked up on our lawn. He looks positively pale, wan, and thin. I told him his name should be Wan Don."

"I'll confess, I'm fond of Don," said Honey. "I admire his happy-go-lucky manner and air of sophistication. But I also have to admit I like him best at a near distance. I like to see him exert his charm on others. Did the light-hearted debauchee make a hit with any of the girls of the summer colony?"

"According to him, with them all, and his weary appearance bears him out. However, he wasn't looking for a prospective marriage partner, if that's what you're getting at. He was looking for a little romantic moonlight, not a permanent rainbow, for thrills, not love."

"You make Astoria City out to be one of those eastern night beats. You know Don only goes to the most exclusive places."

"Sure, sure, I know. I wish Don had been the first today to tell me about his trip, instead of the last. I got off on a bad start, learning about Judge Towner's gambling escapades at Monument Valley. And him a judge once. But do you know Wan Don had a worried look on his face, as if he might face a shotgun wedding this time or fears that he might. Poor guy; he deserves a better break than that after his first marriage fiasco."

"Did he say something you haven't mentioned?"

"No, of course not. That's just it. That's one of the reasons I was hanging from the ropes when I came home. He just looked worried, and I know Don pretty well."

"Well, I have to see that dinner gets on the table," said Honey, jumping up. "Makes one afraid to go away on a holiday, doesn't it?"

"Sure does. I'd rather hunt lions or tigers or elephants in Africa." He took a slow, meditative sip on his martini and then got up and shouted to Honey, who was in the kitchen: "Hey, Honey. I've got a wonderful idea for our vacation."

"OK," Honey hollered back, "but if it's a lost weekend like one of theirs, you can just forget it."

The Witch of Gridley

On the weekend, I visited my friend, Homer Stack-straw, at Gridley, and he told me the most foul, filthy story I've ever heard. It was enough to defile the mind and leave it permanently dirty beyond cleansing, not just the plaster-grey of a hand-towel which defies laundering, but the repulsive color of the putrefying corpse of a rodent fallen victim to a householder's poisoned cheese. I fear that the awful tale will people my dreams with hideous sights and horrid, loathsome shapes for the rest of my nights till the end of time, if indeed I ever sleep again.

Homer and I were school mates at the state university. He majored in English and minored in languages, whereas I studied law. In my final year at school, I wrote a devastating denunciation of the Salem witchcraft trials; absolutely devastating. Homer, who had already gradu-ated and gone to his first teaching job at the little college-farming-tourist town of Gridley, helped me with the composition. The law-school faculty, amazed that I should have chosen such a subject for my senior treatise rather than, say, the avoidance of federal death taxes by means of living trusts and the marital deduction, were unanimous in praise of my criticism of that early, almost-forgotten historic colonial wave of McCarthyism.

I kidded the pants off the ancient, age-old, world-wide, tenacious, unsinkable belief in witches. To tell the truth, I left law school two years ago, firm in the conviction that Evil itself was a complete fiction, an airy abstraction having no place in modern American society, an imaginary viciousness thoroughly outlawed by the Constitution in the Preamble, Bill of Rights, and property guarantees somewhere within "the four corners of the document." That was when I left law school. And everything I had learned since as a junior clerk in an attorney's firm in Sonora Springs had confirmed me in that comfortable assurance. Then I took that bus trip to see Homer at Gridley....

Homer was not a professor but an instructor, no more flush with dough than I. He was living in a fairly nice, furnished apartment in a grand old three-story residence which had been converted into an apartment building. His quarters were on the second floor. There were, he said, two other units on the same level: two above, and two below. At least half the tenants were connected one way or another with the college, which was nearby.

Immediately after my arrival Sunday morning, the two of us went out to breakfast. There were six or more inches of new-fallen snow, and as we trudged through it across the campus, I kept expecting Homer to start a snowball fight or initiate some other form of mischief in accordance with his well-known love of horseplay. No. Well, I thought, he's an instructor now. It behooves him to act dignified. He's older, too, than he used to be. Besides all that, he may have something on his mind.

Talk flowed quite freely at breakfast. We sat in a booth instead of the counter. The waitress was attentive, evidently fond of Homer but as deferential as he was reserved. Homer had changed: older yes, and not just in years; stronger, more solid, more manly. I liked the difference, except that I was baffled and judged that in the new state of affairs, it would be my turn to play second fiddle.

After breakfast, as we sat chatting in Homer's apartment, I heard a curious clucking and cooing going on in the hallway. I couldn't make out the "words of endearment," or even make sure it was a human voice I heard. "What's that, for crying out loud?" I asked.

"That's the woman with the cat. Haven't I told you about her?" The peculiar calls were resumed and were further removed now from the realm of the ordinary and identifiable. "She's a neighbor," Homer said, but he ceased his explanation to let me hear the quick clack of footsteps approaching. I say "clack" because I swear by all that's eternal I've never heard a woman's heels sound like those. The effect wasn't that of hoof beats, but still less was it that of the familiar, homey, half-thrilling click, click, click.

There was a knock at the door. The woman entered with an exhalation of words to Homer and of clucks and gravel-gertie baby talk to the cat. Then, quite breathless, she said, "I saw you and your friend coming back. I wanted to meet him. You knew I would." She looked at me. I looked at her.

I vaguely heard Homer say "Yes, El Worth; Cora Lewison." The stranger's voice took hold of my throat. It was so hoarse and coarse, so breathless or breathy sounding.

"What do you do, Mr. Worth?" the voiceless voice asked me with rude directness. I didn't answer as I stared at the woman's dark eyes, half-dyed gray hair, tall, gaunt, flat figure, knobby ankles, run over shoes, brindle coat.

I heard Homer replying for me: "He practices law." Her response was a snorting emission of air. It was more of a snort than a grunt of acknowledgment.

She turned her interest to the cat. So did I and wished I hadn't. "Do you like Sinbad?" she asked me.

"Is he Siamese?" I asked, trying to find a basis for appreciating the obnoxious beast. That was as much as I could manage.

"Partly, perhaps."

"Mixed with a little of the devil," Homer said in such a matter-of-fact way that I felt slightly reassured.

"I expect so," Cora said. "At night, he darkens to coal-black; all but his eyes." She cackled with laughter, either at her remark or at the jokes she could tell about Sinbad, if she would. And, my reassurance, faint as it was, vanished as quickly as it had come.

I was beginning to feel that both woman and cat were offensive jokes, in utterly bad taste: not rib-splitting ribaldry but vile obscenity. Of the two, the cat was the worst, so much so that one couldn't help but wonder which was master. I almost said which was cat and which was woman. I would have given money, right then, to have been in the presence of a genuine Siamese cat, or just a genuine cat, or even one of those real, blue-eyed, pink-eyed dogs. So help me, I had had about all I could take of these neighbors of my friend. My feelings were so strong that they probably showed on my face (and damned if I care), for the two departed abruptly, the cat silently, his tail defiantly vertical, and the woman with a series of puffs, wheezes, and catcalls.

"Good God," I said as soon as the door closed behind them. "Where did the landlord rake them up? Where did they come from?"

"She is secretary to the Chairman of the Biology Department," Homer said and paused.

"Don't hand me that," I said. "Don't try to pass her off as simply an educated monstrosity. You can't get away with it Homer. After all...."

"No," he said. "I wasn't trying to do anything of the sort. I was wondering where to begin, what to say.

"I met Cora for the first time about a year ago, shortly after your last visit here. There had been a big snow like this one. I went out for Sunday breakfast, as we did today. The steps and the walk had been shoveled, maybe not with perfect artistry but reasonably well. On my way back, I turned in the gate and was coming up the walk when I saw a woman on the steps with a broom. The sun was out, and the snow was melting a little, but it was not warm, only slightly above freezing.

"Here was that woman in nothing but the thinnest of thin smocks or robes sweeping at the few microscopic remnants of snow left by the janitor's shovel. I had seen the woman with the cat around but never face-to-face, never to speak to. I had heard from other tenants that she was a snoop who used the truancy of her cat as an excuse for looking into windows and sneaking around the yard and its shrubbery on summer evenings for a chance to see what she could see that was none of her business. Now here was that woman outdoors in the cold with a broom and a cat. I thought the cat was black this time, at first, against the snow in the sunlight, and damn be if for a split second that the painted wooden broom handle was protruding upward from the woman's legs.

"She was ranting at the absent janitor like a fishwife. I don't know what she was saying. Then I realized that instead of holding her robe or smock closed, she was clasping it so as to keep it from flapping shut. She didn't want me to miss anything. When she ran out of breath and could no longer hiss or steam, I said 'Looks to me like you've finished the job now, Lady, unless you want me to scatter a little salt on the steps.' She said, 'Yes, I guess so. Come in.'

"We went in. She forgot about the salt for the steps; probably hadn't given that any more thought than I had. She showed me her apartment: the living room walls lined with books to the ceiling, few, if any, ever touched; the primitive kitchen; and lastly, the small bedroom and small bed. She took off her smock. I spent the whole of that bright day in the dim recesses or her apartment; didn't leave till evening."

"Don't tell me," I said. "I'd sooner cuddle a toad, a horny toad, a Gila monster. I couldn't under any circumstances put arms around that mockery of womanhood, that resurrected corpse, that regurgitated hank of hair."

"It wasn't easy," Homer replied; and it wasn't till he said that that I began to comprehend that he had done what he said. I shuddered.

"Only that day," Homer resumed. "Never again. That was it; the one and only occasion. There hasn't been as much as a word between us since then. We parted friendly, but we parted finally. Today she came to see you, not me."

"The mere sight of her made me feel unclean," I said. "Did it take you long to get over that—that whole day in the bat-bath? Excuse me. I didn't mean it the wrong way. I'm so horrified, that's all."

"I understand. I avoid her myself, and always will. You've probably gathered that. But for the past, I have no regrets whatever: none, on the contrary." And then, for my sake, he agreed to talk about other things.

A few minutes later, I was at it again. "Homer, how in the hell do you account for her being a secretary in the Biology Department?"

"I tell you, I think Old Doc Haighler finds her most useful in case any student or teacher starts getting too cocksure, too dogmatic or doctrinaire, in his theories about living matter." He didn't need to go further, and from then on I succeeded in keeping the wretch out of the conversation, if not out of my thoughts. It was a relief, though, to get on the bus later, hear it shift into high gear, and gather speed away from the unholy, ghastly, contaminated, haunts of woman and cat. Believe me!

The Witness Wins

Orlando Redondo had lost a good many and won a few cases for the insurance companies he served as attorney, but this morning everything was different. He was a witness in a trial, not an attorney; and yet it was he who scored a magnificent triumph. His appearance to give testimony was an entirely unscheduled affair, and if the newspapers had been reporting this particular battle of wits, which they weren't, he surely would have been labeled a "surprise witness" for the plaintiff.

Orlando took the stand, as the lawyers put it, at his own request. He had been a trial counsel for automobile insurance companies for a score of years, had in his time at the bar seen the average size of plaintiffs' verdicts double and yet remain inadequate. After all that, he was entitled, if anyone was, to a little variety and, if being a witness was what he wanted as a change, why then a witness he should be.

The court and jury convened far earlier than customary to hear Orlando testify. This was out of consideration for the witness who, as everyone knew, had at least a round dozen of commitments in other courts which had to be met and an infinite responsibility to each and every court and client to meet those commitments to the full, to the letter.

There was a little by-play right after Orlando had been sworn in which nettled him intensely and induced in him a settled state of irritability which persisted throughout the questioning. He had been asked to give his name and had given it when the attorney for the defendant interjected in a raucous, rasping voice: "I didn't hear the answer. Did you say Orlando Furioso?" Orlando's red complexion reddened still further with anger but, before he could retort, the judge, with the air of a man only half-awake to his surroundings, said "Yes, you'll have to speak up in a voice loud enough so everyone present can hear: the jury, the reporter, and all. This is not just a private conversation you're having with your lawyer, you know."

Vexed at the manner and tactic of the opposing attorney and bewildered that the judge should think it necessary to admonish a courtroom veteran like him, Ruddy Redondo, as he had done, Orlando hesitated. Then, without realizing what he was doing, he answered, "Yes, Orlando Furioso." His own attorney asked, "Furioso is your middle name? Your last name is Redondo?" His middle name was not Furioso at all, but he let it go at that and volunteered: "Everybody calls me Ruddy."

The skirmishing and jockeying for position between the lawyer for the plaintiff and the lawyer for the defendant let up a little while the former brought out that Orlando seldom drove a car himself; he turned that job over to his wife, for the most part, so he could keep his mind free for more important matters of business. He always went to work on a bus which went past his downtown office, and the accident in question had happened this very morning as he was about to get on board at the stop just down the block from his home. He lived, he testified, on a one-way thoroughfare in a suburb of Sonora Springs known as Pinewoods.

The judge now was looking down over his glasses at the witness suspiciously. The opposing attorney was poised, ready to leap into action with an objection or an innuendo, whichever might suit the occasion. His own attorney asked, "Then what happened?" Orlando repeated, wonderingly, "Then what happened?" and, after the slightest of pauses, continued, "Then he came up over the curb after me in headlong haste, hit me squarely and violently in the seat of the pants, and catapulted me through the air all of thirty feet. It knocked the breath out of me. I thought I'd never be able to get up before he'd be at me again."

"Now, when you say 'he,' Orlando, whom do you mean?" At this strange question from his own attorney, Orlando looked puzzled. The questioner restated his inquiry. "Do you mean Mr. Simnitz, the defendant?" Orlando replied "Yes. No...No. I mean the four-eyed monster with the wide, slender eyebrows that moves along the ground one way and appears to be flying off in exactly the opposite direction." The judge, as if expecting pandemonium to break out at this point, rapped for order with his gavel and frowned sternly at the jury and the few spectators, but everyone appeared intent on the testimony and anxious to get on with the trial.

The attorney for the other side took the silence of the audience as his cue to hurl himself into action. "If you mean a 1959 Chevrolet, say a 1959 Chevrolet, and, if you don't know the answer, say so," he shouted. Orlando was not in the least intimidated. "I don't think it is for me to draw conclusions," he said with a sense of delicacy he scarcely remembered having. "I've described the critter for you. It is for the jury to make the necessary inferences."

Here, Orlando's own lawyer came to the rescue. "What kind of an automobile is it that you have, Mr. Redondo?" The laconic reply of the witness was, "A four-eyed Ford, which is a different breed altogether from that which hoisted me." The lawyer waited, and Orlando went on "I will say just this much further by way of identifying my assailant. This unearthly wagon-dragon that hurtled into me was not finned as is the man-eating shark; nor did it have so many taillights in its collection as to dim the splendor of a sulphur-bottom whale by comparison."

The opposing lawyer was on his feet, fuming and spluttering. "I move the Court that it all be stricken as not responsive to any question put to the witness and as wholly incompetent, irrelevant, and immaterial." The judge nodded sympathetically, but his former appearance of extreme sleepiness had not left him; it had, if anything, become more pronounced. "I was wondering," he said slowly and softly, "what qualifications the witness has to speak of monsters. Aren't they creatures of myth, fantasy, and legend and therefore not a fit subject of testimony by anyone in a court of law unless the witness can be shown to be an expert? Perhaps counsel for both sides can give the Court a little enlightenment on this point, by argument, before he—I mean it—rules."

This turn of events caught the two attorneys wholly unprepared. While they were momentarily speechless, Orlando, quite unperturbed by the judge's remarks, took it upon himself to lighten the darkness in which monsters played around in the judge's mind. "Your Honor," he said with great humility, "is thinking of sea serpents and of the dragons of antiquity. They, indeed, may be more legendary than real. However, I'm not so sure even of that. When I was in France during the war, I often went through a village in a convoy. At the roar and speed of our vehicles, with the drivers gunning the motors, the villagers and their children would scamper to safety and then stand on each side of the narrow street and stare at our sinuous, speeding convoy as if it were some titanic serpent which had emerged from the sea and was rolling, as serpents did at Creation before they were punished for their perfidy and forever consigned to crawling, was rolling across the countryside in sinister, senseless sounding fury.

"But land monsters are unquestionably real," Orlando went on. "They definitely register on the senses, and I assure you, Your Honor, I speak as an expert. First of all, their whirring din inflicts itself upon the ear. Then they emit a stench which poisons the air. Finally, they're ugly to the sight. Maybe the Hudson of 1950, of the Koreano-zoic era, was different, but that's a long while ago, and everything since then has been retrogression. And the Hudson itself has gone with the snows of yesteryear, the dodo, and the dinosaur."

As Orlando was ticking off his scientific little lecture or expertise, one, two, three, he had become increasingly conscious of the judge's inattention. This annoyed him far less, however, than the feeling that an evil eye was fixed upon him. Now that he had finished speaking his piece, he realized it was the gaze of the opposing attorney that bothered him. The latter shrieked at him: "Are monsters useful in getting home from market with a load of groceries?" His high-pitched voice broke on the last word so that the final syllable, the "ies," came out in a sustained, sobbing whimper, e-e-e-e-s.

Orlando was pondering how to frame an answer which would be a perfect squelch, but there was a rough, distracting hand on his shoulder and the answer would not come. Then he heard the bus conductor saying, "Hi, Buddy, wake up. It's the end of the line; end of the line."